SPELL CASTER

ALSO BY JAYMIN EVE

SHIFTER CITY FATED MATES

A Curse of Fate
A Twist of Luck
A Claim of Fortune
A Bond of Trust

FALLEN FAE GODS

Gilded Wings
Crimson Skies

SHADOW BEAST SHIFTERS

Rejected
Reclaimed
Reborn
Deserted
Compelled
Glamoured

SUPERNATURAL ACADEMY

Year One
Year Two
Year Three

SPELL CASTER

JAYMIN EVE

MIRA

If you purchased this book without a cover you should be aware that this book is stolen property. It was reported as "unsold and destroyed" to the publisher, and neither the author nor the publisher has received any payment for this "stripped book."

/||MIRA™

ISBN-13: 978-1-335-47200-7

Spellcaster

Copyright © 2025 by Jaymin Eve

All rights reserved. No part of this book may be used or reproduced in any manner whatsoever without written permission.

Without limiting the author's and publisher's exclusive rights, any unauthorized use of this publication to train generative artificial intelligence (AI) technologies is expressly prohibited.

This is a work of fiction. Names, characters, places, and incidents are either the product of the author's imagination or are used fictitiously. Any resemblance to actual persons, living or dead, businesses, companies, events or locales is entirely coincidental.

For questions and comments about the quality of this book, please contact us at CustomerService@Harlequin.com.

TM is a trademark of Harlequin Enterprises ULC.

Mira
22 Adelaide St. West, 41st Floor
Toronto, Ontario M5H 4E3, Canada
MIRABooks.com

Printed in Lithuania

To those who search for magic.
Here's the secret—it's already inside you.
You are enough.

SPELL CASTER

PROLOGUE

Ragged breaths caught in my chest as I stumbled along the hallway, footfalls quiet against the carpet, which absorbed the blood dripping from my side.

The edge of my vision grew fuzzy, but I pushed forward, aware that the beast wouldn't be held off for long. *Just one more step. Just one more step.* It was a haunting mantra in my head, urging me on, even as I grew weaker with each step, until those words were a mere whisper.

I had a small head start thanks to Belle's spell, but its claws had already done their damage, tearing through my flesh and embedding deep in my magical essence. When I stumbled past the curtains, I decided to get off the beaten path.

Nightrealm Hall.

In my haste to escape one monster, I'd found myself in the lair of another.

With the heat of blood pulsing against my hands as I attempted to keep my insides . . . *well, inside* . . . there was still enough life within me to feel fear. Only this fear tasted different, tainted with hate and regret.

Against all common sense, I found myself stumbling to the one door I'd refused to approach before tonight. The only indication of the powerful and dark being who resided behind it was a carved minotaur in the center of the wood paneling.

With my right hand clutching my ribs, my left rested beside

the minotaur as I swayed forward and almost smashed my head on the frame. When I pulled away, there was a streak of crimson left behind, as if I'd marked this door with my energy. Not that I really had energy left to do more than sway on the spot.

Lurching dangerously forward once more, the scuffle of the monster echoed close by. With no other option, I dug deep for the strength to lift my hand and knock, only to find the door opening before I even made contact. Cold air rushed around me, like a slap in the face, almost waking me up. *Almost.*

In the doorway stood my enemy.

But tonight I needed him.

To fight a monster, I needed a monster.

Unless he was the one who set it on me in the first place. But still, he was the only warlock strong enough to stop this attack.

His cold gaze traced over me, and that perfect face that haunted my dreams grew harder. I opened my mouth to explain, but I had nothing left to give. Swaying forward, I fell, expecting to hit the floor. Instead, strong arms wrapped around me, crushing against the wounds on my side. Even beyond pain, I still felt the weight of his hold.

"Precious?" he murmured, that one word dripping with fury. Maybe it was my sanity failing with my life, but it didn't sound as if his ire was directed at me. For once. "Who hurt you?"

Logan Kingston pulled me close, and I knew that this was the defining moment of my existence. He held all the power, and as darkness won its battle and I closed my eyes, I wondered if my enemy would hand me to the beast or save me.

Time would reveal all, but it seemed I was out of that.

For tonight at least.

CHAPTER 1

Six months earlier

"Paisley! Paisley, get your butt down here this instant!"

My mom's voice woke me from what was turning out to be an excellent dream. There'd been a bar and dancing, a frenzy of heated bodies. I'd found myself pressed into an alcove by a guy who'd been frequenting my darker thoughts lately. I never saw his face, but I knew it was always the same warlock, built like sin, with a *very* talented tongue and . . .

Yep, it had been shaping up into an extremely nice dream.

These sporadic *spicy* dreams had started two weeks ago on boxing day, the day after my twenty-second birthday. That night I'd been watching my favorite K-drama, and when the head-bitch of the storyline took it a step too far, sabotaging the sweetest character on the show, I'd raged and accidentally blew out all the lights in the house.

All witches and warlocks had a magical bloom after their twenty-second birthday. Mine had been very soon after, and power was racing through my veins—yet somehow still inaccessible in my day-to-day life.

There was a rather steep adjustment as magic heated my blood, but at least I finally understood why I'd spent my life desperately trying to ignore the overly affectionate, *borderline obsessive* way my parents acted around each other. Those of us with magic were filled with passion and fire, and without an outlet, I was stuck in the *dream* phase.

"Paisley Hallistar, you can't possibly still be in bed at this hour."

Mom, having exhausted her full range of patience, was now in my doorway. Yawning, I rubbed my eyes to try to wake myself up. "I'm an adult, Mom," I mumbled. "And I don't work today."

I was currently employed at the local skating rink, where I had the honor of pouring drinks and shining shoes. At least the soundtrack was always pumping, and I got free skate hours whenever I wanted, so I couldn't complain. The transition between high school and college had no timeline, and I enjoyed the in-between.

"Brat," Mom muttered. "Always with the sass." The air temperature shot up as she reached out and slapped me right on the ass.

Beth Hallistar was no pushover, having raised four witches and warlocks before me—I was the last of the litter, and I should have known better than to grumble at her. Hopefully she'd blame it on the abrupt wakeup.

Clearing my throat, I pulled myself up to sit. "Sorry about that." I gave her my entire focus. "What did you need to tell me?"

Her annoyance vanished in a whoosh of paper as she waved it in my direction. "You got the letter! Weatherstone."

Like a shot of adrenaline to my chest, any lingering tendrils of sleep were dashed as I leaped from the bed, uncaring that I was clad only in a tank top and panties. "*The* letter? To Weatherstone College? Are you fucking serious?"

"Paisley Hallistar!"

Full-named twice in the span of two minutes was definitely a record. Thank Selene and her moon energy that Dad was away at Weatherstone with my siblings, otherwise I'd have to answer to him for cussing around Mom. The hot-blooded part extended to more than just sex, it was an all-encompassing possessiveness that demanded warlocks destroy anyone who upset their mate.

From the outside it looked like perfection, except children in the relationship often ended up as distant third wheels. Still, we couldn't complain. Dad put Mom first, but she loved us just as fiercely. A love she showed in countless ways, and today it was a firm hug as she murmured, "I'm so proud of you, honey. I knew you'd have the magical aptitude."

Burying my face against her shoulder, I marveled that even as an adult, a hug from Mom would never grow old. There'd been a bittersweet taste since my energy bloomed, knowing these were my final days in our family home, before magical college, which would inevitably lead to a coven.

"I'm not going to lie," I admitted, when we pulled apart, "I had my doubts that my magical essence would be strong enough for Weatherstone. I all but tanked the entrance test."

There were five main magic colleges across America. After their power bloomed, anyone with a drop of magical blood would take the entrance exams and wait for their letter of acceptance. Weatherstone was the oldest and most prestigious of the five, and you only got in if you were exceptional.

I was far from exceptional, and a niggling voice in the back of my head insisted that the letter was only a courtesy to my father, who was a professor at Weatherstone.

"You earned this, honey," Mom said softly, pressing her hand to my cheek. She had the uncanny ability to ease my doubts with only a few reassuring words and her natural calming energy. "Your powers unlocked faster than any witch I've heard of, and your energy will only grow from here. You've got years to find your affinity."

Technically, what she said was true, but my doubts had deeper claws than she could loosen. "I know, and I'm ready to exercise these magical muscles." I made that promise to us both. "I won't waste this opportunity, and I have four years to declare my affinity."

"Are you feeling a draw to anything yet?" Mom asked. She'd asked this question every morning for the last two weeks, and every morning the answer was the same.

"Nope, nothing. I'm expecting I'll be an elemental, because you and Dad are, but so far none of the five elements are responding." Not air, water, metal, fire, or earth.

Mom nodded, and I could see she expected I'd be an elemental too. "Though your sisters are nature sprites, so there's a chance for that as well, just based on the twins." Nature sprites were gentle, communing and energizing with plants and animals, using their familiars to bond with the land.

"I've always wanted a familiar," I admitted, imagining the thrill of an animal best friend who would enhance my magic. "Just as long as I'm not a *necromancer*. Their energy feels wrong to me."

Mom's shiver was visible. "Me too, baby. It's unnatural to commune with spirits and the dead for energy. I don't care how many times they try and tell us it's not dark magic."

Only dark magic could feel that cloying and strange. "Of course," I said with a dry laugh, "I could absolutely be a spellcaster. I mean, the rarest, most powerful of magic, where I can literally draw on the energy of the world itself for near limitless power."

Mom swatted me again. "Don't sell yourself short. You have a spellcaster's attitude."

That had us both laughing because they were rather arrogant. Most of them ended up as leaders in our military and council; fully trained they were nearly unstoppable.

"All of my siblings knew their affinity before college." I sobered up as doubts spilled over once more. "I did expect that after my energy was revealed I'd find myself drawn to fire or water, maybe even discover an animal friend in the forest, but there's been nothing new."

"Many students will be unsure," Mom said, her unwavering confidence bolstering my own, "and the entire point of college is to unlock your true potential and find your coven."

She was spouting the tagline of the Weatherstone College brochure, currently on my desk, but I appreciated it. With a bright smile, Mom placed the acceptance letter beside the brochure and my entrance exam, where I'd managed woeful forty to fifty percentile scores across the magical aptitudes. Eighty to ninety was usually the minimum for Weatherstone, so . . . yeah, as I'd said, unexceptional.

"Get dressed," she ordered as she turned to leave the room. "We're going out to celebrate our final baby off to Weatherstone." When she closed my door, her smile was as bright as last night's full moon.

Snatching the letter off my desk, I read and reread the few paragraphs offering me a college placement. It was signed off by Headmaster Gregor. With four siblings already in the school, I'd heard a lot about the famous necromancer. According to my sisters, he was tough but fair. My brothers were less trusting of him, noting his soft spot for those with affinities in the darker arts.

It appeared I might find out for myself.

Returning the letter to my desk, I pushed doubts aside once more and started to rifle through my clothes for the perfect outfit. All the while distracted by the fact that I finally knew my college. Would I find my true affinity and live up to the very high standards my family had set in Weatherstone's prestigious halls? Doubtful, but I'd give it my very best shot.

For the first time, all of us would be attending college together.

The twins were the oldest; Jenna and Alice were in their final year at Weatherstone, and were nature sprites, collecting animal familiars since they were toddlers. Trevor, my oldest brother, was a year below the twins; he was a strong fire elemental with a secondary skill in air. The fact that he'd almost burned our house down when he was five, eight, and twelve had been a strong indication of his affinity long before he attended Weatherstone. Then there was Jensen, my youngest brother, who was eighteen months older than me, and about to enter his second year. He was a primary water elemental with a secondary in air.

He'd been swimming since he could walk, spending hours in the pool, and holding his breath for ten minutes with ease.

Dad was fire and air elemental, Mom water and earth. It was rare to have two strong elements to call, some might even say . . . exceptional. Hence their acceptance letters to Weatherstone coming as a surprise to no one. Unlike mine.

Well, I'd hopefully find out soon enough. College started next week on the tenth of January—my power had emerged at the perfect time for me to take the entry tests and start in semester one. Still couldn't tell if that was a good or bad happenstance.

Forcing my worries into a box, I slammed the lid closed and pulled on jeans, a thick down jacket, and my waterproof wool boots. The weather was frigid this time of year in Spokane, Washington. It would be just as cold at Weatherstone, which was across the country, out in the wilds of New York State.

For years I'd watched Dad take his daily transport out there, and now I'd get to experience it for myself. It wouldn't be my first time traveling via an energy portal designed by air elementals and spellcasters, but it'd be my first to Weatherstone.

As I hurried downstairs, more than one voice echoed up to me, and I stepped into the living room to find my whole family there—Mom had called everyone back from college to reveal the news.

"Pais! I'm so proud of you." Jenna launched herself at me, throwing her arms around my neck. She was blonde and petite, like Mom, the picture of girl-next-door beauty. Her power, on the other hand, was strongly centered around her bear familiar—she could growl and slap you down good and hard when she wanted to.

"Me too." Alice sounded teary as she joined in on the hug. The twins weren't identical. Alice was my height of five feet nine with darker blond hair. She also had less slap in her power, as the epitome of the gentle nature sprite, with a sheep familiar.

"Our family fucking rocks," Jensen cheered from behind us, and I heard a thud, which no doubt was Dad smacking him up the side of the head.

When the girls pulled away, the rest of my family stared at me, proud and beaming, and I tried not to panic at the very real prospect of letting them down. They didn't expect anything of me, I knew that, and yet I had this terrible urge to try and live up to all their powers and reputations.

Zero freaking chance of that.

"Come on, Little Gem." Dad, also known as Professor Tom Hallistar, patted my shoulder. Hearing that familiar nickname warmed my heart and brought me back to my younger years. From the age of four, I'd collected gems and crystals like it was my life calling. Shelves in my room were filled with my obsession, and if there had been a crystal witch affinity, I'd be set.

"Let's go out and have one last family meal before the nest is empty," Mom choked out around a sob, and Dad was immediately distracted, wrapping her up in his arms.

Dad was a good foot taller, but they never looked awkward together. If anything, despite the fact one was small, fair, and blonde, and the other huge, bronze, and dark-haired, they fit together perfectly.

Trevor, my equally huge and dark-haired brother, draped an arm over my shoulders and steered me out the door. We'd learned over the years that it was best to give our parents space.

"You're going to love Weatherstone," he said with a grin. "And if anyone gives you grief, you find me immediately." The temperature rose as visible flames danced in the darkness of his pupils, before he blinked his power away once more.

I leaned into him. "I'm sure it'll be uneventful. I'm just excited that we'll all be there together, at least for one year."

My sisters clapped their hands, and everyone was excitedly chattering as we waited outside. It was so rare that we had these moments together, all of us in the same place, and I found more joy here than I did in the letter sitting upstairs on my desk.

My family was special, and even if I was the least exceptional of them all, I'd hold on to their strength and energy. Hopefully this would be enough to get me through the next four years.

CHAPTER 2

Forcing myself not to fidget with my long hair again, because messing with the golden-brown strands five times was officially four too many, I stood beside Dad, staring at the imposing Weatherstone gates. Seconds ago we'd been at home, hugging Mom goodbye, and then Dad had called for the transport. The magical ring of energy we'd stepped through had deposited us in a hut to the right of the campus gates. Right was for incoming traffic, left for outgoing.

No one could transport straight into Weatherstone, except maybe the headmaster. I'd heard rumors he had his own personal portal inside his office.

"Impressive, isn't it, Little Gem?"

"Uh, yeah . . ." A picture of the gates had been in the brochure, but it did not do them justice. It was more than their sheer size, standing twenty feet high and at least that wide, constructed from iron, curving and twisting in intricate patterns to reach an arched top. It was the energy emanating from every facet, including the glowing golden script in the center that read *Weatherstone College*. Below, in a slightly duller gold, was the school's motto: *Conquester livara incidium morando*.

The ancient language of magic users was no longer part of our day-to-day speech, but we still used it in spells. Everyone knew the rough translation of the motto: "To conquer life you must first accept death."

It made sense with the knowledge that the two witches who created Weatherstone College, all the way back in the eighteenth century, were both necromancers. Hence the reason a necro always sat as headmaster. Rumors about the pair still swirled to this day, but it was widely accepted that in the end their obsession with death and Weatherstone had gotten them killed. It was believed that their souls remained on this plot of land, trapped, unable to move on to the next plane of existence.

Considering its history, the fact that this was the most prestigious magical college in the country was odd, and yet, *not* at the same time. The afterlife was shrouded in mystery and untapped power, and those of us with magical abilities were always blurring the line between the energy of the living and the dead.

"Ready to start the next chapter of your life?" Dad asked as he picked up my duffel bag, leaving me to pull my suitcase along. The school provided uniforms and all our needs for classes, so I only had to bring some casual clothes and any personal effects I couldn't live without for the next ten months. The hardest part for me was choosing between my favorite crystals, but I'd narrowed it down to ten.

"Yes," I said with more confidence than I felt. "I'm as ready as I'll ever be."

As Dad approached the gates, the shimmery blue field indicating the defensive perimeter grew visible. My siblings told me it ran the entire boundary and was crafted to permit only professors and students.

As this was my first time at the school, I held my breath, wondering if I was about to trigger an alarm. Dad pressed his hand against the center of the iron paneling, right below the glowing motto, and both gates swung open silently, like they were well-oiled. Expanding out from the gates were chalky stone walls standing as high as the gates and much thicker. At one point they'd clearly been white, but now all I could see through the mass of vines that had been cultivated across them was the patina of cracked and aged paint.

If these walls could talk, the history here would no doubt blow my mind.

A fissure of energy caressed my body as we crossed the threshold, but there was no alarm, and we soon made it along the cobbled path that led to the front of the impressive stone and smoky-gray brick entrance. The design of the school was Victorian slash Gothic Revival, and despite many of the wings having been rebuilt over two centuries, the overall facade remained the same. Dark brick with brown stone, turrets, and arches, peaked roofs and columns, dotted across the entire campus.

"Jensen said there's a huge lake at the rear of the college where the water elementals train." I struck up a conversation in the hope of easing my nerves. It was overwhelming to finally be here, feeling a slight sense of unease and excitement as my magic mixed with the unearthly energy of Weatherstone.

"It's beautiful," Dad said with enthusiasm, "and there are forests surrounding the lake on three sides. The familiars are housed in the barracks to the right of the lake, but otherwise it's very natural."

"I'll have to get down there and meet the twins' familiars. I feel like I already know them."

I'd heard so much about this college, of course. Every member of my family had lived here at one point or another, and I was the last to climb the ancient stone steps. History said that the materials used to craft the entrance to the college were imported from the Battle of the Hedons in Germany in 1835. The necromancers wanted to capture the energy of those who died in that battle. There had been many magical wars over the years, some involving humans, and others just between the covens, but the Battle of the Hedons was rumored to have been the most bloodthirsty.

Who knew, maybe these steps were the reason that Weatherstone graduates went on to the strongest of covens, and all but ruled the magical world. Any respect I planned on displaying them though was diminished as my suitcase clunked up each of the treads, and I was struck once more by the thought that I wasn't going to fit in here. Even so, I'd still take the best training in the world, graduate Weatherstone, and find a decent coven.

In the end, that was all that mattered.

Your coven decided your job and financial situation, so the more prestigious your coven was, the better you'd do in the long run. All I had to do was survive my four years here and make it through graduation.

Easy as that.

At the top of the stairs we passed through open metal doors, darker than the brick surrounding them. Dad, who walked these halls five days a week as a professor, entered the building like he owned the place. In truth, with his impressive height and stern features, he always looked like he owned every room he walked into. Tom Hallistar was an imposing warlock, and he never hid his power.

Still, his softer side emerged for those he loved, and while I had no classes with him this year—he taught senior elementals—I had no doubt he'd be around checking up on me.

Inside it was warm, a blazing fireplace in the entrance hall casting dry heat over us. Unwrapping my damp scarf, I examined the room, which was wide with stone floors and walls, covered in thick, rich tapestries. It looked as if it had been modernized a few decades ago, and from then maintained to keep everything pristine.

Dad headed right to the door with *Office* printed across the front panel. He gestured for me to step through first, my suitcase dragging along, and he followed. The office was well lit and clean, dominated by a long desk. Behind it, two witches sorted through paperwork, laughing as they gossiped. Powerful magic usually caused glitches in computers and phones, so for the most part the colleges had minimal technology. There were landline phones for us to call home, but otherwise we would spend our time here talking to each other for entertainment.

"Professor Hallistar," one of the witches cooed, looking up from her papers. "What brings you in here this fine morning?" She looked to be in her midthirties, with a Southern drawl, overly curled blond hair that was piled on her head, and huge brown eyes behind thick black glasses. She wore a lot of makeup and was shooting Dad flirty looks that annoyed me on Mom's behalf.

Dad was gruff as he returned none of her energy. "Ms. White, I'm here to pick up my youngest daughter's welcome pack. It should be under 'Paisley Hallistar.' She needs her dorm assignment and class schedule."

Ms. White eyed me curiously, and I followed Dad's example and kept my face passive and hard to read. "You have the prettiest children, Tom," she said, her smile widening. "Look at those baby blues. I hope you've warned all the boys at the school."

Compared to my siblings, I was no more attractive than the average witch, and I let her words roll off me without settling. This wasn't even about me; she was trying to get a rise out of Dad, and he was stubbornly refusing to give her the reaction she wanted.

"The pack," he repeated patiently, my duffel seemingly forgotten as it draped at his side.

Ms. White's smile eased as she turned to rifle through one of a series of filing cabinets lining the back wall behind the desk. She took a few minutes before we heard, "Aha! I found it." Returning to the desk, she held out the thick cream envelope. "Here you go, dear. Enjoy your first year at Weatherstone College."

"Thank you." My words were polite; hopefully my face followed suit; it didn't always do what it was told.

With a nod and smile, she picked up her paperwork once more and resumed conversing with the other witch as if we'd never entered the room. Dad led me out of the office at the same time as four new students were about to enter. I held the door open for them as they made their way inside. None of them had parents, of course, since they wouldn't be permitted on the grounds, and I thanked Selene that I didn't have to make this journey alone.

When the last of the students, a small redheaded witch, was inside, I went to release the door when Ms. White called out suddenly, "Oh, and, Professor Hallistar." Dad edged back into the doorway to face her. "Headmaster Gregor asked me to pass on a message. I forgot until just now with all the new students." She laughed in a delicate, fluttering way, but Dad's expression remained neutral.

"The message, Ms. White," he said shortly.

Her full lips puckered. "Alright, no need to get snappy. He wanted me to tell you that Rafael Kingston's son is transferring in from Italy this year. He'll be in his third year, but will be teaching a few classes on spellcasting, since he's the strongest of that affinity we've had in a long time. I'm not sure of the significance, but apparently you needed to be updated."

She shrugged, message delivered, and returned her focus to the students waiting for their packs. The small redheaded witch eyed me curiously, and I shot her a weak smile. The aim was to make friends, and since none from my high school were in this grade with me, I really should practice.

I gasped as Dad's hand closed around my wrist, and with urgency he jerked me from the room, the office door slamming behind us. "Dad?" I asked, confusedly blinking at the frantic look on his face. "Are you okay?"

His breaths came out fast and hard. "This changes everything, Paisley." His tone was almost unrecognizable. "You're refusing your acceptance to Weatherstone. We're going home."

With that, he yanked up my suitcase as well as the duffel bag, and marched out the front doors.

CHAPTER 3

My shock lasted a few long seconds. *Refusing my acceptance to Weatherstone?* Okay, someone better tell me who Rafael Kingston was, because that name had triggered Dad out of his sanity.

When my brain kicked back into gear, I raced out of the building and down the steps, following his path. "Dad!" I shouted—he'd almost power walked all the way to the front gate. I cursed as my sneakers slipped on the paved path, which needed a blast from an elemental to clear the icy muck slicking the well-worn stones.

"Dad!" I called again. "Come on. I'm not chasing you all the way home."

His long legs ground to a halt, allowing me to close the distance between us. When I was almost at his side, I noted the way his shoulders heaved up and down as he fought for control. He continued to stare at the gates, no doubt wishing we were on the other side and ready to depart. *But why?*

"Dad, who is Rafael Kingston?" I asked tentatively when I reached him. My breath was visible as I watched students stream through the gates, bags and suitcases in hand. "Dad, you've got two minutes before we no longer have privacy." My voice wavered a beat because I'd never seen him like this, and the longer he was silent, the more I freaked out.

"Rafael Kingston and I grew up together," he finally murmured. He shook his head as color returned to his unnaturally pale features. "Come on, let's get off the main path." I followed him over to a large tree, one of the multitudes of ancient oaks that dotted the college. Despite the weather, it was still a wash of gorgeous red and orange leaves.

"You grew up together . . ." I pushed.

He nodded, his eyes still screaming panic, even if his tone was even. "Our families were friends, and we ended up being the best of friends. Went to Wintergreen together when we started primary at ten, and then secondary, before we ended up at Weatherstone."

A twinge of familiarity filled my thoughts, as if I'd heard this story before, even though I was pretty sure I hadn't.

"His son, Logan, is a few years older than you. Trev's age. You all grew up together, but when you were four, tragedy struck and Rafael's wife, Isabel, was killed in the forest."

A flicker of a memory joined that familiarity. A child's face, arrogant and perfect, staring down at me. I'd . . . tripped in the park. *Logan.* His name raced through my mind, and that one image, but there was nothing more.

"Rafael blamed you?" It was the only explanation I could muster for my dad's reaction right now, since he wasn't known for losing his cool like this.

"He blamed your mother." His voice was cold and bitter. "Isabel and your mom were best friends too, with all of us spending our years together. They were in the forest on the day of the accident. The pair of them were avid hikers, always out in the elements to test their power. Your mom said that she felt a spell and then was knocked to the ground, and by the time she came to, Isabel was gone. They found her body a few days later. Rafael's grief broke him. He accused your mother of delving into energies she couldn't control and drawing darkness to her. But that was his pain speaking."

"Mom never uses her magic anymore," I mused softly. Dad

stared at me for a beat, and I finally put the pieces together. "*That's* why she doesn't use her magic?"

She'd never told me explicitly why, just stating that she preferred to use her physical skills versus her magical ones.

"*Did* Mom cast a spell or call on energy she shouldn't have?" I asked, and then immediately regretted the question as a storm of fury descended over Dad's face. *Shit.*

"Of course she didn't!" he seethed. "She was hurt that day as well and lost her friend. Since then, she's rejected all but the most basics of magic, and for a witch as powerful as your mother, that's painful."

I didn't fully understand that concept yet, with my magic sporadic and uncontrolled, but I believed him. The essence of magical energy inside was innately part of us. The part that separated us from humans, and to cut yourself off from that would be like removing an organ—painful and debilitating.

"Okay, so Rafael hates us, and by extension his son Logan feels the same, no doubt." I shrugged. "What's the big deal? I can ignore him for the year. We're not even in the same grade. I mean, this warning is probably more appropriate for Trevor."

Dad pursed his lips. "You heard Ms. White. He's a spell-caster, powerful enough that they'll have him teaching classes. You have no skills to fight him, Paisley. You're the baby of our family, and I won't risk you."

There was nothing quite like being called a baby when you were twenty-two, but I understood his worry. "Dad, I need to learn and improve my magic. I need to discover my affinity and have a chance to apply for a coven. I won't let this family steal my future like they stole Mom's magic."

He growled, like, a legit growl, and since he wasn't a nature sprite with an animal familiar, it took me by surprise. "There's a blood oath," he bit out, sounding hesitant, as if he knew he shouldn't be telling me this. "Between Rafael and me. This is more than just a mere rivalry that you can ignore. Logan is going to hate you, and through his father's anger, possibly try to hurt or kill you."

I just stared at him. "Surely Weatherstone doesn't just allow students to wander around murdering each other . . ."

That was when Dad grew very still. "Rafael and Logan are spellcasters. I don't know why they haven't come after us before now, but maybe this is a long-term revenge plan. Maybe he was waiting for all my children to be in our old college. I don't know the reason, but . . . I'm worried."

"Maybe Logan doesn't care," I suggested, finding it hard to believe that this was all an elaborate plan. "What if I take extra precautions. Like, I promise not to wander around late at night by myself, and you can magically seal up my room with protection spells."

Everyone got their own dorm rooms, and while the doorways were magically keyed to the energy of the student who occupied them, all spells were breakable if you were strong enough and had the right tools. Dad was powerful though, so adding his energy would give me another layer of security.

He sucked in a deep breath, staring up at the underside of the branches, like the answer lay there. "I'm going to discuss this with your mother," he said softly, "and whatever we decide together will be final. Until then, you can stay here and start settling in. But if you catch a hint of Logan, you get away from him immediately. You hear me?"

The way he said *final* chafed at me, but it wasn't worth arguing with him until I had his decision.

"I promise not to go near Logan," I said. "I'll do whatever it takes to remain safe *and* at Weatherstone."

Dad didn't look convinced, but he was calmer. "Okay, let's go."

We trudged back to the school in silence, joining the dozen

students entering through the double doors. A few glanced curiously at me, noting that I had a parent with me, but no one said anything.

Dad led me toward a set of curved stairs at the back of the entryway. "You have a map in your welcome pack," he said, sounding normal, but I knew him well enough to hear the undertones. He didn't want me here, and he was beating himself up about giving in. "Which you'll refer to a lot to start with, but here's the basic layout. This main building is Writworth Hall, named after one of the witches who created Weatherstone. The building behind it is Ancot Residences, named for the other witch. Ancot houses the dorms, while Writworth has most of your indoor classrooms, along with dining and assembly halls, spell storage, and more. Outdoor classes take place in one of the ten outbuildings. They aren't named but are numbered."

When we ascended to the first landing he directed me toward a set of gorgeous arched gothic windows. I glanced out at the massive expanse of the school campus, catching a glimpse of the lake glinting in the dull winter sunshine. "Stay out of the nature sprites' barracks," Dad said, pointing toward a row of low, wood lined buildings in the distance. "As I said earlier, this is where they house their familiars, and you don't want to unintentionally wander into a zoo without guidance."

I'd always envied my sisters' affinity and their familiars, inbuilt friends and companions for life. Unfortunately, I'd never been able to draw a fly to me, let alone any creature with higher intelligence, so I lived vicariously through the twins.

As we continued, halls spanned in four directions, and despite the chilly day it was warm and homey inside. The stone and tapestry decor continued up here, and the building's innate power traced tingles of energy across my skin.

"This hall is referred to as the *Zoo*," Dad said, pointing out a tapestry of needlepoint zoo animals. "It leads through to the Ancot Residences. The quickest and most direct thoroughfare."

We started along the Zoo and Dad fell silent. He held both of my bags, so I opened the welcome pack I still clutched in my hand. Inside was a much larger brochure than the one on my desk back home. On the front in gold lettering it said, *Welcome to Weatherstone College.*

The motto and short bios of the founders, Writworth and Ancot, were detailed on the inside pages, and I decided to read through all the information later. For now, I needed my dorm assignment. "I'm in Florence Wing," I said, skimming the page. "Room 267."

Dad let out a harried huff. "None of your siblings are in that hall, so be careful. All of the halls intersect with each other at some point. Including Nightrealm."

According to the welcome pack, there were five halls in Ancot: Florence Wing, Spectral Wing, Aura Hall, Ember Hall, and Nightrealm Hall. Officially, your affinity didn't dictate your dorms, but unofficially fire elementals, spellcasters, and necromancers more often than not ended up on Nightrealm and Spectral, nature sprites in Florence and Aura, the others in Ember.

Hence why my father was a touch panicked about my hall intersecting with Nightrealm, and our newest spellcaster. "We'll secure my room," I reminded him. "It'll be fine."

I really couldn't imagine anyone holding on to a grudge for eighteen years. If they'd wanted to attack, it would have happened long ago, right?

Dad huffed but let it rest again, picking up the pace, and I knew he was keen to get back to Mom and tell her what we were dealing with. Realizing this might be my only chance to experience Weatherstone, I peered out of every window, examining the grounds. The college was huge, and if I wasn't yanked out by my parents, I'd no doubt be using the included map more than once.

My future hung in the balance, and it was all thanks to Logan Kingston. I hadn't even met the warlock yet, and already he was a pain in the ass.

That perfect, boyish face flashed across my mind once more, and I wondered what he looked like now. I only had fractured memories of a child, and if fate was kind, his golden skin, laughing green eyes, and contagious smile would have morphed into a dull blob. Maybe a beer gut. Crooked teeth and busted nose would be nice too.

The moon goddess would have my back on this, right? Of course she would.

Hopefully I'd be here long enough to find out.

CHAPTER 4

Florence Wing was beautiful and had its own theme, as did all the other halls. We stepped onto a thick red carpet with an interwoven filigree pattern; the walls were papered in a similar swirling design of faded reds and golds. Between each of the dorm rooms stood intricately carved cream-colored pillars, giving it a very French Provincial look.

"This is amazing," I said as we strolled past doors. "I didn't expect such opulence."

Our house was simple and small, with a large yard that suited our need for nature. Mom hadn't used magic since that day in the woods, which meant she'd had to leave her job with their coven: Blessed Souls of Spokane. She'd been an accountant for their various businesses, but once she halted her magic, she'd been unable to fulfil other tasks.

I'd never heard my parents discuss money, but I had the sense that when the twins graduated at the end of this year and headed into covens to earn their own money, there would be a huge relief on their finances. Weatherstone College had quite reasonable fees—all the magic colleges were heavily sponsored by the covens on the understanding that they were fostering the future of the magical world.

But it wasn't free. Not even for a tenured professor, though he did get a faculty discount that helped.

"Your mother was on Florence Wing," Dad said, his expression calmer now. "I used to sneak in here all the time, because in our day, only witches were allowed on Florence and Aura."

As much as I didn't want to think about my dad sneaking into my mom's room, I was curious. "So, all floors are co-ed now? I know we don't have roommates, but we do share bathrooms, right?"

"Yep, there's two on each floor. One for witches and one for warlocks."

I was well used to sharing a bathroom with four siblings, so this didn't bother me hugely. It was college and we were all adults here, so there would—*hopefully*—be very little incidence of magical sabotage.

It was strictly forbidden to use your affinities against other students, but it was college and not everyone enjoyed following the rules. Hopefully most of us were beyond bullying and toxic behavior.

When we reached dorm room 267, Dad dropped my duffel bag and pointed out the shiny silver panel to the left of the frame. "As long as you're the first to press your hand against the magic scanner, then this room will be yours."

The door was white with ornate detailing and picture framing timberwork. The silver scanner looked out of place, but I appreciated the security nonetheless. Pressing my right hand against it, the icy metal bit into my palm, warming a few seconds later. Metal and earth elementals used the strongest materials from the land itself to create such technologies. This scanner showed no obvious signs of what it contained, but from my studies, I'd guess there was iron, rhodium, platinum, and gold—the best conductors of magic.

"Your energy has been accepted," Dad said.

Jerking my head up, I removed my hand, flexing my fingers against the tingles still skittering across my palm. "It has? How do you know?"

Dad cracked a proper smile for the first time since Ms. White delivered her message. "Well, the door is open, Little Gem."

Oh, right. That was a decent indication. Ready to see my home for the next ten months, I hurried inside to find a sparse, simple, but very comfortable room. The main furniture included a white timber twin bed, small dresser, and desk for studying. The carpet was as plush as the hallway, but a muted gray instead of red. Dad set my suitcase and duffel by the door and followed me over to the window.

"That's the western gate," he said, "beside the apothecary forest."

"Where we'll find spell material," I confirmed, taking note of the landscape.

"Exactly," he continued, "and over there is the Weatherstone graveyard where you'll take a few of your necromancy classes."

Most of the graveyard wasn't visible, tucked in beside the western gate forest. Only the arched stone entrance could be seen, and as I observed it, a shiver traced down my spine. I had no necromancers in my family, and I'd never not feel uneasy around those who communicated with the dead.

Dad turned from the window and perched on the edge of the desk to watch me check out the rest of my room. With its white duvet and thick down pillows, the bed looked comfortable. There was the mild scent of lavender from its magical cleaning. The dresser was empty, ready for me to unpack my bags, but in the small wardrobe to the side, ten or so uniforms hung neatly.

"I hope I can stay," I said to Dad, sinking against the bed. "I just feel there's so much for me to learn here, and a lot of growth to be had as a witch."

Goddess knew I needed it.

"My college years were some of the best of my life," he admitted, with reluctance. "But there are dangers here now." The lines carved around his eyes painted a picture of worry. "You've only just turned twenty-two. You could stay home for a few more years, give us more time."

My heart hurt, but even as he implored me to take this offer, I couldn't. "I love you, Dad, and I will miss you and Mom, but this is the right time for me to leave. Magic blooms when you're ready to step forth, and I won't ignore the call."

We both knew it. Our schooling system was already set up differently to humans, in that we were home with our parents until the age of ten, when we started primary. This was to give us a chance to learn how to exist in a family unit first, which was akin to a coven. It was also designed so that we'd finish primary and secondary school near our twenty-second birthday.

No one really knew why our magic bloomed in that year, but it had been reasoned that children weren't mentally prepared to handle magic, so to keep our species safe, the ancestors had spelled our kind. Or maybe it was the goddesses themselves.

It had been this way for as long as our records of history existed.

Dad's worried expression did not ease. "It's going to be okay," I reassured him. Now that I was here, surrounded by the tingling energy of Weatherstone, I couldn't be torn away from it. As an unexceptional witch, if I missed my chance at Weatherstone, I'd remain unexceptional forever.

"It suits you," he admitted with reluctance. "I'll go now and speak with your mother, before you settle in too deeply."

"Give me a chance," I all but whispered. "That's all I ask."

He nodded. "I love you, Little Gem. I'll cast some protective energy around your room as I leave."

"Love you, Dad."

"I'll see you soon," he promised, before adding with a flash in his eyes, "and don't wander around on your own." He made a show of closing the door tightly.

"Give Mom all the facts," I shouted through the closed door, but there was no reply from the other side, and I wondered if he'd even heard me.

Settling against the bed, I tried not to let stress get the better of me. There was nothing I could do to influence this decision yet, and even though I didn't need their permission as an adult, I also couldn't afford the tuition on my own.

I had to hope Mom would be on my side.

Exhausted but also strangely energized, I bounced to my feet and made my way to the simple white desk. There were two small drawers on either side, with sets of larger drawers underneath each, and a black leather chair. Taking a seat, I opened one drawer to find a collection of pens, while the other was empty. The larger drawers held notepads, textbooks, and a small apothecary kit.

I'd grown up seeing our battered kit in the kitchen, used almost daily between healing, cooking, and small spells. Ours was an all-purpose kit, coded white across the tag, but I knew Dad was desperate for one of the black combat kits.

This was the first time I had a kit of my own, and even as simple as it was, I felt more grown-up and ready for college just staring at it. Almost all witches and warlocks incorporated herbs into their daily lives, and smelling the chamomile tea and lavender ointment was enough to bring me back to my childhood home.

The school kit in its light brown leather satchel held mostly familiar herbs, but there were a few I hadn't ever used before. I assumed they'd be for attack and defense spells. Dried rosemary and angelica were contained in small jars, along with half a dozen others tucked into pockets around the bag.

I hadn't checked out my schedule yet, but considering the kit, there had to be at least one apothecary class. Placing the satchel on the table, I retrieved my welcome booklet, reading through more of the information I'd skimmed before.

First was the map, which I tore free along the perforated line. I spent a few seconds tracing the paths around the huge school, finding Ancot, and noticing that the five hallways of the dorms formed a pentacle shape. Dad had said they all intersected at points, and I noted that my dorm was close to both Nightrealm and Aura.

Setting the map aside, I was about to pull out my class schedule, when there was a knock on my door. The sound didn't come physically though, but in the form of someone placing their hand on my entrance plate. I felt the corresponding intrusion in my energy.

Panic hit me first, before I shook it off. Only Dad knew my dorm room, and he must have returned to impart one last *very important* piece of advice. As I focused on the presence outside, I got wafts of family.

Not just family, but a familiar earthy energy.

It wasn't Dad after all.

As I yanked the door open, Jenna was already in the room—Alice, Trevor, and Jensen right behind her.

"Little sis!" they shouted, and in that moment my worries and nerves vanished.

My family was here, and I knew they'd never leave me to deal with this alone.

That was not the Hallistar way.

CHAPTER 5

As the four of them crowded into the room, I expected the space to feel smaller, but it just felt cozy. They spread out and examined my room like they didn't all have an identical one of their own.

"Pais!" Jenna crowed, my class schedule that I hadn't had a chance to even look at yet in her hand. "You'll be down in the forest for Animal Studies and Their Magical Properties next week. Still my favorite class and professor."

Jenna was in her fourth year and all but specialized now. She didn't have to take any classes not related to her affinity, and it was clear she missed many of her old professors.

Jensen peered over her shoulder. "Hel yeah, you've got Elemental Water 101 tomorrow. That's *my* favorite class. It's basically an hour to swim in the lake and bond with water."

No surprise that was his favorite class. Meanwhile I had zero desire to get into a lake in January. Those with water affinity could heat the particles around them by vibrating the water, but I would freeze my tits off. Jensen must have noticed my concern, and as the sibling I was closest in age with who knew me almost as well as I knew myself, he reached out and patted my shoulder. "The professor will heat the water for you." He looked at the schedule again. "You've got Professor Mordock—he's awesome and taught me so much. You're in great hands."

Jenna nodded. "Very good hands. This is a great array of classes to help you figure out your affinity. Do you already feel more in touch with your energy here?"

"I actually do," I said with a shrug. "But since there's a chance I might not be able to stay, I'm trying not to get my hopes up."

That got their attention. Trevor left the window, where he'd been checking out my view, Alice jumped up from my bed, where she'd been declaring mine was softer than hers, and the other two pushed in closer, my class schedule forgotten.

Trevor stood close to me, arms crossed over his broad chest. "What are you talking about, Paisley? Why the Hel would you have to leave?"

Since I'd already decided I might need their support if the decision didn't go my way. "When Dad was getting my paperwork in the office he received a message from the headmaster about a new student . . ." I told them everything Dad had said to me, finishing up with the tragedy that tore apart families who had been friends for decades.

No one interrupted me, and it was clear by the furrowing of brows and confused expressions that none of them were particularly familiar with this part of our family history.

"So that's why Mom never uses active magic," Jenna said softly, her expression thoughtful. "Now that you've brought it up, I do kind of remember the Kingstons, but clearly Mom and Dad kept the part about the weird death and blood oath from us."

"I don't remember them at all," Jensen declared, sounding pissed. "How old was I when this all went down?"

"Five or six," Jenna said, eyes glazing as if she was doing the math. "Paisley was even younger." She turned to me. "Do you remember them?"

I shook my head. "I honestly didn't remember them at all until Dad started to explain the situation. Then I had this flash of a dark-haired, golden skinned boy standing over me in the park. It happened when he said the son's name—Logan." I shrugged. "I could be making it up though."

Alice cleared her throat, looking uncomfortable. "You're not making it up. Logan looked exactly like that, and you two were inseparable. Even though he's Trevor's age, he just gravitated toward you and was überprotective."

"Even against us, right?" Trevor said, brow furrowing. "Little shit was always sneaking Paisley away, and beating us up for teasing her."

"Yep," Jenna and Alice replied together.

I had no true recollection of Logan Kingston, but there was a twinge in my chest at the thought of his protectiveness. It didn't correlate with Dad's fears that he was going to attempt to murder me on the daily.

"What do you think Mom will say?" Trevor asked, looking between me and Jenna. "And do *we* think Paisley should leave Weatherstone for her safety?"

Jensen snorted. "No fucking way. She should be afforded the same education as the rest of us. Why would she even be in more danger than us? It's not like the vendetta is just against her. It's all of us Hallistars, and I for one am ready to beat the fuck out of this asshole if he steps near my sisters."

Jensen was huge; both of my brothers were just like Dad. One dark-haired, the other light. There was no denying they could be intimidating in a physical fight.

Unfortunately for them, this wouldn't be that.

"He's a spellcaster," I reminded them. "From a family of spellcasters. I think we should consider now that he might be the most powerful warlock in this school." I included the teachers in that assessment.

Both of my brothers shrugged because they were also arrogant warlocks. "We're powerful too," Trevor drawled.

"Against all except a spellcaster," I bit out. This idiot was going to get himself killed trying to play hero.

"This is all moot if Mom and Dad decide she shouldn't stay," Jenna muttered. "We need a plan. A way to convince them that between all of us, we can keep Paisley safe until she discovers her affinity and can manage her magic well enough to protect herself."

Jenna always had our backs, while also strongly encouraging us to stand on our own two feet. As the oldest, she was a typical type A personality, practical, driven, and super successful in every endeavor. As the baby, I was more of the dreamy crystal collector, but the drive was there now. I wanted Weatherstone, and I would fight for it.

"Because this story involves Mom's history, I actually have no idea what decision she'll make," I admitted honestly.

"She's usually the more flexible parent," Jensen agreed, "but you're right about this being a trigger for her."

Trevor ran a hand through his hair agitatedly. "Which means we have no idea how this is going to play out."

Alice hugged me suddenly, it was a fierce, firm hug that had me settling against her briefly, soaking up the comfort. "We'll fight with you, Pais," she whispered. "Even if Dad comes back ready to pack your bags and drag you out of this dorm."

"Speaking of leaving the dorm," Jenna said quickly, glancing at her watch. "It's almost time for the welcome ceremony. We should head to the assembly hall if we want decent seats."

Trevor snorted, a fraction of his anger fading as he raised an eyebrow at her. "You're the only nerd who wants *decent seats* in assembly. Come on, Jen. You've got to learn to relax."

Her glare could have melted the polar ice caps, and Trevor was lucky Morris wasn't here to throw down. "I'll have you know that many students like to sit in the prime positions. Just because you want to be the class clown at the back of the room doesn't mean it's universal."

Trevor's gaze caught on mine, and he shook his head, lips curving into a smirk. He loved all of us equally, but giving Jenna shit was a favorite pastime of his. I secretly thought she enjoyed it too.

"Morris is going to eat you one day," I warned him, and it was Jenna's turn to snort.

"Morris doesn't eat trash."

Trevor slammed his hand against his chest, as if mortally wounded. "I'll have you know, that many a witch has eaten—"

"Shut up," Alice broke through, voice pitched higher than usual. "We do *not* need details about your overactive sex life. My goddess."

Trevor just laughed, enjoying himself immensely, and I was happy to see his annoying personality return. He was always there with his sarcasm and lack of giving a shit. Meanwhile, you'd catch me constantly telling everyone *no worries*, which was a blatant lie—all I had were worries. Especially today.

"Don't stress," Jensen whispered, nudging me. "It's going to work out. I can feel it."

I wanted to trust him, but this was a situation none of us had dealt with before. "Let's go to the ceremony. I need a distraction."

None of my siblings were in their uniforms, so I didn't change out of my jeans and hoodie, enjoying my final hours of comfort. It felt weird to leave the room with nothing, but I didn't have a phone or computer, and there was no need for books and pens today.

Alice linked her arm with mine. "We'll show you the quickest way back to Writworth."

By *we*, she meant Jenna, who was in charge, of course—none of us would fight for the alpha position. In our family, there was a hierarchy based on both birth and power, and we pretty much stuck with it.

She took a right turn into another dorm hall with light golden carpets. The walls were a cream-colored sun pattern and the doors held hues of gold as well. "Wow, this is as nice as Florence," I noted, looking around as my shoes sank into the thick pile. There was a calming element to this hall, and I felt the tension ease in my chest.

"This is Aura Hall," Jenna said. "Our rooms are just down there, so your dorm is close."

"And Ember is over there," Jensen added quickly. He pointed in the opposite direction we walked. "That's where Trev and I will be. You know our room numbers, and if you ever need us, just come running."

Pressing my lips together, I managed not to laugh at how they'd already formed my unofficial security detail. It was annoying but sweet, and I was well used to it. "I've missed you bossy assholes over the last few years."

Trevor huffed out a laugh. "Don't hit us with sentimental words like that, sis, we're all on the verge of tears."

They weren't but they were smiling, and that felt almost the same.

We weren't the only students heading for assembly, and as my siblings closed around me, a few curious glances shot our way. As frustrating as it was to get the *youngest sibling* treatment—Weatherstone was supposed to be my first real chance for independence and to find my own power—I'd take it if the alternative was staying home for another couple of years and delaying my life.

"I won't go looking for trouble," I reminded them, "and I have a pretty good head for danger. It's going to be okay."

They didn't argue, but looks were exchanged between Trevor and Jenna, and I sighed internally. I knew that look, and just like with Dad when he made a decision and dug his heels in stubbornly, those two were the same.

In silence, we passed another intersecting hallway, and for the first time there was a barrier. A black curtain cordoned it off from Aura, as if they were afraid a little sunshine was about to infiltrate their darkness.

As we moved closer, I shifted my position for a better look, hoping to confirm what hall it was. Before I could see anything, the curtain parted, giving me the briefest glimpse of very dark walls and carpet.

The others weren't paying attention as two students emerged, but for the briefest moment my body went cold and then so blazingly hot that I was helplessly fighting flames. My first indication that this wasn't just a random encounter with students was when my brothers ground to a halt, and both shifted in front of me.

Dread settled in my gut as I attempted to see around Jensen's broad shoulders.

"Don't bring your blood oath here, Kingston," Trevor rasped. "We have no beef with you."

My world stopped. The tingles of energy down my spine ceased, and there was not a single sound. But I hadn't mistaken what my brother said. Trevor had felt his power and he knew who blocked our path.

Kingston.
Logan Kingston
Fuck.

CHAPTER 6

I'd barely been at Weatherstone for two hours and I'd already screwed up the part where I promised Dad I'd stay away from Logan Kingston. Not that this was my fault; it was the fault of the asshole who'd stopped us in the hall. An asshole I had no interest in seeing.

Liar.

There were times I wanted to tell my inner voice to fuck off, because I wasn't about the truth right now. This was about staying at Weatherstone, and more importantly, staying alive.

The spellcaster's laughter was a delicious rumble, but there was no amusement. "Hallistars, always so arrogant." His voice was as deep as his laughter, with a slight accent that I couldn't place. Ms. White had said he was transferring in from Italy, but there was more than one country in that timbre. "Why do you hide your youngest? Where is my best friend, Paisley Hallistar?"

His voice lowered over *best friend*, leaving trickles of unease to settle in my gut. It took real talent to make pleasant words sound like a threat. It wasn't a skill I possessed, and even as he terrified me, I had to admire his work.

Needing to know what I was up against, and about done with my brothers' posturing, I ducked between them before they could stop me. With no more barriers between us, my gaze ended up locking onto a set of piercing green eyes. The color was so light it was almost arctic, teaming perfectly with the chill in his expression as he stared me down. Swallowing roughly, all my fighting words died on my tongue.

The goddesses had let me down.

Logan Kingston had not developed a beer gut, crooked nose, or acne.

He was glorious. Absolutely glorious, and completely terrifying.

Taller than my brothers, he towered over the five of us with golden skin and artfully tousled hair that was just a shade lighter than black. A slight smirk played around the edge of lips that were lush but decidedly masculine, and once again there was no corresponding humor in his flat expression.

Realizing he was examining me as closely as I was him, I forced myself to stop running my gaze over his unfortunate perfection and focused on the giant behind him.

It spoke a lot of Logan that I hadn't even noticed his friend until now. A friend who was at least six feet six, with skin a few shades lighter than his buzzed dark brown hair, and built like a linebacker. He hadn't said a word, appearing both relaxed and neutral, but there was a coiled energy about him that told me if needed, he could turn from neutral to deadly in a heartbeat.

These warlocks exuded a darkly menacing aura, hidden under the guise of neutral expressions.

"What do you want, *best friend*?" I managed to find my tongue, faking a bright smile. The air was electric between us. I had no idea what the battle was, or who would draw the first blood, but it was a battle all the same. "We're just heading for the welcome ceremony."

He didn't move closer, but I felt crowded as his gaze narrowed. "I have everything I want, Paisley Hallistar." His repeated use of my full name was crashing into my system, sending it fucking haywire. Bastard was aware of it too, if that knowing smirk was any indication. "Don't you remember our last days?"

Swallowing hard, it was a real effort to keep my voice neutral. "I don't remember you," I said flatly. "I was only four when we were—"

"Torn apart?" he suggested. I found those words odd, and that heat in my veins surged again; my cheeks had better not look as flushed as I felt.

His friend placed his giant hand on Logan's shoulder, and for the mildest of reprieves I wasn't trapped in that gaze. "It's time for assembly," Giant said, words clipped as if he talked only when necessary.

An unspoken message passed between them, and I could feel how tense my siblings were around me, but no one broke the silence, until Logan returned his icy, penetrating stare to me. "See you soon, Precious."

Precious? Did that fuckwit of a spellcaster just call me—?

"What the fuck?" Trevor growled, swiping a hand through his dark hair until it stood up on end. "We should just kill him now and get it over with."

Jenna made a noise that sounded like shock but could have been horror. "Trev! What the Hel is wrong with you. You can't threaten warlocks like that, you'll end up in prison."

At that point, Trevor didn't really appear to give a shit, but he also didn't follow Logan and Giant, who were already halfway down the hall, filling the space between the walls with their broad shoulders.

Meanwhile, I was in the midst of a mini panic attack because it was very clear who had drawn the first blood, and he'd done so with polite conversation.

Jensen looked almost as pissed as Trevor. "That asshole was waiting for us. How did he know we were coming along at that moment?"

"Spellcaster," I reminded them, my voice hollow. "They're in touch with earth magic and can read the energy of others. The five of us leave a distinct essence behind."

Alice nodded, looking pale as she swallowed roughly. "She's right." Her focus turned to me, blocking out the others. "Are you okay, sis? That felt a little confrontational." Her empathy was second to none as she picked through the vibes of the meeting.

Confrontational and deeply unnerving. "It felt like a threat," I murmured, wondering if I was losing my mind. "Why is he focused on me? This is a family vendetta, and yet . . . that felt . . ."

"Personal," Trevor snarled, flames dancing in his eyes. "Which is exactly why we should kill him."

Jenna shot a worried gaze around, but no one paid us any attention. "He *was* solely focused on you," she said, the blue of her eyes darkening. We all had *Hallistar blue* eyes, in varying shades. I wondered if mine were as dark as my siblings' right now.

"Too focused." Trevor was getting more and more worked up. "Of course the bastard would be six feet five and built like a brick shithouse."

"With an even bigger friend," Jensen reminded him.

Trevor breathed deeply through his nose. "I can still take him, don't fucking worry about it."

Before I could advise him to absolutely leave that terrifying warlock alone, Jensen slapped him on the shoulder. "You've got me, bro. We'll deal with him together."

I was surrounded by idiots.

"No!" Jenna snapped. "Absolutely no one is dealing with him. We will ignore the Kingston in the school. We will not provoke a spellcaster. Are you two insane?"

With that, she got us moving again, because we were really

going to be late for the assembly. My watch told me it was nearing 5:00 p.m.

"Why did he move back now?" I asked, my brain stuck in a loop of Logan. Now that I had his grown-up face to go with the name, I was finding it harder to block him from my thoughts. "Dad thinks it might be because we're all in school here. Logan and his father can deal with us in one place."

No one had an answer, but their worried expressions remained as we entered the Zoo and joined the fray of students heading to Writworth. We turned left into a hall and took a set of stairs two floors up to classrooms, their doors open to give me a glimpse of desks and paraphernalia for spellwork. The scent of yarrow and thyme hit us as we passed a room with longer desks and candles set up in pentacles. An apothecary classroom.

The assembly hall was at the end of this row, and when we entered the vast room, noise surrounded us. I couldn't see Logan and his friend anywhere. In fact, there was no one in this room I knew outside of my family. None of my classmates from secondary had made it into Weatherstone, either due to a lack of power bloom or because they'd tested into another college. My best friends, Trina Creston and Olivia Turn, were going to Wicca State, in California.

We'd promised to keep in touch, but the odds were that after a few months the calls would become fewer and further between. College was where lifelong bonds were created in the magical world, because this was where we found our covens. Most of the Weatherstone students would end up in the top covens as well.

As damn depressing as it was, the hierarchy existed for a reason, and it was all about power. Power and connections.

Jenna led us to the front, scowling at Trevor when the first few rows were already filled. We ended up in the fourth back, and my brothers, still riled up, looked like they'd kill the next witch or warlock to look sideways at us.

"Calm," Alice whispered, placing her hand on their arms—she'd sat between them to settle their ire. "We're all upset, but we need to get it together. Trev, you're two seconds from starting a fire with Jensen fanning the flames."

Trevor turned to glower at her, but Alice was just too sweet. "Okay, fine," he groaned. "You're right. I just . . . I don't like that guy. He's not to be trusted."

As he said that, his flinty eyes met mine. "Zero percent trust here," I said, holding my hands up to profess my innocence. "Actually, is there a *less than zero* figure I can use? Because that's where I'm at. He's clearly an asshole, and I prefer to spend my time around people with souls."

A devastatingly gorgeous, broken asshole.

Trevor held my gaze for a few seconds, before he finally relaxed. "We'll see," I heard him mutter, as he turned to face the front.

As the hall grew crowded with witches and warlocks, the college faculty filed onto the stage to sit in a long row off to the side. There were thirty at least, but no sign of Dad, who must not have returned from Mom yet, allowing me the illusion of being a college student a little longer.

The noise of the room died off when Headmaster Gregor stepped up to the small podium on the stage. I'd seen photos of him in the Weatherstone brochure, and he looked exactly as I'd expected: a small, wiry man in his sixties with dark skin and a full head of graying hair. He pushed his thin-framed glasses up on his long nose and swept his gaze across the hundreds of students in the hall.

"Welcome," he said, voice clear and echoing, his magic amplifying the sound so we all could hear. "Welcome to the new year of Weatherstone. I'm pleased to see so many strong magical families returning, and an exemplary influx of freshman." He straightened his orange tweed jacket, and if I hadn't known he was a powerful necromancer, I'd think he was a librarian with how bookish he presented. "Weatherstone will be the home where you find your affinity and coven. Don't waste your time here, use these years to build on your natural gifts and form magical alliances. For you'll need these in the future."

Alliances were everything in our world. Weatherstone gave you the connections you needed to have a future. I knew my dad would never have made it as a professor here without having attended first. Every single professor here was once a student.

"Students need to familiarize themselves with our rules," Headmaster Gregor continued. "They're in your welcome pack, and posted in the office. More importantly, we must reiterate that the safety of our students is our priority. If you have an issue, see one of your professors. Do not take magic into your own hands. The energy we are blessed with is volatile, and in your young ages I know it can be hard to resist fighting back, but there's always a diplomatic solution. We have zero tolerance for using attack spells on classmates. Keep that in mind."

"Logan better keep that in fucking mind," Trevor grumbled under his breath.

I forced my lips together to prevent the snort of laughter emerging. My brother was the epitome of volatile energy, and I really hoped he didn't get himself kicked out this year.

Or killed.

Headmaster Gregor continued with a few more welcoming notes, and then waved his hands to dismiss us with tingles of his dark energy. I shivered at the touch of necromancy, even though he'd done nothing except project his natural power.

"We've prepared a feast for you all, as a welcome. Here's to the best magical year."

Noise erupted once more, and the students were on their feet to file out of the room in a rush. Jenna, of course, wanted to be the first to leave, and I was relieved when Trevor said, "You know, you'd get out first if you sat at the back of the room."

She wrinkled her nose at him. "You just have to move faster. Getting a little sloppy in your old age?"

Trevor lifted his shirt and slammed his hand against his visible abs. "I'll have you know there's not a sloppy bone in my body, including—"

The rest of his argument was lost in the waves of students pushing us forward, and I held on to how normal we were acting. The Kingstons might be trying to kill us all, who the Hel knew, but they couldn't take this away from us. If they ever did, then they'd really have won.

When we reached the dining hall, it was to find a room as large as the one we'd just left, filled with long rows of tables. Students rushed in to grab spots, and I realized how hungry I was. It had been many hours since I'd had breakfast with my parents.

"It's normally a buffet," Alice explained, as she sat on one side of me, Jensen on the other, with Jenna and Trevor across from us. "But tonight they'll feed us family style."

A shiver ran down my spine as magical energy filled the air and huge trays drifted in on currents of air. Air elementals worked in the kitchens to whisk food our way. The trays landed in sync across the room, and when ours landed, it held ceramic blue plates, crystal glasses, silver utensils, and mountains of food. Enough food to fill my brothers and then some.

My stomach rumbled appreciatively, and I snatched up a plate so fast that I knocked Trevor's hand out of the way. "Too slow," I said with a smirk as I heaped food onto my plate.

He shook his head, eyes narrowed. "I still don't understand where you put it all. You outeat me, and you're a skinny little thing."

Excuse the fuck out of me. "Did you not notice the boobs? I am *not* skinny."

Trevor paled and flinched, as if I'd punched him in the junk. "What is wrong with you?" he rasped. "You don't have boobs. Brothers don't notice boobs on their sisters. You need help."

He turned frantic eyes on the others, and they ignored us both to pile their plates with roasted meats, mashed potato, green beans, and whole corncobs.

"Mind your business," I said, waving a spoon at him. "Trust me, the food is going to all the right places."

Jensen snorted. "He looks a little green, sis. I think you finally broke him."

Trevor was a touch green, and for a moment I thought he wasn't going to eat until he shook his head and reached for what was left on the tray. The rest of dinner went down the same way, with delicious food, lots of jokes, and the sense that if the whole year went this way, I'd never want to leave Weatherstone.

When we were finished, it was still far too early for bed, but I found myself sleepy and content, a huge yawn overtaking half my face. "Come on, little sis," Jensen said, all but hauling me up from the table. "Let's get you to your dorm. You've had a big day today, and tomorrow you have classes."

Monday, my first legit day of college. Providing Dad didn't haul my ass out of here in the morning. Tomorrow I'd learn my final fate, and whether my dreams of attending Weatherstone College were about to come to an end.

CHAPTER 7

Hands traced along my skin, the touch firm as he dragged his palms across the hard peaks of my nipples. A moan spilled from my lips, and I gasped as the heat of his tongue flicked over the tight bud of my right nipple. His hold was heavy, pressing me into the bed, and I loved his weight against mine. I writhed against him, needing more. "Please . . ." I moaned. As he lifted his head, the green of his eyes—

Gah! I jerked awake, heart racing as I pressed my hands to my clammy cheeks—my body was on fire despite the cool dorm room. I'd had this dream for weeks now, thoroughly seduced by a faceless male who claimed me as if he owned me, and there'd never been a single defining feature . . . until tonight.

I knew those arctic green eyes. That fucking spellcaster wasn't content with simply ruining my waking hours, he'd now decided to invade my sleep. I squinted at my watch in the dim light to find it was only 2:00 a.m.

Too early to get up for classes, but I was way too worked up to sleep, so I decided to grab a quick shower and wash off the sweat. It wouldn't hurt to cool down my overheated body either.

When I pulled myself out of bed, the moonlight through the window was dull. Crossing to grab my toiletries and a new set of pajamas, I brushed my hand across my crystals, needing their comfort. I'd settled on bringing my favorite mix of amethyst, quartz, obsidian, and moonstone. I'd also packed a necklace that I'd inherited from Granny Helena. I'd never met this particular gran, who'd died giving birth to Mom, but we'd both been crystal lovers.

Tonight, my precious gems were bathing in the moon's glow, recharging their energies. Ugh, *Precious*. And now I was thinking about that spellcaster and the green of his eyes in my dream. Was that a new nickname, or another memory just out of reach? Why did that one meeting with him imply a sense of knowing Logan my entire life when he was nothing more than a stranger? A dangerous one at that.

When I stepped into the hall, it was empty, lit only by a few sconces high on the filigreed walls. I didn't encounter another student on my way, and it was only when I entered the well-lit bathroom that it crossed my mind I'd just broken my promise to Dad by wandering around the halls at two in the morning. For a second I was torn, before deciding that I was already there, so I might as well rinse off.

The bright lights blinded me until my eyes adjusted, and then I grabbed two towels, wedging them under my arm as I headed toward the back where the showers were. The bathroom tiles were sparkling white, cleaned and sanitized every hour—or sooner if a mess was detected by the spells lingering in the walls. That niggling worry about danger faded as I enjoyed the silence, only to reemerge in a burst when I heard a small cry.

I paused, body tense as I waited.

"*Stop!*"

Another weak plea. Broken. Someone was in trouble in this room, and as tingles raced along my spine—magic or adrenaline, it was hard to tell—I decided to check out the situation. If someone needed help and I just ran and left them, I'd never forgive myself.

Shucking off my flip-flops, my bare feet padded against the cool floor as I crept silently. My hands were full, but I wasn't going to risk dropping my shit and alerting them to my presence. As I got closer to the showers, I heard another voice. "You think you're so fucking special," a witch rasped. "Your father got mine fired and destroyed my family. So, now . . . now, I'm going to destroy you."

There was another whimper. "I'm sorry. It had nothing to do with me."

A crack echoed loudly, and I ran. The caress of magic touched my skin, and I tasted electric energy on my tongue. I recognized the power; it was an air elemental.

Rounding the corner, I skidded to a halt to find a red-headed witch on the floor of a stall, half soaked in the water of the shower, and completely naked. Another witch stood over her, slapping air at the crouching witch, her cracks leaving red welts.

As I finally dropped my items, I charged forward. I hated bullies, especially since my second year of primary where I'd been targeted by a small group of assholes-in-the-making. For a solid year they'd made my life miserable, until I'd learned to fight back.

This scene triggered me back to my childhood, and before I even knew it, I was ready to jump in.

The air elemental was so caught up in being the Wicked Witch of Weatherstone, she didn't even hear me coming until I punched her right in the side of the head. Yep, cheap shot, but desperate times when I had no active magic.

Her raged-filled gasp was loud as she stumbled and fell in the water too, leaving her neat blond chignon disheveled. Fired up, I came at her again, and to my surprise she pushed to her feet and took off, slipping on the wet floors, followed by the distant echoing of the bathroom door slamming shut.

Expecting she'd be back, I quickly turned to the redheaded witch, who was staggering to her feet, one arm wrapped across her breasts. "Are you okay?" I asked, snagging one of her towels hanging on the hook and handing it to her.

She took it, sucking in ragged breaths, pupils dilated. "Holy shit," she breathed. "Holy, holy fucking shit." Her breaths grew even raspier, and I wondered if she was going into shock.

"You're safe now," I said in my best calming tone. "I'm sure she won't be back tonight, but if I were you, I'd leave my showers to a time when this room has witnesses."

She stared at me, and then at the towel in her hands, and there was a visible calming as she pulled herself together. "That bitch ambushed me," she bit out, wrapping the white length around herself. Her huge brown eyes, a similar shade to her skin, lifted to clash with mine. "And you saved me. Thank you. Shit, I should have said that right from the start."

"No worries." My favorite phrase was in use again. "I'm just glad I was here."

She shot me a rueful glance. "Would you believe I'm a water elemental? I should have been able to take her out on my own, even untrained, but she was relentless."

The welts from the attack were visible on her flawless skin, and as she moved closer, I realized how pretty she was. Perfect brown skin, long, dark lashes that skimmed her cheeks, and full rosy lips to match the very red of her hair. A color that looked magically enhanced, the darker roots just visible along her part. "I'm Belle," she said, flashing me a genuine smile. "I think I saw you in the office this morning."

"Right, yes, I'm Paisley."

She'd been the curious redhead watching my father lose his mind. Thankfully she didn't ask me what our drama was about; she had enough of her own. "Annabeth must have been waiting for her opportunity. Her father used to work for mine in the High Council of Magic. He got fired two months ago for taking coven bribes. Nothing to do with my dad at all." She tilted her head toward me. "Why did you punch her and not use magic?"

"My magic is not what you'd call particularly reliable."

Or even accessible.

No doubt the next question burning a hole in her brain was *How did you make it into Weatherstone with unreliable magic?* But she was too polite to say anything.

"I'll wait for you tomorrow for our first classes, if you'd like," she said, in another rapid subject change. She jumped around topics a lot, but I didn't mind. "It'd be nice to have a friend to walk with."

"I'd love that," I said. "I'm in room 267."

Not only would it be stupid to turn down a friendly face, since I doubted Annabeth was the only evil witch at Weatherstone, but Belle had mentioned her father was an elder on the High Council.

"Perfect, I'll meet you there at eight." She went to leave, before pausing, "Do you need me to wait in case she comes back to hurt you?"

"Nah, I'll be fine. I've been battling much stronger elementals than that witch most of my life."

If Belle was curious about that statement, she didn't show it. She just waved awkwardly, clutching her towel to keep it from slipping. "Okay, see you in a few hours." She grabbed her pile of clothes, and when she was gone I huffed out a breath. Weatherstone drama was intense, and it was kicking in before classes even started.

At least this time it wasn't a spellcaster with intriguing eyes trying to do me in. I doubted a sucker punch to the side of the head would deter him if there was an attack.

Entering one of the stalls, I made sure the door was shut

and locked, and hung my towels on the hooks. My change of pajamas went onto a small shelf on the back of the door. There was a chill in my bones that had me cranking the hot water and standing under it until I finally felt clean but not necessarily warm.

My chill was deeper than skin. This ancient school, filled with magics I could only dream of experiencing, had already seeped into my essence. Seeped and claimed.

No matter what Dad said tomorrow, I would convince him I had to stay.

CHAPTER 8

Morning arrived far too soon.

"Motherfucker," I mumbled when my watch beeped at me. I'd known to set it after stumbling back from my shower, but now I really wished I'd just forgotten. Rolling over in the bed, I hit the wall and startled awake, remembering I wasn't at home. I was at Weatherstone.

And I had *classes*.

That got me moving. I hauled my ragged ass out of bed and rushed to the bathroom to pee, brush my teeth, and get ready for the day. This time the bathroom was filled with other witches doing the exact same, and there was no sense of dread in the air. It was excitement all around.

Back in my room, I had just enough time to slap on some makeup and braid my hair before I slipped on the uniform and grabbed my schedule. My first class today was Elemental 101, which would test our magic against all element affinities.

"Hey, you look great," Belle said when I all but fell out the door, satchel over my shoulder holding my notepads, pens, and *Beginners Guide to Embracing Your Element* by Professor PJ Witherington.

"You too," I said, shooting her a smile. Weatherstone's uniform consisted of black stockings, a blue pleated skirt that ended just above our knees, a white button-down shirt, and a blue blazer that had the college emblem embroidered over the pocket. It wasn't a sexy outfit, but then again, none of the magical schools were about the sex appeal. They were about learning and furthering your career prospects.

"How is it that you don't look like you were up half the night?" I groaned, wanting to rub at my puffy eyes before remembering I was wearing mascara.

Belle chuckled, and I glared at her cheeriness and near-perfect skin. Witch wasn't even wearing makeup from what I could see. "I'm used to living on little sleep," she said, as if that were completely normal. "I've spent half my life traveling between my dad in Maine and my mom in Panaji, her hometown in India. The constant time zone changes have made me a perpetual night owl, who also doesn't sleep in the day."

Our friendship wasn't at the stage of pry-into-personal-life details just yet, so I didn't ask for any further information. "Guess I know who to call when I need to party at midnight."

"Hel yes, babe. I'm your girl if you ever need a friend in the middle of the night."

I got a stupid rush of warmth at the word *friend*, and it was nice to know that there was a chance of a real friendship.

We joined the throng of students in uniform, the hall a wash of blue, black, and white. Belle, who couldn't be taller than five feet two, set off at a pace that had me near jogging to keep up. "Whatever you're having, I'll take two," I said, stifling a yawn. "Not only do you not sleep, but you're also still energized. My ass has been ripped off and I want a refund. My mom asked me once if I was a cat in my previous life because I had the lounging-around-for-eighteen-hours-a-day part down pat."

She snorted. "My father asked me why I can't *sit fucking still* and my mother calls me her little hyper witch. It's not always fun, especially when I *hyper*focus, but for the most part, if I'm busy, I can keep the rest in check."

Belle led me down a different path than I'd gone with my

siblings, and I kept an eye out for Dad, expecting he'd find me real soon. He wouldn't let it drag on, because the longer I was here, the harder it would be to get me to leave.

When we reached Writworth, my stomach rumbled, and I wondered what the breakfast situation was around here. There wasn't enough time to hit the dining hall, with only ten minutes until Elemental 101, but it would be good to know for tomorrow.

"Quick, if we hurry we'll have time to get to the cart," Belle said, pushing past a couple of students chatting in the middle of the hall.

Cart?

There was no time to ask her what she was talking about, as her tiny figure slipped through gaps in the crowd, leaving me stuck behind a couple kissing like it was their last day on Earth—desperate, drugging, and reminding me that the spark of magic heating our blood was no joke.

By the time I made it to the end of the hallway, Belle was already waiting in the line for what appeared to be a breakfast cart. "You're a fucking angel," I moaned, my stomach rumbling as the scent of coffee and bagels hit me. "I was just panicked about starving through these first classes."

Her face twisted into an expression of horror. "My motto in life is Never Go Hungry. My older sister who graduated last year told me this was the key to sleeping as late as you could. Not that I sleep enough to worry about it, but I do enjoy fast food."

Belle already knew the key to my heart. "I have four siblings at this school, and all of them are going to hear about my lack of knowledge of the breakfast cart." How dare they hold out on me like that? Those bastards would be hearing from my lawyers when I charged them with withholding the truth and miscarriage of justice.

"Is that right, sis?" Trevor swung his arm over my shoulder and jerked me against him in a rough one-armed hug. Throwing my elbow into his side had no reaction, and I was silently fuming that he was too large and strong to easily injure now. "Aw, come on. We would have told you about the cart eventually. It's a rite of passage to starve through the first week of school."

Before I could ream him a new one, Belle held out her hand. "You must be one of Paisley's siblings."

"The best looking, most charming of them all," Trevor said, grasping her hand briefly. "I'm Trevor."

"Belle," she replied with a glint in her eye. "And I'm stressed for the college community if there are three more of you floating around out there."

Trevor wasn't offended. "I like the fire, Red. See you two later."

With that, he cut in line, stole the next two coffees and breakfast sandwiches, biting into them as he walked away. Belle stared after him for a beat, before turning back to me. "Girl, you did not mention that your brother is Trevor freaking Hallistar."

I snorted, taking a wrapped sandwich from the blonde witch behind the cart. I got a coffee as well, moving off to the side to add my cream and sugar. Belle took a sandwich too, but she got hot chai.

"How do you know Trevor?" I asked her. "Do you know Alice, Jenna, and Jensen too?"

Belle blew on her tea, lifting the cup to take a sip. "My sister told me that the Hallistars have tons of gorgeous, powerful kids, and she mentioned your brother won Hottest Warlock last year. Did he tell you that?"

It was interesting to know our reputations preceded us. "He announced it every morning during Christmas break,"

I told her dryly, "as if he was being introduced on a bachelor reality TV contest. *Welcome to the breakfast table, Trevor Hallistar, Weatherstone's Hottest Warlock of the Year.* Trevor is a lot of things, but lacking in confidence is not one of them."

"I couldn't tell," she deadpanned, and we both laughed as we headed for class. As we walked, I alternated between sipping coffee and munching on a delicious breakfast combo of scrambled eggs, hashbrown, and crispy bacon.

It was easier to move now that most students were in class. Belle knew where she was going—she'd been studying the maps for weeks, she'd told me when I asked—getting us to Elemental 101 with a few minutes to spare. This was a freshman-only class, which explained the nervous faces lingering around the door as we entered.

My sandwich was finished, so I threw the trash away and followed Belle into the room. There were a few rows of desks arranged concentrically with everyone staring into the middle. My black dress shoes clicked across the cobbled gray stone floor, which matched the walls. It wasn't well lit, with the main lighting coming from *illumina* globes, high on the walls.

My parents' house was in a human neighborhood, so we used electricity to power our house. But if you lived in one of the exclusive magical communities, you'd use illumina. They were spheres that could be placed into scones or chandeliers, and were created through a combination of earth and fire magic, burning bright for years. They could be dimmed and turned off as needed too.

Belle and I sat in the third row of seats from the center. I placed my almost empty coffee cup on the edge of the wooden desk and lifted my satchel over my head as a light voice echoed through the room. "Doors closing in two minutes."

Energy sprinkled across my skin, and I turned to find a professor dressed in dark robes drifting a few feet off the ground, demonstrating an impressive use of air. She looked to be in her late forties, and under her robes she wore a blue suit similar to our uniform. Her blond hair was pulled back in a simple bun at the nape of her neck, setting off the severity of her dark blue eyes, which observed every seated student.

"I'm Professor Damone," she continued with a no-nonsense snap, "and I'll be guiding you through Elemental 101. I'm a strong air elemental, but I can touch all elements to call, in very minimal capacities. I tend to bring in seniors and other students to help with more advanced elemental training."

She was in the center of the room, staring at us as she moved slowly in a circle. "Time's up," she said with a smile as she clapped her hands, and the doors slammed shut. Exactly two minutes after her last warning.

"Let's begin, shall we . . ."

CHAPTER 9

There was a clatter of bags as students pulled out the textbook, but Professor Damone waved them away. "You won't need that today. First, we need to determine what we already know about your elemental capabilities, and then where we take them from here.

"The elements," she continued, "are air, water, fire, earth, and metal." She produced a spark of each as she ran through them. "As I said, my main affinity is with air, but every one of you should be able to touch an element minutely. Even if you're not an elemental, we all draw from the same magical essence."

As she waved her hands, a breeze ruffled around us, sending pieces of parchment floating to each desk. I studied the diagram sketched on it, a pentacle showing how the five elements were connected, all of them nourishing or quenching, a combination of yin and yang.

"If you are predominantly elemental," Professor Damone continued, "you will use your strongest elements by instinct, but the rest can be accessed if you work hard enough and open those pathways." Belle shot me an excited smile, as if she was more than ready to expand on her water power. "We're all connected through the affinities, our energy, and the Earth. Without one, there would be none."

The class was silent as if the words were as magical as the

energy in our chests. Maybe they were. My sisters told me the best professors here infused their power into their lessons so you left with more than just knowledge. You left with a magical boost.

"Okay," Professor Damone continued, "let's get to the practical fun. Who here already knows their elemental affinity?"

More than half the students raised their hands, including Belle. I tried not to let my envy sprout green across my face, but it would have been nice to have less mystery around that fragment of my life. A niggling part of me still wondered if I might be a dud, prone to occasional emotional outbursts and nothing else.

"Water over here," Professor Damone called, and Belle was on her feet before anyone else even shifted their chairs.

"Holy shit, I've waited so long to specialize in my element."

I reached out and patted her arm. "You go, girl. Show them how you handle your water."

Belle wrinkled her forehead. "Why did that sound dirty? I'm definitely using that line though."

I couldn't help but laugh after she skipped off to join the other water elementals. The room was dividing into five distinct groups, leaving those of us without an affinity or non-elementals at our desks.

"Amazing results already," Professor Damone trilled. "So many of you already strongly connected to an element. Seniors will be joining us shortly to assess your strengths and assign additional element-specific classes based on that. But remember, Elemental 101 will remain for at least the first half of the year. Learning to touch every aspect of the great cycle is important to create well-rounded magical adults."

The door opened to the classroom for the seniors to enter, all of them dividing into the elemental group they were supervising. "The best and brightest elementals will be guiding you," Professor Damone explained. "Learn as much as you can from them."

It wasn't long before we felt the heat of fire, the chill of water, gusts of air, and the scent of earth, along with the clang of metal. We were surrounded by elementals as they bonded, leaving the rest of us to cool our heels and feel left out.

Professor Damone gave us all of her focus. "Let's see if any of you hold an affinity in the elements." Her wind rushed through the room once more, bringing small trays to our desks. Mine landed softly, and I recognized the four items resting on top of the silver base—I'd tried this test before at home and had no results.

"I'll be coming around to each desk to test air personally," the professor said, "but if you've used this kit before, go right ahead and test the others."

I touched the small pile of dirt first, the deep rich brown coating my fingertips. I let the swirl of magic in my center move toward my palms, trying to feel the elements that made up the dirt. But there was no feeling of connection, no way I could manipulate any of the grains on my palms. It was just dirt.

I tried water next, swirling my fingers through the glass, washing away the earth, but again there was no connection. I felt no urge to surround myself with the water. As much as I enjoyed showers, that was where my love for water ended.

Putting water aside, I moved on to the flint and accompanying tinder. The flint was used for initial combustion, but then it would be a fire elemental's job to control the flames. Fire and air often went together, like for my dad, who was almost equally strong in both.

The *equal* part of that equation was what made his a rare magical ability. Usually there was a dominant and a secondary.

The flint struck on the third attempt, and the smallest of flames sprang to life. The heat was low, almost negligible, and for the first time I felt the slightest of draws, deep in my chest, a lingering connection. But no matter how hard I tried to create a larger flame, it remained steadfastly a tiny flicker, before eventually sputtering and dying out.

An echoing hollowness resounded in my chest, and as much as I wanted to cling to that tiny, *tiny* draw I'd felt, I knew it wasn't even close to being strong enough for an affinity.

The final element on the tray was metal. Five rods of differing metals spread out, and I recognized iron, silver, and rhodium. The other two were a mystery, both dark gray and without any shine.

Lifting each piece, I searched for a connection, but once again there was a slight spark with rhodium and iron and nothing with the rest. Why the Hel did a slight spark feel worse than no spark? That flicker of hope hurt even more when it was dashed.

Professor Damone made it to my desk not long after. She observed the elements scattered on my tray, her sharp gaze missing nothing. "No calling from these four," she said, and it wasn't a question.

I shook my head. "Not really. I felt the barest flicker with fire and metal."

There was a shred of sympathy in her blue eyes as she nodded. "Your father told me you unlocked your energy only recently. A lot of the students here have had months, if not a full year to work on their affinity before the start of college. You don't need to worry about finding an affinity for a long time, Ms. Hallistar. It will come when you're ready."

It was a "mom" pep talk if I'd ever heard one, and I felt a pang for my own. I needed to call home and let her know I was settling in, but I'd been waiting for Dad to give me their decision first. It was odd that he hadn't come to find me yet.

"Thank you. As frustrating as it is not knowing exactly where my magic affinity lies, I'm excited for the opportunity to learn and grow."

"An excellent attitude that will take you very far," she replied with a knowing smile. "Before I leave, let's test out air."

The air wasn't visible, but as I closed my hand over hers, I felt it swirl, tickling the underside of my palm. Letting her energy settle against my skin, I shut my eyes, and searched for the draw.

Professor Damone remained silent, and even though my eyes were closed, I felt her focus on me. After a beat, I released the wind, and it drifted back to her.

"Well?" she asked, sounding as if she already knew the answer.

"Nothing," I confirmed. "I'm not an elemental."

Her smile was once again brief. "Not yet. But you'll find your way. I'm sure of it."

With that, she strolled to the next student and left me to ponder her words.

CHAPTER 10

"I feel fucking invigorated. I might not sleep for a week." If I hadn't known water was her jam, I'd have thought Belle was using air to float out of class. "That was the most intense water experience of my life. I can't wait for more advanced classes. They've already added two to my schedule, and I've never felt closer to my element."

"I'm really happy for you," I said, barely able to stop an excessive sigh from escaping. "Meanwhile I feel closer to my chair, because I didn't leave it for the whole lesson."

She breathed out a laugh, shaking her head. "You'll get there. Otherwise, you and your chair can form your own coven."

I choked on my own laugh, covering my mouth with my hand. "Christ. I better invite the desk too, otherwise it'll get jealous."

Belle nodded, forcing a serious expression. "You don't want to know what scorned desks are capable of. Trust me on that."

Students were sparsely dotted around the hallway as we made our way to our next class: Weatherstone and Its History of Necromancy. Another freshman-only class that I was excited about; history had always interested me. "At least our next class isn't an active affinity class," I mused, looking around at the students rushing by. "My power is still playing hide-and-seek, outside of a slight spark with fire and metal."

Belle gave my shoulder a gentle squeeze. "Honestly, I wouldn't stress about it. Mom took eight months to figure out her affinity. She expressed magic early, but then was stuck in her college—Grimsworth University—for almost a year before she developed a craving for the ocean. Her dorm was a few miles from the beach, and she woke one morning knee-deep in the water. It'll happen."

"Fuck, good to know. It's just hard because all of my family expressed clear affinities during their toddler years."

"Your family isn't exactly normal," Belle reminded me. "I'd heard about them long before the Hottest Warlock of the Year came strolling by."

I squeezed my eyes closed briefly. "Please don't ever call him that when he's around. His head is already too big."

The history classroom was five times the size of our last, with cork floors that squished beneath our shoes as we made our way to the stadium seating. We'd arrived early, having booked it out of Elemental 101, which gave us a chance to observe everyone walking in.

There were a lot of faces from our last class, including Marcus Lofting, who I remembered quite well. "It's Fireball," Belle whispered, and I tried to smother my laugh.

Marcus had engulfed half the room in flames before they put it out.

"Or should we call him Aquaman?" I replied, since he'd shown as strong an aptitude for Belle's element too.

"He could touch air as well," she pointed out, and I wasn't surprised that Professor Damone had been fawning all over him. He showed signs of multiple strong elements to call, which meant they'd be watching him as a possible spellcaster.

Spellcasters were hard to classify in college because students could show small affinities in multiple areas and still only end up having a single strong affinity. A true spellcaster could touch all affinities equally except for necromancy. The dead didn't share well with the living.

Belle and I must have been staring at Marcus a little too hard, because he caught my eye and offered the slightest of smiles. I turned my gaze away, trying not to notice that he was quite nice to look at—a few inches taller than me with broad shoulders, messy dark blond hair, and piercing blue eyes.

"Spellcasters are way too much work," I said, before realizing that Belle would have no idea what I was talking about. I'd answered my own damn thoughts.

"Way too much," she agreed, taking that brain slip in stride. "Drama-free is the key this year. We're only at college once, and I'm not tying myself down to any witch or warlock."

"Same."

We high-fived over it, settling the deal the old-fashioned way. It wasn't that I didn't want to date. I absolutely needed to find an outlet for the rage of fire in my veins, lest the dreams keep me awake for the entire year. But nothing serious.

That wasn't my focus here.

"Have you ever had a boyf . . . ?" Belle trailed off suddenly, and I stiffened in my seat, forcing my gaze not to look toward the door. Because I felt what had shocked her. I felt him.

How in the Hel . . . ?

"Who—*and I cannot emphasize this enough*—the fuck is that?" Belle breathed.

"Logan Kingston," I bit out, gritting my teeth as I continued to fight my eyeballs' need to turn his way. Disloyal bastards. "He's both my *best friend* and archnemesis, apparently."

Her gaze snapped to my face, but then she was looking at him again, as if she couldn't help herself. "Are you telling me that gorgeous hunk of power that just walked in the room is your friend?"

The laugh that burst from me was hard. "Did you miss the

archnemesis part? We're enemies, and I don't see that changing anytime soon."

"Did your dad fire his dad too?"

"Something like that," I mumbled, before getting more specific. "His dad has a blood oath against mine. It's a long story, but there's a chance Logan might want to murder me."

She snorted as if I was kidding, but I didn't join her.

From my peripherals, I could see that Belle wasn't the only one gawking. Even if Logan hadn't been a giant, gorgeous specimen of warlock, he was a spellcaster, and power was sexy in our world. What can I say, we're fickle little witches.

Logan must have reached his seat, as Belle's full attention returned to me. "Murder or not, maybe you two should bang it out first. Imagine the hate fucking. That's way too fine a warlock to waste as a nemesis if there's no hate fucking."

It was horror that twisted my features. Absolute horror and nothing else. So help me goddess. "He's legitimately terrifying," I breathed.

Belle shrugged. "The warlocks who fuck the best always are. It's like riding a roller coaster that's never had a safety check. You have no idea what's going to happen, but it's always thrilling."

"Or you end up dead," I said as I rolled my eyes. "Repeat after me, we don't fuck bad boys."

Belle opened her mouth, and then slammed it shut. "Sorry, I can't. My programming is preventing me from lying."

Shaking my head, I had to laugh, and I felt somewhat better about that asshat being in the room. When my neck started to hurt from the odd angle I was holding to avoid him, I turned to face the front, catching a glimpse of Logan out of the corner of my eye. Not just Logan, but Giant, and another white-haired warlock. All three were in conversation, ignoring the gawking from the crowd.

I found myself glaring at his profile, which was just as perfect as the front view. He could really use a bump on his nose—someone should break it for him. As my thoughts grew murderous, and I maturely ignored my irrational anger at a warlock who'd done nothing to me yet, he turned and met my gaze full-on. Like he knew I'd been staring at him. *Gulp.*

A student walked up the pathway between us, breaking the tension, and I was finally able to turn away. *Shit shit shit.* I should not have looked his way. I'd known not to from the second he entered this room.

"Definitely enemies," Belle confirmed, patting my arm. "I vote for enemies with benefits, because there was tension, Paisley. All the tension."

If only she knew that tension might be born of hatred. If Logan blamed my family for the death of his mother, then I doubted we'd ever move past it. All that was left to determine was how much he hated me, and if he planned on destroying my family to sate an old revenge.

"What's he even doing in this class?" I felt completely out of sorts. My uniform was strangling me, my skin clammy under all the layers. On top of that, the swirls of energy in my center were performing a fucking dance. "He's supposed to be a junior and long past freshmen classes."

Belle shrugged. "Did he transfer this year? Because this is a specific class for Weatherstone. Everyone has to take it before they can graduate."

Fuck. "Yep, he did."

The last of the students hurried in as Headmaster Gregor entered the room. He had a blond male professor at his side, who was both younger and taller than Gregor.

"Welcome," Professor Gregor said, just as he'd done yesterday. "This class is designed to give you an overview of Weatherstone and the witches Writworth and Ancot. As a necromancer, blessed to govern this school over the last ten years, there's a legacy of dozens behind me. Those of us who find an affinity in the energy of the dead, cross planes of existence to discover more questions than answers usually. It's not an affinity for those who settle, but for those who seek beyond the norm. With that being said, I will now leave you in the capable hands of Professor Jones, a former necro student of mine."

There was polite applause as Professor Jones took over from Gregor. "It's great to see so many new faces," he said, his voice both deep and with a slight Southern drawl. "I know for many of y'all, this feels like a filler class, but I promise that understanding the history of your world helps you step into the future as a stronger, more well-rounded witch and warlock. With that being said, let's get started."

The next hour was spent delving into Writworth and Ancot, the two witches who started Weatherstone. Professor Jones explained that they were friends, both born into English families filled with elementals. "They were the only necromancers in their small village," he said, "and at this time in history, that affinity had a very dark reputation. Female necromancers were often accused of being witches by humans and burned at the stake."

"Witches and warlocks just cut their heads off, if I remember my history," Belle added in my ear. She was taking diligent notes, and I could already tell that she was dedicated to her bookwork. Meanwhile, I'd written ten lines, and most weren't even legible.

"The lack of understanding almost wiped out our affinity completely," Professor Jones continued. "Rose Writworth and Francesca Ancot escaped in the middle of the night after hearing Rose's father turn them in to the local law enforcement. They crossed the Atlantic, stowing away on a rickety old ship, the SS *Brigade*, which would have met a watery death if they hadn't used their magic to guide it. Once they reached the Americas, they searched for the perfect plot of land to establish themselves, and with one goal in mind—turn necromancy into an affinity with the same respect as the others.

"They were untrained," he continued, pacing as he spoke. "As were all necros in those days. They didn't understand the risks of connecting to the dead, and as they sought to achieve their goals, they did whatever it took for the power. Even drawing on energy from darker souls they should never have touched."

He let the tale settle in the room, and I rubbed at the goose bumps on my arms. He had a way about him, this professor, turning a lecture into what felt like a scary campfire story.

"They used their magic to call for those seeking a different life, drawing them from all over the world. As many of you would have felt already, there's a power here in this school, a beacon to our kind."

I'd felt it from the moment I crossed the entrance gates, that trailing of energy along my spine.

He wrapped his lecture soon after, calling out over the chime of the bell: "I'll continue with their story next week, but we'll go deeper into their backstory first. You need to understand the world they lived in to better understand their motivations. I'd also suggest some independent research of your own. I promise, they're fascinating and terrifying witches."

As I packed my notes away, I found myself looking forward to the next lesson. Belle followed me as we left class, and I ended up strolling next to Marcus, of all warlocks.

"Better lesson than I expected," he said, and I looked around to make sure he was talking to me.

He was.

"It was great," I replied with a quick smile. "I love history, and even though Elemental 101 kicked my ass, it was amazing too."

He let out a low, soothing sort of laugh. "At least you didn't almost burn the school down." A slight pink flushed his cheeks, but he didn't sound embarrassed.

"At least you won't have to form a coven with your desk and chair," I offered.

He shot me a confused look but took the comment in stride. "One fear to cross off the list, I guess."

Belle popped her head in then, smiling broadly. "I'm Belle," she said brightly. "Water elemental."

"Marcus," he replied. "Fire elemental."

He hesitated just a second before his response, and I wondered if he was thinking about all the other elements he'd managed to express today.

"Paisley," I added. "Affinity unknown."

Marcus shot me a nice smile. "The mystery is half the fun. I'll be keeping an eye on you, Paisley. Something tells me that you might surprise us all."

When we exited the room, he peeled off, heading in the opposite direction to us with a brief "See you later."

Belle met my gaze, eyes wide. "Did he just say he's keeping an eye on you? Well, damn. Let's bring him into the dining room coven. He's hot and powerful—I mean, not Logan Kingston hot, but he's also not trying to murder you. Big bonus points."

"All the bonus points," I agreed.

I'd initially dismissed him as a possible hookup, but I couldn't deny that flicker of interest between us. A flicker could fan a fire, and as we headed for lunch, I decided it was a maybe.

CHAPTER 11

Lunch was held in the dining hall, with a long buffet running right through the center of the tables. "This selection is amazing," Belle said, eyes alight like we'd just been given free shopping trips with a limitless credit card. "I'm a vegetarian, and it's usually so hard to find a decent selection."

I tore my gaze from the mashed potatoes. "You ate a breakfast sandwich this morning."

She shrugged. "What can I say, bacon is an evil mistress who won't release me from her grasp. If bacon calls, I must come running. I'm a vegetarian with mistresses."

I snorted. "Well, I hope they don't find out about each other."

Belle smirked. "I'd never be that sloppy. I can keep my affairs in order." I had no doubt she could.

I was momentarily distracted by a tray of my favorite food: "They've got salmon sushi," I gasped, before noting the next section, "and mixed fruit with yoghurt and honey. I'm in heaven."

We made it to a table, plates overflowing, and since Jenna and Alice had the same lunch break, they found me soon after. "Has Dad seen you yet?" Jenna asked after I'd introduced her to Belle. She reached out and stole a piece of my watermelon, shit-eating grin on her face as I glared and tucked the bowl closer. *Nasty witch.*

"Not yet," I admitted, side-eyeing Alice too, though she rarely stole my prec—food. Asshole had ruined that word for me as well. "I don't know what he's waiting for, but I hope this means they've decided to let me stay."

Alice nursed her cup of coffee, taking a drink. She had to have at least three cups a day or she'd show her uncharacteristic *cranky witch* side. "It's got to mean that. There's no way Dad would let you get established like this unless he was prepared to continue it. I saw him before class earlier and he looked relaxed, so I'd guess Mom voted for you to stay."

Mom always had my back, no matter what, and I made a note to call her this afternoon when classes were done.

"Okay, we're off to see Simon and Morris," Jenna said, eyeing the rest of my fruit, so I picked up my fork and wielded it like a weapon. "You need to come meet them soon."

"I will," I promised, waving the fork as one last warning. "Give them hugs for me."

Alice dropped a kiss on my cheek. "Will do," she said, and then she dragged the evil twin away, leaving me to enjoy my lunch in peace.

"Simon and Morris?" Belle asked. "You haven't met their boyfriends yet?"

I cracked up, laughter spilling from me. "They're nature sprites. Simon and Morris are their sheep and bear familiars. Neither of them has a boyfriend." Jenna had come out as gay to us a few years ago, and Alice had no interest in sex at all, preferring to spend her time in nature. They channeled the fire of their magic into nature and the platonic love of their lives, Simon and Morris.

Belle stared at me, her spoon of mac and cheese halfway to her mouth. "They called their familiars Simon and Morris?"

"Yep." I slurp up another piece of delicious fruit. "They're weirdos, but I love them."

Belle's expression softened. "You're making me miss my sister, and she's a real bitchy witch that one. Might call her tonight."

Sibling relationships made no sense from the outside, but everyone understood the rules. We were allowed to make fun of and beat up our siblings, but no one else better lay a fucking hand on them.

We were finished with lunch, so we dropped our trays into the pile near the trash cans. "Are you excited for our next class?" Belle asked.

I shot her a look like she'd just asked me if I liked to stab myself in the hand with a pen. "Are you kidding me? The lake looks freezing, and I have no water affinity."

"I can't fucking wait," she said, cheeks pink with excitement. "Can we head there now?"

Since we had no choice, I forced some cheer into my response. "Yep, let's do it."

We stopped off in our dorms first. I threw my satchel on the desk, and changed into my school-provided, navy-blue one-piece swimsuit, pulling on a pair of blue school sweats over the top.

Elemental Water 101 was a class where we'd be immersed in the water, in winter, because everyone here had a death wish.

I exited the room to find Belle waiting, dressed in the same blue sweats. "Did you grab your towel?" she said, holding up a Weatherstone-branded, striped blue-and-white one.

"Crap, no!" I dashed back into the room and opened my wardrobe to grab one of the four towels neatly folded on the top shelf. With it tucked under my arm, Belle and I hurried along the hall, and took a right turn that led to a set of doors that opened to an external staircase. As we stepped outside, we were assaulted with an icy breeze, and a vast array of scents, including pine, maple, and freshly cut grass.

"Welcome to the western perimeter of Weatherstone," Belle said, as we started down the stairs.

Despite the thick fleece of my sweatshirt, the wind cut right through, and I shivered, but I was at least grateful that we didn't have any snow. Dad had said the weather was relatively mild this year, as Northeast winters went, and I would have ditched this class if I saw even a sliver of ice on the lake.

A swift breeze sent my hair flying around my face, and I pulled it back into a ponytail, resting the towel against the railing. As I stared out at the grounds, I noticed how green a lot of the lawn still was, along with a multitude of vibrant flower gardens. "It must take a ton of magic to keep these flowers blooming all year," I said, snapping the band in place around my gathered hair.

Belle spared the gardens a quick glance and nodded. "Yeah, Kris, my sister, told me that they have earth elementals working here all year." Her focus returned to the lake, and I hurried with her to get to class.

"I almost can't believe I'm finally here," Belle breathed reverently. "Finally ready to step into the next stage of my life and power."

College was the final step before the rest of our lives began, and being here was a big deal. "The fact that I'm even at Weatherstone is hard to believe," I said with a derisive laugh. "My magic is hard to connect with, and I don't show any exceptional skills."

Belle shot me a glare. "If you're here, it's because you earned your spot. This was the right college for you, and I'll kick your ass if you keep talking bad about yourself."

She was a fiercely protective friend, even against myself. And I was grateful to have stumbled into that bathroom at two in the morning. "I'm embracing it," I promised her, "just a little slower than others."

Our gazes remained locked for a few seconds, before hers softened. "Okay, good. Slower is fine. So, what were your sisters talking about before?" Her ability to rapidly subject change was second to none. "About your father. Was that about how he yanked you out of the office yesterday?"

She was far too observant. "He wants me to defer for a couple of years. He tried to pull me out yesterday, but I fought back enough that he was going to talk to Mom about it. I expected him this morning before class, but he hasn't come by yet."

Belle ground to a halt, clutching her towel closer, face wreathed in horror. "He wanted to pull you out of Weatherstone? This college is the safest in the world, right? And the blood oath isn't even between you and Logan."

It was supposed to be safe here, but more importantly, it was the college every magical parent in America hoped their child would attend. No one would pull their children out without evidence of an actual threat against them. "Dad believes Logan is here to fulfil the oath, and that the Kingstons are too powerful to be worried by rules or Weatherstone security. There's a lot more to the story, and it's . . . complicated."

There were so many questions in Belle's eyes; she just stared for a few seconds before schooling her face once more. "Tell me when you're ready, okay?"

"Yep, I promise to spill the entire story after class."

"I'll hold you to that." She let it go, content to play witch-guide along the path. "That zone is where the seniors do alchemy." She pointed toward a set of three buildings with stone walls, no windows, and what looked like a single door for entry and exit. "I've heard it can withstand an atomic bomb. And these are the Barracks." I'd already seen the long wood-lined building with Dad, but from this angle, it was even larger than I'd thought. We could hear and smell the animals within, catching glimpses of white-fenced pens off the side with horses, bulls, bison, and even a giraffe.

"That's the Dojo," she continued, "where we take our attack and defense classes in sophomore year." It was an open-sided building with visible fight rings, octagons, and training equipment. "I'm super not looking forward to that," she grumbled. "Being tiny has its advantages, but not in fighting."

"I've had a little training with my dad," I said. "But certainly not enough to keep me from getting my ass kicked."

We were past the bulk of the buildings now, heading down toward the icy-looking lake. A group was already milling around the water's edge, so we just stood near the back and waited for class to start. Half the students were still dressed in their uniforms, and the other half in sweats like us.

The professor for this class didn't arrive on the path. Instead, he popped up in the middle of the massive lake and zoomed his way across to us. "Welcome, I'm Professor Mordock," he said, marching onto the shoreline. He had an open, friendly face, and I was reminded of Jensen telling me how great he was.

He pushed a hand through his slicked-back, shoulder-length brown hair. He wore only a pair of navy board shorts—nothing else—and there was no sign he was cold. "I'm so happy to see you all down here by the lake." His smile grew. "And I know it's freezing, but I promise that I can keep you comfortable in the water." The crowd spread out, so we weren't so bunched around him. "For many of you who don't have a strong affinity to water, it's still important to find the smaller connections. That's why every first-year takes classes that deal in all the elements, despite many of you not calling it as a primary affinity."

The well-rounded nature of our education here was a part of college life I loved—except when forced into a lake in the middle of winter. This class was much better suited to the summer months.

"Any questions?" he asked.

There was a beat of silence, and then a tall Black girl raised her hand. "Are there any creatures in this lake?"

Okay, excellent question. Thank you.

Professor Mordock's smile never wavered. "Absolutely."

No one laughed, because it was nearly impossible to tell if he was joking or not. I started to back away, until Belle caught my arm and rolled her eyes at me. "Wimp," she whispered.

The professor was the one to break the silence. "Okay, okay," he said with a chuckle. "There's absolutely nothing dangerous in the lake. This is my second home, and I can keep you safe. Now, get into your suits and hit the water."

Belle and I moved to the side, and I shivered harshly when my nice warm sweatshirt was sitting on my towel on the ground. The wind was brutal for all of five seconds, then a warm breeze washed over us. Professor Mordock had been joined by Professor Damone, and she stepped in to give the class a break from the arctic air.

"Told you I had your back," Professor Mordock called out. "Now hurry up, the water is lonely without us."

Belle's face was wreathed in excitement, while I wondered if I could just drop this class completely. "I'm so freaking excited for this," she said, and I could feel her energy surging. It boosted my own witchy powers. They roiled in my chest, settling again soon after.

This was the first time I'd stepped outside since arriving. The power was stronger here by the lake. Traces of energy traversed my spine with force. With them came the slightest sense of unease, no doubt about entering this lake in winter.

Students were already strolling in, including Marcus and his friend Troy, who dove into that torture chamber like it was a heated swimming pool. With the professor's help, maybe it was. "Come on, witch," Belle called, all but running to dive in.

"Slow and steady," I muttered back, warm water swishing around my ankles. It wasn't bath temperature or anything, but it was pleasant, especially with the air still heated around us.

The deeper I got, the cooler the water grew, and I figured that not even Professor Mordock could heat the whole lake. Still, it wasn't freezing, and I decided just to dunk under a couple of times, before sitting my ass in those shallows.

"Feel the water surrounding you," Professor Mordock called. "Let it cover your skin and fill your energy. Try to touch the individual elements of the hydrogen and oxygen particles, so you can control the way they move around you. Once you learn how to draw those elements from the water, you will be able to breathe below. You can also use it to propel you through the water."

A skill he'd demonstrated quite successfully earlier. Almost everyone was submerged now, swimming around and moving farther from the shore and into deeper water. I continued to step slowly until the water lapped at my waist, and I tried to ignore that unnerving race of energy down my spine.

But it felt stronger.

Stronger and uncomfortable.

Was I reacting to the water? Could this be an indication of an element to call? I'd felt very little in class, but this was a much more immersive testing grounds, and my energy was absolutely reacting to the power here.

Bolstered by a very slight possibility of finding my affinity, I shelved all my fears and dove into the lake, enjoying the caress of water against my skin. When I surfaced, I turned to find the professor, but instead caught sight of a familiar figure standing up on the hill near the buildings.

There was no mistaking who it was: Logan Kingston. He

was huge, and even though I couldn't feel his energy from this distance, my chest constricted the same way it had in our previous encounters.

What the Hel was he doing here though? He wasn't in this class, that was for sure, so was he . . . stalking me?

Was Stalkcaster the one responsible for the shiver down my spine, and dread in my chest? It felt narcissistic of me to assume his presence had anything to do with me, and with that in mind I decided to ignore him. Should be easy enough.

Provided my head remained under the water.

Better learn that breathing technique, *stat*, because I was going to need it.

CHAPTER 12

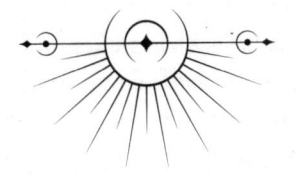

"When you're under the water, move into her depths," Professor Mordock shouted. "Give her a chance to entice you."

I looked to my left to find him waving us farther into the lake, and when I returned my focus to the shore, Logan was gone. The eerie feeling didn't vanish with him.

Shaking it off, I sucked in a deep breath, diving deeper into the water. It was clearer than I expected, the winter sunlight streaming down as I swam in a slow breaststroke. The water itself felt light and silky, and with dozens of students around me, I decided to follow the professor's instructions and push deeper.

Needing to breathe, because to no one's surprise my power hadn't connected to water particles, I popped my head up to find I was quite a distance from the shore now. Belle was even farther out, her red hair flashing as she shot herself up in the water. It was only a foot or so, but she looked to be having the time of her life.

This time when I dove, I focused on connecting to the water, letting that swirl of power in my chest expand. When my lungs were screaming for air once more, I surfaced, sucked in a deep breath, and returned below. I'd felt a slight connection, and I didn't want to remain above for too long.

Diving down, tingles started down my spine and settled low in my gut, and with each kick that sent me deeper, the more I drew power from my essence. The energy of Weatherstone overall was strong, but here, under the water, it really kicked up a notch.

Forcing my power to swirl as hard as I could without busting my brain, I almost choked when a brief illumination shone from my hands. My first sign of active magic since I'd exploded the lights during my bloom.

I have magic!

It was there, but it was caged. I hadn't found the right key yet.

In my excitement, I'd failed to notice how dark the water had grown around me, until I could no longer see my hands. Lungs straining, I kicked hard and rose through the water until it grew lighter and lighter. I popped my head above and took in a glorious lungful of air. Just one single breath.

Before I was jerked from below, a vise around my ankles.

The unease I'd been feeling ramped up until my body was shivering uncontrollably, even as I fought and kicked against whoever grabbed me. At first, I assumed a student was being an asshole and pranking me, but a quick glance below showed no students in the vicinity.

Still, there were more than enough water elementals around who might be using their power against me. But why would they?

The deeper I was pulled, the less it seemed likely this was a simple prank, and as the water grew cold then icy, true panic kicked in. My mind flashed to Logan, who was more than capable of drowning me in the lake, and I fought even harder. But there was no breaking the hold.

I barely managed not to scream, knowing I'd take in lungfuls of water and it'd all be over. Focusing on grasping my energy, I expanded it as I'd done before, but all I got was a flash of light. A flash showcasing the empty space below me as whoever was trying to murder me used their magic and not their hands.

Another flash spilled from my fingertip, and for the first time my fight died off completely. As the last of my oxygen dwindled, I swore that I saw a visage of a creature holding me, long claws wrapped around my ankles. It had deep brown, leathery skin with a head similar to the aliens in those old movies.

Forcing light from my hands one more time with a dying need to know what was killing me, I found the space below was once again empty. As the synapses in my brain exploded in those final moments, I accepted what was happening—acceptance masquerading as peace—and I let the faces of my family flash across my mind. The pain I felt at never seeing them again, at what they'd go through over my death, was worse than the dying itself.

Darkness was almost a relief as I gagged and water filled my lungs. I didn't notice the rumble around me until the depths of the lake erupted into arcs of lightning. I was grabbed again, this time from above, and when a bubble of air surrounded my face, water rushed away from me, drawing from my lungs at the same time, leaving me coughing and vomiting.

Hacking coughs shook me as the two entities played tug-of-war with me and I blacked out, only coming to when the hold on my ankles released. Whoever had saved me pulled me to the surface so fast that they had to be a water elemental, and I tried to wrap my head around the fact that I wasn't going to die here today after all.

Light enveloped us when my head broke the surface. I coughed and sputtered again, choking as my lungs attempted to squeeze up and out of my throat. When I managed to stop coughing, exhaustion had me all but boneless in the water, my savior's tight hold the only thing keeping me afloat. My head dropped back against their firm shoulder.

"Paisley!" Belle's frantic tone had me forcing my eyes open. Her terrified gaze was right before me. "What the Hel happened?" she gasped on a sob. "You were there one second and then gone the next. You moved so fast below that we lost sight of you almost instantly."

Lifting my head, I turned to see who had saved me, expecting it was the teacher—awkward, as I was pressed along the hard lengths of his body to stay afloat in the water—only to meet icy green eyes.

Everything slowed. The noise around me faded to silence, and I was drowning again, only in a completely different way. Logan's glare was as heated as his eyes were frosty. "Trying to kill yourself before I get the chance, Precious?" Weirdly, I expected him to sound smug or satisfied at my almost drowning, but that snap of words indicated he was pissed.

"You tried to kill me?" I choked out.

Had it been him though? I'd thought there was a monster, but I'd also been severely oxygen deprived at that point, my brain freaking out on me. Logan released me so suddenly I almost went under again, but managed to kick my heavy legs to stay afloat.

"I saved you." His voice was inflectionless, and his expression smoothed into neutral lines. "I'm not like your mother. I don't leave people to die." I opened my mouth to protest that, but he was already leaving. "And you owe me one now. Don't forget it."

Noise burst back to life, and I was hauled out of the lake by Professor Mordock in the next second. "What happened?" he asked as he settled me on the ground, a few feet from the water. "Why did you sink into the depths so quickly?"

My throat rasped as I answered, and despite the water soaking me, every part of me felt parched. "I got pulled under." Panic and pain pulsed through me as flashes of dying filled my head. "It felt . . . it felt like bands around my legs as I was dragged down. Are you sure there're no monsters in the lake?"

That last part slipped out because I'd already made up my mind that there were no monsters and I'd had a mental break in the last moments of my life.

The professor stared at me, pale and confused. "Monsters? Like a giant fish? Or squid?"

Sure, or maybe a giant alien from a popular movie in the seventies.

"Are there any of the above?"

Before he could respond, I heard my name, and I turned to find Dad sprinting toward the lake. He was wearing his favorite brown corduroy suit, and had clearly been in the middle of a class. "I called for him when you went under," Professor Mordock said from my side.

"What grabbed me in the lake?" I asked him, keeping my gaze on Dad. Seeing him had my eyes burning as I fought the urge to curl up into a ball and sob, but I needed answers before I fell apart.

"There are no monsters in the lake," he told me quietly. "Small fish, a few amphibians, but absolutely nothing with the strength or capability to drag a student down that fast. I couldn't find you."

"How did Logan get to me, then?"

He was silent, and I turned to see his grim expression. "He's a spellcaster. Even in water, their abilities far outreach mine. You should thank him, because he absolutely saved your life."

Did he though? The facts weren't adding up. Because if it wasn't a monster, and I disappeared faster than a water elemental could track, then it stood to reason that Logan was still the only one capable of the attack in the first place. But why had he attacked and then saved me?

Had it just been a way to break me?

If it was that stalkcaster behind it all, there was no way I'd let him know I was rattled. Fuck that. I'd deal with the darkness settling in my brain and I'd come out stronger on the other side.

"There'll be an investigation," Professor Mordock added, when our silence extended. "I promise you, Paisley. If there has been a magical attack against a student, whoever is responsible will not only be expelled but charged before the elders."

If it was Logan, they'd never find evidence of it.

"Paisley!" Dad hauled my soaking form up into his arms, holding on like his life depended on it. "Sweetheart, you're okay. Thank the goddess. Thank the goddess."

He held me for a long time, and I finally allowed myself a few seconds to fall apart, hot tears soaking my dad's shirt. "What the Hel happened?" he snapped over my head.

"She was dragged under," Professor Mordock replied, voice subdued. "A student called for me, and I went after her, but there was no sign, Tom. The water wasn't murky, and I can see for many feet around me, but it was as if she'd vanished."

Pushing my hand onto Dad's arm, he finally released me, and I wiped away the last of my tears. The two professors were facing off, one puffed up and pissed off, the other looking beaten.

"Logan Kingston saved me, Dad," I rasped.

Dad's face turned a startling magenta, and I hoped he wasn't about to explode fire everywhere. The heat of his power had already dried me and my swimsuit off.

"Impossible," he snapped, flames flashing in his eyes. "Logan had to be the one to pull you down."

Professor Mordock furrowed his brow as he looked between Dad and me. "He wasn't anywhere near the water when she went under. Even a spellcaster would need to be closer than he was. That boy is a hero."

Dad looked about as convinced that Logan was a hero as he was that his favorite football team were making it to the playoffs. And they were dead last on the leaderboard.

"You should get her up to see a healer," Professor Mordock pushed gently. "She was without oxygen for almost two minutes."

And thought she saw a monster.

Dad, those flames still dancing in his eyes, gave me his full attention again. Whatever he saw in my face had the hard lines of his face softening. "Let's get you back to the school, Little Gem. We'll take you to the healers."

"No," I mumbled. "I'm fine, I just need to rest." From the corner of my eye, I could see Belle waiting for me, and I shot her a weak smile while mouthing, *Go.* I'd see her later.

Her worried gaze flashed between Dad and me, before she nodded and blew me a kiss.

Dad wrapped his arm around me, and all but carried me to the school and up the stairs into the Ancot building. "I think you should leave Weatherstone," he said, the first words he'd spoken since we left the lake.

He started to direct me away from my dorm, but I stopped him with a hand on his arm. "Dad, I feel fine. I just want to go to my room. Please."

I expected him to refuse, but as he examined my face, his crumpled. Just this brief moment of grief. "Okay, sweetheart. But I will be sending a healer up later to check on you."

There was no point in arguing, because I had a much bigger problem on my hands. "I'm not leaving Weatherstone, Dad," I said softly through my aching throat. "Logan saved my life so he's not a threat."

"But something is," he bit out. "It's your first day and you almost died. Who pulled you under?"

The word *monster* lingered on my tongue, but I didn't mention my possible hallucination. Dad would have me in the medical wing so fast it'd make the magic dragging me under the lake look like a snail.

"I must have swum too deep and lost consciousness." I had no other explanation or theory I was willing to share with him. "I don't know why Professor Mordock couldn't find me, but maybe he was looking in the wrong place. No one pulled me under, especially not Logan, because why the heck would he save me?" *Unless he was really into torment and had much bigger plans for me.* "It's not the school's fault."

Dad didn't look convinced. "You've got a Grand Canyon of a plot hole in that theory, Paisley Hallistar. You're a strong swimmer, and there's no way you just swam too deep. But I can't argue the rest."

"Mom said I could stay, didn't she?" An unfair segue, but I needed to know. I wouldn't let fear keep me from my future. If Logan had been trying to scare me, he'd show his hand sooner or later.

Dad cleared his throat, flames reappearing briefly, before he deflated. "She did. She doesn't want you to lose yourself the way she has, and she told me that all of life has risks."

Reaching out, I squeezed Dad's hand tightly. "I promise to be careful. I think I'll sit out the rest of the lake classes, if you can clear that with my professors."

"I will," he said as he puffed up once more. "And, Pais, be careful of Logan. Don't let your guard down, even if he is the reason you're still here with us."

"Dad, you don't have to worry about me developing some sort of misplaced faith in that spellcaster. He might have saved me today, but he's bad news. We all know that. I'll be avoiding his grumpy ass as much as possible over the next year."

We were at my dorm now, and I pressed my hand to open it. "I'll be back with a healer," Dad reminded me. "Don't sleep yet."

"I love you too," I rasped, waving him off.

He shook his head, looking like he'd aged ten years in a few minutes, before he leaned in and kissed my cheek. "I love you, Paisley. Tomorrow will be a better day."

Well, it couldn't get any worse. Though, I was still alive, and that was more than I thought I'd have in those last few seconds. Despite my misgivings, there was no denying that Logan had saved my life.

Why? was the only pertinent question left now.

CHAPTER 13

The next few weeks at Weatherstone were gloriously boring compared to my first day. My family barely left my side, each of my siblings freaked by almost losing me, but there were no further conversations about me withdrawing from college. Dad told me he was in the *wait and see* phase, and I wasn't pushing the issue.

The nightmares I expected did come for the first few nights, but Alice and Jenna, squished with me on my tiny bed, got me through the worst of it. The Hallistars never let the demons win; our family stood in the darkness and fought side by side.

Classes went by quickly, and I found myself enjoying the variety of elemental lessons: history, Apothecary and Herbal Studies, along with Intro to Alchemy. All of that kept me busy enough that I didn't think about Logan Kingston more than, say, five times a day. My stalkcaster had turned into a ghostcaster, disappearing into Weatherstone as if he'd never stepped foot in the college.

My burning questions about what happened in the lake remained, but with life growing busier, I managed to focus on the now. My near death was pushed down into the depths of my memory, and I forced myself to embrace the future I almost didn't have.

"So, party tonight," Sara said with an extra wiggle to her

hips. It was the Friday after Defensive Spells for Beginners. Our final class had us whipping up small deflection spells.

Belle and I had expanded our friend group to include two other freshman witches: Sara Collier and Haley Michaels. Sara, a dark-haired witch not much taller than Belle, was born in Romania and moved to Florida when she was ten. We'd bonded over her lack of an affinity too, and I'd found myself clicking with her bubbly, outgoing personality.

"You've got to be kidding me," Haley said with a groan, as if Sara had suggested an after-class dentist trip.

Haley was the opposite of Sara, tall and thin, with light brown hair, hazel eyes, and skin so pale she needed sun protection in the middle of winter. She was also an introvert who'd rather visit her gynecologist than go to a party. "I need to study," she stated, pouting as hard as she could. "And the next book in that witch-warrior series releases at midnight, so I absolutely need to stay up for it."

Belle shook her head, falling in on the other side of Sara, her glorious red curls cascading down her back. "Girl, the fact that you're reading witch stories is disturbing. Humans rarely get the details right."

Sara's laugh burst from her as she tried to cover it with a cough. "I figured that's why she reads them, to laugh at all the bullshit and inaccuracies. If I hear about one more wand reference, I'll probably throw myself off the Lewington Mountains out the back there."

Haley rolled her eyes at Sara's dramatics. "It's called *fantasy* for a reason. I like to escape."

"Yeah, into all of those spicy scenes," I casually added, forcing myself to remain straight-faced. "There were lots of magic wands in the one she was reading the other day, only they weren't attached to anyone's hand—"

Haley let out a little shriek and covered her ears. "Oh my

goddess, you three are the worst." Despite the horror twisting her face, she was smiling. "But you're also not wrong. I'm not opposed to a little one-handed reading at times."

It was such an unexpected comment from our nature sprite that all of us paused and stared at her. Mirth trickled up through my chest, and I fought the urge to ask her what the book title was.

"Well, fuck," Belle rasped. "I'm ashamed to say that it took me a beat to understand what you meant. By the way, what's the name of your book? Asking for a friend."

Belle had resisted no such urge, and all of us laughed, even as Haley shot the title our way. I filed it away because I could always use a new hobby. Collecting crystals, watching K-dramas, and worrying about my inability to express magic were not quite rounding me out as a witch.

"Okay . . ." Sara got back to the point. "The party is tonight, and we're all going. This is to celebrate Selene's energy, and it's the first full moon since we started in Weatherstone. This is a rite of passage, and none of you witches can miss it."

Jensen and Trevor had been carrying on about this event for days, and I wanted to go, even though I had a shit ton of schoolwork and assignments waiting for me.

"Fine," Haley conceded. "I'll stay for an hour. That's all I'm promising."

Belle and Sara's faces lit up, and then Belle rounded on me. "You're awfully quiet over there, Paisley Hallistar. But just know, if you're not back here at six, dressed in your sexiest best, I'll drag you out in your pj's." She blew me a kiss and then raced off down the hall. "See you bitches in two hours."

"Think she meant *witches*?" Haley asked as we watched her sprint off.

"Definitely not," Sara and I replied simultaneously.

After the girls left to get ready, I took a quick shower,

and naked, collapsed onto my bed. I decided to grab a ten-minute nap because the sexy dreams were back in force now that the nightmares had faded, leaving me exhausted.

Sleep came quickly, ending when I was woken by a strong rush of magic tingling down my spine. I hadn't felt anything similar since the lake incident and it had me bolting upright, throwing on whatever clothes lay on the floor and tearing out of my room.

The hallway was mostly empty, only a few students visible in the distance—certainly, no big-ass spellcaster. I *had* expected to see Logan. Since the day at the lake, I'd taken to thinking of that tingle across the back of my neck as a warning of danger. Whether that danger came from Logan or an outside source, I had no idea, but I wasn't about to ignore it.

As I stood there in the hallway, the energy settled leaving me frustrated as I reentered my room.

A quick glance at my watch told me it was already 5:30 p.m., so I forced everything else from my mind and rummaged through my clothes to find an outfit. I settled on black jeans, black boots, a tight red sweater, and a black wool coat to throw on top. It was still freezing outside, but the worst of the snow had passed by now, so we were back to just regular winter. Not arctic.

After straightening my hair until it hung in a shiny golden-brown sheath to midback, I added some makeup, lining my eyes darker than usual, topping it off with red lipstick to match my sweater. This was my first chance to get out of uniform with other students, and I wanted to look good.

At six exactly, my door's sensor pad was pressed, letting me know they were here. I hurried over to find Belle, Haley, and Sara outside, looking gorgeous in jeans and jackets like me.

"Fuck yes," Belle yelled, waving her hands in the air as she danced. "It's party time, bitches."

Haley snorted. "Such a human phrase."

Belle shot her a wink. "I happen to enjoy humans. They fuck different to warlocks. It's hard to explain, but I'm definitely not ruling out a human match in the future."

"Worked out well for my parents," Haley said with a shrug. "I say go with your heart."

As Belle's father was an elder, I doubted he'd be cool with his daughter *going with her heart*, but if I knew my friend at all, she gave zero fucks about it. Outside of that first night when she'd been beaten down in the shower, I'd only ever seen her brimming with confidence, and taking life by the balls. Literally, sometimes, if a warlock got too handsy.

"Do you think they'll have witch wine there tonight?" Sara asked, pulling out a small mirror to check her eye makeup, which was dark and shimmery.

Belle let out a groan, her features exaggeratedly sad. "Not a chance. We'll be stuck with regular alcohol."

Human alcohol barely affected us; magic kept our metabolism working overtime. But witches and warlocks had figured out a way. Starting with O'Hara, an English witch in the seventeenth century, who invented Trunica, the first witch wine. The brew had only been perfected since, coming in a range of flavors and intensities. It was strictly forbidden in Weatherstone, due to its twenty-six-plus age restriction, but in reality, what college experience would be complete without a little underage drinking.

I eyed Belle closely as she danced again. "Are you sure you don't have a secret stash in your dorm?"

"My father would kill me if I sullied the family name that way," she groaned, straightening her back and tilting her chin up. "Us Harpers are from the original witch lines, didn't you know?"

Her dad sounded like a bit of a dick, and I expected nothing less from an elder and councilman. They didn't reach those lofty positions without being both powerful and arrogant. Belle dealt with his control by acting out, and screwing around with humans apparently, but she still struggled to *not* be excellent at everything she did. My best friend already topped our grade in multiple classes, playing right into the role he wanted for her.

"Come on, friend," I said, linking my arm through hers. Her killer black boots with silver buckles had enough heel to bring us closer in height. "Let's get to this party."

Haley and Sara hurried along with us, and we were soon in the middle of students heading for the party. The vibe in the air was electric, and I felt tingles of energy, but they weren't like the day at the lake. This wasn't a warning, it was pure magic filling the air.

Weatherstone was letting loose, and as we descended the back stairs, my own excitement built. Thank the goddess I didn't stay back and study. I wanted to be here tonight. Under the full moon.

The party was located at the back of the campus grounds, pockets of forest surrounding the large, cleared space. Tables were set up, covered in food and drinks, as music blasted from speakers hanging in trees around us. Bonfires were in the process of being lit as fire elementals flexed their muscles, while air elementals, not to be outdone, dragged logs across for seating.

"This is amazing," Sara crowed, voice rising in excitement. "Weatherstone is great and all, but the classes are hardcore compared to my secondary school. We deserve this night to relax."

Haley exchanged a look with me, and I had no doubt she wished she was back in her dorm reading. "One hour," she reminded us grimly. "Come on, let's get a drink."

The first table was groaning under buckets filled with ice and mixed drinks. As predicted, it was all human-made alcohol, so we just grabbed a can of whatever looked good. I opted for watermelon vodka, holding the icy can as I followed my friends back to a log near one of the larger fires.

As we sat, Sara nudged me so hard I almost dropped my drink. "Marcus is looking at you," she hissed.

Spurred on by Belle, Sara and Haley had noticed his efforts to chat with me after class, and now the three of them were in cahoots to get me laid. My gaze drifting across the crowd, I found him on the far side of the bonfire, relaxed against a log with his best friend, Johnno.

Marcus shifted his long legs in front of him, sipping a beer as our gazes caught. There was the slightest shift in my stomach, a murmur of attraction. Only an idiot would deny that Marcus was hot, but I kept holding back.

It wasn't as if the heat of my magic had cooled—thank you, sexy but annoying and clingy dreams—but I hadn't acted on it. Maybe tonight it was time to let go and just get laid. I wasn't a virgin by any stretch, even if my experience was somewhat minimal compared to Belle's.

It was unnatural for us not to seek out sex after our magic bloomed. The heat in our blood could drive us crazy otherwise, and I could already see more than one couple hot and heavy in the forest. There'd be sex everywhere tonight, and if I played my cards right, I could be one of the lucky ones.

"Go to him," Belle said as she lifted her daiquiri and took a sip. "Go and have some fun. You're far too uptight."

I snorted out a sad little chuckle. "Under-fucking-statement of the year. My magic is fire in my veins without an outlet. I don't know what my issue is though. Maybe I'm waiting for him to make a move."

My natural confidence had been known to take a back seat

when it came to sex. I liked the warlock to take control, to take what he wanted. Within reason.

Sara prodded me harder than before. "Paisley Hallistar, do not waste that fucking sexy warlock tonight." She turned to Haley for backup, but the introverted witch who identified as a book witch already had her nose stuck in a paperback.

"Haley even agrees," said Sara with a shrug, taking her on as a wingwitch anyway. "We all voted, and you lost, so go and get your fucking warlock."

I got the sense that if I didn't move my ass, one of them would drag me over. The push I needed was coming whether I liked it or not. "Okay, why the Hel not." As I got to my feet, I could see above the bonfire, and my gaze locked on three warlocks standing there drinking.

A heavy tugging in my gut almost knocked me over.

Logan, Giant aka Noah, and the third of their crew who I'd coined Weasel, due to his beady eyes, stood right behind Marcus. This was the first time I'd been close to Logan since the lake, and I almost ran right for him to demand answers before I remembered it was a party.

None of us wanted to chat about *almost dying* at a party.

Turning away before they noticed me staring, I returned my attention to Marcus, only to find him deep in conversation with a witch.

A very pretty witch, with long blond hair and a flirty smile.

Ah, fuck.

There went that plan.

CHAPTER 14

"I'm getting another drink," Belle announced. "Anyone else want one?"

We'd been at the party for thirty minutes; our countdown time updated by Haley in ten-minute increments. Especially after Sara made her lose the book. "That's not the point of being here," she'd scolded her gently, and Haley had conceded.

"I'll take one," I said to Belle. After my chance to chat with Marcus fizzled out, I'd focused on drinking and absorbing moon energy with my friends. We'd chatted to other freshmen who crossed our paths, but for the most part it was a chilled-out night so far.

"We're fine," Haley and Sara said, and Belle headed into the crowds around the tables.

Turning to Haley, who sat stiffly, hands playing in the hem of her sweater in what looked like a nervous gesture, I sought out a topic of conversation that might distract her. "How are your family? Did your dad get his work situation sorted?" She'd mentioned a few days ago that there might be cutbacks at his job.

"Good," she replied, her voice softer. "His hours got cut, but he's not out a job completely. Which is a relief."

Haley grew up poor. Her mother was a human who fell in love with a warlock she met in the mall. He was an air elemental and worked on the docks, but the pay sucked—no doubt because while it wasn't uncommon for one of us to marry a human, it did come with a certain stigma.

A stigma that I had no doubt had also followed Haley through school, even though she was a near genius and was neck and neck with Belle for top of the classes.

When she wasn't forthcoming with more information on her family I changed the subject. "What's this book series you're waiting for tonight?"

My question wiped away the semimiserable expression she'd been wearing. "Oh, it's amazing. It's about gods who were banished from the world for centuries, and now they're back and want revenge. The first book was fucking perfection, and left me with a moderate cliffhanger, so now I'm desperate. If only there was a spell to get these books out faster, but I can't really complain."

Sara shook her head at us and went back to flirting with the fire elemental on her right. He had the sort of golden surfer boy looks she liked, and at least one of us was on their way to getting some action tonight.

"She's one of my favorite authors," Haley continued, "and is independently published, which allows her to release at least four books a year. I don't have the patience to wait for these yearly releases."

I wasn't what you'd call a reader. I loved the concept of it, but getting my brain to focus long enough to finish a novel was hard. I'd started and abandoned more books than I could remember. "Maybe you can recommend a series for me to start." Haley's enthusiasm was addictive, and maybe I just hadn't found the right books yet.

Her eyes grew even wider, and she bounced on the spot. "I've been desperate for a friend to share books with," she gasped as she rapidly hugged me, pulling away just as fast. "This might be the best day of my life."

"Just point me in the right direction," I told her. "Did you bring all your paperbacks with you to college? Do your parents mail them to you? How do you get these new books when they release at midnight?"

Her lips twitched. "The hardest thing I've ever done was leave my books at home. I smuggled in a few for emergencies." She patted her pocket, because apparently a party was an emergency. "For new releases, I've figured out how to manipulate my e-reader to prevent it shorting out around magic. Back home I live in a human suburb so there's no issue. Here, thankfully, it's holding up so far. I have a second, backup one, of course, if you want to borrow it." Her genius was showing, and I loved that about her.

"That would be amazing. Make sure you load your favorite sexy series on there for me to start."

Haley bounced to her feet, shoulders back with her new mission. "I'm heading to my dorm to get it ready for you."

"We'll walk with you," Sara said, getting to her feet as well, with the help of a surfy warlock. Turned out our resident party girl had found a new interest, and she was out of here.

"I'll wait for Belle," I said, shooting them both smirks. "Enjoy the rest of your night and I'll see you both tomorrow."

Sara leaned down and pressed a kiss to my cheek. "See you later, witch."

"Be careful," I murmured, and she shot me a cheeky smile. "Always."

The three of them exited the party, just shy of Haley's one hour, and she couldn't have looked happier about it.

Alone now, I noticed Jensen in a crowd with his friends, and missing my brother, I was about to head in his direction, when Belle stumbled toward me. She held two cans in her hands, but her face was pale, and in the flickering light of the fire I noticed shiny tracks on her cheeks.

Panic grasped me as I rushed to meet her. "What's wrong?" I asked, taking hold of her shoulders to examine her closely. "Are you okay?"

"Annabeth," she rasped, sounding both pissed and in pain. "Sh-she jabbed me with an iron attack spell, and it knocked all air from me. I didn't even see it coming."

She pressed her hand to her ribs, and then worked up the side of her green sweater so we could both see the dark spatter of bruises already forming.

A litany of curses spilled from my lips as I raged at that fucking witch. An iron attack was designed for blunt force trauma, and could break ribs if wielded by a strong enough witch or warlock.

"It looks bad," I said, barely keeping it together. "I'm going to fucking kill her. I don't know how, but if I have to throw her into the lake and watch the monster take her down, I'll do just that." I'd told my friends about my hallucination, and while none of them believed it was real, I'd had to mention it anyway.

Belle laughed briefly, before it died under her groan. "Fuck, remind me not to do that again. I mean, not that I don't appreciate your possibly mythical lake monster taking her down, but for now can we just get out of here?"

"You need a healer," I said shortly, my gaze darting around to see if I could find Annabeth.

Belle didn't argue, which told me how much pain she was in. "I can go back on my own," she huffed, holding her side. "I don't want to ruin the party for you."

I leveled my best glare on her. "Like I would let you walk back alone while injured with that psycho witch running around out there."

"Come on, killer," Belle said with another strained laugh, noticing me still checking the crowd for Annabeth. "I love you for caring, and as badly as I want to see you smack her around again, it's not worth putting you in her crosshairs. She's been avoiding you, and I want to keep it that way."

Belle was the best friend a girl could have hoped for, and I thanked Selene's light that Dad hadn't dragged me out of college. I was closer to Belle, Sara, and Haley in a few weeks than I'd been with Trina and Olivia in years of friendship.

Friendships were weird in that way, but I wasn't going to question it.

As we set off to leave, Trevor intercepted us. "Sister!" he exclaimed, sounding as if he'd indulged in more than plain old beer. "Where in the warlock have you been?"

"Brother," I shot back dryly. "We're heading out. I'll chat with you later."

"But the party's just started," he complained. "Stay for one drink with me. I've waited forever for Baby Sis to make it to Weatherstone."

Drunk Trevor was annoying and adorable, and I wasn't surprised when Belle caved. She hadn't said anything to me about it, but there was this weird tension between her and my brother, even as they shot jabs at each other more often than not. "Stay, Pais. I can get my way back, and I probably don't even need a healer."

"You're injured," I said, crossing my arms as my stubbornness kicked in. "I'm taking you to a healer."

Whatever intoxication Trevor had been displaying vanished like magic. "Injured?" He focused on my tiny friend, his gaze running over her as he assessed for injuries. "What happened? Are you hurt as well, Pais?"

"I'm fine," I said. "This stupid witch is bullying her, and she got Belle with an iron attack."

Trevor pressed closer for a more thorough inspection, but

Belle waved him off. "Hands to yourself, warlock," she said. "I'm fine. Just some bruises on my ribs."

My brother's hands twitched at his sides. "Paisley is right, you need to see the healers. I'll walk with you to make sure you get there safely."

I waited for Belle to object, her dark eyes watchful. "Thank you. I'd appreciate the escort."

Whoa, okay. That was odd. Trevor better not ruin my friendship due to his playwarlock ways, or he'd be the one with bruised ribs.

The three of us headed away from the party, and near the edge of the forest, a hand landed on my shoulder. I spun, fists flying up, and Marcus jumped back, hands held up before him.

Trevor was already in front of me, but I grabbed his biceps before he could do anything serious. "No, wait. He's my friend," I said quickly. Leaning around my brother, I smiled. "Sorry, Marcus. Belle here was just attacked by a witch, so we're a little on edge."

Trevor relaxed enough that I could step around him, and I saw Belle tugging on his hand. "Paisley will catch up," I heard her whisper. "Let's give them a second to talk."

He didn't want to leave; I could see that quite plainly, but when I narrowed my eyes with a clear *fuck off, brother* in them, he grimaced and pointed a finger at Marcus. "Hurt my sister and I'll rip your fucking arms off and beat you with them."

He didn't wait for a response, turning to march off with Belle, not bothering to look back. *Cranky asshole.*

Marcus, to his merit, didn't leave, and he showed no indication that my brother's threat phased him. "Sorry about that," I said, clearing my throat. "My brother is a tad overprotective, and a giant dick, but I love him."

He tilted his head. "Can't fault him for being protective of you. I shouldn't have just grabbed you like that. I'm the one who's sorry."

Damn, he was smooth. "Why did you grab me?" I asked, cool breezes ruffling my hair as they whistled through the trees nearby.

A fraction of his confidence fell as he rubbed a hand over his face. "I've been wanting to chat with you all night."

And yet he hadn't approached me until now.

"How are your classes going?"

Great, we were talking about school. Excellent start. "They're going better than I expected," I said with a shrug. "The amount of information we're learning is intense, but I enjoy it. I like flexing my magical muscle."

"No sign of your affinity yet?"

That sprinkling of unease that swirled in my energy swelled. "Nope. There was a low-level bonding moment with a dog in Nature Sprites for the Newly Bonded, but not enough to call it a familiar. My strongest reactions have been during the lake, where I almost drowned, and during Necromancy in the Wild, in that forest—" I waved my hand to the eastern perimeter "—I actually felt the heat of my power emerge."

"Being a necromancer would be a great affinity," Marcus said, and it was clear that he meant that. "If I end up being a spellcaster, I'm almost disappointed not to explore that final frontier of energy."

"Professor Longhorn hasn't indicated that he's seen a necro affinity yet, but my magic is locked away. We're all searching for the elusive key."

Marcus's eyes softened. "You're too hard on yourself, Paisley. It's only been a few weeks, and from what I can tell, you're doing pretty well for a witch without an affinity." His words replaced the unease with warmth. "You've got your entire four years of college to figure out your affinity. It'll probably take them that long to declare mine too."

For a vastly different reason to mine. Marcus showed a strong aptitude for too many affinities, but the classification of a spellcaster was a lengthy process. "Logan Kingston is a spellcaster," I said suddenly. "His first class is this coming week. I wonder if you'll find a resonation with his energy during the lesson."

He shrugged, taking a sip of his beer. "Whether I'm a spellcaster or not remains to be seen, but I am looking forward to this class. How often do we get firsthand experience with a powerful spellcaster? I heard that Logan is classified as one of the strongest in the world, and he's not even finished college."

Of course he was. I'd expect nothing less. Wishing I hadn't brought that warlock up, I was trying to figure out a subject change, when Marcus stepped closer. "Would you like to catch up on a weekend? Just . . . the two of us?"

I stared at him, wondering why I wasn't jumping at the opportunity. Maybe because I'd been looking for mindless sex to quench the fire, but his question and the way he stared at me spoke of more. "That sounds—"

An explosion rocked the party grounds, and Marcus grabbed my shoulders, spinning me behind him while he searched for an attack. Near the largest bonfire, I saw a kaleidoscope of lights followed by shouts as a fight broke out. "Shit." Marcus shot me an apologetic grimace. "My friends are in there. I need to help them, but I'll find you after, okay?"

"Go, help your friends," I said with an encouraging smile. If my friends were here still, I'd have been right on his ass to help them. "I'll catch you later."

Marcus still hesitated, but as the fight grew louder, he shook his head and took off. Jostled by others, I was pushed farther back in the crowd, until I stood at the edge of the forest again. Exhausted, I decided to catch up with Belle and Trevor. If I took the shortcut, I might catch them before the healers.

Walking along the side of the building, I stuck to the shadows, wondering what stupidity had made me take the darkest, eeriest path. Not that I was worried about an attack, with everyone distracted by the fight.

As if those thoughts tempted the Fates themselves, when I turned the corner a roughly hewn bag was jerked over my head, cutting off my screams. It tightened around my neck, and I panicked and clawed at my throat, before I was cracked on the head, pain exploding through my brain as everything went fuzzy.

CHAPTER 15

My attacker was an air elemental, using their energy to lift us both, and send us hurtling across the campus. The throbbing in my head worsened with each breath of air I tried to suck through the burlap bag. It stuck to my sweaty face, and I fought not to pass out again through sheer panic.

My attacker was bigger and stronger, and their hold was tight until they stopped suddenly and released me to slam against a hard surface. Winded, my lungs ached along with my head as I gasped for breath, but that didn't stop me from rolling to the side and clawing at the ties at my throat.

The psycho warlock laughed, a deep chilling sound, as he wrapped his hands around my throat. Blindly swinging my arms, I tried to claw him, but he wasn't strangling as I'd expected. He released the ties on the bag. When he yanked it off, my head slammed back with a crack against whatever I rested on, and I turned to find it was a headstone.

My attacker had brought us to the Weatherstone graveyard.

Tingles raced along my spine stronger than I'd ever felt—this warning system I'd developed the moment I stepped onto these college grounds. *Little too late this time.* Scrambling to my feet, the back of my head felt warm, and I had a suspicion I was bleeding.

Which wasn't the worst of my worries as the full moon

crested to the peak, washing its calming energy over the graves and illuminating my attacker:

Weasel.

Tilting his head to the side, he shot me a smile any serial killer would be proud of. "You're a pain in my ass," he said conversationally, sounding less deranged than he looked. "A distraction. An annoyance. And I'm sick of seeing your fucking face. Kingston will thank me for this."

He twisted his right hand, and the air I'd been quite happily breathing was restricted in my lungs and throat. Choking, I clawed at my neck, as flashbacks of drowning in the lake hit me hard and fast. Only this time, there was definitely a monster attacking me, and since he was of the warlock variety, I could fight back.

Dropping to my knees, I fought through my panic, desperately searching for a weapon. My palm hit a rock, half-buried in the dirt, and I clawed it loose, pitching it as hard and fast as I could. I'd spent two summers playing baseball with the kids on my street, and I had a mean fastball when I wanted.

Weasel dodged it, but not the second one I shot at him just as fast. The tennis ball–sized stone slammed into his gut, and when he doubled over the elemental hold on my body ceased. Leaping to my feet, I didn't stop or think, sprinting in the direction I hoped the gate was. I couldn't see it from this angle.

Of course, a witch with no active magic against an asshole with control over the elements meant I was far outmatched. Air wrapped around my body, holding me in place, before he lifted me a few feet off the ground, and slammed me down face-first onto the hard, rock-filled grass. Compacted dirt bit into my skin, scraping where my clothes didn't protect. Weasel repeated this movement over and over, until I could taste blood, and my head was spinning and screaming at me.

When he stopped, he left me sprawled on the ground in a

broken heap. "Are you planning on killing me?" I choked out, wiping blood from my lips. Little beams of light shone in my hands, but it was so far from an active power I might as well have been holding a firefly. "They'll execute you."

"Not if they can't find your body," he snarled as he slammed his foot on my back, pushing me until I tasted grass and more blood. "You're just an annoyance and a distraction, and I think the plan is much better this way."

A strangled scream escaped me as I tried to push up against him, but I was hurt too badly to have any fight left. As it was, I could barely whimper.

"I'm going to enj—"

"What the fuck are you doing?"

Another whimper escaped me, as shouts rang out. Students had left the party, and judging by the chill of their energy, some necromancers had decided to visit the graveyard on their way back to the dorms.

My face was pressed into the ground, so I couldn't see who had arrived, and even when the weight of Weasel's foot disappeared, I didn't move. Didn't or couldn't, it was hard to tell through the blaring pain. Gentle hands touched me a few seconds later, and I flinched.

"It's okay," a witch said carefully, her voice pitched low and soothing. "We're here to help you."

I was lifted, and I couldn't help my cries as the pain intensified. Tears burned my eyes, and I squeezed them shut and prayed to the goddess for a little relief.

"You need to hurry," the witch said to whoever carried me. "She doesn't look good."

Excellent. At least I looked how I felt.

The warlock who held me—I could feel his hard chest—moved faster, jolting my broken body. I gritted my teeth and tried to be thankful I was alive. Feeling no pain would have meant I was dead, and once again the reaper had kept its claws out of me.

Not that I knew why I was being hunted by that scythey bastard, but it wasn't my time yet apparently.

Why did Weasel attack me? Was it on Logan's orders? He'd said Kingston would thank him, and yet it hadn't sounded like he had been directed to attack.

It made even less sense for Logan to save me at the lake, ignore me for weeks, and then let his asshole friend beat me to death. There'd been no new torture in that period of time. Nothing that would justify saving my life at the lake for a great plan.

The light grew brighter behind my tightly closed eyelids, and I soon smelled antiseptic, lavender, peppermint, and other herbs. Healing witches and warlocks were almost always nature sprites, using what nature provided, along with spells and their internal energy, to accelerate our bodies' healing.

It was quiet at first, until a witch let out a loud gasp. "Oh my goddess." Her voice was low and sweet. "What happened here?"

"She was attacked in the graveyard," the warlock holding me said. "We didn't see her attacker clearly, but it was another warlock."

"Quickly, get her on the bed, and then can one of you fetch the headmaster for me?"

I was placed against a soft surface, but I was in too much pain for anything to feel comfortable. "It's okay, dear," the witch told me in gentle tones. I attempted to open my eyes, but every time I tried the pain grew worse.

The warmth of her energy surrounded me as she started to chant a healing spell, and for a second it hurt worse than ever as I fought back a scream. "You're doing amazing," she whispered. "Your injuries aren't the worst we've seen, but you do have internal bleeding and a few fractured ribs. Don't worry. I'll have you as good as new in no time."

She chanted again, and I did nothing except attempt to hold on to my sanity, until eventually, there was some blessed relief from the agony. When her hands lifted, and the heat faded, she rubbed cool, lavender-scented paste across my arms and side, leaving me sore but not dying any longer. I slumped into the bed, exhausted and emotional, wondering what I was going to tell my dad when he came raging into this room.

"Rest, sweetie," the healer said. "I'll check on you soon."

The need to sleep was a normal part of the healing process, and I let myself drift off, hoping that by the time I woke up the rest of the pain would be gone. My theory almost worked, until I heard a frantic "Little Gem" beside my bed, and I opened my eyes to find Dad and all of my siblings standing pale faced around me.

"Almost missed the family reunion," I joked, voice raspy against my dry throat.

Dad took my hand and squeezed it gently. "Sweetheart, why do I keep finding you in these situations?"

"Magnet for trouble?"

Dad's frown deepened, even as the fire in his eyes eased. "Maddy, the healer who first attended you, said you had severe bruises, some internal bleeding, and broken ribs. She's got most of the healing under way, and you should feel much better in a few hours. How's your pain?"

I took a second to assess my injuries, shifting on the bed, relieved when it was all down to a dull ache. "Honestly, not too bad. A few bruises and aches still, and I could really use a glass of water, but other than that I'm going to be fine."

"Who did this?" Trevor growled, hands gripping the metal railing beside me. Unlike Dad, the flames in his eyes roared.

"I don't know his name," I told them the truth. "But I'm going to find out, and I'll report it to the headmaster."

Dad looked over his shoulder, before coming back to my gaze. "Victor was just here, but he must have stepped out again. You will absolutely be reporting this warlock, and we will make sure he's charged to the full extent of the law." I had no issue with that, but I did have an issue with Dad's next words. "And if we don't find him soon, I'm taking you home, sweetheart. No negotiations."

"We'll find him," I promised darkly, deciding I'd search the entire fucking school daily until I found Logan and demanded a name. "I know his face. I just need the name."

My sisters pressed in for hugs, and I wasn't surprised when Alice cried into my side. "I'm so sorry this happened. We should have been at the party."

"I shouldn't have left her at the party," Trevor rumbled, and the heat in the room shot right up, giving us all a free sauna along with healing.

"It's okay," I told them all. "I'm a grown witch, and I should be able to take care of myself. This is not on any of you, it's on that asshole who jumped me. And he will be dealt with."

"I want his name," Jensen said, wrapping his huge hand around mine, and holding tightly. "I want his name, and five minutes with him in the lake."

It wasn't like my brother to be so bloodthirsty—not that brother anyway. The difference between water and fire was apparent in their personalities, but tonight they were both infernos.

"I want his name too," I assured Jensen, noting how his jaw was clenched.

"Make sure you tell me first," he bit out, squeezing my hand.

"I love you guys," I whispered, jumping when Jenna pressed

a cool glass of water in my hand. The first sip tasted like nectar, and I finished the entire glass in seconds.

"We love you too, little sister," Trevor said, brushing his hand gently over my head. "We'll kill this bastard, don't you worry."

It was hard to tell if he meant that literally or not. When the fire took him over, darkness clouded his gaze, and for once Dad didn't reprimand him about it.

My family stayed until the healers kicked them out so I could get some rest. "She'll be released in the morning. Come back at 8:00 a.m.," Maddy told them. With reluctance and final hugs, they left the room, and the cool, dark silence surrounded me.

"Okay, one more round of healing before you sleep," Maddy said as she added more energy and tinctures to my body, before leaving me to rest.

In my drowsy state, I was almost asleep when I felt a power brush across my skin. It wasn't the power of the healers; it was much stronger than anything I'd felt tonight, forcing my blurry eyes open, I searched for the source, and found a hulking shadow to the side of my bed.

I thought I caught a glimpse of green eyes, but when I focused again, the room was empty of shadows and scary spellcasters.

Exhaustion dragged me under as I succumbed to the sleep my body required to heal.

CHAPTER 16

"Just think of us as your personal bodyguards," Trevor said the next morning when we left the healing wing. "Outside of getting to class, from now on you're not traveling anywhere on weekends or after hours without one of us present."

As much as I wanted to protest, I wouldn't, not if it meant staying at Weatherstone. "Your mother wants to see you," Dad told me, face serious as he stood with my siblings. "I know you've been chatting to her on the landlines, but with this being the second attack on you in the first month of school, she'd like to physically see you."

"Organize a weekend home for us all, Dad." Jenna's face lit up at the thought. "I think we could all use the break."

Dad nodded. "Okay, I'll square it away with Victor, and let you know when we're heading home." He pressed a kiss to my cheek. "We have a staff meeting about the attack now, so I'm leaving you in your siblings' capable hands. Get some rest."

A Saturday staff meeting, that was some serious shit.

"Promise, Dad," I told him.

"She'll rest if I have to sit on her to make it happen," Jenna called after Dad's departing back. My ribs, still mildly bruised, ached at the mere thought.

True to their word, my family walked with me, and if I wasn't mistaken, all of them were channeling their power closer to the surface. Jenna and Alice's hands were stained green and brown, which meant they'd been cooking up some spells. Jensen's energy felt cool, the particles of water and air hovering across his skin. And Trevor was all heat, offsetting the cool calm of the others.

"Should we take shifts outside her door while she rests?" Trevor asked like I wasn't standing right there with them.

"Absolutely not," I cut in before anyone else could say a word. "I'm safe in my room. I doubt that asshole will attack again while the school is in an uproar over it. A Saturday staff meeting, guys. They're taking it seriously."

I fully intended to report my attacker, because I'd seen that look on his face last night—he planned on killing me, and he would not be happy that he'd failed.

Kingston will thank me for this.

"He hasn't been caught yet," Alice reminded me with a waver in her voice.

"I know." I grasped her hand. "And I'm so sorry. I know how freaked out you all must have been. I'd have lost my shit if it was one of you hurt. But I'm just going to rest in my room. I promise."

They left me with reluctance, after searching my room twice and promising they'd be back very soon to check on me. "I love you, guys," I called after them.

"We love you too, Pais," Jenna said. "Don't scare us like that again."

Trevor's expression was hard and feral, and I knew he still blamed himself for leaving with Belle. My brother, for all his bravado, was a protector, which was why I gave him an extra hug as he left. "It's not your fault," I whispered. "You've always protected me, and this is no different."

His chest made a deep rumbling sound, and I had to pull

back when the heat grew too intense. "When I find out who did this, I'm going to kill them." He repeated the threat from last night, and there was no indication he was kidding.

"You'll have to get behind me and Simon first," Alice said fiercely, and all of us stared at the gentle sprite who was threatening Weasel with her sheep.

"Come on, let her rest," Jenna called, already outside the door. "We'll be back in a couple of hours."

"Okay, bye," I said.

When they were gone, I closed the door firmly and checked the lock. Exhaling one long breath, a few minor pains let themselves be known, but it was nothing compared to last night. The healers had done an incredible job, and with rest I'd be as good as new. Although, rest didn't arrive for a while as Belle, Haley, and Sara banged on my door not ten minutes later.

Belle was already crying, fat tears slipping down her cheeks as she rubbed her red nose. "I can't believe we left you. I thought Marcus would have stayed with you." She sobbed as I hugged her tightly.

"A fight broke out and he got pulled away. I was the one who made the decision to take off back to the school on my own. This is on me." She sniffled hard, pulling back. "How are your injuries?" I asked, checking in on her as well.

Wiping her cheeks, she forced a smile. "Actually, fine. We went to the healers first, and then Trevor convinced me to speak with Headmaster Gregor. He took me seriously, and Annabeth . . ." She took a deep breath. "She got expelled. I came to your room first thing this morning to tell you, and that's when I found out what happened." She sniffled loudly. "I burst into tears and tracked Trevor down for all the updates. Your brother wasn't a complete douchenozzle last night."

"Yeah, he can be decent when he wants to. But that's

amazing news about Annabeth. Now I just need to figure out who Weasel is."

"Weasel did this to you?" Haley asked me, pushing herself up from my desk chair. "Logan's friend?"

I nodded. "Yep, the bastard. He jumped me when I left the party and used his air energy to zip us to the graveyard. Where he could beat the crap out of me in private."

All three of them raged and cursed for a few minutes, before Belle shot to her feet. "I'm going straight to the headmaster. He'll deal with this just as he did with Annabeth."

"Wait," I said, scrambling after her as she raced for my door. "Don't go to him yet. Let me get a few hours' sleep, then we can figure it out."

Sara crossed her arms, face thunderous. "We won't let him hurt you again, Paisley. This ends today. Let us know when you're awake. We'll just be in Belle's room down the hall."

"Okay," I said, before a yawn overtook my face.

They left me then, with hugs and kisses on the cheek, and I spent ten minutes holding my crystals, drawing in their soothing energy. I didn't touch them daily, as I used to, but today I needed them.

After that, I crashed into bed for hours, and to my surprise didn't have any nightmares; the aftereffects of being healed kept me in a deep sleep. When I finally woke, I was left with a desperate need to pee, and a worry that I shouldn't be leaving my room alone. The healers had exchanged my bloody, ruined clothes for a set of light gray cotton pj's in the healing ward, and I left them on as I poked my head out of my doorway.

For a Saturday afternoon, there were plenty of students around, and I felt I should be safe to duck to the bathroom quickly. I made it there without issue, finished up quickly, and washed my hands. I also splashed water on my face to hopefully add a little color back into my cheeks.

On my way back to my dorm, I stopped to grab a drink from the wall-mounted fountain. It tasted like heaven on my parched throat, and as I dropped the paper cup into the recycling, a shadow washed over me, sending me stumbling back against the wall, arms raising to defend myself.

Logan didn't react to my defensive pose, and he wasn't close enough for me to feel threatened, so I cleared my throat and straightened my pj's in an attempt at dignity. "You really shouldn't sneak up on a witch who got jumped last night."

His expression remained neutral as he ran his gaze over me, but I couldn't miss the darkness in those icy eyes. Energy radiated between us, almost visible in the air, and it wasn't my imagination that the lights flickered as Logan's power seeped from him. He wouldn't attack me in a crowded hallway, right? There was no way he'd be so stupid.

"Logan, I'm tired and hurt, what do you actually want?" He might terrify me, but I refused to let him know that.

Moving faster than I could react to, he grasped the edge of the flimsy pajama top, and slowly lifted it. Maybe it was shock or curiosity, but I found myself frozen and watching as he examined my ribs, which were still painted in faded yellow and green bruises.

Logan's hand twitched, his bare skin brushing against my side, and I flinched. But it wasn't pain. It was a dark, drugging sensation, caressing my skin, and burning into my energy. I tried to breathe normally, to hide his effect on me. "You don't look surprised," I choked out, needing a distraction. "Did you thank him, as he said you would?"

To deflect how this spellcaster destroyed me with a simple graze of skin, I'd gone straight for goading—a *brilliant move* when he was a billion times more powerful and possibly trying to kill me. Still, I did need the name of his friend.

"Walter is no friend of mine." His voice was flat, that flare in his eyes from before as strong as ever.

Walter. Surely that would be enough to find that bastard.

Logan released me suddenly, and I shivered at the loss of his energy. Mine had been frolicking nicely with our *best friend*. The spellcaster noticed the goose bumps. Of course he noticed. He yanked his dark hoodie off, leaving him in a nicely fitted black shirt that hugged his muscled chest, and I choked out a surprised gasp when he gently dropped the warm material of his hoodie over my head, the length falling down my body.

"You're cold and still healing," he said as he stepped back. "Don't leave your room again tonight."

He was gone before I could get my addled brain to form words. I slumped against the wall, desperately sucking air into my lungs. With that air came the scent of Logan, surrounding me in his hoodie. It was a combination of minty evergreen, and energy so rich it heated my blood. A desperate need to tear it off overcame me, but my fingers remained tangled in the hem of the soft material, and I was still wearing it when I made it back to my room.

By this time I was exhausted, so I fell back into bed, and despite the absolute chaos of my energy and equilibrium—*thank you, Logan Fuckface Kingston*—I slept like the dead once more.

When I woke early the next morning, the pain was almost completely gone, and I pulled myself out of bed. As I stood, Logan's hoodie fell down my body, and with a grumble I ripped the freaking thing off, neatly folding it and shelving it in my wardrobe.

I *would be* giving it back to him later.

After a quick shower and change of clothes, I marched

through the school to the front office. Ms. White was the only witch in there today. "Hello, dear," she said, glancing up from her paperwork. "How can I help you?"

Her expression gave no indication that she remembered who I was.

"I need to speak with Headmaster Gregor." I forced a polite smile. "It's about the attack on Friday night."

Her face fell. "Oh my goddess, was that you? I'm so sorry, dear. Let me see if he's free."

She got to her feet, and hurried to a landline phone, and I was reminded once again that I needed to call Mom. Dad kept her updated, but I should reassure her that I was fine.

My siblings were probably freaking out too, even though I'd left a note on my door. They wouldn't be happy about me wandering around on my own, but this was important. I wouldn't feel safe in Weatherstone until I dealt with Walter the Weasel.

"He's on his way down," Ms. White said as she hung up. "You can take a seat back here." She led me into a room with a round table and four chairs. I took a seat but didn't have to wait long before the door opened for Headmaster Gregor.

His energy was stronger than usual today, and with it tingles trickled down my spine. It felt like the warning energy, and I wondered if all of this was somehow tied to necromancy. In a college like Weatherstone, that would make sense.

"Ms. Hallistar . . ." The headmaster's face was wreathed in concern. "I'm so sorry about the attack. I checked in with the healers throughout your recovery. How are you feeling today?"

He sat across from me and I pushed down the chill I always got around his affinity. "I'm feeling much better. Almost fully healed. I just wanted to come and let you know the name of my attack—"

His smile was brief. "It's already been dealt with."

I blinked. "Already? But I haven't made a statement."

He steepled his fingers before him, peering at me over the top. "The student in question, one Walter Allomore, air elemental, has been expelled from Weatherstone, and external disciplinary action is underway. He was turned in by another, quite well-connected student, and I can promise you that he won't be back on these grounds ever again."

I stared even harder, trying to figure out how this could have happened so quickly. "Who turned him in?" My first instinct said Logan, but there was also no reason for him to care enough about my safety to get rid of his friend.

"I'm not in a position to reveal their name, but rest assured, you're safe at Weatherstone now. Walter is no risk to you, or anyone else, any longer."

With that, he stood, and offered what felt like his first genuine smile of the meeting. "Rest up, Ms. Hallistar. You went through a traumatic ordeal, and you shouldn't rush to get back into college life. Take as much time to heal as you need. All of your professors are aware of the situation."

He left before I could utter another word, and I just blinked, wondering what the fuck had happened.

Walter Allomore, aka Weasel, had already been removed from the school? Before I even reported him?

It wasn't adding up.

None of this was adding up, and I hoped that next time I saw Dad he'd have more information for me.

CHAPTER 17

Dad didn't know more than what the headmaster had told me, stating that he'd heard Walter had confessed and would be going to jail for a very long time. The council had facilities across the country that held witches and warlocks, no matter their affinity or how powerful they were.

"As long as he's gone," Dad said, "the rest are details. I just want you safe here, Little Gem."

I agreed that was the most important part and let my worry go.

Later that week in apothecary with Belle, Sara, and Haley, the four of us were at our table near the back of the room, our kits set out before us.

Professor Kary wandered between the rows. "Great work last week," she said. "But we have new spells to work on today."

The professor was a voluptuous brunette witch, with a penchant for bright red lipstick and outfits that hugged her ample curves. Most of the warlocks in the class lusted over her, and I couldn't blame them. Her sex appeal was innate, but my favorite part of the class was her spell crafting abilities. I'd never met a more capable witch in that regard, and I'd already learned a lot.

Apothecary for Beginners was turning out to be one of my favorite classes, and I found a weird sense of comfort as I crafted spells in the steamy classroom.

"I love that necklace," Belle said as I leaned forward and

the crystal encased in a silver frame fell from my shirt. Releasing my bundle of sage, I pressed my hand to the thick silver chain. "It was my Gran's. I never met her, but Mom made sure to pass on some of her pieces to me. It's an amethyst."

"Amethysts are supposed to have psychic and spiritual properties," Haley piped up. "Or so I read. I've never had much to do with crystals."

Most witches didn't because there was no need. If you disregard the few spells which required a crystal bowl, usually quartz, we never used them in our magic. "Hopefully I don't commune with any of the spirits," I joked, because we all knew that not even a house built of amethyst would give me necro abilities. It was the one discipline where there was no cheating, unless you wanted to go all the way dark with some blood sacrifice. Which was a hard no from me because I enjoyed my soul mostly uncorrupted.

Our conversation died off as we focused on the spell, and I barely noticed the time passing. My worries faded until I was holding four parcels of protection herbs. "Keep small sections of it in your pocket," Professor Kary called as we packed up. "It could save your life. See you all next week."

Packing away the unused ingredients into my kit, I slung the bag over my shoulder. "Is anyone else nervous about this spellcaster class?" Haley asked. "I mean, why do we only have a few random classes with Logan throughout the year? What could that possibly teach us?"

"I heard that Logan flat-out refused to take more than that," Belle whispered. "Boy may be hot, but he's scary, and no one even attempted to force his hand."

I tried not to think about Logan, or that fucking hoodie that I'd found myself sleeping in most nights this week. It was soft and comfortable, and there was no other reason I kept putting it on.

I'd always liked comfort, and for some reason, his was softer than any of my hoodies.

"I'm mostly looking forward to staring at him for an hour," Sara said casually, slinging her bag over her shoulder too. "He's been starring front and center in my dreams lately, and I would bite off a piece of that warlock with nothing more than a crook of his finger at me."

My magic flared, heat overflowing inside me, which I ignored as I forced myself to act normal while we headed for his class. These special spellcaster lectures were held in the same room as necromancy history. They needed the stadium seating because there was no way everyone wouldn't turn out for this.

The four of us took a seat, with the rest filling up quickly. I saw Marcus off in the distance, but he was chatting to his friends, and I tried to ignore the twinge in my chest. He'd seen me briefly after my attack to check I was okay, but he'd made no mention of us hooking up again. I had no idea if it was guilt or if he'd lost interest, but either way . . . our budding friendship had fizzled out already.

That might be a record.

Once the room was full, Logan entered without fanfare, striding in, the door slamming closed behind him. If you weren't already in the room, you clearly weren't getting in.

"Silence," he rumbled, and to my great surprise everyone shut the fuck up. He wasn't a professor, but our magical essence recognized the apex predator in the room.

"I don't want to take this class," Logan continued, his disdain seeping out. "It was part of my deal to transfer to Weatherstone, and with that being said, I'm here to give you all a brief understanding of the affinity that is spellcasting."

"Fuck me dead," Sara groaned softly. "This dude could recite the alphabet and I'd be there." She was dating blondie surf warlock, but apparently there was no substitute for a spellcaster.

Forcing myself to focus on Logan, I noticed the slightest twitch to his lips. "Lesson one," he said, and without moving from the center of the room or lifting his hands, he sent all of our seats shaking.

There were screams and gasps as the entire stadium seating lifted about five feet off the ground, before dropping again a moment later. The silence that followed was heavy as we acknowledged the predator.

"We control the matter of the world," Logan continued, showing no strain despite the fact he'd just lifted thousands of pounds of witch and warlock. "And if you understand science at all, you know that everything is made of matter. Of elements and cells. Of energy I can manipulate. Don't get me wrong, I have the limitations of my body, and if I attempted to, say . . . throw the Earth's axis off, my magic would be exhausted and I would die. But on a smaller scale, we don't have many limits."

That heavy silence lingered, and I wondered if I was the only one whose heart pounded like I'd just run a marathon. It was a fear response, plain and simple. Sara fanned her face, giving zero cares that he could kill her with a thought.

"I could destroy you all with ease," Logan continued, and he smiled. Creepy asshole. Though most of the witches in the front row were leaning forward with keen interest. "Some of you could hold out for a few minutes, if you had a strong grasp of your own affinities. In larger numbers, you could fight back, but remember I control the same affinities that you do. Using water against me won't do much when I am stronger and can counter it. The only way to beat a spellcaster is to have enough witches and warlocks, and enough power, to overwhelm them. Not that I'd suggest trying it."

I studied him as one would do when faced with a creature of unknown origin. Logan might be a warlock, but he was unlike any I'd ever known. My gaze was drawn to that golden skin, and the flash in eyes so icy green that they were as unnatural as his power. Why had he sought me out in the hallway after my attack? Why had he refused to defend Walter?

It made no sense.

More importantly, why couldn't I stop thinking about him?

What the Hel was wrong with me? *He hates me.* His family had a fucking blood oath against mine, and yet . . . I found myself innately curious about him. The second he pulled that hoodie over my head, I should have taken it to Trevor to burn to cinders, and yet . . . I couldn't let it go.

"Lesson two . . ." Logan continued, and I wiped those other thoughts because I had no idea what he would do next.

Thankfully, there was no more attempting to move the building, but he did demonstrate his control of air, fire, water, wind, animals, elements, weather, tides . . . it was a ridiculous list.

"Can you use necro energy?" a student called from the back of the stands. "Since you dominate all the other affinities."

Logan lifted his head in the witch's direction, expression almost bored. "No one can touch the planes of existence and nonexistence unless they are necromancers. It is their one true calling, and while I have some control over the dead they summon here, I will never be able to call spirits to our plane of existence." The slightest chink in the spellcaster arsenal.

"Can you feel a student's affinity if they don't know what it is yet?"

I jerked to the side to see Belle with her hand in the air; not that she'd waited for him to call on her. *What the fuck are you doing?* I mouthed at her with a glare, but of course she ignored me.

Logically speaking, considering she was well aware of her affinity, that question was for me. Logan knew it too, as he fixed his penetrating gaze on my face. "I've never done so, but I don't see why I couldn't."

Belle lifted my hand. "Paisley volunteers."

Oh my goddesses. "I'm going to kill you," I muttered from the corner of my mouth. "And then find a necro to resurrect you so I can kill you again."

She snorted, before coughing to cover her laughter. "Come on, we might as well make him useful. And we both know you're desperate to find your affinity."

"*Desperate* is a little harsh," I breathed, but she wasn't entirely wrong.

"You're powerful, Pais," she whispered as she nudged me. "I know it, you know it. We just need a little boost to unlock your potential."

All possibly true, but not from Logan Kingston. He'd been associated with my two near-death experiences, and I trusted him as far as I could throw the stadium seating.

"Sure," he said, shocking the shit out of me. "Come down here, *Ms. Hallistar.*"

I felt the flush of heat in my cheeks as every single person in this room stared at me. He'd thrown out a challenge, and since I refused to witch out, I got to my feet. Sidling out of the row, I descended the four stairs to the main floor. Logan didn't move, his gaze still firmly on me, the echoes of a smirk on his lips as he made me go to him.

This power play had me clenching my teeth hard enough to crack them, but I'd come too far to back out now.

"No affinity," he said softly when I stopped before him. "Poor Precious, always rushing to catch up."

His face in that park flashed through my mind again, and I wondered if I'd fallen because I'd been chasing him. With no further memories forthcoming, I'd probably never know. Especially as my current dreams about him were very much in the present and very much *not when we were children.*

Standing close to him had my energy swirling hard and tingles racing down my spine. Not those disturbing ones, but the sort I was coming to recognize as strong magic. "Are you going to do anything or just stare at me?" I snapped, annoyed with the entire situation.

Witches gasped around the stadium, and I barely stopped myself from sneering and asking why their brains were in their vaginas today, before I realized how hypocritical that would be. I was hardly immune to Logan's many charms.

"Brace yourself," Logan rumbled, and then he lowered his voice until I was fairly certain these next words were just for me. "Try not to gasp too loudly, Precious."

I wanted to snap at him again, this feeling of being out of control grating against my composure, but his power locked around me before I could utter a word. The strength encased me whole, as if I were bound in metal. I couldn't move, or scream, or even pee myself through sheer terror. Logan wasn't hurting me, but that didn't make it any less terrifying, especially as the sensation of him digging into my essence increased.

He held me in stasis for what felt like an hour but couldn't have been more than a minute. His expression morphed from indifference to annoyance to frustration. His brows drew together, and he was standing close now. "Your energy is unlike any affinity I've felt," he said, and I was thankful that this time he kept his voice low. "I need to go deeper."

"No," I groaned, pushing through his hold. Or maybe he released me.

His hands grasped my biceps, and I was surrounded by minty evergreen as his touch burned through the material of my uniform. There was a brief pause, as if the universe held its breath along with everyone else in the room, and then I was struck with an inferno of his energy.

Wind howled through the room and water drenched us both, followed by multiple flickering flames above our heads, as if we'd set off fireworks.

Half of the students rose out of their seats, but I was too busy staring at Logan to notice what they did next. His eyes narrowed on me, and standing this close I could see a darker mossy ring around his pupils. Releasing me slowly, he waved a hand and dried us both, all the while that penetrating stare never wavered.

"You've been holding out on us, Precious," he drawled, his bored expression returning.

I shook my head. "I—I don't understand."

Did my power bring those elements out to play? If so, why in Selene was I so useless in class? Logan dismissed everyone soon after, and I remained in a shocked stasis, trying to figure out what had happened. I felt him turn toward me, but unable to deal with the intensity, I shook my head and raced from the room.

A few seconds later the girls found me, and thank the goddess they had my bag. I'd completely forgotten it was even in the room. Sara's eyes were wide as she opened and closed her mouth, attempting to speak but failing.

"What she's trying to say is that was really intense," Belle explained dryly.

At least I hadn't been the only one feeling overwhelmed by the sheer energy we'd created together.

"I don't know what happened," I whispered, and none of them appeared to know either, as we all just stood in silence. Belle had been trying to help me with her question, but I was more confused than ever about my affinity, and more importantly about my connection to Logan.

The spellcaster affected me, and despite his snarky "best friend" moniker, we hadn't seen each other in almost twenty years. We'd been children the last time we were together.

There had to be more here, an explanation for our connection.

I just couldn't remember what it was.

CHAPTER 18

That evening as I walked with the girls to dinner, I couldn't shake the feeling of being watched. It was that eerie energy times a hundred, as if the very walls themselves were stalking my steps. "What even happened in spellcaster class?" Sara asked, finally recovered from her shock. "I swear, you used multiple elements. Was that from Logan's power? Or yours?"

I didn't want to talk about it, and at the same time it was all I'd thought about since. "I wish I knew. I really wish I knew. All I felt was an explosion of power, and then the elements were everywhere, and I couldn't tell if it was Logan or me."

"Or both, but either way, you were involved, which means you're powerful enough for an affinity," Belle said with a casual shrug. "It's just about figuring out the key to unlock your magic from wherever it's bloomed and hidden. It makes sense to me that not every witch and warlock accesses their energy through the same paths. I have zero doubts that you'll get there."

"Love you," I told her, and I really meant it. Her unwavering support meant everything to me. Even with Trina and Olivia, friends I'd known for most of my life, there was a distance between us. It was probably more my fault than theirs, since I was content to hang with my family, but I didn't feel that distance with Belle. Or Sara and Haley, if I was being honest.

"Love you, babe," Belle said, her face all soft as her eyes grew shiny. "All of you guys."

"Same," I added.

"We love you too!" Haley said, getting in on the love. "If I swung that way, I'd totally wife one of you up."

I cracked up but couldn't disagree with her. Warlocks were drama, but unfortunately for me I wasn't even a one on the bisexual scale.

"Come on, future wifeys," Sara said, "I'm starving. Let's get some dinner."

Haley groaned, "Holy shit, I hope they have the lasagna." She clutched her paperback to her chest, and I noticed it had a different cover to the one I'd seen her with yesterday. Today's was mostly black, with a foiled skull and hissing snakes nearly jumping off the page at me.

"You and your pasta obsession," Belle said with a shake of her head. "Meanwhile, I'm hoping eggplant parmigiana is the special of the night."

"Also Italian," Haley sniped back, before clearing her throat. "And delicious. I'll have it also."

My favorite remained the salmon sushi, but I enjoyed those other two dishes as well. Weatherstone was not letting us down in the food department, that was for sure. Nothing would ever be Mom's home cooking, but it came close here.

The buffet was crowded, so we waited our turn, and as if the goddess herself heard us, all our favorites were there tonight. Even Sara's, which was steak and mashed potato. "They're too good to us here," she moaned, shoveling in another forkful of creamy potato. "What the fuck is even in this food? Crack?"

Laughing around another delicious bite of sushi, I startled when a hand dropped on my shoulder. "Oh shit!" Jenna backed up a step. "Sorry, Pais. I know you're still a little jumpy."

I was, but not for reasons that she expected. Sure, the attack might still occasionally add a new dream into the sex rotation, but it was more the feeling of being watched that had me on edge.

"All good. Did you eat already?" I asked her.

Before she could answer, Alice, Trevor, and Jensen all strolled over, and I was staring up at my four very protective siblings. "Yep, already done," Jenna said, ignoring them. "We're about to head down to the Barracks. Did you want to come?"

I hadn't had a chance to meet their familiars yet, what with all the *almost dying* drama, and I knew I should, but I had so much homework waiting for me. "I wish I could," I groaned. "I've got three assignments that I have to deal with tonight. Rain check?"

Jensen swooped in and kissed my cheek. "Baby Sis, you work too hard. I'm feeling neglected."

I shoved him away with a scowl, even though his puppy eyes were adorable. "You've been swimming every night, J, and not always alone, I might add. I think you're doing fine. I was waiting for Dad to organize a family trip home, but until that happens, we should have lunch on the weekend."

"It's a date," Jenna said sternly, before they all pat me on the head like their puppy and leave the dining hall.

Sara let out a sigh. "As an only child, can I just say that I hate you? I mean, as previously established I love you, but I also hate you, because that was just too sweet."

Lifting my last piece of sushi, I raised my eyebrow in her direction. "Look, I love them more than fucking anything, and I'd kill and die for them without a second thought, but let's be real here . . . they're giant pains in my ass."

"Would they be related to you if they were anything less?" Belle said, spooning the last bite of eggplant into her mouth. "Siblings are put on this Earth to break us down to our foundation, forcing us to rebuild ourselves into a stronger version. It's how the species survives."

Sara shrugged. "Maybe I was already my strongest, most perfect version. Hence no need for siblings."

All of us laughed and Haley threw a spoon at her, which Sara dodged.

After dinner, with assignments in mind, I decided to check out the library. I hadn't been to that building yet and needed to do additional research for Defensive Spells for Beginners. The professor tasked us with finding the best overall defensive spell that could be used in under ten seconds.

The girls were already up-to-date on their homework, so I walked through the halls alone. Halfway along the Zoo, I rubbed at my neck to ease the tension building and fought the urge to glance behind me. I'd already done that ten times, and the hall was completely empty. There was no sign of a stalker, no sign of danger, and no reason I should feel a dozen eyes on me.

Maybe the attack had had more of an effect on me than I'd thought. The physical injuries were healing but the mental ones were digging in deep. Creeping from my dreams into reality was playing dirty though, and I wondered if I should talk to someone about it. I'd give myself more time to work through it, and if it didn't ease up, I'd see about talking to the healers.

When I reached the library, using my paper map because I didn't have Belle, I examined the building from the outside. A standalone structure close to the Barracks, it used to be a religious shrine to Hecate and Selene, before the chapel was relocated into a larger building in 1927. Since then, this old shrine became the library.

It wasn't wide but it was clearly long, and as I ascended the dozen steps to reach the front doors, I found myself curious about what it would be like inside. I might not be a reader, but as I opened the double doors and stepped through, a sense of peace eased my tension.

Thousands of books filled hundreds of dark wood shelves, spanning into the distance. I loved the peaked roof and lofty ceilings, with shelves built into every nook and cranny. Two librarians hurried past me then, and I felt the currents of air as they used their affinity to move books to their appropriate shelves.

It was still early evening, and all the desks in my immediate vicinity were occupied, so I lifted my bag higher to ease the heavy load and moved through the rows.

The lighting inside wasn't too bright, just a calming glow, and with my tension completely gone—along with that sensation of being watched—I decided I'd be spending a lot of time here.

I reached another section of desks surrounding a huge fireplace designed to exude heat in all directions. It had a glass protector, and its flume exited the highest point of the ceiling. Peering around, I thought I was out of luck again, only to find one desk in the corner still unclaimed.

Dropping my bag on it to reserve my spot, I hurried off to find the books I needed. The classification system here was brilliant, and it took me less than ten minutes to find *The Highest Protection Is the One You Create* and *Defending Your Energy: Magical Spells for Those Who Want an Extra Boost of Defensive Power.*

Feeling quite pleased with myself, I was returning to my table when a shadow loomed over me. Strong hands wrapped around my arms, and I was hauled deep into the stacks before I could utter a sound. Screams built in my throat, as memories of that bag being jerked over my head pressed in on me. "Breathe, Precious." His low voice broke through my ragged breaths, and for some fucked-up reason, I calmed. As I lifted my head, I found Logan staring at me.

His expression was hard, but his eyes weren't as icy as usual.

Shaking him off, I backed away as far as I could go until I hit a shelf. Fighting the urge to rub at my arms where he'd touched me, branding his energy into my skin, I glared at him. "What are you doing, Logan? Do you want your fucking hoodie back?"

Goddesses be damned, Paisley. You're an idiot.

Logan tilted his head, and whatever softness I'd imagined was gone. "Explain yourself."

Wondering if he was about to attempt to murder me thrice, I started to sidle down the aisle, only for him to growl and slam his hands on either side of my head, effectively trapping me. "Explain," he gritted out a repeat of his last statement.

"Explain what?" I shot back, clutching the heavy textbooks in my hands, debating if I should swing them into his face. He was too close at the moment, so I pressed them into his chest, which didn't move him in the slightest. Even worse, as I touched his shirt, there was a spark of energy that had me yanking them away.

Logan didn't appear to notice. "You come here pretending to have no affinity, to barely have power, and then you touch all the elements in one class. Are you a spellcaster?"

It finally clicked on what his irritation was about; this suspicious asshole thought I was a sleeper cell of a witch, pretending to be a lame little lamb. "Sorry to be an annoyance," I told him blithely, and it was a straight-up lie, because I loved to annoy this prick, "but I genuinely have no idea what my affinity is. What happened today was because of your spellcaster energy and nothing else. It wasn't me. It was you, bro, so you might want to back off."

"I am not your bro," he seethed. "And you better stop lying

to me, Precious." He brushed a strand of my hair back, grazing his fingertips over my ear and sending tingles through my energy. "I abhor liars."

Swallowing roughly, because my throat decided to dry up, I snapped, "I abhor assholes, so I guess we're even." Realizing how that sounded, I hurried to add, "And I'm not lying. I have no reason to lie. Also . . . stop calling me *Precious*. Where the fuck did you even get that from?"

The light green of his eyes briefly flickered darker, that mossy ring expanding. "Precious Gem. You don't remember?"

Gem.

"My dad is the only one who calls me Gem," I whispered, trying to figure out why I was panicking so hard. Those memories that were just out of reach had my pulse racing. My breaths were harsh and rapid.

Logan leaned back suddenly, lifting his hands. "I know. I know everything about you, Paisley Hallistar."

Forcing a normality in my tone that I didn't feel, I chuckled darkly. "You thought I was a spellcaster. You don't know shit about me, and I really need to study, so . . . get out of my way."

Logan eyed me for a long moment, and just as it appeared he was about to back away, tingles raced down my spine. The bad ones. The *I'm being stalked in the hallway* tingles. With it came a feel of heat in the necklace hanging under my shirt.

Unable to help myself, I turned left and right, searching the long aisles of shelves.

Logan missed nothing, his sharp gaze turning to look along the shelves as well. "What did you feel?"

Moistening my lips, my breaths were ragged as I shook my head. "Nothing. I'm just reacting to being trapped in these shelves with a psychopath who's already attempted to murder me twice."

Expecting more anger, all I got was a slow smile as he played with the ends of my ponytail, running it through his fingers. "If I wanted to murder you, Precious, you'd be dead."

Jerking my head away from him, I felt the heat of my power, and there was a cracking sound as Logan's head jerked to the side. He blinked, and a rumble filled his chest as he stared with a look of disbelief. "Did you just witch-slap me?"

"N-no," I stuttered out, because there was no way I'd slap a spellcaster. I might despise him, but I knew Logan could crush me like a bug. "Unless my magic did that on its own. I don't have an active affinity, and I certainly don't have any control over it."

Logan showed zero shock, and to my surprise he didn't look angry.

Nope, it was even worse.

He was intrigued.

"I've learned a lot here tonight," he said, as he examined my face. I was so caught up in him that I didn't notice the creepy feeling was gone until I took a step to the side, and he let me.

"Whatever you think you know, you're wrong," I said, wanting the last words, even if they were lame.

"I don't think so," he murmured, and I doubted I'd ever get the last word with this controlling asshat. "I believe I'm finally seeing clearly."

Before I could wrangle up my next witty comeback, he strode away, leaving me to slump against the shelves, almost losing my grip on the textbooks. *Holy goddess.*

That was unnerving, and I had no idea what to think about Logan. He wasn't acting as if he wanted to kill me, but he was certainly interested in my power, which made no freaking sense. Unless there was a game at play here that I wasn't clued in on.

Stumbling back to the table, the *Logan bubble* burst, and I was once again immersed in the busy and noisy room. Students were chatting, spells were being stirred, and the librarians were racing around shelving and retrieving books. It was as if those minutes in the stacks never happened, and yet I could feel his energy and heat burning into my skin. My power was volatile too, just like my pulse.

What had happened with Logan? Had my magic slapped him? Had there been a presence stalking us, or was this all tied to his spellcaster energy?

More importantly, what was in our brief past together that had Logan acting the way he did? The nickname was one part to the equation, but another was the sense of familiarity between us.

It wasn't just the dreams. It was so much more than that, and I feared that if I didn't figure out what it all was soon, I would find my end at the hands of Logan Kingston.

CHAPTER 19

Strong hands pressed my thighs apart, pushing them firmly into the bed, and I cried out as his tongue swiped over my clit, circling it slowly. Desperate to move, I tried to ride against his mouth, but he held me so firmly I couldn't move. Those continuous swirls of his tongue were unrelenting. My cries grew louder, and when he slid one finger inside my slick heat, and then another, curling them up to stroke against my G-spot, an orgasm ripped through me—

I woke up with my hands in my panties, coming so hard that I felt like my body was locked in a place of pure pleasure. "Holy goddess," I breathed through a sob. This had to end. I couldn't handle the dreams any longer, especially when the warlock behind them had ghosted me harder than I'd ever been ghosted before.

Even if he was my mortal enemy, the fact that Logan and I had barely crossed paths in weeks frustrated me to no end. I'd expected that day in the library to find myself constantly dodging his observations in his quest to unravel my secrets. Instead, it had been endless weeks of catching glimpses of him and nothing more. He taught his classes, but he never once glanced my way, and I couldn't figure out why it pissed me off so much.

I should be happy about his disinterest, because there was no point I stopped believing Logan was dangerous.

He was the thorn in my side in an otherwise amazing year—with the exception of nearly dying . . . twice. *So far.*

I'd settled into college life like I'd been born for it: classes were going well, my friends were amazing, my family were all happy, and Dad had stopped staring at me like I was about to be kidnapped out from under him.

Everything felt settled, and yet . . . the roil of my useless magic only grew stronger. Along with the dreams. This wakeup, thankfully, was only ten minutes before my alarm, so I rolled out of bed, grabbed my bag with my showering items, and made my way to get ready for the day.

An hour later, Belle met me for defensive spells class. "You look like shit," she said, by way of greeting.

"Feel like it too," I mumbled around a yawn. "Fucking dreams."

Her smile was sympathetic, but she couldn't relate to my frustrations. Recently she'd started hooking up with a fire elemental in the grade above us, and her situationship with Micha appeared to be working out quite well.

"Ava joined us last night," Belle said suddenly, and I forgot my sleepiness for a beat, and blinked at her.

"As in *joined*, joined you?"

Belle snorted. "Uh, yep. I mean, I wasn't expecting it, but I wasn't objecting either. We're going to see how the three of us fare for these hookups."

Micha had more than one *situationship*, and the clever bastard had figured out a way to bring them both together. "As long as you're happy and getting all the orgasms you need . . ." I said, wanting to ease her expression. She wore a look like she thought I was about to judge her. "Then I'm fucking happy for you." She had two sex partners, and I was just over here with dreams and sadness. I knew which one of us was living her best life.

"Love you, bestie," she said, hugging an arm around my shoulders. "I couldn't do this college life without you."

"Ditto."

We set off down the hall, and I rubbed at my tired eyes, already planning an afternoon nap.

"Any progress on figuring out the creepy feeling?" Belle checked in as she did every few days.

"No progress. It's just so random, and I can't find a single pattern." I'd caved and told the girls about it. None of them had felt anything similar, and for the most part believed it was my energy reacting to Weatherstone. My magic wasn't following any rules, and they thought this was just one more oddity.

"What if you do have a stalker?" she asked suddenly. "I mean, that could be another reason we don't feel it. Their energy is directed at you. It could even be a tracking spell, if it's a powerful enough witch or warlock. Like . . . Logan maybe?"

We hadn't talked about him recently, and I'd never mentioned the library incident, but somehow she still knew how often he was on my mind.

I shook my head. "He doesn't seem the type to be this sporadic, or let it drag on for months. It's connected to Weatherstone and the energy it holds. It only ever happens to me here."

My siblings and I had gone home last weekend to see Mom, and there'd been zero dark or creepy energy. No weird shadows that I caught a glimpse of but when I'd turn there'd be nothing there. I'd even caved and visited the healer to see if I had head trauma still, but Maddy gave me a clean bill of health. It was either psychological or . . . *who the fuck knew.*

"Okay, well, I'm back to it being your magic, and how it's locked away." Belle nodded as if that solidified her theory. "You show an aptitude for necro, and I'm guessing that could feel creepy when it's not fully . . . uh, developed. I wouldn't panic about it."

My aptitude for necro wasn't strong enough for an affinity, but there was a vibe. Especially near the graveyard. The professor explained during class that inside those walls the veil between the planes of existence was thinner. There were a few spots around Weatherstone like that, including the lake. It had been part of the old battlefield that this college was built on, with skeletons littering the lake bottom. Lovely.

We pushed through the students to find Sara and Haley waiting for us at the cart. They'd already grabbed our favorites, and I could have kissed them both. Sara and I needed coffee to function as civil witches, while Belle generally got chai, and Haley enjoyed chocolate milk.

"Because I'm still mostly twelve with my food choices," she'd explained. Not that any of us cared—not liking chocolate milk was the first sign of a sociopath, as far as I was concerned.

"You are angels," Belle breathed, closing her eyes as she took her first sip of tea. "I needed that."

"Looks like you might need a double shot today," Sara said as she handed me my cup, laughing when I gulped down a mouthful, scalding my tongue.

"The dreams," I croaked, shaking my head.

"You need to get laid," she told me sternly. "This is not good for you."

I didn't disagree with her. I'd attempted to get laid on three separate occasions.

Brenton, a third-year who was friends with Trevor—hence why that one ended before even starting.

Lewis, in our grade, who had a habit of talking about himself in the third person. By the time he said, *Lewis is ready for some fucking*, I was out of there.

And finally Damien, who was in our year as well, a water elemental, who ironically was as dull as dishwater.

"I need to find a warlock who gives me that spark, you know?"

Haley sighed. "Good luck with that. I haven't even found a warlock here who can carry a decent conversation, let alone give me a spark."

I chuckled sadly. "Girl, ain't that the truth."

We walked to class, munching breakfast bagels and sipping our drinks. Breakfast was served in the dining hall as well, but we loved the cart. Outside of Belle, it was my longest relationship on campus.

"I finished that book last night," I told Haley as I chewed. "It was really freaking good. That cliffhanger though . . ." I breathed heavily. "I almost threw your e-reader across the room. When is book two out?"

Her entire face lit up. "Oh my goddess, I'm so excited that you enjoyed it. It releases in June, so not long to wait."

Grinding to a halt, the other three turned back to stare at me in surprise, but I was too busy glaring. "Haley Michaels," I finally growled. "It's the end of April."

She pressed her lips together but refrained from laughing at me. "I know, friend. But I promise, it'll be worth the wait. This author always delivers."

Haley had done the impossible and converted me. I'd had no idea there were books filled with the sort of desperate love that I craved, along with action, adventure, snark, and all the sexy, *sexy scenes*. While they didn't exactly help the dreams, they did keep me occupied when my mind wouldn't shut up.

"I thought we were friends," I said with a sad exhalation. "How could you hurt me like this?"

Haley's laughter couldn't be contained any longer, and she spilled her milk on her hand. "I promise not to send you incomplete series from now on. How does that sound?"

I huffed for a few seconds, before settling down. "Sounds like a plan."

After mopping up her hand with the napkin, she linked her arm through mine. "Come on, yell at me about the cliffy as we walk."

I did just that, and when we reached our defensive spells class, all four of us threw our breakfast trash in the can and took our usual seats.

This was one of my favorite classes, and today we were perfecting an all-round defensive trio of spells, one that would cover a whole range of attacks and could be used quickly. Other spells were more specific, such as the *lingher trestoria* that we'd studied last week, which was literally used to ward off an attack from ants.

Yep. Apparently, if ants banded together, they'd destroy every living thing on Earth.

Who knew?

Today was *fringal*, a simple spell that covered a range of attacks. "We don't recommend this one in an attack situation if you know a more specific spell," Professor Zander said, starting the class without preamble. He was a serious warlock in his sixties with a no-nonsense style of teaching. "More specific is more effective, and fringal can drain you easier if you use it on an attack too strong."

He looked around the class, and Dawn, who was a brainy student currently battling Haley and Belle for top grades, put her hand in the air. "Why do you teach it if it's effectively useless in an attack?" she asked after the professor called on her.

"It's not useless per se," he told her. "If you find yourself in a situation without the knowledge of a specific counterspell, then this gives you a chance to deflect and escape. It could still save your life, and my aim is to ensure all of you live long and healthy lives."

Good enough reason for me. A general spell felt *very* useful, because the odds of being attacked by ants were still low.

"Low but never zero," Belle said with a snort when I mentioned it.

I shrugged, because there was no way to argue that.

"Get your stations ready," Professor Zander called, returning to his desk at the front of the room. "You have fifty minutes. Make sure you read step three very carefully."

There were forty of us in this class, spread out around high desks, with a good three feet between each of us. Belle was on my right, Sara on my left, and Haley beside her. We all got to work arranging our candles first. Lavender-infused witchdrake candles were set out in a pentacle carved into the wooden table. A fire elemental made their way around the class to light them, and as soon as the scent of the candle filled the room, my body relaxed.

I'd grown up cooking, and mixing tinctures with my mom, and this part of witchcraft settled well with my energy. It wasn't a hugely difficult spell, but there were multiple steps, which included various herbs. Step three we'd been warned about pertained to the order of the herbs, and the timing of the incantation in the ancient language.

If you got all of that right, there should be a puff of white smoke and then a puff of black smoke, before the pentacle would visibly join with a light beam.

I got it on the first try, and when I wrapped up step six, waving my hand over the candles to douse their flames and release the spell, I felt calmer and more at ease with the events of my life. The result of my spellwork was a small pile of ash. Or, what looked like ash, but would work as a defensive mist when cast across the danger.

"You did that so fast," Belle complained, still trying to get step three right. "Can't I just go and play in the lake? I honestly think the rest of these classes are a waste of my time."

"I'll help you," I said with a laugh. This was one of the few classes where Belle's vast intelligence didn't come in as handy as my solid knowledge of cooking and mixing ingredients. Her parents had never let her in the kitchen, but I enjoyed helping her. It was nice to excel in one class.

The day passed by quickly, and even though my only successful magic was with the defensive spell, I finished up the day feeling relaxed. Weatherstone was the guide in the magical world that I'd always hoped it would be, and even without a clear affinity, I had no doubt that I'd graduate from here a stronger witch.

By the time I headed for my dorm, a raging party had spilled into Florence Wing, and as one exhausted witch, I wished they'd chosen another night. It wouldn't be long before the professors broke it up though, so I decided to take a walk and get some fresh air. Today had been a lot of classroom work and research in the library, and I was due to stretch my legs.

It wasn't quite dark yet as the days got warmer and longer. I loved the early evening balminess in the air. Maybe I'd even venture into the lake again, staying in the shallows this time. My path around the school brought me to the edge of the forest, and when I saw the graveyard, I was reminded of my attack.

It felt like it happened years ago, but also yesterday at the same time.

It had been hard to return to that location—my first necro class had triggered me so badly I'd raced off to vomit in the bushes. But I'd been determined to return the next time, and I'd been forcing myself to stay ever since. Walter the Weasel wasn't going to take one more piece of my life away.

With that in mind, I crossed closer to the arched entrance

gates and stepped inside as the last rays of sun washed over the headstones. Like in class, I found my energy expanding as I sought to touch the veils of existence. There were tingles. There was heat and light. But like always, my magic was too weak to behave as a true affinity.

This evening, the tingles of my energy were stronger than usual, and I glanced up to see the full moon again. I'd been so exhausted and stressed out with classes, I'd forgotten the cycle. It was sacrilege not to know when we should be communing with Selene.

My skin glowed softly, and I felt that urge to release my energy.

If only I could figure out how.

I found myself reaching down to press my hands to the ground, which was stupid, because the energy of the dead wasn't found literally under our feet. You had to cross the veils between the five planes of existence. The living, where we existed; purgatory, for those who could not cross over and were not welcome into the afterlife; the dead zone, for those on their first journey to the afterlife, to be judged and given their path; Hel, for those souls condemned to an eternity of suffering; and the eternals, where those with light in their energy would enjoy an eternity in the blessing of our beloved goddess.

Necromancers could not draw from the eternals or purgatory. There was no true explanation for why, but any who tried were destroyed by the energy. The other two zones, though, were prime for the taking of energy.

Hence why there was a sense of unease when I felt a necromancer's power. Primarily, it was drawn from souls. Some light, but others very dark. Necros on occasion would lose control of the energy they borrowed and turn into what we referred to as a *necroils*. Dark witches and warlocks, who delved deeper and deeper, taking the blood of life to do so.

They generally required a spellcaster to take them down and remind us all why we didn't mess with blood magic.

Not if we wanted to live to tell the tale.

CHAPTER 20

As expected, there was no response to my touching the ground, and when I stood a strong wave of exhaustion pressed in on me. Surely I'd given them enough time to party back in the dorms. I needed to get in some study and sleep.

I headed for the arched gates, and was almost there when a pair of warlocks hurried past. I came to a halt, recognizing them both. Logan and Noah were in the middle of their evening run—running for fun explained a lot of what was wrong with both of those assholes—when the moonlight washed over them. There was this stupid pain in my chest at how I'd been ghosted. My dad was freaking ecstatic at Logan's obvious lack of interest in me, and I should have been too.

"Logan!" A witch screamed out his name as she raced across the grounds. She wasn't alone either, two of her friends trailing behind her. "Wait up. We didn't finish our conversation."

Logan and Noah stopped, wiping the sweat from their foreheads. The witch leaned into him, and I recognized her as the pretty blonde who had been talking to Marcus at that first full moon party. Rage bubbled in my chest, and I was shocked to see light spilling from my fingertips.

The instant fury made no sense, and needing to get away, I slinked back into the graveyard. "Bastard asshole of a fucking warlock," I snarled, and kicked rocks between the headstones.

My anger wasn't rational. I could only attribute it to the

fire of my magic, which swirled so hard that my chest ached. I tried to force it out, but the way it was locked down only increased my anger. All I ended up with was hands and arms glowing as I grasped my crystal necklace, desperate to find a calm again.

A tingle caressed my neck and raced down my spine. I was struck with the unnerving sense that I'd pushed too far into the tombs and headstones. My new location had brought forth the creepy stalker vibe.

Danger, danger, danger.

Like a flashing light above my head, my warning systems were on full alert, telling me to get the fuck out of there. The fear demolished my rage, and I found myself unable to move, my hand fused to my pendant as I searched for danger. I'd made a stupid rookie move and let myself get complacent. Nothing good ever came from this creepy feeling, and here I was in the middle of a graveyard under a full moon. Alone. Wait, no . . .

Logan and Noah.

They were just outside the gates, and as much as I didn't want to run into him, Logan was my best chance of avoiding whatever haunted my world. I just had to push past the debilitating fear and move my feet.

Gripping the necklace tight enough that it cut into my palm, I closed my eyes and summoned up every ounce of strength, managing to lift my foot as the snap of a branch alerted me to a presence.

My eyes shot open, and I found myself staring at a nightmare.

The creature dragged itself through the graves. It had two huge clawed hands, while the rest of its body slithered on the ground like a snake. My breaths were just short of hyperventilation as I stumbled back into a crypt. The snakelike head of the beast came into view, with dozens of teeth. It crawled toward me faster than should be possible as it navigated the narrow spaces between headstones.

This time I couldn't blame a lack of oxygen. Unless I'd slipped, hit my head, and was unconscious, there was a real, *honest to fucking goddess* monster coming at me. It didn't look like the one in the lake, but it did arrive with Logan's presence. Just like the last one.

Was he dealing in dark magic? As a spellcaster, and one of the strongest warlocks in the world, had he crossed a line?

The snake monster cut off my panicked thoughts as it snarled and came closer, bringing with it a distinct scent of ash and sulfur. Its beady black eyes were focused on me, unwavering, and I managed to take one step, and then another, almost falling over exposed rocks.

Goddess, help me.

I had no idea what I could do here, and the creature was only a dozen feet away. Releasing my crystal, it fell against my chest, and with its warmth my sanity returned.

My sanity and ability to get the Hel out of there.

With the monster between me and the entrance, I sprinted deeper into the graveyard, chancing one very brief look over my shoulder. A strangled scream escaped when I found the monster close behind. Its pace was intense. There was no way I'd make it out of here before it caught up.

In my panicked state, I searched my pockets for anything that might help, only to pull out a small vial of ash. *Oh, thank fuck.* I still had the defensive spell from class today.

I uncorked the jar right as my luck ran out and I clipped my shoe on a stone hidden in a patch of grass and went tumbling forward. Somehow, I managed to keep hold of the jar, and only a little ash spilled.

Flipping over, I screamed again, this time with much more intensity because it was on top of me.

That snake head darted forward as I jerked my hand and let the ash fly in its face. I screamed the incantation, instinct driving me, even as my mind remained locked in fear. If I survived tonight, I'd have to send Professor Zander some flowers or my firstborn child because I owed him big-time. In his fussy way, he'd drilled this spell into our heads all week, and under pressure, I'd remembered it.

My magic burned within me, and when I threw the ash, I pressed my hands against the chest of the creature and prayed I could send enough energy into it to knock it away. All I needed was a chance to escape.

Its skin was scaly and hot to touch, and as magic raced through my palms I knew I'd made the right decision to open a pathway through touch. The light grew bright enough to blind me, and while I closed my eyes I didn't stop expelling magic.

The light faded, and I opened my eyes to find that I was completely alone. The monster was gone, and so was the creepy sensation. My arms trembled as I pushed myself up, looking at every dark shadow, waiting for movement or another attack. Instinct told me I was safe, but I wasn't about to take chances.

Once on my feet, I ran out of the graveyard like my ass was on fire, to find that not a single student was nearby. A glance at my watch had me blinking . . . 9:00 p.m. How in the world was that possible? It hadn't been more than seven when I'd wandered down.

When I entered the dorms a few minutes later, it was quiet, no sign there'd been a party at all. I gathered up my clothes and toiletries, knowing that I needed a shower, even if there was a monster lurking in the halls. No way could I go to bed covered in grass, dirt, and possibly snake-monster drool.

Peering out of my room, the hallway was empty, so I speed-walked as fast as I could to the bathroom with only a moderate level of panic. The monster attack had my head a mess, as I wondered if I hadn't imagined the alien in the lake after all.

I'd explained away the first monster encounter easily enough—a hallucination caused by a lack of oxygen. But now with this second one . . . ? There was a pattern here, especially when both were accompanied by a sense of danger tracing down my spine. But how did it all tie in to my stalker vibes as I walked through the halls? Was there a student—or professor, couldn't discount them—gunning to kill me? Waiting for opportunities as I walked around the school?

Could it be Logan . . . ? Or Noah . . . ?

One of his friends had already beat me half to death, so it stood to reason that the other could try as well. I hadn't made any enemies that I was aware of, having only punched one witch, who was no longer a student here.

But there was a threat out there.

By the time I finished showering, the tremble in my limbs had eased under the hottest water I could stand, but I was no closer to an answer. Dressed in pj's with my wet hair wrapped in a towel, I raced through the hall. No one jumped out at me, and my heart only calmed when I was once again safe inside my room.

Putting my bag away and tossing the dirty uniform into the wash bags that we dropped outside our doors to be laundered once a week, I crawled into bed and let myself fall apart. My chest shook as I drew in a ragged breath, and even as I attempted to cry, to ease the ache in my throat, no tears came. I was beyond tears, trapped in a moment of terror, as that attack flashed before my eyes.

Part of me knew I needed to tell someone—my dad, siblings, or Mom for example, but I had no doubt that a single mention of another attack and they'd pull me from school. As far as I was aware, I was the only one *almost dying* on the regular at Weatherstone.

I should leave. I knew that with every part of my being, and yet . . . I hated to let those bastards win. Weatherstone felt like home, and the education was second to none. I mean, Defensive Spells had saved my life tonight.

As exhaustion wrapped around my brain and dragged me into sleep, I decided not to mention anything until I could do more research. I'd never heard of any magic that could create monsters. I needed to know more. We might exist in a world of magic, but there were no mythical creatures, dark or other.

Knowledge was my power here, and I would be proactive rather than reactive.

I also needed to whip up another defensive spell.

That shit had really come in handy.

CHAPTER 21

The next few days I was jumpy but managed to keep it together for my friends. I got through my classes in a daze, trying to figure out who hated me enough to dabble in dark magic and create monsters.

Logan was the obvious choice, and later that evening when I was racing through the hall to shower, he stepped into Florence Hall and we almost collided. He caught me with ease, before I lost my footing and toiletries. "Precious," he said, voice a smooth rumble. "Why are you sprinting like you're being chased?" He looked over my head as if checking for a pursuer, but clearly there was none. I was just a hot mess seeing shadows and monsters everywhere.

"You don't already know?" I choked out, because he was far too close, and I was far too frazzled to hide my usual reaction to his presence and magic. His touch confused and destroyed me in equal measures, and maybe I was actually losing my mind.

His brow wrinkled as he shook his head. "You're just as fucking weird as you were as a child. You're making less sense than usual, Paisley. Are you injured? Did you hit your head?"

I'd show him who was weird. "No, I didn't hit my head. I don't have to injure myself when there's someone else out there ensuring it happens. Now, if you'll excuse me . . ."

I tried to wrench myself free, but his grip tightened.

"Who?" he asked, in a softly dangerous tone. "Who injured you?"

This guy did my head in. "I don't know, Logan," I replied. "I mean, last time it was your bestest buddy, so maybe this time it's you. Or . . . your other friend."

No change in expression. "Walter was taken care of long ago, and if Noah wanted to hurt you, you'd be in much less—" he eyed the long expanse of leg exposed by my shorts "—pristine condition. So, I repeat, Precious, who the fuck hurt you?"

The way he said *Walter was taken care of* settled uneasily in my chest. "You got rid of Walter? Did he end up in prison?"

His eyes twinkled, and I could have sworn he was amused. "No, he's missing. No one has seen him in weeks. Answer my question, Paisley."

Missing. That wasn't good when I felt a stalker on my ass. Was it possible for him to sneak into the grounds somehow and try to take me out for good this time? Or was he sending the monsters through the barrier?

"No one hurt me," I said, desperate for Logan to let me go. Or pull me closer. *Fuck.* I was such a mess. "Can you let me go . . . ?"

For a moment, it didn't seem he was going to release me, but then he relaxed his grip and stepped aside. I scampered away before he could say another word, and forced myself not to look back, even as I felt the burn of his gaze on me.

Tomorrow, no matter what classes I had, I'd find time to research the magic required to create monsters. And find out if it had to be a spellcaster.

After that night I did nothing except go to classes, see my friends, and live in the library. I had all but exhausted the supply of dark magic books, and had a ton of theories about how the monsters were being created, though nothing concrete. It didn't take a spellcaster per se, but it did take a dark warlock or witch to be able to bring nightmares to life.

In a text on the history of dark magic, I'd found an obscure paragraph that suggested there was a way to draw beasts from one of the planes that none of the affinities could touch. Which should eliminate Logan as a suspect, but the part about *going dark* was the key. If you dabbled in magics you shouldn't, you touched energy you shouldn't.

"Pais!"

I lifted my head, rubbing at my bleary eyes. Half of these texts had tiny freakin' writing. I was going to need glasses if I kept this research up.

"I've been waiting for you for an hour." Belle's voice was low and vibrating with annoyance. She placed her hands on the back of the chair opposite me, and I noted how nice she looked. Her hair was shiny and straight, makeup darker than usual and on point, and she was in a cute little black dress and heels.

That was when it clicked on, and I let out a gasp. "Holy fuck. I'm so sorry. I got totally caught up in this research and spaced on the time."

I'd promised that I'd ditch the library for one night and go to a party in the gardens. This one was school sanctioned, so I'd felt safe in attending, but then the library books had dragged me in and time had slipped away.

Pushing to my feet, I started to apologize again, but she got in first. "Honestly, I'm worried about you. You're obsessed, not sleeping, and barely eating. You look like shit, friend."

Her bluntly honest words hurt, and I felt the need to react defensively. "There's a darkness stalking my steps, Belle. I've felt it, and I think . . . maybe I'm in danger." This was the most

I could tell her without coming out with the whole monster thing. "I need to know why and how, so that when it happens again I can deal with it."

She just shook her head. "I've never felt what you do. None of us have. I'm not saying you aren't in danger, but I think this might be PTSD from Walter's attack. That's all. You need to talk to someone."

This wasn't the first time she'd suggested I get help from a professor or maybe a magical therapist. They could use healing energy to soothe the brain, especially when there had been real trauma.

"I don't think it's PTSD." I rubbed at the ache in my temples. "I'm not crazy. I know what's been happening to me."

Belle nodded, without any real emotion. "Okay, Paisley. I get it. But I'm done waiting for you tonight. I'll see you tomorrow."

She was gone before I could open my mouth to offer another useless apology. Her words, though harsh, were not unfounded—I hadn't been a very good friend for a while now. That recent attack in the graveyard had taken a piece of me, and now I didn't feel safe in my own life.

The lake I'd excused away, and Walter was a deranged psychopath, but a legitimate monster had me spiraling . . . and keeping it all to myself wasn't getting me anywhere.

Knowing I'd get nothing more productive done tonight, I returned all the books and left the library. As I stepped outside in the balmy night, I basked in the glorious warmth, the chirp of cicadas off in the distance. Party sounds echoed across the grounds, resurrecting my guilt and sadness. I hated letting my friends down.

Maybe I should have gone into more detail about the graveyard attack with her. I'd mentioned that I thought I was in danger, and that someone had been there with me, but left the monster part out completely, lest she think I was crazier than she probably already thought.

Heat swirled in my chest as I fought my emotions, trying to calm down. I'd been practicing calling my energy and had improved enough that there was a whisper of talk that I might possibly be a late-blooming spellcaster. I could touch most of the affinities, but I hadn't found the key to my power yet. It was as if I forced small slivers out through the keyhole, but it was never going to be enough for an affinity.

Dad was proud, glossing over my lack of true active magic. Mom, when I called her last, had been just as excited. "I told you, honey," she'd said. "You will grow into the amazing witch I always knew you could be. But don't let the pressure of being a spellcaster get to you. Your path is yours alone, and it will be clear when the time is right."

Then she'd promised to send a batch of my favorite choc-chip cookies with Dad, and I'd found myself desperate for home, for one of her hugs. The reality of maturing and searching for my future, while simultaneously missing my childhood and old life, was disconcerting to say the very least.

In my dorm, I opened my window for one last breath of summer air and let the moonlight wash through the window. My crystals sparkled, and I picked up the large moonstone piece, with its unusual emerald flecks embedded. This was my most comforting crystal, and here, in my room surrounded by its energy, I felt a peace and safety that was lacking outside these walls.

As I went to return the moonstone to my desk, a scream rang out so loud that even in my dorm I could hear it. I almost dropped the crystal, catching it before it slipped through my fingers, and placed it back in its spot. Another scream echoed through the room, fracturing the peace I'd found, and unable to stop myself, I raced to my door and peeked out to see what was happening.

The noise amplified as soon as I cracked the door, and there were dozens of students streaming along as more screams rang out—this was not a normal fight.

Stepping out of the room in my skimpy pj's since there was no time to change, I joined the crowd. Most of them wore pajamas and confused expressions too. No one knew the source of the chaos.

When we crossed into Aura Hall, the screams were so loud they were almost deafening, and as a shadow reared up, I choked on my breath, grinding to a halt. A creature filled the hallway, squished down by the ceiling, as it jabbed claws in front of it. At first glance, it looked like an armored praying mantis, its grasping legs serving as serrated weapons. It was black, just like the last two monsters I'd seen, and it was grappling with a warlock in the hallway.

The relentless screams came from a group of witches, who were using elements and other magic to try to knock the beast off a warlock. I caught a glimpse of Jenna in the group, and panicked that she was about to get hurt, which was the only way I could move again.

"I'm going to fetch a professor," she shouted before I got too close, and then she was gone. Alice joined her at the last minute, and I was relieved that they were out of harm's way.

"Use air to send it flying backward," a witch shouted.

The air elementals moved closer together, and the wind in the hallway picked up until my hair flew around me. They blasted the creature in one shot and managed to send it skidding back only a few inches. These monsters were strong, and as I tried to push through the crowd, my newly procured defense spell burning a hole in my pocket, the monster lifted its head and screeched loudly.

"Watch out," I screamed, but it was too late. The creature struck out with its grasping leg, the serrated edges slicing through the warlock, tearing him near in two.

If I'd thought the screams were loud before, it was nothing as the blood spattered across the walls, covering half the students standing nearby. It wasn't just blood either. The monster viciously tore that warlock into so many pieces there was no way he'd survive.

As shock and terror held most of the students immobile, I was able to move this time, because I'd felt this before. I knew the fear tracing my spine, and I knew how to push through it.

We could mourn that student later, but right now everyone here was in peril.

The incantation raced through my mind as someone grabbed my arm. I spun to find Belle, her eyes filled with tears, clinging to me. "I'm so fucking sorry," she sobbed. "This is the feeling, right? That scary shit that has been chasing you. I can feel it now, Paisley! I feel it!"

She was half-hysterical, and I knew we'd debrief later, but I couldn't let anyone else die. "This is it," I confirmed. "I need you to get back to your dorm now. This monster is deadly."

She didn't release me. "Not without you."

"I know how to get rid of it," I said in a rush. "Wait here." I turned to wade through the crowd, which was harder than it should be as students moved in both directions—the braver ones toward the creature, and the rest away. The creature scuttled across the hall, and everyone backed up.

"Let me through," I called. "I know how to get rid of it." In their panic, no one was listening to me. Or more accurately, I couldn't be heard above the screams.

The scent of death, a heavy copper, amongst other disgusting aromas, had me gagging, but I didn't back away. One warlock was dead, but it wasn't too late to save everyone else.

When I finally got close, a familiar ash and sulfur smell filtered through the death, and I had no doubt this was created through the same energy as the one in the graveyard.

The beast let out another ear-piercing screech that almost drove me to my knees. There was power in both their presence and their calls, and wishing I could press my hands to my ears, I instead uncorked the vial, and tossed the ash at it, repeating the incantation.

My panic this time was less intense, having faced a creature like this before. My brain knew what to expect already, and how to deal with it.

As the ash landed on the monster, I sent my energy out with it, but I was too far away to touch it. My hands lit up, illuminating the hallway, and I lost sight of everyone. When my energy eased, I expected the monster to be gone, only to find a massive, serrated leg jabbing right for me. There was a split second where I registered that I was about to die, *a-fucking-gain*, only to feel a solid weight slam against my side, knocking me out of the way.

We landed hard, the air forcibly ejecting from my lungs until I gasped and flailed like a fish out of water. Whoever had saved my life was on their feet in another heartbeat, and I managed to roll over, clawing my way into a sitting position.

A deep, familiar voice rumbled throughout the hallway, and once again it was Logan who'd ripped me from death's grasp. "Everyone get down," he bellowed.

We were all blown back by his power, and the light it emitted made mine look like darkness. I shielded my eyes until the radiance faded, and when I opened them again, Logan was gone, and so was the monster.

CHAPTER 22

Headmaster Gregor called an emergency assembly the next day. The crowded hall was a somber space, as students huddled in their seats, faces drawn. "We lost one of our own last night," he said, his expression grim. This was the most like a necromancer I'd ever seen the friendly headmaster act. "And if it wasn't for the brave work of students in holding the creature back, it could have been worse."

Logan, who sat in the third row, was the subject of even more attention now. Not that he showed any unease, even as hundreds of students turned to stare at him. Noah was at his side, the two of them looking as if they could take out monsters for breakfast and be in class before lunch. There was a capability about them, a strength and power that I'd rarely ever seen in adults, let alone students.

"He should mention Logan," Belle muttered, staring at the spellcaster too. Most of the college had been gawking at him since he destroyed the monster.

"Yep," Sara added. "He's the real hero."

Sara and Haley had thankfully missed the monster, but we'd told them all about it on the way here this morning. I hadn't been sure my father and siblings were even going to let me out of my dorm for this meeting, but eventually they'd relented. Their panic last night after the attack, and before they found me safe and well, had been next level.

"Gerard Donovan was a third-year," Headmaster Gregor said gruffly. "He was a necro student and showed exemplary magic and skills. His loss will be felt greatly in this community, and the wider magical world. There will be no classes today as you all take a mental health break to mourn the loss of a friend and fellow student."

A student raised their hand just in front of us, and though the headmaster jerked his head in surprise, he did call on him. "What will be done now about safety?" the warlock asked. "Do we have any idea how that creature got into the building?" *Or what the Hel it even was.*

He didn't ask the question, but we all thought it.

There was a moment where it seemed the headmaster wasn't going to answer, the skin around his eyes tightening as he pressed his lips flat. "We're investigating the incident still, Mr. Lochin. Rest assured, your safety is our top priority. We have elders and magical military on campus now for both security and to investigate this tragedy. We will be doing everything in our powers to ensure there is never another incident like this at Weatherstone. At the conclusion of our investigation, more action may be required. Including a possible magical blanket to limit any strong energy. For now, just take this time to be with your friends, and remember your fallen classmate."

He dismissed us, and the noise picked up as everyone got to their feet. Logan's name was called by multiple witches and warlocks, but he ignored them all, exiting with Noah.

When we made it outside, needing a hit of sunlight and fresh air after the crowded assembly, Haley asked, "What do you want to do today?" She clutched her paperback so tightly her knuckles looked white.

"We need to go to the library," Belle said fiercely, brown eyes nearing black, as her anger took over. "The dark energy

Paisley has been feeling is because someone is creating monsters here on campus. She's been telling us for weeks, and we kept dismissing it as her unpredictable power or her imagination. And now a warlock is dead. We need to help her with research."

Sara and Haley nodded, their faces somber. "We're sorry we dismissed you, Pais." Sara's voice wavered. "It wasn't that I didn't believe you, it's just hard to imagine anything dangerous in Weatherstone. I mean, outside of students like Annabeth, but when it's an unknown and unseen threat . . . I really thought it was your power awakening."

"It's not your fault," I said, and I meant every word. "I've thought often that it was connected to my fickle, uncontrollable powers. I also didn't tell you guys everything. I skimmed over the 'monster' part of the equation because I wasn't sure if I was losing my mind. I'm sorry I didn't tell you as soon as I was attacked in the graveyard."

During our walk this morning Belle had asked me why I'd thought that defensive powder would work, and I'd had to explain the graveyard attack. All of us decided it was more than a little worrying that this creature hadn't reacted the same as the last.

"Now that we know everything, we can do better," Belle said, as fiercely as before. "Now we know that stalking, icky feeling you get at times is a dark magic–wielding asshole, who managed to figure out how to create killer monsters straight out of our nightmares."

We reached the library to find it was deserted, most students too traumatized to spend the day catching up on homework. After grabbing as many books as we could, we lugged them to a table near the fireplace. It might be summer, but that didn't mean the fire ever died off in here.

Today it was comforting, working together with my friends to keep the darkness at bay.

"Why did you think that defense spell would work?" Sara asked as she opened her book, *Monster and Myths*.

Opening my own book—*Spells to Turn Insects into Weapons*—I told them in great detail about the attack in the graveyard. "Maybe it was a weaker monster," I finished, staring off into the stacks as I thought it over. "Because it didn't look like the praying mantis one."

"It looked like a snake though," Haley repeated my description back. "What did the one in the water look like?"

A part of me couldn't believe we were even having this conversation, that my friends were on board with the monster theory. I'd been carrying this around by myself for so long that there was an almost out-of-body experience in revealing it all.

"I caught only the briefest glimpses," I admitted. "For the most part, it wasn't visible to me, but I think it looked like the aliens from those old Sigourney Weaver movies."

Belle, eyes moving rapidly as she speed-read through pages of her book, said, "I think you should tell the professors about the monster in the lake and the graveyard."

She was right, but if I did, my father would yank me out of school. Me as a target was completely different to a general attack in a dorm hallway.

"It can't be Logan, right?" Sara said suddenly, her book opened before her, but she wasn't looking at it. "I know he's got enough power to do this, and clearly it's someone who is targeting you. Hello, blood oath, but . . . he's saved you twice now and banished that creature last night."

I'd spent most of my sleepless night after the latest attack running everything through my head, trying to figure out what was happening in Weatherstone. "He's the most confusing, infuriating, frustrating—"

"Gorgeous," Belle added, and I shot her a flat stare, even if she wasn't wrong.

"I don't know what to think about Logan," I admitted. Outside of lusting after that asshole in my traitorous dreams. "But there's still a chance that he might be behind it all, and these little heroic moments are all just building up trust until he levels the college—or murders me. He's here for a reason. No one just transfers in their third year."

Belle lifted her book. "Hence why I'm deep-diving into defensive magic. We need more power than you had last night. We need the full shebang."

Haley and Sara nodded, faces set in grim but determined lines, and then we all fell silent as we plowed through text after text.

"Apparently there are spells that can manifest creatures, but they're built almost entirely on dark magic," Haley said suddenly, on her fourth book. She moved the giant tome, wrapped in a musty red leather, to the center of the table so we could see the depictions. None of the monsters shown looked like the three I'd seen.

"Are there shadows above them?" I asked, peering at the grainy image.

"Possibly," Haley said, squinting with me. "I wish we had the internet. This old school shit is too slow for my liking."

Haley was our book nerd and tech girl. In the outside world, she loved to game, and spent years building up her worlds in role-playing games. Here, though, in the world of magic, that part of her life was left behind. The best she had was her rigged e-reader, and she never made it a secret that she missed technology.

"When we have our next break, we'll all do more research," Sara said, leaning over to read the text closer. "I don't think this is the same sort of monster. It's clear how the dark magic is animating it in these images, and from what you all described, that beast last night didn't carry any aura of that."

She was right, so we all went back to our books.

"I know we haven't explicitly said this," Belle said a few minutes later, "but we're working under the theory that the monster in Aura Hall was after Paisley as well, right? She's had too many close encounters with these creatures to be a mere coincidence."

My insides twisted horribly, and even without a feeling of dread, my body was on alert.

"Most likely," Haley agreed.

Sara nodded. "Either way, Paisley shouldn't go anywhere alone from now on." She grasped my hand, squeezing it briefly before she let go. "You were alone in the graveyard when they attacked, and last night if the hall hadn't been filled with students, they'd have gotten to you much quicker. We need to travel in a group whenever possible."

In theory, I loved her suggestion, outside of possibly bringing danger to my friends. "I should be telling Dad," I said, "but provided he believes me, I'd be yanked out of college before we see the sunrise tomorrow."

"No!" Belle gasped. "I think we need more information. We don't even know for sure they're targeting you. Maybe your magic is sensitive to what's happening in the school. If they were targeting you, surely there'd have been more attacks than just these couple. We're over halfway through the year."

"All good points," Haley agreed, pressing her pen hard into the notepad she had in front of her. "At minimum I think it's worth seeing what the headmaster discovers. If the monsters are out in the open now, it's going to be more difficult for this asshole to keep bringing them into the school."

I didn't want to leave Weatherstone, so I ran with their suggestions. "Yep, I'll wait and see what the officials discover. Until then, let's go with the *travel in groups* plan."

Belle relaxed now that we'd agreed on a plan that wouldn't get me yanked out. Even though it had been her suggestion in the first place. "It's going to be difficult," she said, tapping her finger against her chin, eyes unfocused. "We don't share all the same classes, now that we have our affinities." She shot apologetic eyes at me, as we were all reminded of my uselessness.

"We'll figure it out," Haley said, forcibly. "I think the main point is that we can't be as relaxed as we were before. No more late-night wanderings into cemeteries."

The three of them leveled their gazes on me, and I snorted. "Yeah, yeah, Moms. Keep your hair on. I promise to stop wandering aimlessly and giving monsters a chance to eat me."

"Excellent." Belle dropped her pen, rubbing a hand over her eyes. "In better news, I think I've found the strongest defense spell we have the capability of creating and utilizing. We'll need to get herbs from the apothecary store because this is beyond fourth-year advanced spellwork."

Since it was late afternoon, and we were all exhausted and starving, we returned our books and gathered up the copious pages of notes we'd taken. Then we followed Belle as she marched from the library and headed for the Stores, the small hut containing all the herbs, potion mixes, candles, and other materials required in potion making.

Students couldn't just help themselves to whatever they wanted, but when we showed Madam Craney, the witch who ran the apothecary, the spell we were studying, she was more than happy to help us out. No talk of it being too advanced, she was all smiles as she waved her hands. "Oh, yes, dears," she said, pushing back the huge purple glasses that framed her wrinkled eyes. Her hair was bright purple too, lovely against her brown skin. "After last night we could all use protective energy around us."

It had been twenty years since the last death at Weatherstone, when a spell had missed its mark and taken out a second-year. The monster murder last night was a thousand times worse, and it would take this magical community a long time to get past it.

"His parents are with the headmaster now," Madam Craney continued. She'd always kept up a constant stream of chatter whenever I'd come in here for supplies. "I hope they don't take them to Aura Hall until the investigation is complete. They questioned that poor Logan for hours, and he is such a hero." Her eyes twinkled as she looked back our way. "Handsome too."

That was Logan, the handsome hero.

Her monologue trailed off as she delved into the shelves to find what we needed. The familiar scents of an apothecary eased the tension in my shoulders, reminding me of being back in Mom's kitchen.

"Rosemary is my favorite," Sara said, breathing as deeply as I was. "It reminds me of home, and the early mornings when Mom would mix up her healing elixirs in the kitchen."

Haley's smile was genuine, for the first time today. "It's oregano for me. Mom enjoyed using it for every-freaking-thing. Not even joking. Cooking, spells, my homemade toothpaste."

"My dad was into sage," Belle said with a shrug, conveying that he wasn't her favorite person. "Mom liked to grind up ashwagandha, which isn't as strong in the scent department, but that earthy smell always reminds me of India."

It was my turn, and I brushed my fingertips across the leaves of the mint plant on the front desk. "Mom doesn't use active magic these days, but she has all the herbs you could imagine.

Lavender, thyme, oregano, sage, lemongrass. You name it, it's growing somewhere in the house. Jars everywhere, windowsills crammed. I kind of miss all the greenery."

"No active magic?" Sara queried, and I nodded. "Yeah, it's to do with whatever happened with Logan's mom in the forest that day." I'd told them why there was a blood oath between us, or as much as I knew anyway. "But it doesn't diminish her capabilities as a witch."

"It wasn't her fault," Belle said fiercely. "Logan is dumber than he looks if he believes otherwise."

Madam Craney returned with a box of items, and I had a thought. "Would it be possible for me to take a few of the potted herbs? I'd love to keep them in my room."

Her whole face lit up. "Dear, you can take as many as you like. Our magic is stronger when we immerse ourselves in nature."

All four of us ended up with a few trays of potted herbs. On our way back, each of us stopped in our room to drop off the plants. I set my tray on the windowsill and hoped I'd inherited my mom's green thumb, because I now had babies to keep alive.

When we were done, we snuck into the defense spells classroom, needing the pentacles and insulated walls in case we screwed up the spell. With classes canceled, there were no students in this part of Writworth, minimizing our chances of getting caught.

"It's complicated," Belle warned, as she set down each piece of the spell before us. "We need to work slowly, and all of us can check we're getting every step correct."

"Especially Paisley," Sara added. "She's killing it in spell making classes, and is top of the grade."

I'd never been top of anything, and without an active affinity I certainly wasn't going to be for most classes here, but

I enjoyed this niche in spells. Hopefully my new skills were enough to get us through a spell of this caliber.

"Okay, we need to swap out the candles for ones with sage, fennel, and lavender," Belle said quickly, checking her notes. "They should have a dark wick laced with black basil."

We checked to make sure Madam had given us the right ones, and thankfully their shiny surface and black wick were as described. We placed them on the grooves in the pentacle and used the multitude of flints nearby, left for those who weren't fire elementals.

"Light them now," Belle said, and in a few seconds we had five eerily dark flames.

Next, she separated the herbs. A similar array to what was in the candle, with an addition of salt, dragon's blood—powerful at warding—and red pepper.

"You take the salt," she told me. I read the instructions over her shoulder and grimaced at how quickly we had to move. A single witch or warlock couldn't have done this on their own. It would take at least two or three to be safer.

Holding the salt in the palm of my hand, I followed the instructions and flicked it in a counterclockwise motion across the herbs on the table, purifying and mixing it through them all before we began.

"Okay, this is the order," Belle said, voice steady, even if her eyes held an edge of panic. "I go first, and then within two seconds, Haley, you drop the lavender . . ." She gave us all our tasks, one by one, before taking a deep breath. "Are we ready?"

Belle didn't give us time to freak out, barking out the orders again.

To no one's surprise, with a spell this complex, we failed twice. When we were down to what was our last stock of herbs, we sat in silence, staring at each other. "Okay, this is it." Belle barely looked as if she was breathing, wiping sweat off her forehead. "One last time, learning from all of our mistakes."

This time she remained quiet because we had the order memorized now. Somehow, this time, desperation etched across our faces, all four of us managed to hit every action, direction, and time frame. As if the moon goddess herself were watching our backs.

When we were done, there was an extended silence, and I was the one wiping sweat as my blood pumped with adrenaline.

"How do we know if it worked?" Haley whispered, as we watched the middle of the pentacle closely.

"We'll know," Belle replied, her focus never wavering. "The last step that didn't happen the last two times will give us the sign."

A puff of smoke emerged from the center, where the herbs swirled, and with a loud pop that had my frazzled nerves bouncing, the smoke shifted from white to the darkest of grays. As it filled the room, there was no scent or acridity, and when it cleared, all that remained of the multitude of herbs was a thick stem.

In the dim light of the candles, I examined it closer to find a dozen lethal thorns scattered across the length.

Belle reached out hesitantly, grasping a small section without thorns. "You need to stab this into the monster." She twisted the stem to show us shades of brown, gray, and silver embedded in the points.

Stabbing meant we had to get close, so it wasn't the safest option, but it would come in handy if we got pinned.

Using one of the metal stirrers, Belle broke off sections of the long thorns for each of us, sliding them into glass vials so we didn't accidentally stab ourselves. "We'll split them," she said. "That way, no matter who is with Paisley, we all can help her."

"And yourselves," I added quickly. "Even if the monsters are targeting me, and we don't know that for sure yet, they are indiscriminate with who they destroy on the way."

Belle nodded. "I know."

Slipping my thorny weapons into my pocket, we all promised not to leave our rooms without them. Last night's death meant we had to start taking this seriously.

If I wanted to make it through the rest of this school year alive.

CHAPTER 23

Our stomachs went on strike after we finished, demanding equal food for work, so we packed up and left the room. In the dining hall, to no one's surprise, the twins found me not five minutes after I sat.

"Where the Hel have you been, little sister?" Jenna demanded, shuffling my friends along so she could drag a chair in beside me. "I know we saw you last night, but there's still a monster on the loose. I was worried about you."

"Sorry, we were in the library all day trying to figure out how someone created that creature on Weatherstone property."

Her fierce expression eased a touch. "Did you find anything?"

"Nope, it shouldn't be possible," I said, trying not to let the darker thoughts creep in. "No affinity can do this without using dark magic."

"And dark magic leaves traces," Belle added, listening in.

Alice nodded, taking a seat on the other side of me. "That's what Dad said when I spoke to him earlier. The professors are in crisis mode, and the school is all but locked down until they figure out what happened. The council should be here tomorrow."

Weatherstone had no options but to take this seriously; a college of this reputation would do almost anything to protect itself. The death of students was not a good look.

"I've missed you, little sis." Alice hugged me, and I sank

into the familiar warmth of her embrace. Herbs might remind me of home, but my family was home.

"I missed you too," I mumbled through my emotions, chest tight. "Have you heard from J?" Jensen was away for a month at the beach, as part of more intense studies he'd taken on for his element. I didn't like the feeling of him being in another state, and I tried very hard not to think about the end of this year when the twins would graduate.

Alice chuckled, her eyes lighting up. "Dad mentioned that he's hooked on life under the sea, and we'll probably never see him again."

"Disloyal bastard," I tried to joke, but it fell flat. As much as it hurt, I would never deny Jensen his chance for happiness. Even if it meant we lost him to a Californian or Floridian coven when he graduated.

"Trev did say he might join us tonight," Jenna said, pulling her bowl of carbonara pasta closer. "But I would have expected him already, so his study group for his Magma Studies class must have run over."

Magma Studies. The fact that my brother could handle literal magma and not lose a limb would never not be odd to me. Those of us without elemental affinities didn't always understand the ones who walked with the natural elements of the world.

"Are you both free this evening?" I asked, deciding that I wanted to hang with them for a few more hours. "I still need to meet your familiars. I should have done it months ago, but there's just been so much going on, and I don't want to be too busy to make time for what is really important."

We fell silent for a moment, all of us caught up in last night's death. That warlock had his whole life ahead of him, and then he was gone. Just fucking gone. I refused to put off these important moments any longer.

"We've been waiting so long to introduce you," Jenna said, and she looked younger as her face softened. "Let's go right after dinner."

"I'm done," I said, pushing what remained of my fried rice away. "Let's go."

Belle, Haley, and Sara, who had been chatting while I caught up with my sisters, turned as we got to our feet. "I'm going to the Barracks with the twins," I said, patting my pocket to remind them I had our new spell. "I won't walk alone."

"We'll keep you safe." Jenna looked mildly affronted.

Belle smiled briefly. "Go, have fun. But good to see you're sticking with our new pact. No one walks alone."

Jenna's expression relaxed when she realized it hadn't been a dig at her ability to look after me, but a reassurance to my friends that I was sticking with our plan. "Good idea, girls," she said as she swung her bag over her shoulder. "You can never be too safe these days."

They waved us off, and we headed to the Barracks. I'd passed this building so many times, heard the animals, seen the animals, and sure as heck smelled the animals, but I'd never been inside. The Barracks was exclusively used by advanced nature sprites who had claimed their soul-creatures.

Jenna and Alice used the side entrance near the forest, and I gaped at the sheer size of the Barracks. "It's deceptive from the outside," I breathed. The ceilings must have been thirty feet high, wood slats extending for a mile in every direction I looked. "It's the size of a small town."

Alice chuckled, looking around as if she'd forgotten the grandeur. "It sure is, but there was no way any of us would dump our animals in a cage when we're not with them. They get accommodations as good as or better than ours."

"That's what I love about you nature sprites."

We walked along the main aisle through the building, and I could see into the animal enclosures as we passed them. The polar bear had what looked like an acre of actual ice, snow, and a large pond. "They also go out into the wild every day," Jenna said as I peered inside. "Our familiars are humanized, so they pose no danger to witches or warlocks. But they're still wild at heart and need to revel in their freedoms."

Having heard them talk about their familiars, and then seeing the truth of it here, was so vastly different that I found myself filled with questions. "Do either of you stay with Simon or Morris at night?" I asked, noticing that most enclosures had a bed set up in the corner. Even the snowy ones.

"Yep," they said together.

"More often than not," Jenna added, voice a little dreamy, and I was taken aback by how calm she appeared. The Barracks soothed that frantic need of hers to overachieve and control every aspect of the world.

As we walked, they ran through a list of animals and their witch or warlock companions until we reached their familiars. Morris and Simon were next door to each other, and we entered the sheep's territory first. Inside, it looked and smelled like a farm, with grassy fields, a watering tank, and bales of hay scattered around the edges. I could see Alice's bed set up in a far-off corner, and as soon as she stepped past the gates Simon beelined for Alice. I tried not to laugh, because I'd never seen a sheep run, and there was more than a little waddle in his gait. His cream-colored coat was short at the moment, no doubt shorn for summer, and when he got close, Alice dropped to her knees and held her arms out for him to bound into.

He was freaking bounding, and it was adorable.

The pair remained locked as her magic sparkled the air, a light dusting of happiness and tranquility. The nature sprites were the least intrusive and combative of affinities, but they were strong in other ways. They created peace, and I still believed it to be the toughest and most elusive magic of all.

"Simon," Alice said as she stood, one hand on his head. He appeared larger than a regular sheep, standing waist height on her. "This is my sister Paisley. She's our best friend too, just like Jen."

Simon strode forward and I marveled at the sheen of silver in his cream coat, even while his face was darker. He stopped before me, and I shot a quick glance at Alice, wondering about the etiquette here. "Should I pet him? Is that rude?"

She laughed. "Not at all. He loves a good scratch behind the ears."

He absolutely did. Butting against my hand, I ended up spending thirty minutes scratching his head, telling him how beautiful he was, between chatting with my sisters, who were deep in conversation about their process of applying to covens.

"It's a lot like college," Jenna said, her voice wavering, stress tugging at the corners of her lips. "You have application exams—a practical next month that will take us away from the school for a week—and then endless questionnaires to determine where you fit. We have to list ten jobs we're hoping to secure after graduation. I didn't know it would be this intense, to be honest, but at least our college work is wrapping up. Just a few larger assignments are all that stand between us and graduation."

"What covens have you applied for?" My question was soft, because I was internally freaking out. Hundreds of covens were scattered across America, across the world, and once you were initiated, your coven became your family. We were all heavily involved in our parents' coven, Blessed Souls of Spokane, attending events over the years.

"Blessed Souls, of course," Jenna told me, and I worked

very hard not to let my relief flood my face. "Along with Ancient Mages of America, The Sisters of the Moon, and Sprites of Spokane."

With each name, my relief grew. All those covens were local to our area, with the farthest only in the next town over, which was less than an hour away. "We didn't want to be too far from home either," Alice said gently, reading my emotions in her way. "We like the comforts of visiting Mom and Dad, and our animals in the forests around us. All those covens are amazing. They'll offer us the job placements we want in the animal shelters and zoos, so we're set."

Feeling like ten tons had been lifted from my chest, I breathed easier, and left Simon so I could give them both hugs. "While I love that our lives are changing, and we're growing up," I admitted, when we pulled apart, "it breaks my heart to know it'll never be the same again. We'll never all live at home with Mom and Dad, and race into the living room to watch TV together or eat an afternoon snack or pet your bunnies in the forest."

We weren't kids any longer, and with that, our lives would be forever different.

"But our kids will do that," Jenna said quickly, voice thick. "When we all have babies, they're going to grow up together. I'm determined."

The thought of having kids was so far off for me that I could barely envision the future she was suggesting, but *damn* it did paint an awfully nice picture. Even though change was inevitable, we could still hold on to what made our lives so wonderful growing up.

Eventually we said goodbye to Simon and ventured next door to find Morris. His territory was more foresty, with visible caves set back in the corner. Elementals helped them build these animal territories, and they did a damn good job.

Morris appeared when Jenna called him, a huge black bear poking his head out of a cave. He ran for us, and it was only a touch more terrifying than Simon. When Jenna greeted him, he wrapped his arms around her, careful of the lethal-looking claws, and lifted her into a—

"It's a bear hug," I cooed, barely suppressing my *awwww* afterward.

Morris was terrifying, standing at least eight feet tall, but as soon as Jenna introduced us, his intelligence and understanding were clear in his huge black eyes. He patted me on the head, like I was the cute puppy, and while there were no ear scratches, I figured we were buddies by the time we were done.

"You need to visit more," Jenna said when we left, heading for our dorms.

"I do," I agreed. "The study load has been intense, and there's always some danger lingering around the edges, but I promise to make more time for you. I love you guys so much."

All the shit in my life was making me sentimental, but since the attack, and the Logan stuff, I felt as if my emotions had grown into this volatile mess of destruction. Zipping around me in intense arcs, which took me by surprise more often than not.

Alice patted my shoulder. "Don't be hard on yourself. You're doing amazing. How is your search for an affinity coming along?"

I hesitated briefly. "They're talking spellcaster, but also not, because I have this small penchant for necro, which as you know, no spellcaster can do. The biggest issue really is that I don't express enough power to be a spellcaster."

"The fact that they're even discussing spellcaster for you—" Jenna shook her head, the blue of her eyes boring into me "—means that you're showing plenty of power. Everyone develops in their own time, and your energy released so close to your birthday . . . you could be a full year behind other freshmen."

At some point I'd stopped beating myself up over my *slower to develop than normal* affinity. "I'm just going to let it all work out in time," I told them. "I have faith that sooner or later I'll know my place."

Mom would be proud of my newfound maturity, achieved mostly through the exhaustion of constantly questioning myself rather than personal growth. Or maybe it was a bit of both.

The twins left me in my dorm, and I felt their peace for a long time, even as I stared at Logan's hoodie and debated wearing it to bed. That stupid length of material had become a comfort for me, but I decided tonight I would put it back in the wardrobe and return to my tank top and shorts.

Feeling more relaxed than I should when there was still a dark warlock or witch on the loose creating murderous monsters, I settled into bed and let my mind slow. Tomorrow I'd worry about it again, but tonight, I'd sleep.

CHAPTER 24

"Ahhhhhhhh!! It's so fucking good to be home."

"Trevor!" Mom admonished, as he threw himself onto the couch. "You're not at college now, son."

It was the Festival of the Moon Goddess holiday weekend, and Weatherstone gave all of us Friday off so we could visit family. Dad had opened our transport not twenty minutes ago, and after dumping our bags in our rooms, we were making the most of our time together.

Jenna and Alice had already headed out the back to greet the various squirrels, rabbits, birds, and other creatures living in the forests behind the fence. The rest of us were sprawled around the living room, settling in like those *old times* I'd been mourning.

"Mom," Jensen whined. "I'm starving. Please tell me you're making tacos. And paella. And lasagna."

Goddesses, I'd missed Mom's cooking too. Even though Weatherstone was amazing, nothing compared to Mom's food. Her salmon sushi, made completely from scratch, was the meal I'd request for my last dinner on Earth.

Mom stood in the doorway with Dad by her side, his arms wrapped around her waist. If they were in a room together, they were touching. She smiled as Jenna and Alice stomped inside once more, ditching their muddy boots at the door. "I'll make all your favorites." Her voice rasped. "I'm just so happy you're all home."

Blinking away the heat in my own eyes, I tried to remember what Jenna had said. These moments might be coming to an end for us as a family of six, but eventually we'd find new traditions and moments. It wasn't a loss, it was change and growth, and I'd embrace it just as fiercely.

Our first night at home was one of the most relaxing I'd experienced in a long time. No monsters, no eerie feeling of being watched, no dreams of Logan fucking Kingston. We watched movies until midnight, we ate everything Mom put in front of us, and we chatted about our lives. Jensen told us in detail about his time at the ocean, and the animals he saw beneath the surface. We also learned about Trevor's new girlfriend. "She's an elemental too," he said, and fuck if his cheeks weren't a touch pink. "We've been dating for a few weeks."

The fact that he was even mentioning her to us meant that he liked her. His expression closed off after that though, so no one got anything further from him.

"Any news on the monsters or attack?" I asked Dad, scooping up queso with a corn chip and shoving it into my mouth. I'd been eating all afternoon, and my stomach reminded me that we were at our limit and should stop. An excellent idea that I would not be taking into consideration.

"They're investigating." Dad leaned back in his chair, eyes darkening with a brief whoosh of heat from his energy. "They want to blanket the energy of the school, lock down any magic that's stronger than level two. But that would also inhibit their ability to track whoever created that monster in the first place. So, for now, we're in a holding pattern."

Level two was basic spells. Enough for most college-level

magics, but nothing strong enough to call a murderous insect on steroids.

"They're not using their affinity to create monsters," Jenna said with a shrug. "There's no affinity associated with monsters. If it were me, personally, I'd be checking the library to see who touched books about dark magic."

I almost choked on my next chip but managed to keep myself together. My energy would be found all over those books if they followed that route, because I'd been trying to research these monsters for months.

"There are no books in our public library which would detail this sort of magic," Dad said seriously. "We think a student is being fed the magic *and/or* the means to do this."

"Like from a parent?"

Dad nodded at me, and I let that marinate. That possibility was why Logan remained on my list of suspects—Rafael Kingston.

Mom was quiet through the conversation, and I didn't like that blank look on her face. She'd checked out, so I decided to check her back in. "Mom, are you okay?"

Her expression softened, and life returned to her eyes. "It's just . . . this feels very much like that day in the forest where *we* were attacked." She didn't mention Logan's mom, but she was part of the *we* in that sentence. "I mean, it was a shadow of energy but—" She cleared her throat, and Dad rubbed his hand across her shoulders in a soothing manner. "She was torn apart in the same way. With Logan in the school now, it just feels close to home."

Dad huffed. "I haven't dismissed the Kingstons' involvement. But I've been watching Logan, and he's not shown any signs of abusing his powers. Not one time. Even if he was pretending to be the perfect student, it's been months. Hard to hold a facade for that length of time."

It would be hard, but not impossible, especially if you were as capable and powerful as Logan. The Kingstons had eighteen years to plan out their revenge, and I wasn't buying into the few months of Logan's hero act. He remained on my list and would until there was another truly viable suspect. The girls and I had made a list of students in the school, and evaluated whether any of them had the power to do this. Outside of maybe one or two, there were none, but we didn't know their parents.

In that case, it could be anyone.

When we eventually went to bed, I lay there for a long time unable to sleep. The spellcaster was on my mind, icy green eyes haunting my waking hours along with my dreams now. Part of me hated him, my chest burning with a rage hotter than Trevor's magma, but there was another part, small though it might be, which hated myself more.

Because I couldn't fully hate Logan.

Why the Hel did he have to be powerful, gorgeous, arrogant, and smart? Oh, and as an added bonus, the bastard was also tall. It was too much. The goddess wasn't supposed to give with both hands. Though, he could possibly be evil, which was a massive checkmark in the turnoff column.

Eventually I fell asleep, clutching a large piece of uncut jade to ward off bad dreams. With a touch of luck, it would ward off all dreams so I didn't get caught up in sexy times with my hand while at home. Thinking about Logan before bed was absolutely a mistake, but the goddess had mercy on me that night, or the crystal worked, because the next morning I woke late and without a single dream.

Saturday was spent in a similar fashion to Friday night, with more food, more movies, and a delightful afternoon nap. Just before dinner, I found myself in the attic with Dad as he cleaned out a bunch of boxes Mom wanted him to drop at the dump. "She wants to put in a new crafting room," he explained. "She's moving on to knitting and yarning."

Mom dabbled in crafting, and our house was filled with the different projects she had started and succeeded at over the years.

"What's even in these boxes?" I asked, coughing as I shifted one and a cloud of dust emerged.

"I have no idea. Have a look through and see if there's anything of yours, otherwise it all has to go."

Most of the boxes I opened were junk. Broken kitchen appliances, old clothes from when we were kids, and a lot of our old artwork. I kept a few pieces that I found hilarious, like the one where I'd drawn Mom with huge boobs and Dad with a bald head. I was three at the time, but memories lasted forever.

Dad started to haul the boxes down the stairs as I went through them, and by the time the last one was waiting for me to check, he called up that he was having a break, and he didn't care what was left up there.

"You used your magic half the time, old man," I called back.

His chuckle wafted up to me. "Don't tell your mom that. She's about to rub my shoulders."

Thank fuck he said *shoulders*. Though knowing them, it was still too much information. I knew shoulder rubs were only the beginning. Or I *would* know, if I wasn't currently in the worst dry patch of my life.

"Don't hurry back," I shouted down, sitting on my butt beside the last box, ripping off the dusty, yellowing tape.

This box looked older than the others we'd cleared, and as I opened it a sweet floral scent arose. There was no mustiness with it, which surprised me. On top sat a black-and-white photo of an unsmiling witch. For a beat I thought it was Mom, until I read the caption to find it was *her mom*. Gran. I'd never met her, but she looked so much like Mom that it weirdly hurt to look at her photo. The thought of my mom dying was too much to bear.

Placing the photo to the side, I found a bunch of letters below, all addressed to Beth Hallistar. I paused at the sight of Mom's name, realizing that Gran had written letters to her, but they were all unopened, the yellowing envelopes sealed up completely. Since it wasn't my place to snoop through her memories, I placed them to the side as well, and looked at what else the box contained. It was mostly photos and patterned teacups, but in the bottom I found two silver necklaces with crystal pendants attached that had my greedy heart leaping as I tried to figure out if I could claim them.

Leaving the crystals on my knee, I shifted through more photos, looking closer this time. I was surprised to find many of them were of crystals and gems—not that I should have been since her obsession was as well-known as mine. There were short sentences on the back of pics, and some of the specific pieces I recognized, as they were in my collection. My largest piece of quartz, which was shaped almost like a rose, had the words: *Use quartz to draw in moon energy and increase power.*

A few of the other photos showed Gran again, wearing a crystal necklace. In one, she was wearing all three. The two I'd found in this box and the one Mom had already gifted me.

"Paisley, dinner is ready!" Mom called, and I hurriedly packed everything back into the box except the two necklaces. "Wash your hands, honey," she added as I strode into the kitchen.

She pulled a dish out of the oven and caught my eye, her smile turning into a chuckle. "On second thought, maybe you should have a quick shower."

I felt grimy, and no doubt looked even worse. "I found

these necklaces in a box of Gran's old stuff," I said, holding them up. "The stones aren't familiar, but would it be okay if I wore them?"

Mom barely glanced at them. "Absolutely, baby. You know I don't have any sentimental value to Mom's crystals."

Losing her mom at such a young age protected her from sad memories, so she mostly mourned the concept of having a mother. She always told me that Pops had been an amazing substitute, raising her by himself, and when he died last year, every single one of us lost an important part of ourselves.

Mom never lacked love growing up, but I knew she would always grieve the mother she should have had. "There are some letters from her for you up there as well," I felt the need to add, already guessing that Mom wouldn't care.

She smiled at me over the stove, stirring stew in the large silver pot. "Thanks. I'll check them out later."

I highly doubted that, but it was her right to do what she wanted with them. Maybe she was afraid that she'd find a new pain inside those scented pages. I couldn't blame her for trying to avoid that. Since that day in the forest, Mom had made a decision to live in her protective bubble, and as long as she was happy, I was happy.

She knew her limit, and mental health was important, so she'd get no argument from me. She'd managed to exist for well over forty years without her mother's words, so there was surely nothing urgent in there anyway.

Dinner went by in a flash, and then we were down to our last day at home.

"Tomorrow we visit Blessed Souls," Mom reminded us as we traipsed up the stairs for bed. "To send our thanks to Selene. Dress nicely."

Like the twins, Blessed Souls was my top choice for a coven too, and since they rarely took in candidates not from

Weatherstone—the largest sponsor of their programs—I finally had a real shot at the future I'd always hoped for.

Provided a monster didn't take me out first.

Being home had stoked the fire in my belly. I was no longer content to passively sit back and wait for another attack. All the research was one thing, but I'd also decided to start actively tracking Logan through the school. Dad put the idea in my head, but he was also a professor who couldn't just hang around students in their private hours. Logan was very unlikely to show his true colors in classes, or at official events.

Nope. It would be after hours. In the dark. When he thought no one was watching.

Which was perfect. From here on out, I'd be at the parties and behind the scenes however I could. Stalkcaster was about to find himself with his very own stalker.

Lucky warlock.

I was going to stick to his ass like glue and hope his secrets unraveled before me.

CHAPTER 25

When we returned to Weatherstone on Sunday, a tingle of energy crashed into me so hard I almost tripped and fell on the cobbled pathway. "Whoa, Pais." Trevor caught my arm as I stumbled. "Are you okay?"

Straightening, I rubbed the back of my neck, trying to dispel the overload I'd been hit with. "My body appears to have forgotten how strong the magical energy inside is," I said, trying to laugh it off. "I'll be fine once I adjust."

My siblings stared at me with varying degrees of concern. "I'm fine," I repeated, with a little more force. "I've always been sensitive to the magic here. No doubt because my own magic is a finnicky bitch who wants to keep playing the affinity field. Girl needs to settle down, but she's just not ready."

With a soft snort, Jensen took pity on me, removing Trevor's hand with a flick of his energy. "Leave her alone, guys. Paisley is more than capable of dealing with her own shit, and she'll come to us if she needs us."

He wrapped his arm around my shoulders, getting us moving again. "Thank you," I murmured, as we joined the crowd of other witches and warlocks returning from break.

Dad wouldn't be back until tomorrow, so thankfully he'd missed my stumble. My siblings' suspicions were already hard enough to navigate, but it wasn't anything new to be affected by Weatherstone's energy. That one just took me by surprise.

"You will come to us if you need us, right?" Jensen said, for my ears alone. "If you know anything about these monsters, sis, you need to tell someone. Don't take this on alone. That's why you have a family, so we can support you."

He was always able to read me the best of my siblings. "I will come to you, I promise."

The second I had anything concrete to share with them, I would, but all I had now were questions. Jensen squeezed my shoulders, and we walked the rest of the way in a comfortable silence. My family left me at my dorm, and I hadn't even made it past the threshold before Belle came barreling at me, throwing her arms around me. "Witch, I missed you!" she cried, and I hugged her tightly.

"I missed you too."

She followed me into my room and flopped down on my bed, watching as I added the four crystals I'd brought from home to my collection, along with my new necklaces. I'd also thrown in a pile of the photos, wanting to read through the notes Gran had jotted on the back of each in her sloping writing.

"Hope you had a nice break," Belle said. "Mom showed up and it was so good to see her. Dad worked for ninety percent of the holiday, so there was no need to split my time."

Belle was closer to her mom, and counted India more as home than here. She'd told me she planned on trying to find a coven there as well as in America, so she'd still always be part of both worlds.

"That's frustrating with your dad," I said, dropping into my desk chair. "He works a lot, doesn't he?"

"All the time," she grumbled. "Fairly certain that's why my parents got divorced. Oh, he's also stubborn and calculating, and able to suppress emotions with the skill of a sociopath. Compounding factors, I'm sure."

"I think that goes with the territory of being an elder. It can't be easy keeping all the magic assholes across America in line." It took a lot of magic, and attention to detail, to make sure the covens remained safe, and operating within the rules of our covenant.

Belle snorted. "Oh, I know. He tells me all the freaking time. The only time we did talk this time was about the Magic Covenant."

The covenant was an ancient set of rules, blessed by witches and warlocks of the twelfth century. It had been amended and adjusted to modernize over the years, but the basic principles remained the same.

"What's happening with it?"

She blinked at me. "You know . . . I don't even remember. I tuned him out for most of it, but I can assure you, it was as dreadfully boring as you'd imagine."

I tried really hard not to laugh, because her dad's attitude hurt her deep down. "Maybe next holiday you can come stay with the Hallistars."

Belle's entire face lit up, her flawless skin shining. "That would be amazing. Your family sounds like a fucking dream. Hard to believe they're even real."

We weren't perfect, but I'd fight the goddess herself for them.

Pulling herself higher, Belle was focused in a way she hadn't been a second ago. "Okay, our evil-monster-creator problem. What's the next move?"

"More research, I'm sure," I said, but in reality we'd almost tapped out the library's resources. "And I'm going to spend a little more time keeping an eye on Logan."

Her eyes snapped to me. "You going deep-cover-007? Seduce that spellcaster, please."

I groaned through my laughter. "You're terrible. As delightful as that seems, I prefer to fuck warlocks who don't hate my guts."

She tilted her head, this smug little smile on her face. "Come on, bestie. We're past the point of lying to each other. There's a lot between you and Logan, for sure, and some of it might very well be hate, but it's not the strongest emotion. Not by a long shot."

I chose not to address her insinuations. "He's hiding a lot of shit. I'm going to figure that spellcaster out."

Her lips twitched, but she let it go. "Dad said that it won't be long until they wrap up their investigation, and then the college will incorporate a blanket of energy while they conduct external searches. If that happens, not even Logan will be able to perform the sort of magic to create the monsters."

We were on a time crunch, and while a blanket spell over Weatherstone would make us safer, it wouldn't solve the problem of who was behind it. Despite their hopes, I was under no delusion that the professors or the council were going to figure it out. Not after this amount of time.

"Okay, so research and stalking the spellcaster." Belle nodded, nothing but confidence in her expression. "I'm cool with these next steps." She bounced off my bed, smacked a kiss on my cheek, and said, "See you in the morning."

After her abrupt departure, I got ready for bed, and when I was snuggled under the covers I looked through the photos from Gran's box. There was enough light through the window for me to just make out the words.

On the moonstone she'd penned: *Don't use in the height of the moon, because the power is too great.* The amethyst stated: *Strongest when teamed with aquamarine, for true power boost.* The jade: *Deadly to those who wish you harm.* The agate: *Will call strongest.*

There were quite a few others, and with each image came

the real sense that my obsession with crystals might have more to do with my magic than I'd ever believed. Were there witches and warlocks out there who did use crystals to strengthen their affinity? Had Gran been one? If that was possibly true, why had I never heard of them before, and which affinity did they mainly fall into? Maybe that was part of the issue with my energy lock and finding the perfect key.

Next time we had a weekend at home, I'd ask Mom if I could read the letters she'd been left. Maybe there were answers in them after all.

Classes started with a bang the next day, the professors informing us that we were over halfway through our freshman year, and if we wanted to make it to sophomore year we should have started studying two months ago. "Not like we've been dealing with monsters and murders," Sara muttered from my right, as we desperately took notes in Flora and Fauna Studies.

Apparently, that was a *fail out of freshman year* attitude, and from that point on we were nose to books, trying to catch up on all the spells we should know by now. My plan to tail Logan had to take a slight back seat due to the sheer workload we were handed, but we did have one of his rare spellcaster classes coming up soon. It wasn't really an ideal place to observe him, but it was a start.

"This is weird, right?" Haley whispered, clutching her Kindle to her chest. Her textbooks banged at her side in her satchel, but her Kindle was always safely in her hands. "We haven't had a spellcaster lesson in weeks. Do you think it's because of the attacks?"

"That's what I'm assuming," Belle added, as we hurried through the halls. "Maybe he's going to give us some tips on how to stay safe."

Ironic if he was the bastard creating the monsters.

The class was full and weirdly quiet, with only a few low whispers as we entered. Since the attack, there was a sense of unease filtering through day-to-day life, and with no answers forthcoming, the tension continued to ramp right up.

A few minutes later Logan strolled in, confident as always, as if he owned the college. My traitorous hormones did a stupid flip at the sight of him, heat settling low in my body as I noticed the way his uniform stretched across his broad shoulders as he walked.

Evil or not, the outside was perfection.

His dark hair was shorter, artfully messed on top of his head, as those icy eyes surveyed the room. "Quiet down." His expression was flat. "Headmaster Gregor has asked me to add another class to explain how I destroyed the creature in the hallway." He shrugged off his jacket, presumably to counter the slightly warmer than expected day, and draped it over a nearby chair. When he rolled up the sleeves of his shirt, my mouth went dry, while other parts of me *very much did not*.

He had tattoos.

I'd never noticed before under his full uniform, but with each roll of that white shirt, more of his colored ink came into view. It wrapped around his wrists and spanned up to where the shirt cut off on his forearms. Belle cleared her throat and shifted in her chair until her mouth was right near my ear. "Excuse the fuck out of me? He has tatts too. Unfair. We should riot."

I was too busy smacking my hormones down to respond, but rioting didn't sound like the worst idea.

Logan ignored the girls fawning over him like the arrogant shit he was. "The amount of power it required to banish that creature is more than most of you will ever know. But I'll explain the process to you, nonetheless. Just don't expect to survive an attack using this alone."

With that uplifting pep talk behind us, Logan went on to demonstrate how he drew upon various energy sources to blast the creature into pieces. That was the first time I realized he hadn't banished it, or reversed the spell used to create it, he'd simply injected enough power to literally disintegrate it.

"He's genuinely terrifying," Haley murmured, her voice wavering.

"Would still fuck him though," Sara said casually, keeping her voice low. "He's very fuckable."

Belle scoffed. "Guys, come on. He might be evil. Get some standards." I side-eyed her since she was constantly talking about me taking a roll in the old enemies-to-lovers trope.

Sara shrugged again. "I mean, I wouldn't take him home to meet the family, but I feel like he'd destroy me for all other warlocks. I'm in a dry spell. I could use some destruction."

All of us were single, Belle's and Sara's previous situationships had fizzled out. At least Haley and I weren't alone in our angst any longer. In some ways, college was exactly as I'd expected, but in others there was way less sex.

By the time the lecture was over, there wasn't a single witch or warlock under the misconception that they could destroy those monsters. We walked out feeling slightly inadequate and entirely terrified of spellcasters. "I've got water studies by the lake," Belle said when we reached the hall.

Sara nodded. "I've got air with Professor Damone."

Haley hitched her bag higher. "Yeah, I'm going to be late for my daily stroll through the forest."

"We're doing fucking excellent at this sticking-together thing," I said with a shake of my head.

Belle's shrug was casual. "At least it's the middle of the day and we're surrounded by students. Meet you all for dinner?"

"See you then," we chorused, and all of those with affinities and specialty classes took off, leaving me to figure out the rest of my afternoon.

A plan fell into place when I caught sight of a tall, dark-haired spellcaster in the hallway. He'd been held up by a few students who wanted to fawn over him, but he'd brushed them off and was out of there.

Hitching my bag on my shoulder, I tried not to act suspicious as I casually strolled through the crowds of students, following him. He left Writworth and headed into Ancot, and I let out a disappointed sigh when he entered the darker hallway of Nightrealm. Peeking through the curtains, because there was no way this would work if I didn't take risks, I caught a glimpse of him placing his palm on his door scanner, and jerked back before he could turn and see me there.

I couldn't follow him into his room, so I spent a solid minute cursing at the ornate curtain, trying to decide what the Hel to do now.

"Are you okay?"

I jumped a good foot, embarrassing myself completely. If the warlock behind me had been a monster, I'd be dead. Spinning, I lifted my gaze up and up. "Noah," I bit out. "What the fuck are you doing?"

He showed no reaction to my rude response, just watched me in that calculating way. It took real effort, but I managed to hide how intimidated I felt around him. He was as scary as Logan, and considering he wasn't a spellcaster . . . Maybe it was his sheer size. He was a beast of a warlock, with an unsettling energy.

I'd never even seen him talk to anyone except Logan.

And now me.

"I'm trying to get into my dorm," he replied in a calm rumble. Unlike Logan, he had absolutely no accent, as if he'd been trained to conceal everything about his origin. "You're staring at the curtains like they're hiding a monster from you." He peered through them. "Did you see another monster?"

For a crazy moment, I imagined a hint of concern in his voice. "No monster," I said, easily. Not entirely true, but Logan wasn't the sort of monster he was referring to. "Do you know anything about the monsters? Any idea *who* might be creating them?"

The slightest of smiles played at the corners of his lips, but it was gone just as fast. "I know as much as you, Paisley Hallistar. And it might be best if you don't wander the halls alone, especially not in Nightrealm."

It was hard to tell if that was a threat or concern for my safety. "Don't worry, big guy." I patted his hard chest, and he glanced down at my hand, as if unsure what the fuck I was doing. Snatching it back quickly, I cleared my throat. "I've got no plans to get myself eaten by a monster. I'll see you around."

Forcing myself not to race away, I could feel his eyes on me all the way along Aura. I had no idea what to make of that odd encounter, but at least Logan hadn't caught me, which meant my stalking plan was still in motion.

CHAPTER 26

Over the next week, while the college was still filled with council members and elders investigating the attack, I did the minimum study, shelved personal research, and focused completely on stalking Logan Kingston. Yeah, it broke the pact, but I was too embarrassed to mention it to the girls. No doubt they'd think it was my obsession with him and not the very real fear that he was up to something suspicious.

Most of the time I watched Logan *and* Noah because they had quite the bromance going on. Even conversing in Italian, which generally ended in one of them getting punched. So I could only assume they liked to sling their joking insults in foreign languages.

It would be adorable, if I wasn't desperate to know what they were chatting about.

In other regards, I'd learned they enjoyed the gym, working out for two hours every morning, dressed in tanks and shorts. This was the point I kicked myself for not figuring out this plan earlier—I almost died at the sheer volume of ink on Logan's body. I hadn't gotten close enough to make out any of the images, and I absolutely didn't want to know.

Liar.

After they tormented me at the gym, they took a swim in the lake, and then attended most of their classes for the day. It was growing more apparent to me why I never crossed paths with him in general. He didn't seem to enjoy the confines of the buildings, spending most of his time outside. He also never ate breakfast, which was about the closest personality trait I'd seen to finding his psychopath side.

Every other part of him was normal. So. Freaking. Normal.

Normal and powerful. That part was innate, as he went about life as a spellcaster, blessed by the goddess to use the energy of the world itself. It surprised me how rarely he took shortcuts though. He never used magic to assist in weight training, which explained the corded muscles under the canvas of his tatted arms. He also never used it to power himself through the lake as he swam laps. He was disciplined, calculated, and appeared to consider every decision before he made it.

By the time Friday night rolled around, and I was once again staring at the curtains of Nightrealm Hall, I found myself frustrated, both sexually and otherwise. This was a stupid-as-fuck plan, and it wasn't working.

Logan was the perfect student during the day, and I couldn't access his room at night to know what he was up to. My last hope was to catch him leaving his room at night, which meant I had to sacrifice precious sleep and wait him out. It was risky, of course. For the first time, my stalking wouldn't be during daylight hours, but desperate times and all that jazz.

After getting ready for bed, I slept for a couple of hours, groggily coming awake when my alarm beeped at midnight. Dressing quickly in dark jeans and a black long-sleeved shirt, I threw my sneakers on and made sure the thorny spell was in my pocket.

The last second before I left the room, I grabbed all three of my crystal necklaces, and slipped them over my head. *Help me out tonight, Gran*, I prayed silently.

This was the first time I'd worn them since returning, and

as I pressed them to my skin, there was a buzz of energy along my spine. I hadn't had time to delve into the crystal theory yet, but part of me already believed they could elevate my magic. I hadn't forgotten that when I got rid of the monster in the graveyard, I'd been wearing a crystal.

My conclusion was that the reason the spell didn't work the second time was my lack of crystal connection.

Leaving my room, I closed the door quietly and moved as stealthily as I could into the dimly lit hallway. Witch lights were scattered enough that I could slip into shadows on my way toward Logan's room.

The curtains were closed as always, and I peered inside to find that there wasn't a single light in this hall. A void of eternal darkness. I shook off the tingles along my spine. They weren't the bad ones yet; this was general unease.

I couldn't sit outside of his door, so I made my way over to a small window seat in Aura, set in a wall recess. This spot kept me out of sight but let me view the Nightrealm curtains. Knowing this was going to be a long night, I settled in, wishing I'd thought of bringing coffee. Even cold leftovers from dinner would have helped.

At some point, despite my best efforts, I drifted in and out of sleep, and this time my dreams were much darker than usual. Silver tendrils of the inkiness that had filled Nightrealm chased me through an endless hall, and when I jerked awake I realized that my hands, which were wrapped around the necklaces, were glowing.

Releasing them, I shook my head to clear it, and that's when I felt it: my warning system was in full swing, the tingles racing down my spine. Too scared to move, but knowing I had no choice, I shifted forward a few inches and heard a scrape from farther down Aura.

Holding my breath and praying I'd imagined the sound, I moved slowly until I could peek around the side of the window seat. *Please be a student.* Even before I saw it, I knew from the energy roaring through my body that my silent plea had failed.

It was another monster, slinking through the hall, moving from shadows to light. Terror choked me, rising from my chest into my throat, as the horrific creature leaped and landed ten feet away from me. Scrambling to my feet, I blinked as it disappeared again, almost as if it'd never been fully here to start with.

Too petrified to scream, I groped in my pockets for the vial, and when I pulled it free I popped the lid to remove the thorn. The monster appeared in the light once more, rearing up on its hind legs. This beast was nothing like the other three, with antlers, huge and webbed, standing three feet above its head. A head that was cylindrical in shape, and I swore only one huge eye blinked at me before the creature flickered and then vanished again.

How did it keep vanishing? The others hadn't done that.

My brain came back online, and I turned to sprint, only for it to reappear and slam its heavy weight onto me, knocking the air out of my lungs as I landed hard. Feeling my chin split, I cried out and dropped the thorn, but managed to find it again, almost stabbing myself in the process.

Its weight vanished, and I flipped to my back, to find it flickering into existence once more. This time it attacked, a clawed front arm emerging from its fur, slicing across my shirt, leaving an agony of burning in its wake. The pain was instant and excruciating. Shocked cries spilled from my lips, as I forced myself to keep moving.

If I stopped fighting now, I'd be dead in the next few seconds.

I slammed the thorn into its skin, with only a momentary panic that its thick, dark hide might repel the attack. It sank in with ease. My incantation breathless as my power surged, and I fought the pain and darkness dancing on the edge of my vision.

The creature reared up once more, but it didn't strike, backing away and desperately gnawing at the thorns in its arm. The spell hadn't disintegrated the monster as I hoped, but it gave me a chance to escape all the same.

Pulling my body along the floor, leaving an impressive bloody slide that would get a serial killer hard, I managed to gain some distance and stagger to my feet. Adrenaline kept the pain manageable, and by *manageable* I meant absolutely destroying me with each step as I clutched my ribs. It was a deep wound, warm blood pulsing against my hold.

Ragged breaths caught in my chest as I stumbled along the hallway, footfalls quiet against the carpet, which absorbed the blood dripping from my side.

The edge of my vision grew fuzzy, but I pushed forward, aware that the beast wouldn't be held off long. *Just one more step. Just one more step.* It was a haunting melody in my head, urging me on, even as I grew weaker with each of those steps, until those words were a mere whisper.

I had a small head start thanks to Belle's spell, but its claws had already done their damage, tearing through my flesh and embedding deep in my magical essence.

Fear faded with each drop of lifeblood that escaped, and when I stumbled past the curtains, I decided to get off the beaten path.

Nightrealm Hall.

In my haste to escape one monster, I'd found myself in the lair of another.

With the heat of blood pulsing against my hands as I attempted to keep my insides . . . *well, inside* . . . there was still enough life within me to feel fear. Only this fear tasted different, tainted with hate and regret.

Against all common sense, I found myself stumbling to the one door I'd refused to approach before tonight. The only indication of the powerful and dark being who resided behind it was a carved minotaur in the center of the wood paneling.

With my right hand clutching my ribs, my left rested beside the minotaur as I swayed forward and almost smashed my head on the frame. When I pulled back, there was a streak of crimson left behind, as if I'd marked this door with my energy. Not that I really had energy left to do more than sway on the spot.

Lurching dangerously forward once more, the scuffle of the monster sounded close by. With no other option, I dug deep for the strength to lift my hand and knock, only to find the door opening before I even made contact. Cold air rushed around me, like a slap in the face, almost waking me up. *Almost.*

In the doorway stood my enemy.

But tonight I needed him.

To fight a monster, I needed a monster.

Unless he was the one who set it on me in the first place. But still, he was the only warlock strong enough to stop this attack.

His cold gaze traced over me, and that perfect face that haunted my dreams grew harder. I opened my mouth to explain, but I had nothing left to give. Swaying forward, I fell, expecting to hit the floor. Instead, strong arms wrapped around me, crushing against the wounds on my side. Even beyond pain, I still felt the weight of his hold.

"Precious?" he murmured, that one word dripping with fury. Maybe it was my sanity failing with my life, but it didn't sound as if his ire was directed at me. For once. "Who hurt you?"

Logan Kingston pulled me closer, and I knew that this was the defining moment of my existence. He held all the power, and as darkness won its battle and I closed my eyes, I wondered if my enemy would hand me to the beast or save me.

Time would reveal all, but it seemed I was out of that.

For tonight at least.

CHAPTER 27

Heat woke me first. My body arched on the bed as the pain slashing through my side added to the sensation of being lit on fire. A shadow washed over my face, and a scream ripped from me before I recognized the flash of icy green.

The heat was from Logan, his hands pressed to my side as power flooded into me with enough intensity I wondered if he was planning on finishing the job the monster started. My screams faded into whimpers, and Logan met my gaze. "Breathe, Precious. Breathe through the pain."

Easy for him to say.

I arched again, fighting the urge to punch the warlock trying to save my life. "The monster?" I managed to gasp, sweat pouring off me from the power.

"You weakened it," he rumbled. "I finished the job."

My relief was short-lived, before I was back to the pain again. Every nerve ending in my body was lit up, flames razing them to the ground. "Am I dying?"

Logan's unamused laughter rasped over my sensitive and burning skin. "Your life has been in my hands for years, and I'm not ready for it to end yet."

Yet. "This is why people are afraid of you," I sniped, but my breathless voice took away the bite.

"That's not the reason," he replied, "now stay still so I can save your life." *Again.*

There was another burst of energy, and after I arched into the power, the searing pain in my side finally eased. Logan lifted his right hand into a higher position, but when it brushed over the crystal we both jumped from a strong shock of what felt like electricity.

Reaching for the stone, I found it resting against bare skin—Logan must have removed parts of my shredded shirt to assess the injuries. My bra was still on at least.

"Did your crystals just zap me?" he asked, a wary expression creasing his face. I tried to sit up, and he placed a firm hand against my chest, and I swear I got as much voltage from that touch as I had from the crystals. "Lie down. You're not completely healed. The internal injuries remain."

Which explained why my lungs ached with each deep breath. "I just want to remove the crystals."

We didn't need to be zapped on top of everything else. Lifting my head enough to get them off, Logan grabbed their chains, careful not to touch the crystals as he placed them on his side table. He eyed them for a long moment, assessing, before returning the full force of his gaze on me. It was too much. Caught in his focus, I half wondered if I might not have been safer with the monster.

Still, choices made in a dying moment couldn't be held against me, so I relaxed and let him press his hands to my side once more, that all-consuming heat filling me. When my insides started to knit together, I jerked and caught myself on one strong, inked forearm. His eyes snapped to meet mine, but I couldn't let go. It was an anchor stabilizing me in the storm of his power.

His power burned but it wasn't fire; it was creation, and beyond what any of us should control. My energy responded to his, now that he was sending it deeper, and just as it had that day in his first spellcaster class, my power rose, bringing with it a completely different sort of ache.

It started with a pulse in my core, until need shattered through my gut and out into my limbs. Visions of my dreams filled my mind, those mornings waking with the echoing memories of his hands on my body. In real life, we'd never touched like this, but in my dreams he knew me intimately. "I didn't know you had tattoos," I whispered. Even in my dreams, that part of him was always in shadow. His eyes were the only part that reflected clearly.

"Why would you?" He assessed me. Delved deeper. Stripped back the essence of my being.

Unsure if this was blood loss, or the pure presence of Logan, I tried to shake off the need flooding me. Shake off the familiarity that had me wanting to lift my head and press my lips to his. His perfect full lips that haunted me.

An animalistic rumble shook his chest, and when my hand on his arm started to glow, I was close enough to see his eyes darken. "Logan," I mumbled, lifting my other hand toward his face.

There was a moment, as his eyes deepened to moss, that I swore he was going to kick me out of his room. Instead, he leaned closer enough that minty evergreen invaded my nostrils.

"What are you doing, Paisley?"

The way he asked that question, it was as if he already knew the answer. An answer that was carved into our bones, as permanent as the power within us. Later, I'd blame my next actions on almost dying and being hopped up on our combined powers, but for now I was beyond such rational thought.

The driving force within me was need, desire, and desperation. The dreams had brought me to my knees, *literally*, many times, and tonight their hold was relentless. I lifted my head to find the pain manageable, the movement bringing me closer to Logan's face. We both stilled as energy crackled between us. "Fuck it." I lost my mind and thrust myself forward to slam my lips to his.

There was a beat where his mouth parted, and then another beat where we were locked together until he tore away. Shame crashed into me as hard as the lust had, and Logan stared down at me as if he had no fucking idea what I was. Feeling the flush of embarrassment coat my cheeks, along with most of my body—this was *big shame*—I was about to stammer out an apology, when another low rumble escaped his body.

His hand shot under the back of my head faster than I could track, pulling me against him as his tongue parted my lips. The kiss deepened so fast that my head spun, and without conscious thought my fingers tangled in his shirt, desperate for more.

Logan was an immovable wall when he wanted to be, so I tugged against him. "You're injured," he bit out.

"More," I demanded, mindless with the sensations filling me. "This is healing me."

We both felt the heat of his power knitting my body back together. Our kiss brought our powers closer, and I couldn't have stopped now. Not even if a monster burst through the door.

Logan lifted his head and examined my side, his brow furrowing as he found evidence of my words. "You want my power like this, Precious?" he asked.

His power. *Him.* Every fucking part of the spellcaster. "I need it," I admitted. There was no way I should be this vulnerable with my enemy, but in this moment I was base instinct and desperation.

With my consent expressly given, Logan's kisses turned demanding, drugging, and they tasted like power.

He pressed me into the bed, hands tracing across my skin, skimming the top of my bra before it all but dissolved under his touch. Spellcasters, able to manipulate energy, could create and destroy as easily as that. But he hadn't destroyed me . . . yet.

He kissed along my neck and down my chest, his mouth burning against my skin as I shifted against the sensations driving me out of my mind. If I didn't get an orgasm out of this night, Logan would have wasted his time on the healing, because I was about to combust.

His lips closed around my nipple, tongue sliding across the hard peak, and I felt a pull all the way to my pussy. Even my clit throbbed in response. "Goddess be damned," I moaned, the heat consuming me.

Or was it Logan? One and the same, really.

He explored every inch of my skin and was thorough, just like the dreams, leaving me with a disconcerting sense of familiarity. This was a billion times more intense, as if I'd felt everything before tonight through a filter.

Logan and I were strangers, and yet he'd been in my mind for months, in my dreams, even longer, and destroying my world with barely any effort at all. When his touch smoothed over my black panties, the lace on the sides strained against his initial tug. His teeth scraped over my lower stomach muscles and I arched against him, and almost sobbed when his power dissolved my underwear, leaving me bare.

Bare, and at the mercy of a powerful spellcaster, my enemy who kept saving my life, confusing me.

Logan kissed along my thighs so slowly that I went a little insane, and when his huge hands wrapped around them, he parted my legs just as slowly. Logan hadn't said a word since *You want my power.* I expected it to feel awkward, but all I had was the pulse of our powers as they crashed together.

I cried out when his tongue, hot and firm, grazed across my clit, sucking the sensitive flesh inside his mouth. Low mewling slipped from my lips as I rocked against him, and his grip on my thighs tightened, holding me so he had the access he desired.

The pleasure was already circling too fast and hard, and there was no way I could hold on to an orgasm, not when I'd been desperate for this for months. The sexy dreams had driven me to the edge of my sanity, but the real Logan . . . he was sending me right over.

Grasping the sheets with both hands, my cries grew louder, but I was past caring who might hear us. Logan groaned into me as he plunged his tongue inside. When he pulled away, he licked from my ass to the top of my pussy, and I could hear how wet I was.

My days stalking Logan had already clued me into his discipline; he did nothing by halves. Eating pussy was no exception. He settled between my thighs and explored my body so thoroughly that when pleasure shattered me into my first orgasm, he just drank in everything I offered, his relentless mouth-fucking sending me over the edge again.

Releasing my hold on the sheets, I threaded my fingers through his hair to hold him, and he finally freed my thighs from his grip, allowing me to ride his face. I cried out as once more I exploded.

Dreams and reality collided, and Logan drew out the pleasure until I felt as if I was about to black out. When my limbs collapsed bonelessly onto the bed, the fire of his power released me and he pulled away. As my eyes flew open, I found him standing fully dressed on the side of the bed. Dread mingled with pleasure; he'd never even gotten naked, while I was completely and thoroughly destroyed.

"What—" I had to clear my throat. "What happened?"

"Our power." His lips were glossy, and I found my gaze locked on his full bottom one. "Your healing demanded extra energy from us both, and that's how it manifested. But you're healed now."

Ouch, okay. Message received, dickface.

I was the one getting the orgasms, sure, but his attitude pissed me right off, and if it wasn't for the impressive and obvious erection in his black sweats, I'd have wondered if he was affected by me at all.

My legs shook as I stood, but I forced my limbs to cooperate. Logan reached for another one of his fucking hoodies, and before I could tell him to *get fucked* he pulled it over my head. Glaring at him when my face came into view, I tried not to enjoy the soft material and minty scent that wrapped around me. I lusted for the scent and power of this spellcaster, but I'd die before I let him know that.

"Well," I said, searching for a distraction in his room. There were three or four guitars against the wall in the corner, which gave me a reprieve from my embarrassment. Was Logan a musician?

"Well . . ." he pushed, and I remembered I'd started to speak and never finished.

"Thanks for saving me." And destroying me.

Logan watched me, and I could have sworn our powers were connected still, just from the tension between us. Needing to escape, I grabbed my crystals and slipped the chains over my head. I was almost at the door, the spellcaster still silent and watchful, and I found a question slipping out before I could stop it. "Are you creating these monsters?"

If I'd just signed my death warrant, there was no impending feeling of doom.

His expression shuttered, and grew even colder, if that was possible. Moody fucker.

With a sigh, I twisted the handle of his door and opened it to step outside.

"They're not from my power." His deep voice stopped me. "And I'm not sure they're being created. They're called here."

Turning back to him, I tried to read further, but he gave nothing else away. My mind raced with implications of what he'd said. *Not being created.* "I read that there are monsters in one of the planes of existence, but it's one that necros can't touch. How are they called here? And who would have the power to do that? Dad said it might be a parent feeding dark magic to their child."

The door opened wider without me touching it, a clear signal for me to get the Hel out of his room. "Your dad isn't who I'd go to for magic advice," he said, a snap of anger in his tone. "Get back to your dorm, Paisley. I'll keep the monsters away for the rest of the night."

Smoothing my hands over his hoodie, I forced my hurt into a box and slammed the lid shut. Logan's dismissiveness should not bother me. We were not lovers. Fuck, we weren't even friends. What had happened in his room was a magical healing, and I'd broken my dry spell at last.

My body was fully healed and without pain as I raced through the halls to my room. The feeling of being watched stayed with me, but this time it was Logan.

Keeping the monsters away.

When I was safe in my room, I collapsed against the door, sucking in deep breaths. I'd almost died tonight. I'd almost died, and Logan saved me again. He'd also given me the most mind-blowing orgasms of my life, and I was once again in his hoodie. My life was weird.

Despite the healing burst of power from Logan, exhaustion pressed in on me and I stumbled to bed, crashing out with the scent of mint and power surrounding me.

Chapter 28

"You're in so much trouble," Belle growled.

It was lunchtime before I dragged myself out of bed. Belle found me in the dining hall, and I spilled everything that happened.

"You promised you wouldn't go anywhere on your own," she whisper-yelled at me, "so why the fuck would you think it was okay to get out of bed at midnight to stalk Logan?"

I felt like shit. "I know. I'm so sorry I didn't let you all know. I was trying to take control of the situation because it's exhausting constantly living in fear. Jumping at shadows. I need answers."

Her fierce expression remained for a few seconds, before it softened minutely. She took a sip of her tea, and I found the scent of the herbs soothing in their familiarity. "I understand what you're going through, but I also love you and wouldn't function without our friendship. You can't be so casual with your life. I mean, what if Logan had chosen not to save you last night? What if he was the one hunting you in the first place?"

"It's not him." I was sure of it now. "We need new suspects, and they have to be powerful enough to drag monsters out of the planes of existence and into ours."

"What about Logan's dad?" Belle stared at the wide beams lining the ceiling. "Maybe he's controlling a student who is weaker than Logan. Noah?"

I'd considered this theory, but it didn't feel right. "It's possible, but I don't think it's Noah."

"Did he really say that he doesn't believe the monsters are being created? They're being called? What the fuck is happening, some weird evil Pokémon battle?"

A snort escaped me as I played with the rim of my coffee cup. "Makes as much sense as the rest of our theories."

The briefest of smiles lifted her lips, before she grew somber again. "Are you sure you're completely healed? No lingering pain? Maybe we should visit the healers."

My stomach wasn't exactly happy with me today, but I didn't have any pain. Picking up the chicken salad sandwich I hadn't even touched, I took a bite and chewed while I mulled over my thoughts. "I checked my body this morning, and there's not a damn mark on me. The healers didn't even come close to this thorough a healing when I was hurt in the graveyard. Spellcasters do it differently."

If only I could stop thinking about just how differently.

Her lips twitched. "Maybe we should let them in on the secret, right? A few mind-blowing orgasms by the hottest, most powerful warlock in the school will bring a witch back from the brink of death." The twitch turned into a smile, and I waited for what smart-ass quip was coming next. "You guys went all enemies-to-lovers. Haley will be fucking thrilled."

I pressed my lips together and resorted to throwing a napkin at her. She cracked up, and I couldn't help my own laughter. It was cathartic. Not that we had any reason to release our worries and tension, but at times your body made the decision for you.

"What's the plan now?" Belle sipped her tea again. "The defensive spell didn't work, which means we need a new spell or a stronger one."

"I have no idea," I mumbled around my sandwich. "We

need to get more proactive about figuring out how they're bringing in these monsters. Once we have that knowledge, we might discover who's involved."

"I was talking to my dad about it," Belle said, finishing up her tea and pushing the cup away. "He rang last night to talk about the monster issue, and I explained what's been going on."

"Did he have any thoughts?" I asked, sandwich forgotten.

"He said the council and elders are doing a lot of work behind the scenes to figure out what's been happening. It's quite the uproar out in the magical world. He did say he'd do extra research for us, and would pass along anything he learned during parents' weekend."

I'd completely forgotten about the event, which was a huge deal for obvious reasons. "That's next weekend, right?"

The magical barriers around the school would ease up to allow parents a chance to enter the school and observe their kids at Weatherstone. Mom had mentioned it multiple times in our last call.

"Yep, next weekend," Belle confirmed. "Barriers will allow parents in from nine Saturday morning until five Sunday afternoon. Most parents don't stay overnight, but will come back the second day for another visit. Dad said he'd actually make it, which is wild."

I was happy for her, because no matter how blasé she acted over her father's lack of presence in her life, I could tell it hurt her. This show of effort was a big deal, and maybe as a bonus, he'd discover information that would help with our research and investigations.

When Belle left to grab another cup of tea, I started on my sandwich once more, only to have Logan drop into Belle's vacated chair. Well, not so much *drop*; he casually sprawled into it, his huge body filling the space around him. "What do you want?" I asked as I swallowed roughly, almost choking on some chicken. After last night, I'd have bet my left arm he wouldn't seek me out for the rest of eternity.

The air hummed between us, and even though his stare was almost lazy, those icy eyes missed nothing. "Is that any way to greet the warlock who saved your life?" He was the king of faked affability. This side of Logan was the hardest for me to handle. I never know what to do because his words never sounded threatening, but they were filled with undercurrents. Treacherous ones. I only ever got half the story, half the picture, and I had to guess the rest.

"Apologies, oh powerful savior," I managed to say with the same level of faked friendliness. "Pray do tell, why have you sought my company in this hour?"

He flashed a hint of genuine smile before it was locked down again. "Firstly, the headmaster is aware of what happened last night."

I almost fell off my chair as I gaped at him, wondering which part he was talking about. "Last night?"

There was a feral snarl in his expression. "Right, the part where I found another monster and dispelled it."

Holy goddess. He'd done that on purpose, and I debated if I could stab him with the butter knife beside me. "If my dad hears I was attacked again, he'll pull me out of Weatherstone. Did you mention my name?"

Logan watched me closely, taking in every minute change in my expression. When he locked me in his gaze like this, I couldn't breathe or think or process as I wanted, so I forced my face blank. "Of course not, Precious. What sort of best friend would I be if I ratted you out?"

"The kind who's mentally deranged because you're not my best friend." The bite I wanted to infuse into my words just wasn't there. I was frankly too tired for our usual snark.

He waved me off. "I'll ignore those hurtful words for now,

but I expect an apology when your memories return." What the fuck was he talking about?

"Was this the sole reason you sought me out?"

"I wanted to let you know that you should be safe from now on. They're casting a blanket across the school's energy today. Which will cut off strong magic. It'll remain until they make headway on tracing the magical essence."

My chest felt tight as Logan stepped in and solved another problem for me, almost as if he'd done it on purpose—when I was sure he didn't give enough fucks to make my life any easier. "That's good news," I managed to say.

"It is, isn't it." His tone and expression remained light, but the moss around his irises was back. "I don't want you to grow complacent, though, so in light of your continued involvement in almost dying, it might be time for you to stop following me around and start working on your affinity. You almost got yourself killed last night." The moss grew and grew until I was staring into darkness.

"Following you around?" I wondered how hard I should be denying it, and also if I could manage to throw myself out of the window by the buffet before anyone stopped me. That was how badly I needed this conversation to end. "A little cocky, don't you think? I have better shit to do than stalk the amazing Logan Kingston."

A genuine laugh rumbled from him, and I liked the sound far too much. "Playing dumb doesn't suit you. I'm a spellcaster. I felt your energy from the first day you trailed my steps, and you're one of the worst stalkers I've ever come across. I'd suggest you don't bother with that as a future career if your affinity never kicks in."

He was just jabbing at wounds today, wasn't he? "Appreciate the career advice," I sniped back. "So, oh powerful savior, how do you suggest I go about honing my magic and figuring out my affinity? I've been trying, you know, but my energy won't cooperate. Surely, you've heard, since you're aware of . . . *everything*."

Logan leaned in closer, and I tried desperately not to breathe in his scent. Why did he always smell so good? I should have searched his room for an aftershave brand and ignored the guitars. "You will train with Noah and me." Any mirth he'd displayed was long gone now.

"Wait, what? Train with you and Noah?" No fucking way. I couldn't even be in his presence for two minutes without turning into a hormonal mess; the last thing I needed was daily contact. I had to remain immune to Logan if I wanted a hope of staying away from him.

"Cute that you think it was a request—you will train with us. I'll be in touch soon, so until then, no wandering the halls at midnight."

The stubborn glint in his eyes told me I wasn't getting anywhere today by arguing, but there was no way he could force me to do this, so I just said, "We'll see. Also, will your father be at parents' weekend?" Now that the event had been brought to my attention once more, I was concerned with Mom, Dad, and Rafael all in the same location.

His expression closed off, and I wasn't looking at my "best friend" any longer. This was a scary spellcaster, a virtual stranger. "My father is none of your business," he said, and he was on his feet and gone before I could kick him in the shin.

Noise returned, and I wondered if everyone had fallen silent when Logan appeared, or if I'd been trapped in his powerful bubble. He had a way of silencing the rest of the world when he was around.

"What. The. Hel. Was. That?" Belle dropped into the chair Logan had vacated, staring at me. "Did he seek you out? Did he mention last night? Are you two going to be hooking up now?" She was two seconds away from hyperventilating, and I had to laugh at her eager expression.

"Calm down. Logan stopped by to tell me that they're casting a blanket over the school today, so we should be safe for a while, and he also . . ."

"Also what, witch?" she shrieked.

"Told me that he will be training me until I figure out my affinity."

She just stared at me, and stared, and stared until I felt uncomfortable enough to add, "It's not that big of a deal."

This time she snorted, looking more like herself. "You must be kidding yourself. This is a huge deal, Paisley. He's a spellcaster. They never train anyone. It's almost as if he's worried about you. When is your first training session?"

For my own sanity, I ignored the *he's worried about you* comment. "Apparently he'll *be in touch*, but I would guess soon."

She sighed like I'd just eloquently spilled a beautiful love story. "Come on, weirdo." I shook my head and got to my feet. Belle joined me as we dropped our trays into the mess, and as we left the room, students stared our way. Stared and whispered.

I was pretty sure I knew why, but I still checked. "Do I have food on my face?" I looked down at my shirt and skirt, making sure I hadn't gotten my period and bled everywhere.

Belle barely even gave me a once-over. "It's Logan. None of us have ever seen him sit with a witch in the dining hall. The rumors were wild while you two chatted." She side-eyed me. "Even with the blanket, you might need the same level of protection. Logan just won the Hottest Warlock this year."

My groan was audible. Of course he fucking did. Now I'd have to deal with Trevor complaining about his dethroning on top of being stuck with Logan for this training.

Ignoring the multitude of morons in the room with too

much time for gossip, we headed for Ancot. I caught sight of Trevor and Dad in the distance, but they were deep in conversation, so I left them to it.

"Are you going to tell your parents or siblings what happened last night?" Belle asked, following my line of sight. "Should I not mention it to Trevor if we cross paths?"

They were friends, so it wasn't a weird question. But her face was twisted in a way that I didn't understand. "With the blanket going up, I think it's best not to stress them out with what might have happened. I didn't die, and we all should be safer now. I don't want to leave yet, not when I'm closer to figuring out my power."

Her expression was softer than it had been all morning; she'd finally forgiven me for not telling her about my midnight plan. "I'd be heartbroken if you weren't here, but I also don't want you getting hurt. Having Logan train you might be a good thing, Pais. Worst case, you can ride his face—"

I shoved her before she could finish that sentence. We weren't exactly in a private space.

She snorted laughter, and I had all the regrets over spilling my guts about last night.

Even if it was all I could think about.

CHAPTER 29

"Mom," I cried, wrapping my arms around her and holding on tight.

There had been no drama in Weatherstone since the night of my attack, so the blanket was holding. And while the students complained ad nauseum about the limitation on their powers, everyone breathed a little easier at the safety that came with it. Parents' weekend didn't lift the blanket, but the barrier around the school was tweaked for the duration of the event.

Mom hugged me hard, only letting go so she could hug my siblings too. We were near the front gates, along with dozens of other students—Sara was off to the side chatting rapidly in Romanian with her tiny mother, who looked a lot like her.

Belle had walked out with us, but I couldn't see her or her father in the crowd. My curiosity was about more than just seeing the elder—I needed to know if he'd discovered any information that might help with our investigations into the monsters. The blanket couldn't stay on the school forever, and the college didn't appear to be any closer to figuring out who was behind it—according to Dad anyway.

"It always feels weird to be back here for these parent weekends," Mom said, looking around, taking in the bright green lawns and oak trees in full brilliant foliage. The late summer weather was perfect, the heat easing as we were gifted perfect blue skies for days, with the lightest breezes ruffling our hair. We were all in uniform; you couldn't show off a school with us dressed as peasants, but I'd ditched the tights.

"Come on, Mom," Trevor said, linking his arm through hers. "Dad said he'd meet us at the banquet later, so we should explore."

Mom set off chattering about her time here, and how it felt like yesterday and a million years ago at the same time. The next few hours were spent wandering the grounds. We stopped to check in on Simon and Morris. I'd been upgraded to bear hug status with the former, which I was *almost* used to. Nothing quite like feeling the strength of a bear wrap its arms around you, even if he was infinitely gentle.

Dad joined us when we settled on a grassy area near the east of the lake to watch dozens of water elementals entertain us with their magical skills.

"Look at J," Mom cried, clapping her hands as Jensen flipped what felt like a hundred feet in the air. On days like this, surrounded by love and sunshine, the tingles of warning down my spine felt like a bad dream. Not that I'd experienced a single one since the blanket.

"Go, J!" I shouted, when he flipped again, a crest of water beneath him, safely guiding him around the lake.

When their impressive display of magic was finished, it was time for the welcome feast in the assembly hall. Jensen, dry and dressed in his uniform once more, joined us as we entered the fray of students also heading for food. It took a lot longer than usual, with parents buffing up the numbers for dinner, but no one minded. This was family time, and we got to chat and catch up as we walked.

"I got a dozen new potted herb plants," Mom said as we crossed into Writworth. "I'm in touch with a witch from Sweden who claims to have cultivated some ancient varieties that you can't get anywhere else. If I can source seeds from her, I'm going to be able to expand our inventory."

I could totally relate to the joy and excitement on her face. I loved my stupid herbs like they were my babies, petting and talking to them daily. I was lucky I didn't have a roommate; with my weird quirks I'd have a lot of explaining to do.

"I hope you can get some, Mom," Jenna said, eyes lighting up. "Imagine the spells that have been lost to us because we no longer have the materials to craft them. Could open up an entire new magic."

Our ancient spells had been adapted to suit modern materials, but that didn't always mean it was an improvement. Generally, we ended up with a weaker, less potent variety of the original.

When we started up the stairs, I asked Mom if she'd read the letters from Gran. They'd been on my mind ever since I'd found them. She furrowed her brows, appearing confused. The letters clearly hadn't crossed her mind once since I'd mentioned them in the kitchen. "No, honey. I honestly forgot they were even there. Why's that?"

I shrugged with an easy smile. "No real reason. I'm curious about Gran, really. I know she loved crystals, so I wanted to learn as much as I could." Like if I could use them to help release my magic. It hadn't escaped my notice that I'd used more of my magic during the times I wore my crystal necklaces.

"Are you talking about Mom's mom?" Jenna asked.

Mom nodded. "Yeah, Paisley found some old letters that Mom wrote to me. I really should give them a read. It's just hard not knowing what they contain, and whether it's going to break my heart. The heart is a fragile organ, you know."

Dad pushed between us, and wrapped his arms around his wife, reacting to the catch in her voice. "You don't need to read them," I heard him murmur. "Nothing she says there could change anything now. She's been gone for more than forty years."

I decided then that I wouldn't bring it up to Mom again. She didn't need the extra emotional stress in her life, not when I could take a tiny peek at one myself and see if it was worth opening them all. As shit as it made me feel to pry into Mom's personal life, if she had no real interest in her mother's words, then what did it hurt for me to open one . . .

When we finally reached the assembly hall, Headmaster Gregor was at the door greeting everyone personally. I hadn't had a chance to talk with him since my graveyard attack, but so far he lived up to my dad's description of him as professional, affable, and pretty lenient with his students. While somehow keeping the college from falling into chaos.

There was a reason Weatherstone was the most prestigious college in America, and I couldn't see Gregor letting that reputation tarnish anytime soon. Even a murder hadn't dulled the school's shine.

"Welcome, Hallistar family," he said, smiling broadly as he shook Dad's hand and then Mom's. "It's nice to see you again, Beth. We need to catch up soon."

Mom's smile was genuine, and I wondered if they'd all known each other before Dad became a professor here. "I'd love that, Victor. It's been too long."

The line spanned out behind us, so we moved on quickly, finding a table inside with enough seats for us to sit together. I ended up between Jensen and Alice, and as I settled in and looked around, I noticed Belle a few tables over. This was the first time I'd seen her since this morning.

Curious about her dad, I tried to view more of him, but his back was to us. He looked tall and thin with short, gray hair, artfully parted on the side, and slicked down. Belle noticed me and waved with a broad smile, which had her father turning in my direction.

My smile slipped from my face the moment his cold, dark eyes met mine, and as my hand dropped I tried to shake off the dark vibes he exuded. He stared in a way that was both assessing and absolutely judgmental. With pale skin and sharp features, he didn't look like his daughter, but I could see they shared a similar nose and lip shape.

"You okay, Little Gem?" Dad asked, noticing my stare-off with my bestie's father. "Do you have an issue with that elder?"

Belle's dad dismissed us, releasing me from his glare and turning to face forward. "That's Belle's father. I'm not sure of his name."

"Elder Monroe," Mom added, narrowing her eyes on his back. "I've never been a fan of that man. He's cold and calculating, and some of the rulings under his watch are downright cruel."

All the hopes I'd had to chat with him about our issue at the school were gone now. In fact, I kind of wished Belle had never talked to him about it, because he was clearly making judgments. My fingers itched to steal my friend away, but at least she seemed content, smiling happily into his face as he gave her attention. For once.

It wasn't hard to understand why she preferred her mom's company, though, to be fair, as I watched him lean forward and grab her hand, he wasn't as bitingly cold to his daughter as he'd been to me. I wondered if his coldness toward me was because he thought I'd put Belle at risk by not speaking up sooner about the monsters.

I was distracted when dinner arrived, served family style on huge wooden trays. "I love family weekend," Trevor said, adding a second serving of everything to his plate. "They always bring out the best foods to impress the parents."

"We need to do this at least once a month when we graduate," Jenna said, reaching for roast chicken. "No matter where we all are in the world, we need to make the effort to be together."

As long as we had access to the witch portals, we could cross vast distances easily. Even if Dad had to organize and pick up those of us who hadn't graduated and therefore weren't tapped into the network.

"I hope we do this until we're old and gray," Alice said with a sniffle. "I don't want to lose this feeling."

Mom lifted her napkin and dabbed at her eyes. "Dad and I lucked out with you five. And I can't wait to add more little witches and warlocks to the dinner table. This is just the beginning of your journeys, kiddos. There are so many wonderful new memories to make."

We were an emotional bunch, caught up in the melancholy of these milestones and final experiences. The days that felt like the *good old days* but were stepping stones to the future—an unknown and possibly terrifying future.

After dinner, we walked with Mom and Dad to the gates. "I'll be back in the morning," she said as she hugged each of us. "I hear tomorrow we get a display from the fire elementals, and I can't miss Trevor and the rest of your dad's students." His advanced students were supposed to be impressive, what with all the magma juggling and creating infernos within the palms of their hands.

After they left, all of us crashed in the twins' room, not quite ready to let the family togetherness end. We played cards and binged on junk food that Trevor *procured*—aka stole—from the kitchens. By the time I was in bed, I marveled at the perfection of the day we'd had.

Only to wake up the next day to an absolute shitshow.

I'd just left the dorms heading down to meet my family when I ran into Belle and her father.

"Pais!" she called, waving me over.

Elder Monroe was dressed in a different gray suit, his hair as prim and slicked back as it had looked last night, and his gaze just as cold. "Hey, friend," I said, forcing a smile. No way would I let this arrogant elder see me sweat, even if he was acting rude as Hel. "It's nice to meet you, Elder Monroe."

There was a slight twitch along his jawline, as if the sound of his name coming from me bothered him. "Nice to finally put a face to the name, Ms. Hallistar. Belle has told me a lot about you, and the—" he cleared his throat "—happenings around the college."

I nodded, pushing down my unease as I decided to ask him if he had any information; he couldn't hate me more than he clearly already did. "She said you might have some insights for us, a way to figure out who is creating these monsters or how they're getting into the school."

He smiled and I got strong shark vibes, as if he'd scented blood in the water. "This isn't the first time there have been monsters such as these in our community, Ms. Hallistar. You should read *The Reapers of Purgatory*, and then investigate the witch massacres of 1859. I think you'll find it quite interesting." The air virtually crackled with tension as he stared me down, and I refused to look away. This asshole was almost at Logan's level of threatening me without uttering one threatening word. It also hadn't slipped my attention that he'd said *nice to put a face to the name* and not *nice to meet you*.

"Dad's a history buff," Belle said cheerily, missing all the undertones in her dad's reply. "If he says to check those books out, we definitely should."

I nodded, wary.

Belle continued in her typical A-type personality way. "Are there any spells we should be practicing to protect ourselves?"

"The only way to protect yourself is through the death of

the witch involved," he drawled. "You need to cut her head off to ensure she's not able to practice her dark magic."

"You keep saying witch," I said, still meeting his dark stare unflinchingly. "Do the elders have a suspect?"

Whatever fake animation had been in his face vanished, leaving just those dead eyes. "It's always a witch. Learn your history, young lady, or I might think you're at Weatherstone due to a certain professor and not your own abilities."

"Dad!" Belle snapped, taking a small step back as though he'd slapped her. "Don't talk to her like that. Not only is Paisley powerful enough to be at whatever college she wants, she was almost killed three times by these creatures. She's the victim here, and we don't victim shame."

Like a pixie of happiness bopped him on the head, his smile brightened, and that threatening vibe he'd been shooting my way vanished. "Absolutely, sweetheart. I just want to make sure you're safe."

Belle relaxed, buying what he was selling, but I wouldn't be letting my guard down around him any time soon. "The blanket is up, Dad, so we shouldn't have any incidents for the rest of the year. We'll do more research in the meantime."

Elder Monroe brushed his hand lightly over her red hair. "I know, and with that, we should leave your friend to find her family. We have a breakfast date before I must leave for the council meeting."

Belle's lips pulled into an apologetic frown as she faced me, but I just smiled. No way was I letting this asshole come between us. "I'll see you later."

She leaned over and smacked a kiss on my cheek. "Find me tonight."

Elder Monroe showed no sign he was disturbed by her warmth toward me. He took her hand and off they went for breakfast. But I found myself uneasy all the way to the front gate.

Where another disaster was in the process of exploding over the grounds.

Mom and Dad had arrived, and they weren't alone. Logan and a tall warlock that I could only assume was his father were facing off against my parents.

For fuck's sake. Apparently, this was the day for assholes to rain from the skies. No wonder today was gray and stormy, after yesterday's perfect blue skies.

Picking up the pace, I had the feeling that this confrontation was going to make meeting with Elder Asshole feel like a delightful catch-up. Sprinting through the students, I came to a skidding halt beside Dad, hoping I could cut this off before it started.

Logan's expression was the affable amusement he perfected so well, hiding the dangerous beast inside. Case in point, his eyes were flecks of glass, light and iced over. "Nice of you to join us, Precious," he drawled. "We were just discussing you."

Logan's dad turned his gaze on me, and I felt every hair on my body stand on end. He had the same piercing eyes as his son, though his were dark. Almost black. He was fairer than his bronzed son, but there was no denying the resemblance between them. I stared at the older version of Logan, still handsome, tall and broad.

But, despite Logan's icy exterior, I'd seen warmth in him on those rare occasions when we were alone. In those moments, he'd saved my life and used his power to heal my body.

Logan had fire in his power, but his father was all icy darkness. A void of warmth, obliterating everything in its path. He reminded me of the monsters we'd seen in that text, with the shadowy aura over them.

This spellcaster was dark, and utterly, utterly terrifying.

CHAPTER 30

"Talking about me?" I said, forcing a casual tone while on the inside I was all terror and panic. "All good things I'm sure."

Rafael, better at hiding his feelings than Elder Monroe, smiled as if we were old friends. It was apparent who'd taught Logan to hide his calculating manipulations under a cloak of civility. Only, the jury was still out on Logan and how dark he truly was. "All good, Paisley. We were discussing this little monster issue the college appears to be having. Weird that it started this year. Your freshman year."

Smoothly done with the accusation there, Kingston, but since I was fairly sure I'd know if I was summoning monsters, the bite didn't really have any teeth. "The year Logan transferred in too," I replied, smiling so pleasantly my jaw hurt. "Definitely a *weird* coincidence."

I swore there was a brief twitch in Logan's lips even as his expression remained hard, his focus on his scary-ass father. "I'm so happy you survived Walter's attack. He's a strong air elemental. How did that happen, Paisley? Also, you wouldn't happen to know where he is? His family is worried sick."

I blinked, trying to keep up with his segue and rapid questioning. Was he talking about Walter the Weasel? *Kingston will thank me for this.* I'd already been on the edge of a panic attack, but the implication that all along that attack might not have been directed by Logan slammed into me, and I couldn't help but burn a hole in the side of Logan's face with my gaze.

His father noticed too, his grin satisfied in a way that hurt my stomach.

"Why would I know where he—?"

"Leave her alone, Rafael," Dad finally cut in, done with the warlock's baiting. "Paisley was attacked by the monsters, she's hardly the one bringing them to the school. You always were quick to blame our family for any wrongdoings."

Mom was quiet, and so pale that I was worried she was about to faint. We needed to end this conversation immediately, before it did more emotional damage.

"I wouldn't dream of blaming anyone. We all know your family is above such reproach." Rafael's reply was smooth, the digs subtle. "How are you, Beth?" Dad shifted his stance to block Mom, not that it stopped Rafael. "Still ignoring your magic?"

"We all lost Isabel that day," Dad snarled at his former best friend. "Beth was hurt too, remember? We have all suffered, none more than my wife, who saw her best friend get torn to pieces."

"She was *my* best friend," Rafael snapped, and for a moment the darkness in the spellcaster blasted like a beacon. "*Mine!* And she was taken from me. I have never bought your innocent act regarding Beth's magic, and now your daughter is neck-deep in a situation where another was torn to pieces. I don't believe in coincidences. You need to stop blaming others for your fuckups, Tom. Not even our years of friendship can excuse what happened that day."

Dad's laugh was strained and without humor. "That blood oath clued me in on the lack of forgiveness, Rafe. We just want to be left alone."

"I think I should leave," Mom murmured softly. "I don't want to remind anyone of their loss."

Her compassionate words only made Rafael angrier. The heat around him rose, and I wondered if it was harder to hate someone who so plainly suffered for what happened that day.

"I'll take you home," Dad said, keeping her partially hidden behind him as he wrapped an arm around her shoulders. "Paisley, let your brothers and sisters know, and stay away from the Kingstons."

"With pleasure," I said, shooting Logan another glare. I'd asked him point-blank if his father was going to be here and he'd ignored me all so his father could ambush Mom.

Asshole.

A *duet* of assholes.

There wasn't a chance in Hel I'd be taking those extra training lessons with him. Not now, and not at any point in the future.

I hugged both of my parents, furious our time was cut short, but happy they'd be away from the spellcasters. "Be careful," Mom whispered as she held on tight. "Don't go anywhere alone while he's here."

"I promise," I whispered into her shoulder, the warm clean scent of her clothes comforting.

My parents didn't exit the gates until they saw me reach the steps of the front entrance, and that was when I turned once more, and made sure they got out safe. Logan and his father didn't move, and their conversation didn't look pleasant. Probably discussing how they planned on taking over the world this weekend.

I was briefly distracted when Trevor and Jensen stepped down the main steps, followed by Alice and Jenna. I'd been early to meet our parents, which was lucky considering what

I'd walked in on. Not that my presence did anything at all, but I was there for support.

"Where's Mom?" Trevor asked, looking around.

Shaking my head, I quickly detailed exactly what I'd walked in on. "Fuck," Jensen muttered, and that pretty much summed it up.

For the rest of the day, I had a four-person bodyguard team. We skipped out on the shows and feasts to stay in the twins' dorm, as it was larger than the normal rooms. By the time Jensen and Trevor deposited me at my front door, the school was once again locked down to everyone except students and professors, and I found myself pulling crystals from my desk and placing them on my bed.

I needed comfort tonight, and wished I could sneak to the phones and call Mom to check on her. But along with a blanket on our energy, there was also a curfew in the halls at night, so the call would have to wait until morning.

Eventually, exhaustion dragged me under, but it only felt like seconds later I was startled awake, my breaths coming out in rapid huffs. I still had periodic nightmares from the attacks, and at first I thought that was what woke me, until I felt tingles racing down my spine. Along with those fear-inducing tingles, I noticed immediately that there was also no cloying press of the blanket against my power. Ever since that magical protection had been enacted, it felt like my powers were contained in a small space. Whenever I expanded them, they'd collide with the walls of the blanket, but now . . . there was nothing holding them back.

Fear held me in place for a second, before I crawled out of bed and crept to the door, listening closely.

Too afraid to venture out, I hurried back to my bed, prepared to hide under the covers like a proper five-year-old afraid of the dark. Lifting the crystals I'd fallen asleep with, because they were scattered everywhere now, I moved them back to the desk, catching sight of a shadow outside the window.

Wait, no. It wasn't a shadow. It was a monster.

Holy fuck!

It slipped into the forest, and then another emerged, and another. Over and over. Closing my eyes, I forced my pulse to slow, wondering if I was dreaming. Pinching my arm hurt a lot, and I knew that this was no nightmare.

When I opened my eyes again, the monsters were still there, emerging from the forest and drawing closer to the buildings.

There were too many. They were going to destroy the school and kill everyone inside. Who had lifted the magical blanket over the college? Had it been Rafael before he left? Was this his way of telling us he was responsible for the monsters?

Knowing that I had to warn someone before they got inside, I opened my door and glanced along the hall to ensure they weren't already here. I huffed out in a rush when the hall was clear of any darkness, and taking a fortifying breath, dashed out of my door and sprinted, turning right. It was only when I reached the black curtains that I realized I hadn't headed for the professors' dorms.

Despite my fears and misgivings about him, instinct had still sent me straight for Logan.

As frustrating as it was to ask this asshole for help, he was thus far the only warlock or witch to be able to banish the monsters. He would know what to do.

Lifting my hand to knock, I noticed my blood had been cleaned from the door. Why that bothered me I had no idea, but there was no time for a mental break here. I had to save the school. Before I could knock, the door was opened, and this time he was dressed in a pair of pajama pants. Just pants.

Holy fucking goddess.

The ink. His ink was . . . everywhere.

Monsters, Paisley.

Right, right. I needed to get my head in the fucking game. There were monsters surrounding the school and this was no time to be devouring the broad expanse of bronze skin, marked with an array of darkly enticing tattoos. The few images I could see spoke of a true artist's hand, with the soaring raven across his right shoulder drawing my eye.

"Paisley," he said, his gaze sliding down my body as if he was checking for injuries. I looked down as well, cursing when I noticed I wore his hoodie.

"It's fucking comfy, get over it," I snapped, before he could say a word.

Crossing his arms over his chest, he leaned against his doorjamb. "And you're here for more of my clothes? I don't wear underwear, if that's what you're after." His gaze rested on the bare expanse of leg sticking out from under his hoodie, as if he was wondering whether I had panties on under there.

If the monsters didn't get me, embarrassment was about to straight-up murder me. *Don't think about him without underwear. Don't fucking do it.*

"There are monsters surrounding the school," I blurted out.

His casual indifference faded as he lifted his head, towering over me. "The blanket is intact. That can't be possible."

Intact. Wait, what? It had been down. I'd felt that pulse against my magic, but . . . I expanded my power and it hit the cloying sensation. The blanket had returned.

"I think it might have been down for a few minutes," I whispered, trying to piece it together in my head. "The power pulse woke me, and I saw dozens of monsters outside my window." Logan's room was an interior, so it didn't have a real window, only a magically created one. "I'll show you in my room."

He didn't move, and I was done with his shit for the night.

"Don't tell me you're afraid of a few monsters, Kingston." Shooting a sneer at him, I left his dorm and ran for mine, hoping that he'd be curious enough to follow.

To my immense relief, I felt the burn of his power not ten seconds later. At my room, I pressed my hand against the palm reader, cursing at how long it took to open the door. "Calm," Logan said, placing his hand on top of mine to ease my jittering.

Calm was about the last thing I felt when Logan touched me, but he was strong enough to ease my hold. When the lock finally clicked, I raced over to the window and flung a hand out to show him what lay below. "The monsters are everywhere," I rasped. "They're surrounding the school."

He was a huge warlock, so he filled the window as he looked out. My body was trembling beside him as I tried to ignore the large tattoo on his back which looked a lot like a giant mountain lion, and instead focused on a plan to destroy dozens of monsters. If we woke the whole school, could the professors help?

"Paisley . . ."

I jerked my head to find him calm and staring out the window as if still searching. Pushing into his space, I drew on strength I didn't know I had to ignore the heat of his naked, tatted chest in lieu of finding the monsters.

Only there were none.

Not a shadow. Not a creature. The moonlight was strong and bright, its energy washing into my own magic until it swirled inside.

"Where?" Logan said shortly as he backed up a step. "Where are the monsters?"

I swallowed roughly and spent another minute frantically staring around the grounds. "They were everywhere," I whispered, rubbing my head as I panicked that I was actually losing my mind. This was the incident in the lake all over again, only this time cranked in intensity. "Dozens of them. Some that looked like the ones I've already seen, but a lot of different ones as well."

Logan arched an eyebrow in my direction, and this time when he leaned closer to look out the window, he spanned his arms on either side of me, trapping me in front of him against the windowsill. *Fuck fuck fuck.* "Show me them, Paisley."

I couldn't even breathe, let alone do anything else. I also couldn't show him monsters that were no longer there. Logan's big body surrounded me, his hard edges and all that power and strength pressing against my back.

A squeak was the best I could manage, and his laugh was husky. "If you wanted me in your dorm to finish what we started the other night, you only had to ask, Precious. No need to make up stories about monsters."

I was starting to hate the word *precious*. Especially when it came out of Logan's pretty mouth. His arrogance did return my voice at least. I whipped around in his hold and slammed my hands against him to push back. "Listen up, asshole, I would never pretend there were fucking monsters to get your attention. It might come as a surprise to you, *Hottest Warlock of the Year*, but I don't want your attention. I wouldn't touch you with a ten-foot pole."

The unflappable asshole shot me a slow burn of a smirk. "Wouldn't touch me with a ten-foot pole, hey. That's not what you said when my tongue was buried in your pu—"

"Enough!" I choked out as my fingers flexed against his skin. "That was healing magic bringing us together. Tonight has nothing to do with it, and I swear to you there were monsters everywhere. I don't know what happened to them . . ."

Maybe it had been a nightmare that I'd taken a few seconds to wake from. I'd sworn there had been no blanket on the school, along with those telltale tingles of dread down my spine, but now everything felt calm. Either I was going crazy or someone wanted me to think I was.

"Whoever brought them must have gotten rid of them," I mused, rubbing a hand over my tired eyes.

Logan watched me closely, his expression assessing in that dissecting way he had about him. "You should get some sleep." There was no bite, just a soothing tone as he finally released me from his hold. "It was a stressful day, and tomorrow isn't going to get much better. Our private classes start in the morning. Be fucking ready."

Before I could conjure a smart retort, he left the room, taking his immense energy with him, and I all but collapsed against the window. When I caught my breath, I took one last look out at the grounds. The monsters truly were gone. Unless they now roamed the halls of the school, there was no sign they'd even been here at all. Amazing. I'd made a fool of myself in front of Logan again, and I couldn't forget what he'd said to me: *our private classes start in the morning.*

Why hadn't I told him I had less than zero interest in training with him after that shit his father pulled on Mom today. He didn't get to order me around, and I had to stop going to him when danger hit. It was confusing to us both, and I had no idea why I was so drawn to him.

Tomorrow, when he tracked me down for training, I had to be strong enough to resist his pull. If I wasn't, that spellcaster would destroy me. He might not be behind the monsters, but there was more than one way to break a witch.

And I was pretty certain Logan was an expert at them all.

CHAPTER 31

The next day started off slow, and I couldn't remember the last time I felt this tired.

"Excellent job, Donna." Professor Damone clapped her hands, sending gusts of air across the classroom.

Donna was a petite witch with dirty-blond hair, who'd reached the point of gathering air around herself and twirling it into a mini tornado. She was halfway up one of the cylindrical glass tubes, storm energy surrounding her. Students always stayed behind the glass because their control was shit.

"Nice work for you as well, Paisley," the professor said kindly, as I managed to extinguish a candle with a swish of my hand. Donna and I, we were totally the same.

"You're using the element at least," Sara said, yawning widely. "You manage to touch most affinities in class. I don't understand why nothing stands out a little stronger."

"I have power." I was finally sure of that. "It's just locked away, and I haven't figured out the freaking key."

"You'll get—" Her words were cut off by another huge yawn.

Waving the flame out again, I chuckled. "Late night?"

She all but slumped forward onto her arms. "You have no idea. My parents stayed until the midnight cutoff, and then I couldn't fall asleep."

I'd been expecting a more exciting story, but that one was kind of cute. "I'm glad you got to see them."

Her smile was gentle, eyes glassy with what looked like happy memories. "Mom never wanted me to leave for college. She wasn't ready, but it was so nice to catch up with them. Being here, with all the drama and coursework, I forgot how it feels to be with people who love me unconditionally. I needed this weekend with them."

I nudged her. "Hey, I love you unconditionally."

She managed to crack one of her eyelids to peer at me as she blew me a kiss. "Love you too, bestie. But you know what I mean."

"Yep, I was on the phone with Mom this morning. The transition is harder than I expected."

During our call, Mom had assured me she was okay. *He's always like that, honey. It's nothing new. I'm just excited to get started on this new yarn pattern I found. And my seeds should arrive this week.* She'd sounded the same, her voice light and open, but I was under no illusion. She would put on an act to keep me from dealing with her drama, and no matter what she said, yesterday had been difficult for her.

When Sara and I were finished with our elemental class, we hurried along to History of Necromancy.

I'd never expected to enjoy this class, but it was turning into one of my favorites. Professor Jones had this way of revealing history to us, almost as if it was a thriller novel and we had no idea what was coming next. It was cleverly done, keeping me hooked, and I enjoyed learning more about Weatherstone and its ties to necromancy.

A lot of my necromancy classes were becoming fast favorites. On Friday, when we'd been in Necromancy in the Wild and one of the students had accidentally unearthed bodies from their graves, I'd found myself intrigued rather than disgusted. Professor Longhorn got it sorted in a few seconds, of course, and then proceeded to show us how to *sample from the energy of the undead but don't call them topside.* An important lesson to learn.

When we raised the dead, they were nothing more than animated corpses. There was no magic to return them to who they'd been before death. The worst part was if you lost control of them, you were in big trouble. Think zombies munching on people and all the bad stuff.

In History of Necromancy, Belle and Haley had saved us seats, so we settled in next to them and waited for Professor Jones. Logan strolled in late, the top two buttons of his shirt undone, and no tie, because he didn't care much for their rules here. He also got away with it.

He never looked my way, but I felt his presence as if he'd sat by my side. My body recognized his energy now, and it was starting to become a problem. Just like my current hoodie obsession.

"Okay, where did we leave off last lesson?" Professor Jones said, a thankful distraction as he tapped the side of his face. "Oh, right. We've finished going back through their childhoods, the covens from that age, and now we will continue with Writworth and Ancot arriving in the Americas. They'd just battled the deadly seas, saving themselves with their magic many times. With salt in their hair, and determination in their hearts, they traveled our amazing country, searching for a beacon of power to call their own."

His eyes twinkled. "Does anyone know why this is the location they chose for Weatherstone?"

"Not yet," a witch in the front row said. "We're waiting for the big reveal."

"Right, right." He nodded, as students laughed. "They'd

been traveling for months, trusting no one, as you know they'd been hunted from their country of birth. They were determined never to allow another to have that power over them again, so they searched for an area where the veil between the living and dead, the five planes of our existence, was thinner."

A shiver traced my spine once more, but it was muted thanks to the blanket.

"They decided building an army was the key to success," he continued. "When they stumbled onto this plot of land, it was sparse, almost barren outside of the surrounding forests. That piqued their curiosity, so they set foot on it only to feel the plethora of death that had taken place. So much death that no vegetation had regrown in the blood-soaked fields."

Goose bumps added to the shivers down my spine, but I was intensely hooked.

"Ten thousand perished here in the two-year conflict," Professor Jones's whisper still boomed somehow, "and as this soil absorbed the bodies and blood of the fallen, it left behind an energy that called to the necromancers."

No wonder it was the most prestigious college in America, if not the entire world. There was an energy of death here, and life forces were the strongest energy of all.

"They called the dead first to be their army, to protect them and build the original buildings for the college. From the moment they came up with their plan, they decided that for an army to be truly loyal, they needed to be the ones to train them. So, the college was born. They sent magical envoys across the worlds and invited all witches and warlocks, provided they had enough power, of course."

Of course. No one wanted an army filled with weaklings.

"Across the world?" someone asked. "Before they had transports to get around so easily?"

Professor Jones nodded. "Oh, yes. It took near another year

before students arrived, and then ten more years before the college grew in reputation, and they no longer had to recruit."

"And so their training began," Logan drawled. "Until they created their own version of the power and control which had been stolen from them."

Professor Jones observed the spellcaster for a beat. "Why, yes. Favoring necromancy, as was to be expected, to contain the absolute plethora of death that exists below our feet. If a headmaster controlled this school who wasn't a necromancer, who knows what might happen."

That made me think about the monsters I thought I saw last night. "Did you feel the blanket drop around the school last night?" I whispered to Belle.

She lifted her head from where she was taking notes, giving me an assessing look. "No, I didn't. What time? I can check with Dad."

Yeah, he was about the last person I wanted to discuss any of this with now. "It's okay, don't bother your dad about it." I shot her a reassuring smile. "Totally not important."

She narrowed her eyes but didn't argue, finishing her notes as the professor wrapped his story for the day. The bell chimed, so it was time for lunch, and then water class by the lake. I still sat out of this lesson, so I decided to skip and take the time to research—I needed to find the book Elder Monroe had mentioned.

He'd been trying to make a point, and I wanted to know what it was.

"Ready for lunch?" Belle asked as we exited into the hallway.

"Yep," I said in a rush, my stomach grumbling. "I just need to visit the library quickly—but I'll meet you there."

"Actually, she won't be meeting you. Hurry along, little water elemental."

Belle's mouth fell open at the interruption, and before I could blink there was a warlock on either side of me. Mint and evergreen intermingled with leather and oak as their strong energies collided with mine. Tilting my head back, I wasn't surprised to see Logan and Noah caging me between them, but just because I wasn't surprised didn't mean everyone else wasn't. The noise and traffic ground to a halt around us, and I ground my teeth in response.

"Excuse me." I injected every ounce of *go fuck yourselves* into those two words. "Are you two in charge of my schedule now?"

"We are," Logan confirmed cheerfully, "and you're booked in for extra training."

My friends stood there, looking between me and the boys, no doubt wondering what I wanted them to do. "How does 'fuck off' sound? It has a certain ring to it, and I think you might enjoy giving it a sho—"

Logan grasped my right arm, Noah my left, and before I could drop every four-letter word in my vocabulary, they lifted me off my feet and started marching through the hallway, students parting for them.

"Call if you need some help," Belle yelled after us, sounding like she was laughing.

Traitor.

"No need," I snarled. "I'll murder them on my own."

And enjoy every second of it.

When we reached Ancot, I cleared my throat. "You can put me down now. I get your point." They'd expertly demonstrated that I was a bug compared to their size and strength, and there was no way for me to fight their command. Best to just shut up and fall in line.

To my surprise, they did place me back on my feet, and I rubbed my arms. Not that they'd hurt me, but their energy was strong enough to leave an invisible residue behind. "That was completely unnecessary." I straightened my uniform. "But you've made your point. We're training. What's first?"

"First, you're coming to the gym with us. You can eat after you work out."

Logan strode off, and I fought down my next argument. I needed this shit over so I could get to the library and find that book. Noah lifted an eyebrow, remaining behind me as a living cage, and I wrinkled my nose at him. "Your master left. Hope you're not on a choke chain."

My aim was to create a little dissonance between them, but Noah just threw his head back and laughed. "Move your ass. This dog bites."

I bet he did.

He trailed me all the way to the gym, and I debated throwing myself into the lake on the way just to get out of this. It wasn't that I was an unfit person—I'd been in modern dancing, ice skating, and roller-skating for years—but I hated the gym. Lifting weights looked horrific, and why the Hel would I run unless I was being chased?

Inside, they led me to the female locker room, and apparently I had my own locker, filled with brand-new sweats and a sports bra. All in my size. Because that wasn't creepy.

Back in the weights room, surrounded by equipment that I couldn't name under the threat of death, I was tortured by two assholes. Logan and Noah took turns working out and barking orders at me, handing me weight after weight, all the while counting reps of suffering. Most of my time was spent breathing, internally crying, and imagining all the ways I'd destroy them when I figured out my powers.

"For you to be strong enough to handle your powers, you need to be physically stronger," Logan barked at me, while Noah bench-pressed the equivalent of a small car nearby.

"There's literally no evidence of that," I huffed as my arm shook. "I might be a nature sprite, and need to be gentle."

Logan shook his head. "Do you even pay attention in class? All affinities are built from a similar source of power. From the magic of our ancestors, the world around us, and the dead realms. How it emerges from our bodies depends on genetics and fate, but all of us need the same strengths. Even the sprites, gentle as they may be, are strong enough to call the wild creatures."

Fucker. I hated when he made sense. I preferred to argue with him. Us agreeing went against the laws of the very nature we drew power from.

When they were satisfied that the physical torture was complete for the day, he gave me ten minutes for water and a sandwich, but my stomach was churning, and I couldn't bring myself to take a bite. "You need to eat, Precious," Logan said, demolishing his three sandwiches. Noah had four.

I leveled him with my best glare, hoping I wasn't as green as I felt. "Should have thought of that before you made me do burpees. I think I'd prefer you to bring the monsters back to kill me next time."

His eyes flashed mossy, but he didn't say anything as he nudged the plate toward me. I managed two bites before we moved on to the next part of the training: affinities. One by one, he used his power to draw out mine, as he'd done those months ago in spellcaster lessons.

It worked too. When his energy drew on mine, I could touch all the elements strongly. I went from a small puff of air that blew out a candle, to a tornado that almost took out the wall in the sparring room. Logan and Noah got that fixed up, and then we moved on.

"How the Hel do you do this to my power?" I held a large ball of fire in my hand.

Logan withdrew his energy and I watched the flame die down into a flicker. Without the key, the magic was dulled. My new aim for the week was to find a key that wasn't Logan Kingston.

"I don't get it," I said, slumping to the padded mats with a groan. The weights were an hour of torture, but the affinity lessons might have been even worse. "Have you ever heard of another who needed this sort of key to unlock their power?"

Logan and Noah stood over me, looking as if they could train for the rest of the day and not break a sweat. If I hadn't been completely destroyed, I'd be embarrassed by my general lack of stamina and muscles.

"I've never heard of it," Noah said with a shrug. "But that doesn't mean it hasn't happened before. It might not be common, but it also isn't impossible. You're living proof."

Logan crouched down until we were eye level. "You're a puzzle," he said. "You were when you were four, and you remain so now. Don't expect to fit in the same slot as everyone else." He straightened abruptly, and I refused to admit that I missed the heat of his energy. "But you're also woefully underdeveloped in magic and muscle. You need to strengthen every part of yourself. Training again on Wednesday, don't make us track you down."

As they strolled off and left me a sweaty puddle, I knew that if I tried to get out of this again, the next time, I wouldn't be escorted quite so politely.

CHAPTER 32

That night as I crawled into bed, muscles aching in places that I didn't even know had muscles, I tried to get comfortable enough to sleep. Those bastards were master torturers, and I wondered if I'd survive our next training on Wednesday.

The air through my open window was cool. I enjoyed the change of season as we headed for fall and the end of the year. I was no closer to finding my affinity, but I'd grown a lot as a witch since the day I first walked through Weatherstone's gates. Grown, but there was a part of me that felt more lost than ever before.

Especially about Logan.

Dad's fears regarding the spellcaster might not have come to fruition, but that didn't mean he hadn't completely impacted my year anyway. He was still a riddle wrapped in a mystery inside an enigma, or however the idiom went. He was a stranger, and yet our energies worked together as if we were the best friends he ironically called us.

Were we still enemies? I had no idea.

We certainly weren't friends, but maybe we'd evolved into friendly enemies? There was no creepy chill down my spine around Logan, but there was a scorching energy that completely messed with my internal composure.

If I hadn't been borrowing our fathers' war, I would have known long ago that it wasn't Logan's magic creating the monsters. I'd felt it enough now to recognize the subtle tendrils, tinted in a dark untraceable energy. Logan's power was as blazing as the summer sun, and as dangerous if you got too close.

He didn't hide in shadows; he had no need to.

Rolling over in bed, I hugged the pillow against me, and tried not to mope over the fact that I wasn't wearing his hoodie. I'd been angry at his arrogant handling during our training, but now I missed the soft lengths against my skin.

Eventually I drifted off, the cool breezes caressing my face as I snuggled deep in the bed. Sleep was restful until my mind shifted into the dreamscape.

His mouth pressed against mine, and as our tongues tangled I wondered if I would die from the heady taste of the warlock. He was dominant, demanding control, demanding everything. My body thrummed as he stroked his hands along my sensitive skin, and I felt the brush of the thick head of his cock poised at my entrance. He pushed slowly inside me, spreading my pussy to its limits with his size. "Logan," I sobbed, shifting my legs so they were wider apart, giving him the access he demanded.

"Shhh, Precious," he murmured. "Don't fight me any longer."

That sentence settled uneasily. I hadn't fought Logan for months. As he slid until he was fully seated, I moaned and completely forgot that thought.

"Isn't this much better than mons—?"

A large crack of thunder woke me, the rain pouring as the scent of storm and ember drifted through my window. Jerking myself up in bed, my body felt as if it were literally vibrating. My hands glowed as I held them up before me—the first time I'd ever woken to my magic spilling. Pressing my hands against my sweaty forehead, I tried to bring myself back to reality. But goddesses be damned, that felt realer than any sex I'd had in my life.

My legs shook as I stood, muscles aching, but not as bad

as the ache between my thighs. Unsure what to do, I was debating the danger in showering off the sweat, and possibly finishing what the dream started, when I felt a press against my door's entrance pad.

His energy hit me as I hurried over on shaky legs to wrench the door open and come face-to-perfect-chest with Logan's artwork. Lifting my gaze, I reached his face, and blanched. It'd been a while since I'd seen this particular expression, dark and feral. The spellcaster looked half out of control.

He pressed into my personal space, and I was too stunned to move away. "What the Hel are you doing to me?"

He was covered in a sheen of sweat too, his chest heaving as if he was winded, when I knew the warlock could easily run for two hours. "Doing to you? I'm doing nothing to you," I bit out, wishing I didn't sound so breathy. "I haven't left my room since dinner."

He pushed into me again, and this time I took a step back. "You're haunting my dreams, Precious," he rumbled, like a legit rumble spilled from the wide expanse of his chest. "When I close my eyes, you're there."

He was still stalking forward as I backed away, until I felt the wind and rain hit my back through the open window. "Haunting your dreams?" I echoed, blinking a few times. My frazzled brain was finally putting some of it together. "We're having the same dreams?"

That took him by surprise, but he recovered in an instant. "Tell me about your dreams."

The demand had my chest heaving, the hard peaks of my nipples pressing against my white tank. At this point, I'd have taken the embarrassment of wearing Logan's hoodie over my braless state. "I dream about you," I whispered, breathing so deeply our chests almost touched. "All the fucking time." *And it's driving me insane.*

The unsaid words were as heavy as those that slipped past my lips.

Logan rested his hands on the windowsill on either side of me, caging me in as he'd done the other night. He hadn't touched me yet, but I was surrounded by the heat he naturally exuded. I had to clench my fists to stop myself from grabbing him and dragging him between my thighs.

He was close enough to read the arousal on my face, his gaze sliding over mine. The ice darkened to moss as he cursed. In a flash, his hands captured my face, and before I could part my lips for my next breath, his lips collided with mine.

I swear time stopped, this single beat where Logan tasted my mouth like a drowning man, and I wondered if I'd fallen into dreamland again. My body, still throbbing from the unfulfilled dream, opened to him like he was the very nectar of the goddesses. The kiss was devastating, and desperate, and he dominated the pace as he always did. One of his hands slid down my ass, and I gasped when he lifted me with ease, resting my butt cheeks on the ledge of the sill, my poor herbs shoved to the side.

Logan stripped away my clothes in one swipe of his energy, and lowered his head to capture my right nipple, while his fingers worked the hard tip of my left. "Fucking Hel!" I tried to muffle my cry, unsuccessfully.

By the time he kissed along my stomach and pressed his mouth to my clit, I was ready to explode. I tilted my hips to give him access, and his movements were jerkier as he ran his tongue over me and groaned, tasting me in an uncontrolled way, taking what he wanted, driving me to the brink of sanity.

Sliding my hands into the thick, soft strands of his dark hair, I tightened my hold and rode his face, half of my body out the window. I'd have fallen if Logan didn't have an unbreakable hold on me.

The swirls in my stomach exploded and I cried out, jerking against him. He tightened his hands, his tongue relentless as he plunged it inside me, lapping up my orgasm. He wrung out every ounce of pleasure and then some, and when I was hanging limply in his arms, breathing heavily, I wondered if he was about to leave just as he had done last time.

Well, last time he kicked me out, but same same.

I gasped when he slid his hands under my ass, gripping me and lifting me into his big body. Logan was a monster of a warlock, huge everywhere. Even with his pants on I could feel his long, hard length pressing into me. I wrapped my legs around his waist, that orgasm barely taking the edge off. We had months of pent-up dreams between us, and there was no stopping what needed to happen tonight.

"Are you spelled against pregnancy?"

Half out of my mind, I was coherent enough to answer. "Yes." I arched against him. "Spelled and free from sexually transmitted diseases."

This time the rumble from his chest was primal. "I'm free also," he said, and with that one sentence, the barrier of his pants disappeared as he thrust inside me.

Holy goddess.

Holy fucking goddess.

I wasn't a virgin, but Logan's size didn't just thrust easily, though he gave it his best shot. The burning stretch was a torturous ecstasy, much more addictive than any substance I'd known in my life. After a minute of those slow but firm thrusts, he was fully seated inside, a wild light burning in his eyes.

"Ready, Precious?" I wondered what would happen if I said no. Not that there was much chance of that, since I was already nodding. "Say it," he growled.

"Fuck me, Logan."

The feral in his gaze spilled across the rest of him, and when he thrust it was hard and fast. His powerful body entered mine, slamming my back against the wall beside my bed, and I could do nothing but hold on, pleasure rolling over me in waves. Once again, I barely lasted more than a few minutes before I broke apart. Orgasms from Logan were destructive perfection, and I wondered if I'd survive the next one.

Pleasure stole my sanity for what felt like an eternity, and I barely noticed Logan dropping onto the bed. He lay back and brought me with him to straddle either side of his powerful thighs.

I'd never had sex in this position before, but instinct lent me a helping hand, as my hips moved of their own accord. It all came down to chasing the next orgasm and finding the place to grind against him, stimulating both my clit and pleasure points deep inside my body.

Okay, why the fuck haven't I had sex like this before? This might be my new favorite position.

Logan let me set the pace, his hands taking the weight of my breasts, large enough to cup them as the rough skin of his thumb caught on my nipples. Eventually, his controlling nature kicked in, and his hands gripped my hips to hold me in place while he thrust hard and fast, sending me into a screaming orgasm. My third, but who was counting.

Me. It was me counting.

I'd been waking for months in the midst of an orgasm, and often with his name on my lips, which made tonight surreal in more ways than one. Familiar but also not.

Logan slowed his thrusts, and I wondered if I could lose my mind from the slow sensuous slide of his body into my still pulsing and sensitive pussy. "Why are you haunting my dreams, Paisley Hallistar?" When he locked me in his focus like this, I couldn't remember my fucking name, let alone answer questions. "Tell me why?"

"I don't know," I sobbed, unable to handle this feeling. "I can't expl—explain it."

Logan's body tensed as he came, and the moment I felt the pulse of his cock, followed by his power, I couldn't help but tumble into that pleasure with him.

My body was spent as I slumped forward to rest against his chest, the thud of his heart under my ear comforting. He wrapped me up, holding me close, and I wondered if all along the dreams had been trying to bring us together, to drive us out of our minds with months of sexual frustration and need, culminating in what happened here tonight.

In my exhaustion, I drifted to the beat of his heart and pulse of his burning power, and when I woke the next morning, I was alone. Alone and wondering if I'd dreamed all of that again.

Except, I woke in one of his hoodies. A deep green one, close in color to the moss his eyes turned when he was channeling strong emotions. I woke surrounded by minty evergreen, with new aches between my thighs.

CHAPTER 33

"Move faster, Paisley!"

Logan's voice was a snap, and it took every ounce of my control not to throw the flames in my hands at him. Since the night our dreams drove us together, Logan and I had fallen into a weird relationship. There'd been no repeat of the best sex of my life, but he watched me closer now, with this fire burning in the icy green depths of his eyes.

Whether that fire was need or hate, I really couldn't tell. He was expert level at schooling his features.

The one constant, though, was my training.

My power had grown under his, and I could do much more now than call the elements. Animals came to me in the forest, and whenever we got close to the graveyard, I felt layers of darkness. Layers I couldn't sort between, but I felt them.

Today we were by the lake so Logan could throw fireballs at me. His touch unlocked my energy, but he didn't need to stay touching me now. Once he initially released my power, I was able to access my magic the same as everyone else. This distance allowed additional training. Like throwing a fucking fireball at me. The first time he did, I'd shrieked at the anticipation of my hand melting, only to catch it like a harmless ball.

"Your abilities are lazy," he drawled. "The power is there, but the desire to express it remains lacking."

"Incorrect," I shot back. "The desire to express my power is very much . . . unlacking. Or whatever. I want to use my magic, I'm sick of being limited to chants and spellwork through herbs."

I released the fireball in his direction—he wanted me to be quicker, right?—and muttered an incantation under my breath while I clutched the amethyst and aquamarine I'd stashed in my pocket earlier. Gran's photos indicated those two would give me a power boost.

Logan, deflecting the fire like it was nothing more than a fly, then jolted at the extra blast of my power which followed. "What are you doing?"

"Shouldn't you know, spellcaster?" I shot back, continuing with the incantation. This particular spell required it to be said five times while channeling power. My magic swirled and heated, my other hand glowing bright, and with a thunder-loud crack, Logan was flipped upside down and tethered to the branches of the oak tree above.

"See you at next training," I called, strolling away as Logan glared down.

There was a thud as he landed a moment later, too strong to be contained by a simple spell, but at least I'd used an active magic. If I could just figure out the way to use the crystals to enhance what I already had, and maybe unlock my magic without Logan, I'd finally come into my own.

It was late Friday afternoon, and when I made it back to the dorms the school was buzzing. There was a huge party, college-organized this time, tonight in the chapel. It was the Blue Harvest Moon Festival, a night for some of the strongest energy. Under the blue moon we would bathe in her power and renew our own.

There was no debating whether I would go or not; Belle would hex the shit out of me if I didn't. She'd gotten very good at underhanded spellwork, and her current obsession was with hex bags. She needed to stretch her magical muscles, but not in the same way as me. She was already excelling in most classes, leaving her to strive for more.

We all enjoyed the subtle yet destructive magic of a good hex.

When I reached my room, as predicted there were three witches waiting outside the door. Sara and Belle chatted while Haley read a paperback.

"You got your book order?" I said to her, excitement twirling in my stomach. "Any good ones?"

She jumped, so absorbed in her book she hadn't heard me approach. "Pais! Oh my God, yes." She pressed a hand to her chest. "The one I finished last night is absolutely perfect for you."

Haley was in her paperback era at the moment, deciding she needed the scent of a real book. When she finished a series, she gave me the good ones to read, and to my absolute shock, I'd read at least thirty paperbacks so far this year. I'd discovered a lot about myself at Weatherstone, but nothing more bizarre than my bestie turning me into a book-witch.

Haley rummaged in her bag, and I peered inside to see at least five books; any less and there'd be a real risk of running out of reading material.

"This one," she said, thrusting it forward. "Fair warning, the sequel isn't out yet, but it's about fae and these powerful gods who . . ." She swallowed roughly. "Look, they do this thing with their tongues and have very interesting, uh—" her voice got very low "—dicks. Anyway. I'm going to need you to read it so we can discuss."

Trying hard to suppress my smile, I took the proffered book, noting the pretty cover, the title in large typography with glittery symbols around. "No sequel yet though?"

I'd also discovered I was not a patient person, and the wait for the next books in a series drove me a little insane.

"Just read it," she snapped, before calming herself once more. "Please."

I laughed, unoffended. Her passion for books was one of my favorite parts of her personality. "You got it, Hales. I'll get back to you with my thoughts soon."

Belle, who had no time or interest for fiction books, tapped her foot impatiently. "You need to get your ass ready, Paisley Hallistar. The event starts in thirty minutes."

"I'll be ready in twenty," I promised, and with that I hurried into my room and the girls followed. While they sprawled out on my bed, I rushed to the showers for a quick rinse, brushed my teeth, and slapped on some makeup.

We were nearing the end of my favorite month: October. All Hallows' Eve was around the corner, where we would not only party, but partake in a mass spelling through the school to raise our collective energies on the night when the veil between the living and the dead was the thinnest. In a school built by necromancers, it was highly celebrated, and was graduation day for us all.

It was hard to believe we were so close to graduation, but for now I was focused on this party.

Dressed in jeans and a tank top, I threw a black leather jacket over top and slipped on my black boots. My hair was left down, and it was freshly blow-dried—thanks to Sara's air power. She might have taken a while to claim her affinity, but was more than excelling at all air related activities these days.

"Okay, we good to go?" Belle asked, face lit up with excitement. "I'm ready for a boost." The blanket wouldn't stop us absorbing the moon's energy, but it would stop us doing anything too fun with the extra power. "Oh, and, Pais, I asked about that book in the library. The one Dad mentioned, and they don't have any record of it. Did you find out?"

We hadn't spoken about her father since parents' weekend. I'd checked long ago with the library and knew they didn't have a copy. Haley hadn't been able to find it in the bookstores her family ordered from for her either. It was growing abundantly clear that this information wasn't easy or simple to track down. I planned on searching harder when I returned home and could get to some of my favorite witchy stores.

"Can't find it anywhere," I admitted.

Belle's face fell. "What about the witch massacre he referenced?"

Now that one wasn't as hard, but it was as equally frustrating. "Found it, but not enough information in the text to make sense. I have all these questions, but the answers are vague and confusing."

"I hate vague and confusing," she muttered, and I was right there with her.

"I found it mentioned in multiple historical tomes, but only in the most minute of details. Odd, considering they keep referring to it as one of the largest witch massacres in our history. Witches killed by our kind. Allegedly these witches were dabbling in magic they shouldn't have, and they referred to them as demon-witches. Then they cut their heads off."

"Demon-witches . . ." Haley wrinkled her brow. "What does that mean?"

That was the frustrating-as-fuck part. "I have no idea. I read every single text but there was never more detail than that."

"We need that book," Belle said decisively. "I bet that has more detail. I'm going to push Dad over the break." As much as I wanted to call off her talking to her dad about it, he already had all the information, so we might as well make him useful.

When we were on the way to the festival, Belle's worried expression eased up as we joined the hundreds of students streaming outside. This was a night to relax and absorb this moon energy that only flowed once a year. With no threat of monsters hanging over us, we could enjoy this college milestone.

Unless, whoever was behind the creatures, was waiting for a night like this. Waiting to use the preternatural boost of energy that I already felt ebbing and flowing in the air. If there was ever a night for the culmination of a monster plan, it was tonight.

After that terrifying thought, I felt *very relaxed*, and didn't jump at random noises around us. *Right*.

"You seem jumpy," Belle said, side-eyeing me when I flinched. A student raced past, already half-naked, eyes glazed from the power.

"What, no," I replied in a rush. "Very calm. I . . . just need a drink."

Or eight. Regular alcohol would not get the buzz going that I desired.

At a college-sanctioned party, there'd be nothing stronger, so I'd just have to drink hard and fast. Even a small reprieve from my brain would be better than nothing. Not that I wanted to be pissed off with myself, but why did my mind choose this year to start attacking me? The bloom of my magic brought sexy dreams, uneasy darkness trailing down my spine, and wonky magic into my life. It was a lot—and not enough at the same time.

We moved around the students scattered across the grassy area and inside the massive chapel. The chapel itself was longer and wider than the library—aka former chapel—and easily housed the full four years of students and professors at Weatherstone. When we entered the building, a warlock with curly red hair rushed right over to us, and I caught the distinct scent of lavender as he held a tray out to us. Along with a telltale sign of that pearlescent foam to indicate that they were serving witch wine.

"Seriously?" Belle gaped, looking at me.

I nodded. "I see it too," I breathed.

"What in the love of Selene is happening?" Sara asked, already reaching for a glass.

The warlock's grin was lascivious, and it bothered me. "It's limited," he drawled, "the glasses are spelled to look like regular wine, so don't mention it, okay?" The smarmy wink at the end was not needed. We already got he was a creep.

We picked up glasses, mostly so we could get away from him, and I took a small drink. I'd only ever had a sip before of my parents' wine, and as soon as that burn trailed down my throat and heated my chest, I knew I needed to go easy.

If this was a prime time for another monster encounter, I couldn't let my guard down.

The four of us strolled around the chapel, Belle and Sara downing their first glass of wine in gulps, while Haley followed my example and gingerly sipped at hers. It was earthy, not like dirt, but filled with fresh herbs and an energy that I'd never tasted before.

When I was half a glass in, I'd more than achieved my desired buzz, my stresses fading away. We explored all the energy inside the glass-ceilinged chapel and then left the building to chat under the direct moonlight. The blue-tinged orb was huge in the clear sky, the air crisp, as the landscape of the college tinted in shades of blue and black.

I let my head fall back, feeling the brush of preternatural energy across my skin. Weatherstone was a beacon for power, and every time I set foot in this place, I found myself energized.

Terrified and energized.

"Little Gem!" I opened my eyes to find Dad and Jenna in front of me.

"Dad, what the freaking Hel are you doing here?" I rasped, before clearing my throat. If I didn't calm my ass, he'd be on to the witch wine in seconds. He eyed me closely and I cursed myself, knowing it was too late. Leaning forward, he sniffed at my glass, recognizing the scent as I had.

"Witch wine," he grumbled. "And on the night when I'm one of the warlocks on duty."

I waited for his anger, and to have the wine swiftly confiscated, but he shocked me when he leaned forward and kissed me on the forehead. "Be careful, sweetheart," he whispered against my hair. "Go and have fun with your friends."

Swallowing roughly, I stared at him. "You're not going to confiscate all the wine getting around?"

He shook his head. "If I don't see it, then I can't know it's there." His wink was subtle. "I was young once. Limit yourself, though, and be careful."

Jenna grinned. "Very careful, little sis. This is the bootlegged version. I think it's even more potent than the usual stuff."

Bootlegged, hey. That might explain that undercurrent of darkness.

Jenna's hug was firm, an all-encasing hug that she'd been giving me for as long as I could remember. She wrapped up every part of me and felt like home. As she released me, she was already falling into conversation with Dad again, the pair walking off discussing her coven choices for next year.

I found myself smiling like a weirdo who knew how blessed she was to have such an amazing family. Turning to find my friends, I locked eyes with Logan, who stood just behind me with Noah, close enough to hear that conversation but not so close that I could tell if they were deliberately listening in.

My stomach tightened, and I wished I had no explanation for it, but I knew. There was a draw to this infuriating spellcaster that I couldn't explain. Not even my freshman year of college had cleared up any of the confusion. If anything, it was worse than ever,

I took a hesitant step toward him, unsure what the Hel I was thinking, but as his jaw tightened and he shook his head, I ground to a halt. *Wait*. Nope. That asshole didn't get to dictate when we talked. Or . . . engaged . . . in other activities.

I wasn't his dirty little secret.

With another dark glint, he turned and walked away, and by the time my feet moved to intercept him and demand answers, there was no sign of the powerful warlocks. Even if they were both taller than the general population of warlocks here.

Dammit.

You can run, spellcaster. But I would not let him hide.

I'd find him at some point tonight and we'd have this long overdue conversation. The witch wine had me braver and determined to get to the bottom of the Logan mystery. This chick could only handle so many mysteries in one year.

Taking another sip, I was just under the halfway mark, and could most likely keep a nice buzz all night just from this glass alone. Of course, the best-laid plans often go off course, especially when one fumed about a warlock. A useless fucking mysterious powerful asshole of a warlock.

Two hours later, on my third glass of witch wine, I found myself buzzed to the point of sloshed, and there was only one person to blame.

Logan. The bastard.

"Who the fuck does he think he is?" I raged sloppily.

"Treating me like I'm nothing. Then fucking me the next night. He thinks I'm just his booty-witch, and I tell you what . . ." I threw my glass in the air, sloshing the sticky wine across my hand. "I'll put a stop to that very soon. It will only happen at least four more times, but then I'm done."

Belle grasped my hand, swaying. Or was I swaying? Maybe it was the ground. Yep, the ground was swaying. "That barth-turd," she slurred. "Youith perfect. He's perfect. Wathis the isshoo here."

"Exactly," Sara crowed from my other side, also on the swaying ground. "How dare he hurt our friend. We should hex him."

What could I say, we were big into hexes. "Great idea," I declared, attempting to take a step, but the ground decided to also dip as it swayed. What the fuck? Were we dancing here or something?

"Not a great idea," Haley said with a snort of laughter. She'd somehow managed to sip only a quarter of her witch wine, and was very far behind the rest of us in this race. "I think maybe we should get you back to the dorms now."

"I could shleep here," Belle said, yawning suddenly. "It's a nice rocking boath."

The air grew cooler as water coated her skin, and I looked up for rain, but it was just her power soaking up the moisture in the air. "Definitely time for the dorms," I muttered, shaking my head in an attempt to sober up. A failed attempt. "Okay, let's go."

Looping my arms around Belle, I held her against me, and as the drunk led the drunk, we stumbled through the students. Over them too, as many were with Belle, wanting to sleep on the *nice rocking boath*.

When we reached the steps leading up to Ancot, we stared

at them, wondering if it was even possible for us to make it to the top in our current inebriation. Placing my foot on the first step, it shook worse than the ground.

The moon's energy was really having a party with the Earth tonight.

"No, you're drunk, you idiot," Haley said, shaking her head. "I told you three not to keep taking glasses of wine. You're going to regret this tomorrow."

"Tomorrow, tomorrow," Belle sang, very off-key, and I'd found one of the very few talents she didn't possess. Girl was not making choir, that was for sure.

Swallowing hard and trying to focus through blurry vision and swaying ground, I lifted my foot to take the next step and immediately toppled backward, taking Belle with me. I grunted when my arm and side slammed into the ground, and not even a second later, I forgot my pain as I was hauled up against a hard chest, a recognizable scent surrounding me. "Logan," I murmured.

His laughter was as dark as that fucking witch wine. "Precious, you're always testing my limits."

I mumbled another lot of nonsense but managed to ask about Belle.

"Noah has your friends," he said as he strode up the stairs. My head spun hard at the motion, and I couldn't tell if it was the wine or the spellcaster. Both were completely intoxicating.

"Why do you hate me?" I mumbled, eyes closing.

Logan didn't answer, continuing up the stairs, carrying me like I weighed nothing. Which was absolute horseshit. I was not a small woman. I was tall and had curves and liked to eat.

He showed no sign of strain. Dammit. Why was that hot? Stupid witch wine and hormones.

"Who said I hated you, best friend?" I'd come to learn that he used the *best friend* nickname when he wanted to deflect. "Let's get you to bed, Paisley. Before you find yourself in trouble."

"Trouble's my midd—"

There was a bang from behind us as Logan reached the landing. He turned and I managed to pry my blurry eyes open. "Fire?" I breathed. "Is it an elemental?"

Before Logan could even respond, my eyes closed once more, and I lost the battle with consciousness.

CHAPTER 34

I was dying.

Again.

Only this time the monster was me. Or my lack of restraint when it came to witch wine, to be more accurate.

A relentless hammer slammed into my head, pounding as my stomach rolled in ways that couldn't be normal. I'd thrown up in my trash can once already, leaving nothing in my stomach except the aftereffects of the wine.

"Fucking Hel," I groaned. "What's happening?"

When they'd said witch wine was potent shit, they'd vastly understated just how potent.

Bleary eyed, I pulled myself to stand, swaying for a second before balance kicked in. When I was sure I could walk without vomiting again, I headed for the showers, and almost drowned myself for an hour, drinking water straight from the showerhead. My body was so parched that no matter how much water I drank, my mouth remained a desert, and my breath could have melted paintwork.

"How many times have you brushed your teeth?"

This question came from another witch standing at the sink, toothbrush in hand.

"Three," I mumbled. "One for every glass of wine I had. It's not getting better."

She groaned, her blond hair lank around her face, dark

circles ringing her eyes. "I know. Who the fuck let me drink witch wine?"

"I fully planned on stopping at one glass," I said, giving up on the toothbrush because I was wearing my teeth out at this point.

"I had four," she choked around her own toothbrush. "And now I'm planning on crawling back into bed and trying not to die."

Goddess be damned. "Girl . . ."

That was all I could get out, because three felt like death, so four must be way worse.

When I was done, I left the bathroom clad in a robe and slippers, my hair wet and stringy. The hot water hadn't completely revived me, but I did feel slightly more awake and alive. In my room I dressed in pajamas and picked up my favorite healing clear quartz. Pressing it against my chest, there was instant relief as the pounding headache and churning gut eased.

As I settled into bed, someone knocked on my door, and with a groan I dragged my ragged ass off my comfortable mattress. When I opened the door, Jenna, Alice, Trevor, and Jensen were standing in my doorway.

They looked grim.

"What?" I burst out, my hangover not exactly forgotten, but pushed way down. "What happened?"

"Dad's been suspended without pay." Trevor never was one to beat around the bush. He pushed his way into the room. "We need to get home and find out what happened."

"Suspended without pay," I repeated, shaking my head. "What? Why?"

Jenna pressed her hand to my forehead. "I told you to go easy on the wine, Pais. You look like death."

Waving her off, because we had far larger problems than a hangover, I repeated my question.

"The witch wine," Jensen said grimly. I turned my gaze on him to find his eyes blazing, frantic. The coolheaded water elemental was nowhere to be found. "The chapel burned down last night, and they found out about the witch wine. Dad oversaw the event, and he was reported to the headmaster as having known about the wine and not putting a stop to it."

"The chapel burned down . . ." I breathed, confusion adding another layer to the pounding in my head. "How?"

There was a brief flash of memory, that red against the sky, and . . . Logan. He'd carried me back to my room. He had to be the one, because I'd woken in another one of his damn hoodies again. A factor I'd been ignoring over the more pressing need of *not dying from witch wine.*

"Quite a few were injured, and the library was damaged down one side, but thankfully it was minimal," Alice whispered, her skin pale and dark circles ringed her eyes. I got the feeling hers weren't from the wine.

"You said someone reported Dad to the headmaster. Who? A student?"

How could they have known, except if they were nearby when Dad sniffed my drink. Could it have been Logan or Noah? They'd been behind me and had all the reason to want to destroy the warlock with a blood oath against him. Dad was the sole money earner in our huge family, at least until the twins graduated. We'd be in trouble without his salary and benefits.

If that asshole had been playing the long game all along, I was going to fucking kill him. Later, though, because we were heading home to see our parents first.

"Give me five minutes," I said, shooing them out the door. "I'll get dressed."

Throwing on jeans and a dark green sweater, I swept my hair back into a ponytail and slapped on a little concealer for the dark circles. Stepping out of my dorm, my family stood stiffly in the hall, none of them saying a word. "Let's go."

Jenna set off first, marching through the hallway. "I've organized the transport, since Dad left early this morning. His access to the school is revoked pending their investigation."

I was freaking fuming at this point. Dad hadn't been the only one in charge last night—I'd seen at least three other professors. "Were the other professors on last night suspended too?"

"Only Dad," Trevor growled, running his hand through his dark hair until it stood on end. "The others claimed they were unaware, and since there were no complaints about them knowing, their word was taken for it."

There were spells to determine if someone was telling the truth or not, but unless you had a court order, it wasn't enforceable. Those three probably allowed the truth spell, but Dad couldn't, for obvious reasons. No matter what happened, he would look guilty now.

Jenna picked up the pace, leaving the rest of us to rush after her. We made it through the college and out to the front gate in record time. Students glanced our way, but most were as bleary eyed as I'd been not an hour earlier. Outside, a scent of ash and smoke lingered in the air, mild, but distinct enough that I knew the fire had happened. As that scent settled inside, dread settled in my gut.

I had a bad feeling about this. The sort of bad that could irrevocably change our lives. "Is there anything we can do?" I asked, since my siblings were still walking in this unnatural silence. "Go to the headmaster ourselves and tell him that there was no way for Dad to know. As the wine was spelled to look like regular drinks."

The warlocks with the trays of drinks had it all worked out as well. They carried two trays with them, and any time a chaperone went for a drink, they switched out to the regular alcohol.

"We need to talk to Dad first," Jenna said, her bite of impatience growing into a chomp. "Talking to anyone now could make it worse for him."

The gates opened for us, and when we reached the hut for outgoing travel, the panel was already geared to Jenna's magic. All she had to do was press her hand to it and the swirl of energy appeared. Stepping through, we found ourselves on the back porch, where we usually transported. The back yard was private, the forest blanketing all sides.

The door was open, as always, and when we marched inside to find Mom and Dad in the kitchen, coffee in hand, they didn't look surprised to see us.

"Dad," Alice cried, hurrying around to him. "I'm so sorry."

She threw herself at him, as if she were a young child still, and he stood in time to capture her in one of his famous bear hugs. Morris's came close, but nothing compared to a Dad hug.

"It's okay," he said to her, voice soothing. He lifted his head and took us all in. "It's going to be completely okay. This is standard procedure after a complaint was issued, but I'm sure it'll all be sorted soon."

He sounded so calm. He looked calm too, with none of the panic I expected to see or hear in his words. Mom got to her feet with a gentle smile. "Coffees all around?"

"Oh my goddess, yes," Jensen crowed, falling into one of the dining room chairs. "I'm exhausted."

Mom shook her head, but bustled around the kitchen filling cups for us, knowing each of our preferences for milk, cream, half and half, and sugar. She knew I loved mine milky and sweet, and piping hot. She knew us better than anyone in the world, and these little moments made me appreciate my family so much.

Showing our love through kind gestures was part of the Hallistar way, and with my hangover fading away with each sip of my perfect coffee, I gave thanks to the goddess for her blessings.

"Do you have a backup plan if they decide to fire Dad?" Trevor asked, nursing his cup but not drinking yet. He was the most pessimistic of us all, and despite the relaxed atmosphere we'd walked into here, he wasn't buying it.

"They won't fire him," Mom said reassuringly. "He's worked for the college for over fifteen years, and he's one of their most valuable dual elementals. The headmaster will no doubt call him in for a meeting on Monday, and we'll have more information."

"Who told him about the wine?" I asked Dad. "Or more importantly, who told him that you knew about it and let it slide?"

Mom shook her head but didn't look disappointed that I was ignoring her advice to let it go for now. She'd expected me to dig further, and if anything, hints of amusement played around the corners of her lips.

"I have no idea," Dad said. "I should have put a stop to it though. We're lucky no one was killed in the fire."

"Because of your father," Mom added, bite coming into her tone as she defended her soulmate. "He wasn't even on duty at that point, but he hadn't left for home yet. He felt the elemental surge and raced back to bring it under control."

Dad shook his head. "It was magically enhanced, so all I could do was hold off the flames long enough for everyone to get out with minimal injuries. But I couldn't save the building."

"You saved the library though." Dad was a book lover, and he'd freak out at the thought of all that information being lost to fire.

"Most of it," he said with a smile. "But that building has many protective spells on it anyway."

"Why didn't the chapel have the same protections?" Trevor demanded.

Dad smiled at his son's ire, recognizing the flames. "Because it's a much newer building. The older ones still have the protection of the elders. They just never get around to blessing the new ones the same way."

"This fucking sucks," Trevor groaned.

"Language," Mom admonished. "Now, are you all staying the night?"

"Absolutely." Alice crossed her arms, elfin features uncharacteristically stubborn. The rest of us didn't bother to answer, because she spoke for all on this matter.

After that was decided, further chat about the fire and Dad's suspension was off the table, and we had a somewhat normal family day. Normal, but with sharp edges hanging over our heads, waiting to slice through our moments of happiness. Mom and Dad never let their worries show, but I sensed deep down they were putting on a show.

We weren't little kids any longer, but they protected us as if we were. I guess we would always be *their* kids.

Later that night, I woke dying of thirst once more—someone had better hex me if I ever touched witch wine again—and headed for the stairs so I could get water from the kitchen.

I paused when I heard voices.

"It's going to be okay, Tom," Mom said in a soft voice. Even knowing it was wrong, creepy, and invasive, I silently stepped closer.

"If I lose my job, we won't be able to afford the coven tithe," he replied, voice rough. "And there aren't many jobs available to those without covens."

"Then we get jobs in the human world," Mom suggested, a hint of her inner strength in those words. "I all but live as a human now, and I can do accountancy and crafting anywhere."

Dad's laugh was strangled. "I don't think there's much call for a teacher in the art of fire magic out in the human world."

"It's going to be okay," Mom repeated, and I wondered if she was trying to convince Dad or herself. "Let's get some sleep. There's nothing more we can do to help tonight. Tomorrow, we'll contact Blessed Souls and get some legal advice from the lawyers. We're not out of the fight yet."

There was silence for a beat, and I thought I heard kissing, so I crept back up the stairs and went to my room.

I knew they'd been putting on a brave front for us, but clearly if Dad lost his job, life was going to get much harder for the Hallistars. All the covens required a sizable yearly tithe, which was used to keep facilities functioning. This yearly contribution paid for protection, employment opportunities, and a multitude of other benefits. Including medical.

Not being able to pay the tithe meant you were removed from the coven. They were all due in January, so we had to get this dealt with before the start of the new school year.

Fucking great.

CHAPTER 35

When we returned to school for our last official week of college, I was midway through class on Monday when I realized that in my stress over Dad's suspension I'd forgotten to check out Gran's letters.

Not that it was a huge priority, with my focus now on figuring out how to get Dad's suspension lifted. My first point of call was Logan fucking Kingston, but he was doing his usual elusive bullshit. I'd even knocked on his door last night, but there had been no answer.

"Ms. Hallistar, you're not focusing," Professor Damone admonished as she walked past.

I'd moved on from fanning the flames of a candle out to lifting the lighter and lighting the wick all with my energy. I could manage it quite easily now. Logan, for all his annoyances, had succeeded in forcing my focus.

Focus and ability went hand in hand, and in most of my classes now I demonstrated moderate aptitude with that affinity. All of the affinities.

The professor paused as I lifted the lighter with ease and lit the candle before sending a puff of wind across to extinguish it. "Are you progressing this way with all the other elements?" she asked, and I nodded.

"Yes. Strangely, it's all clicked into place recently. I'm moving ahead finally."

She pursed her lips. "Interesting." With a sudden flick of her head, she waved her hand. "Marcus, come here, please."

Outside of a few polite words, Marcus and I had barely spoken in months, but I was aware that he'd been officially claimed as a spellcaster, one who showed promising growth as a powerful warlock. "Professor. Paisley," he said, flashing us a polite smile.

"Marcus, I'd like you to shadow Paisley here through her classes for the remainder of the week. She's showing signs of being a late-developing spellcaster who needs to learn how to manage her magic. It would be helpful, as a fellow emerging spellcaster, if you could give us a report on what you notice so we can discuss amongst the professors."

I wanted to protest, because it felt weird to be assessed by a fellow first-year, but I was worried that if I did, they'd ask Logan, and I'd be stuck trying not to murder him for eight hours a day. I needed to talk to him, but I didn't want to see him more than that.

Liar.

Shut up, Inner Voice, you horny bitch.

"Though," Marcus said, and to my surprise, he didn't sound annoyed. "I've wrapped most of my end-of-year assessments, and Paisley is great company."

I shot him a grateful grin; he was clearly going out of his way to not make me feel like a child with a babysitter. Professor Damone nodded. "Paisley has most of her assessments on Friday. We're giving her as much time as possible to control and release her power. We'll make the final judgment about her affinity in the assessment and be able to assign her classes for next year."

The final assessment was when we were tested on our affinity. It was undertaken at any point in October, and many had already completed theirs and were moving into different classes as a prelude to next year. Hence why none of my friends were in this class with me today. Marcus was only here because he was helping Professor Damone with another group.

Marcus returned to his group for the rest of the class but found me just as the bell rang. "Okay, so what's next for you?"

"Normally history, but because all non-assessment classes are done, it'll be our water elemental class by the lake."

"So, we've got a few hours," Marcus said with a nod.

"I planned on practicing for the assessment. It's crept up on me, what with all the . . . shit going on."

The smile faded slowly from his face. "I'm really sorry about your dad, Paisley. If it's any consolation, I think this was an unfair and out-of-line punishment, considering he wasn't the only chaperone."

I agreed, but as my throat grew tighter, I decided I really didn't want to talk about this today. I had to focus on assessment, or I wouldn't even be here next year.

"You up to helping me run through the affinities?"

Marcus smiled. "Absolutely! Lead the way."

I nodded, before the niggling in my chest forced me to say, "Actually, would you mind terribly if I ran a quick errand first. I can meet you at the lake in, like, twenty minutes?"

His smile never wavered, and I wondered how we'd let this friendship crash and burn so fast. It would have been nice to have another ally here. "Sounds good. Take your time, I can wait as long as you need."

He strolled off, and I changed directions, racing along the hall and down the stairs to the office. Barging in, three witches were behind the desk, including Ms. White. "Yes, dear?" she said, barely lifting her head. From a quick glance, she was filing assessment tests, and my low-level panic for the end of the week flared, but I pushed it down. There'd be plenty of time to have a breakdown later.

"I need to speak with Headmaster Gregor," I said, keeping my voice even.

This got her attention, as she peered at me over her glasses. "Regarding what?"

"My father."

Everyone in Weatherstone was acting normal. There was barely any chatter even about the party and the fire, and outside of the charred remains of the chapel I'd spied through the window, you'd never know anything had happened.

And yet Dad was still at home, and I'd heard nothing about his fate. Had he already had his chat with the headmaster? I needed to find out.

Ms. White's face softened a fraction, and she nodded. "I'll see if he's available."

She disappeared from the office for a few minutes, and when she returned, I was disappointed to find her alone. "He'll see you," she said, shocking the shit out of me. "He's in his office. You just take the stairs directly to the right of our door and go all the way to the top."

"Oh, okay, thank you!" I hurried out of the office, wondering how I'd missed the stairs all the other times I'd been here.

When I moved to the right of the door, there was only a tapestry depicting one of the wars draped over stone walls. Reaching out, I pressed my hands against it, and felt a swell of magic. Adding my energy to the magic, the stairs were suddenly visible, and I almost fell into them.

The headmaster used a concealment spell, and a strong one if it got around the natural ability witches and warlocks had to see through such spells. I hurried up the stairs, and was a little breathless by the time I reached the top. If this were one of my training sessions with Logan, he'd be snarling at me for my lack of stamina. Hard-ass.

At the top, I crossed the small half-circle landing to reach the ornate brass-and-wood door. Lifting the tarnished knocker, I let it bang twice and waited.

"Come in," Headmaster Gregor called.

The door opened quietly and then closed again behind me without me touching it at all. I stepped into a warm space. The office was lined in dark timber and smelled of mahogany. There were a couple of bay windows, but every other surface was covered in shelves, filled with ancient books. I wondered if the particular text I had been looking for was here all along.

Headmaster Gregor sat behind his desk, which was as ornate and dark as the rest of his room. He stood as I walked toward him. "Ms. Hallistar," he said. "I'm happy you decided to check in personally about your father's situation."

"You are?" It had been a last-minute decision after talking with Marcus. I couldn't just sit around and do nothing. "I figured you'd tell me it was official Weatherstone business and to get back to class."

"Not at all." Gregor was always so magnanimous, while giving me the creeps. It was an interesting contradiction. "It's terrible business about Tom," he continued, peering intently at me. "We're doing everything we can to clear it up, but unfortunately the complaint came from a very highly ranked member of the community, and they're pressing the issue." He cleared his throat. "They're asking for a lot more than just his termination as a professor."

"Like what?" I asked, feeling chilled despite the warmth of the room. "Because I promise you, I was at the party, and the witch wine was well concealed. None of the professors knew." I'd lie all day if I had to for Dad.

The headmaster nodded. "I understand, and in all honesty, every single professor at this school has turned a blind eye once or twice to underage drinking, illegal spellwork—within reason—and other standard college behavior that might not always align completely with our rules. It's just unfortunate in this situation that there's more than just my judgment involved."

This didn't sound good, and my thrum grew too large to be contained by my internal box any longer. This could derail my parents' entire lives. "What was the extra they asked for?" I forced myself to ask, needing every bit of information, even if it was bad.

"They asked for all Hallistars to be expelled from the college," he said quietly.

I wrinkled my brow, trying to understand. "Why would they want that?"

The headmaster's eyes glittered, so dark and biting. "They believe you're a dangerous family, and that it was no longer in Weatherstone's best interests to have you all here." He shook his head. "Absolute rubbish though. I've never had an ounce of trouble from any of you, and you're all exceptional witches and warlocks. There were no grounds to involve you in the situation, so for now it's all resting on your father."

The fact that this *highly ranked member of the community* wanted all of us gone made it more likely that Logan was behind it all. This was about punishing more than Dad; this was about punishing all Hallistars.

"Thanks for the update," I finally said, feeling worse than when I walked in. "I can supply witnesses who will attest that all witch wine was distributed without the knowledge of the professors." Most of them had no idea that Dad had seen my cup. "Under a truth spell."

The headmaster nodded. "Thank you. We're still in early stages of dealing with this, but I'll keep that in mind if we take it to the elders."

I nodded, knowing that was all I could do for now.

Gregor called out as I turned to leave. "Oh, and, Ms. Hallistar, have you had any further issue with monsters in the college?"

That question felt like a weird segue, given the current situation, and I examined his expression, only to find it neutral . . . almost blank. "No," I said shortly. "Not since the blanket was erected." Not totally true. Parents' weekend was still on my mind—when I'd been sure that monsters roamed the grounds.

His intensity eased up a fraction. "Great to know. The blanket will lift just after graduation."

That made me pause. "Because you've figured out who was behind it?"

"Unfortunately not," he sighed, "but having it up for so long is impacting the ability of students to fully touch their affinities and magic. The elders believe it's not in Weatherstone's best interest to keep it up any longer."

Translation: students' lives weren't worth more than the reputation of the college.

"Hopefully it'll all be behind us next year," I said, with a shrug that spoke of a nonchalance I did not feel.

"I'm sure it will be." The headmaster was more confident. "Good luck with your final assessments, Ms. Hallistar."

He sat once more and returned to whatever he'd been doing at his desk, and suitably dismissed, I stumbled from the room and took the stairs down. My head was teeming with questions and worries, and a thrum of panic that wouldn't fade.

The release of the blanket of energy, when nothing had been solved in the issue of monsters, meant that we'd be right back to danger. Right back where we were that night we lost one of our own.

I had to find those books. I had to figure out what Belle's father had been implying with his sharp and cryptic comments. I had to do it before anyone else died.

CHAPTER 36

Despite running dangerously close to being late to meet Marcus, I took a few extra minutes to exit near the chapel. There was no real reason for me to check it out; there was only ash and debris left behind. But I needed to see the scene that was costing us all so much.

Two witches and a warlock were in the zone, shooing everyone away. This close, that scent of ash and fire was much stronger, and there wasn't a single part of the scene that could help clear Dad's name. The fire happened. It happened because of the witch wine, and elementals losing their brains. That part wasn't up for debate.

What needed to be discovered was who reported Dad and was now pushing for maximum penalty.

Leaving the scene, I raced around the buildings and down to the lake, only to find two spellcasters waiting for me. Logan's expression was flat, more closed off than I'd seen from him in months. Marcus didn't look much more welcoming, and I wondered if they'd argued in my absence. "Paisley." The hard lines of Marcus's face eased. "Ready to get started."

My attention was on Logan, as per usual when he was around. He was in uniform today, without any variation, and I itched to roll those sleeves up to reveal that glorious ink. While another part of me wanted to throw a hex at him so he couldn't walk for a week because he might have finally achieved what his father wanted all along.

To destroy my dad.

"What are you doing here?" I asked Logan, ignoring Marcus.

"If you need a spellcaster," he said, a dangerous edge to those words. "Then you use me."

I could see Marcus's confusion. He glanced between Logan and me, no doubt inferring a whole bunch of truths that were really lies. "The professor asked Marcus to help me before final assessment." I shrugged, acting a hundred times more casual than I felt. "If the college didn't ask you, it might be because you're hardly ever here, hardly ever in class, and rarely want to help without getting something in return."

"What have I asked from you in return?" Logan said, his laser focus reducing me to ash, just like the chapel. "As you're well aware, I'm more generous in giving than receiving."

The flush was instant, heat unfurling through my body. Maybe I'd inferred more from those words than I should, but all I could think about was Logan giving me pleasure. Through that, though, I noticed an odd cadence as he spoke. His energy felt darker, and he looked . . . tired. I'd never seen Logan look anything other than perfect. A flaw wouldn't dare mar the powerful warlock. But today was different.

"Are you okay?" I asked, suddenly wishing I didn't care.

He blinked, and I saw the surprise he hid a second later. "Fuck, Precious. Go with Marcus. I'll be close by if you need any help." His gaze drifted to the lake behind us. "Especially if you're going in the water."

I reached out as if to stop him, but he moved too fast. I hadn't even had a chance to ask about Dad. Logan perplexed me in the worst kind of ways, and I lost my brain.

Marcus released a low whistle. "Holy shit," he breathed. "I don't know if you can feel his power, but it's scary intense."

That caught my attention. "You can *feel* Logan's power?"

Marcus scrubbed a hand over his mouth. "In my bones, Pais. Spellcasters can recognize each other, and we know who the bigger predator is. That guy . . . you should stay away from him."

He wasn't telling me anything I didn't already know, but what Marcus was unaware of was that I felt Logan in my bones too. Like he was permanently etched in the marrow, and I'd never get him out. My destiny with Logan had been set in mud, all those years ago in the park.

The details of which I still didn't know for sure, but I knew they were permanent.

At least these classes with Marcus were a distraction. "Water is just like every other element," he said as I followed him into the lake. "It's all about controlling matter, and the particles that connect the energy of the Earth and the moon."

I drew the water to me, droplets rising from the lake until they danced around me in an arc. "Perfect," Marcus said with a nod. "The element is drawn to you."

"I can't do much more than that," I warned him. "Not without a boost of energy to unlock the full potential of my own."

He assessed me for a beat, turning his head from where we stood side by side. "How do you get a boost?"

An arm wrapped around my waist, and I barely stopped the gasp leaving my lips. "Like this," Logan said softly.

His power crashed against mine, merging with ease. We'd been doing this for weeks and had it down to a fine art. My body swelled, and needing an outlet for this power, I clapped my hands together, and then slowly drew them apart in an attempt to part the water of the lake. I'd expected just to pull a few feet around us, but I hadn't taken into account how intimately Logan was pressed against me.

How connected our powers were.

He'd never touched me like this in our training before, a branding against my skin, and it felt as destructive as any monster who'd sliced through flesh and bones.

The entire lake parted, all the way down to sections so deep I couldn't see the bottom. If we'd have wanted to, we could have walked our way across that mud and made it to the other side.

"Fuck," I cried out as shock shook the hold on my power, and I released the water to crash together.

There was a rush of heat across my skin as Logan and Marcus used their magic to prevent a tsunami, and when the lake was once again calm, Logan's hand flexed against my skin. "This is the true potential of your energy," he murmured.

"Our energy together," I breathed.

He leaned in, and I turned to find him close. I drowned in that icy gaze and lost coherent thought. This was want and need, and I wanted and needed him to kiss me.

"I think I've got all the information the professors will require," Marcus said, voice distant.

Logan broke our hold, releasing me as suddenly as he'd touched me in the first place.

"She's a spellcaster," he told him, looking completely unruffled, while I was a desperate mess. Marcus nodded.

"I agree. I'll let them know that you still need to figure out the trigger for your release, but when you do, your power is strong."

Now that I wasn't wrapped up in whatever fucking spell Logan cast over me every time we were close, heat infused my cheeks. Embarrassment drove me to explain myself to Marcus, but he was already striding from the water, and I felt the air give him a little boost so he was gone in a flash.

Crossing my arms over myself, I tried to hide the tremble in my hands. "You did that deliberately," I said to Logan, refusing to look at him. His eyes were bewitching, ironically. "You're controlling and manipulating my life, and I can't tell yet if it's to help me or make everything much worse."

His gaze burned into the side of my face, taunting me to look at him, but I held strong. Mostly. "When have I made your life worse, best friend?"

Deflection. We were back to deflection.

"Answer me this, Logan. Why have you been helping me when your father made it clear that my family is scum? When your father got mine suspended from school and on his way to being fired? It doesn't make sense."

"Look at me," he demanded. Whatever strength I'd been channeling was yanked away in that one command.

My gaze met ice laced in fire, the green all but swirling with power. "Hear me now, Paisley Hallistar. There's always only been one endgame for us. The journey might vary, but the end will never fucking change. Our endgame was written when you were four."

He was repeating what I'd thought only minutes ago, but somehow it still felt as if I'd been struck by lightning, my cells threatening to explode from the intensity. I reached out to grab him, to demand answers, but he disappeared on me. Just as Marcus had done, he stole the elements, and let them whisk him out of the water and over the hill toward the school.

"What the fuck, Logan!" I shouted after him. "You're the most infuriating asshole."

My heart was pounding. I couldn't explain why, but his words had created a visceral reaction that seeped through my body like poison. Or fresh, foreign blood infusing with my own and leaving a new witch in its wake.

It took a long time to get myself under control, but after I left the water, I spent the rest of the day searching for Logan. When I found him, I would not let him leave without answers. No more cryptic bullshit. He knew more than he was telling me, including all the weird shit that had happened in Weatherstone this year.

Of course, there was not a single sign of him anywhere in the school. Or Noah, who was also on my list to corner and demand answers from.

"You okay, Pais?" Belle asked that night as I played with my dinner, moving roast potatoes around my plate. Beside us, Sara and Haley were in a lively debate about a book that Sara had finally caved and read. She'd hated it, and Haley was taking it personally, which would have been hilarious if I wasn't so distracted.

"Worried about your dad?" Belle pushed as she popped a carrot into her mouth and chewed slowly.

"Absolutely," I said, because it wasn't a lie. "I overheard Mom and Dad talking, and they said if he loses his job they might have to leave their coven. And you know what happens when we don't have a coven."

Belle pressed her lips together, her eyes shinier than before. "Damn, Pais. You should have told us sooner. I'm so sorry. I'm going to ask Dad to put in a good word for Professor Hallistar. This is not fair."

Normally I'd be thrilled by an elder speaking up for Dad, but Elder Monroe had shady motives when it came to me and my family. "You're amazing," I said, clearing my throat against a tide of emotions. "But your dad is so busy, it doesn't feel right to involve him. At least not before we know the school's decision."

Belle, thankfully, didn't show any sign that she thought this was a weird rebuke. "Just let me know. Dad and I have been getting along better since parents' weekend. He's calling constantly, asking me for updates about everything, and my friends, and it's . . ." Her smile got all misty. "Like I finally have a real father."

Every warning alarm in my body went off. It wasn't the trickle down my spine, because this wasn't monster related. Or it was a monster of a different kind. Belle went back to eating, happy again, and I wished I'd found that book already. I needed to know what her father knew so I could figure out what his *endgame* was. As much as I hated that word tonight.

I had some goals when we returned home after graduation. I'd be getting a job to help financially until sophomore year started, I was going to read those letters from Gran, and I would find that book Elder Monroe mentioned.

I had just over two months to get it all done, and I was determined not to return to Weatherstone as a naive witch in January.

"How did all your assessments go?" I asked Belle, changing the subject.

"Excellent." She smiled, relief relaxing her shoulders. "I've been studying my ass off, and it's so nice to have a break. The assessors said that I'm a powerful water elemental with a strong aptitude for curses and hexes." She shrugged. "No real surprises. I hope that when we graduate, I might be able to find a job in an apothecary."

"I was thinking of a similar job," I said with a spark of excitement. "I feel at home surrounded by herbs and nature, mixing up spells. I'd like a touch of peace in my life."

Belle grasped my hand, genuine happiness creasing her features. "Let's put all our focus in apothecary studies and start planning for the future. Maybe we can work together after senior graduation. When are your final assessments? Friday still?"

I nodded. "Yep, and I'm shitting myself. They asked Marcus to tail me for classes so he could assess the possibilities of me being a spellcaster, but Logan interfered at the lake today, so I barely got to show him anything."

Belle leaned closer, eyebrows drawing together as her happiness morphed into concern. "Logan interfered?"

"That's got to mean something, right?" Sara chimed in, having finished arguing with Haley, who was pouting and clutching the book to her chest, like she could protect it from Sara's harsh critique.

"He's jealous," Belle decided, nodding her head. "I've seen the way he watches Paisley. He likes her."

He did watch me, but she missed that darkly calculating glint in his gaze. This wasn't just a simple case of lust or chemistry, though we had an overabundance of both. It was more. "I don't think it's that he likes me," I told them. "I think he's trying to work out the mystery of my power. I'm a riddle that he must solve. Once he does, he'll lose all interest."

Our endgame was written when you were four. Those words were on repeat in my head, but I couldn't let them sway me.

"If they think you're a spellcaster too," Haley said, since they were all aware of this rumor, "is there a way that all spellcasters connect? Maybe that's why Logan is drawn to you?"

"Marcus could feel his powers," I admitted.

"Marcus, who is also attracted to you," Belle reminded me, though I wasn't sure that was strictly true after months of him ignoring me. "Dad told me that spellcasters can feel power but they can't connect to each other."

We all looked at her, and she shrugged. "He's been raving on about the spellcasters lately. There's some dissension in the European ranks, and the elders are worried they might be planning on rising up. Which could spill over here. But they can't all connect their power up. I don't know what is happening with Logan and Paisley, but it's not spellcasters connecting."

I hadn't heard about any dissension, and it should have been big news. The elders must be trying to keep it contained, because if spellcasters rose up against the magic community, it would be bad.

Destructive-war bad.

"Did he say who led this uprising?"

Belle shook her head. "No. He's actually sharing secret elder business, so let's not talk about it until they release the news to the covens." Not that there was anything we could do if war was brewing on the horizon.

I had more pressing issues much closer to home.

CHAPTER 37

"Your dad had a meeting this morning," Mom said, voice tinny through the phone. "He spoke with Victor and two Weatherstone officials, gave his side of the story, and now we have to wait."

"Please don't tell me he admitted to anything," I said, keeping my voice low as I made sure no one was close enough to listen in.

"He didn't," she assured me, "but they were talking about enforcing a truth spell."

"What?" I lowered my voice further. "That's not allowed in informal investigations."

Her sigh was loud. "I know, sweetheart. But this is receiving much more widespread interest than any of us expected. The elders are involved, and we can't go against their rule. Victor and your father are very good friends, so we just have to hope that in the end the headmaster will have final say."

Resting my head against the wall, the phone pressed hard to my ear, I fought back tears. "Okay, Mom. Well, I love you. Give Dad a hug from us, and I'll see you in a couple of days."

"We love you too, honey. Don't worry about us, this will all work out. Just put your focus on final assessments. Let me know how you go."

"I will."

When I hung up, I remained with my head against the

wall, eyes closed, the consistent burn behind my eyes leaving me wrung out. Only my awareness that there were less than ten of these landlines available for students around Writworth had me moving along the hall and letting the next student have their chance.

My first stop on the way to my dorm was in Nightrealm, but Logan once again was out of his dorm, or ignoring me. Slamming my hand against his door, a frustrated curse slipped out, and I felt a thousand years old.

"He's off campus today."

I spun with surprise and tried not to pee myself at the same time. Noah stood three feet away, dressed all in black, because that wasn't creepy. "We need to get a fucking bell on you," I said with as much snarl as I could manage. "Stop sneaking up on me."

He didn't react, just stood there, hands in his pockets, observing me like I was more interesting than he'd ever expected. Noah didn't draw me in like Logan, but my curiosity about him was almost as great.

With my pulse now thrumming an iota below stroke level, I took my chance to question him. "Why is Logan off campus?"

If Noah thought I was out of line, he didn't show any sign of it. "His family is extremely wealthy, controlling one of the largest corporations in the world. His dad sometimes calls on him for business help. He has obligations."

To no one's surprise Rafael was as rich as he was powerful. Wouldn't have expected anything less.

"How do you even know Logan?" I said, crossing my arms over myself, back pressed against Logan's door. "You clearly transferred in this year with him."

Noah still hadn't moved, but his presence was large enough to be intimidating, even with space between us. "He's my brother in all ways except blood." He didn't elaborate, and I didn't push my luck on that topic. But there was another question that I had to ask.

"Is Rafael bad news? Should I be worried about him?"

"Yes." I jolted because I expected a vague answer or outright lie. "Stay away from him," he continued. "You and your family are not safe with Rafael."

"What about with Logan?" I asked, finding myself desperate for this answer above all the others.

Noah moved so fast that if he wanted to, he could have ripped my heart out before I even saw it coming. This time at least, he only patted me on the head, like a puppy. "Depends on your definition of *safe*. Now get out of Nightrealm, Paisley."

He was gone before I could yell and scream at him, which is what I wanted to do. If Logan wasn't here though, that meant I was done with distractions and had to focus on my assessments.

Grabbing my textbooks, I staggered to the library and settled in for the rest of the afternoon. Marcus found me later that night, asleep with my head in my arms. When he gently pressed my shoulder, I lurched up and almost clocked him in the face. "Fuck!" I gasped, heart slamming in my chest. "Can you make some noise when you move. I didn't hear a thing."

For the second time today, a powerful warlock had crept up on me. Marcus let out a soft laugh. "I really wasn't that quiet. You were sleeping, Pais. What were you reading, *Accounting for Witches*?"

"Ha ha, my mom is an accountant, asswipe. But yep, that would have been the most boring text I could find." He laughed with me, and I took a second to wipe my face in case I'd drooled. "I was actually reading *Harvesting Moonlight for Alchemy* and I can't believe I fell asleep. This is one of my favorite classes. I love the concept of creating magic with your hands and base metals. It's fascinating."

Marcus observed me, closer than felt comfortable. "You're an interesting witch. Most of us here just want to boost our power, but you show an aptitude for the subtle magics." I shrugged—one had to adapt when their active magic was defective.

"Did you need me for something?" I asked.

He reached into his blazer pocket and pulled free a wad of cards, all covered in tiny, neat handwriting. "Here are my notes from my assessments. I forgot to give them to you before I left the lake."

Flipping through the few cards on top, my eyes heated once more because this was a kind gesture from a warlock I really hadn't put much time or energy into this year. "Shit, thank you," I said. "Your notes are so detailed."

He'd listed everything under each subject, giving me points of what he thought was important. "Every assessment is different," he said, peering closer, "catered to us as individuals. But if they're considering you for spellcaster, then you might be on a similar path."

"I really appreciate this," I said, holding the cards up. "I'm taking tomorrow to go over everything, so if you need to check on me I'll be here or in one of the element rooms." The library had lined rooms designed to handle study with the elements.

He ran a hand through his hair, face less stoic than it had been a second before. "Look, I'm sorry I bailed at the lake, and really, at the party all those months ago. I like you, Paisley. I've liked you from the first moment we were introduced, but you're hard to get to know. I get mixed signals, and I don't deal well with those, so I tend to bail. Past damage, not yours. But in light of our impending finals and the end of the college year, I just wanted to warlock up and tell you that I think you're fucking awesome. Beautiful, powerful, and kind. If you ever want to hang out again, and give this a real shot, let me know."

My mouth wasn't exactly ajar, but I had not expected that speech. Sure, there'd been a flicker between us, but so much time had passed and that flicker had died out. "Everything is complicated in my life," I said softly, hoping we'd be able to remain friends. "I think you're awesome too. Powerful, kind, and not bad on the eyes." His grin grew. "But I'm in no position to be dating. I'm a hot mess."

He took my rejection well. "If you need help with that as well, Paisley, especially to do with your dad, well, I have some friends who might be of assistance. Let me know over the winter break. I'll see you back here in January."

"See you then," I said, wondering what sort of friends he meant. Marcus had always been a bit of an enigma too, and maybe I'd overlooked an ally that I should have brought into the fold.

Trusting didn't come easy, though, so I'd wait and see what the new year brought.

It was past dinner now, and I was starving, so I gathered my books and notes and dropped them off at my dorm before heading for the dining hall. It was time to fuel up and sleep, so I could do this whole study thing all over again tomorrow.

"Ms. Hallistar, we'll see you now."

It was Friday morning and the butterflies in my stomach had the wings of eagles. Assessment shouldn't be this terrifying; we could fail and have to go to another college, but it almost never happened. Assessments were used to figure out where our skills and affinities lay after freshman year. Still, all the reasoning in the world didn't ease up the nerves.

"Thank you," I said stupidly, walking into the large multi-themed classroom they were using for freshman assessments. It had been spelled into six distinct areas, one for each of the major components they'd be testing me on today.

In the room were two assessors, and neither were professors I'd had before. "I'm Professor Halver," the tiny blonde female said. She couldn't be taller than five feet, with delicate features and wispy shoulder-length hair. She looked like a pixie, if such a creature existed outside of fairy tales.

"And I'm Professor Garrickson," the male said. He was a Black man with graying hair and a very serious expression.

Both professors wore navy robes, covering their clothes beneath, and the lack of expression on their faces really exacerbated my nerves.

"It's nice to meet you," I said, forcing myself not to fiddle with my uniform. We didn't bring anything into the assessments, and I'd have killed for a bag to hide behind.

"We're both independent contractors, brought in by the magical college board," Professor Haliver continued. "We go between all the college first-years, and give assessments based on a national average. Are you ready to get started?"

I nodded, pressing my lips together. My throat felt too tight to contribute much more.

Professor Haliver studied a clipboard, nodding a few times. "It says that you're showing an aptitude for spellcasting but have energy that is reluctant to release without a little prompting. With that in mind, we'll take you through all six areas and give grace for your energy. That's in addition to the grace already extended for the blanket across Weatherstone."

"Thank you," I repeated.

She finally smiled, brief but warm. "Okay, let's start with fire."

The fire area was made entirely of stone and multi-layered glass. "The flame will be lit for you," Professor Garrickson said, standing on the other side of the protective glass. "Manipulate it through the path on the wall."

The wall was a heavy gray stone with the *path* clearly sketched out in black ink or paint. A dark purple flame burned low, in an ember candle, and I knew I was finally seeing an everlasting wick. The color of the flame gave it away. Unless extinguished with magic, it would remain alight forever. They were rare and expensive, though Weatherstone could clearly afford them.

Closing my eyes briefly, I let my energy seep slowly from me, a skill that Logan had made me perfect. Forcing myself not to think of him, because the missing warlock was a distraction I didn't need, I connected to the essence of the fire, to the matter that created the flames.

The heat flooded my veins, filling me with the earthy power and rage of this element. Dad was fiery in a way Mom would never be, and I knew why. The fire burned within him, and while at times it was small and other times an inferno, it always burned.

Slowly, I lifted my hand, wafting it upwards, and the fire followed my path, moving higher while remaining anchored to the candle. Blocking out the rest of the world, I kept my focus on the flame, guiding it left and right, binding it to the wall, until I had almost reached the end. My energy was stable as I allowed it to trickle out in minute increments, even as it took all my concentration to manage without Logan.

Near the top I missed a right turn and it broke my focus, until there was a fizzling pop and the flame disappeared.

"Is the candle extinguished too?" Professor Haliver asked suddenly.

I glanced at the everlasting wick and took a step back. "It is."

What the fuck? Was I mistaken about the candle they were using?

Heavy silence followed, and I panicked thinking that maybe there was a chance I'd be kicked out of Weatherstone today. "Thank you, Ms. Hallistar. I think we are finished with fire. Let's move on to water."

Breathing through my nose in quick rapid breaths, I nodded jerkily and exited the fire area.

For water, I was in another glass cage, this one sealed on all four sides and above my head.

"You must survive for ten minutes," the male assessor told me. "If you run out of breath, you can use that button to drain the water."

He showed me the large red button that was impossible to miss.

As soon as they stepped back, the cage sealed and water poured in on me. Taking a deep breath, I was fully submerged in less than ten seconds. I hadn't been in water like this since the day I'd almost drowned in the lake, and I'd been expecting some unease, but it was panic. Full-blown panic, triggering me back to those moments right before I almost passed out.

I reached for the button, needing to escape, but for some reason I couldn't push it. I couldn't witch out like that, not in the middle of an assessment. *Come on, Paisley.* Closing my eyes, I let the sensation of water wash into my energy. Like fire, it had particles that I could feel against my skin, and breaking them down, I was able to move a fraction of the liquid away from my mouth.

Taking a tiny breath, I kept centering myself.

"Six minutes remaining."

The update came through loud and clear even under water.

Pushing more of the water away from my face, my nose was now free, and I drew in more shallow breaths.

"Two minutes remaining."

My relief was immense as I joined in with a mental countdown, chanting as loudly as my brain could handle, determined to make it through.

Whoosh. The water drained away with a loud crash, and I stood there soaked for a beat, still unable to master the art of completely drying myself.

"Excellent, Ms. Hallistar. Next we have earth."

I got through all five elements, showing a solid general aptitude for all. Next was spells, and I had no trouble whipping up the five requested. Even better, all of them worked exactly as they should. Alchemy was last, and I felt no nerves now. I formed a strong talisman using liquid metals.

"Excellent work, Ms. Hallistar," Professor Garrickson said as I stepped out at the end. "Your professors were right—I think we have another spellcaster on our hands. We'll inform Headmaster Gregor."

He didn't wait for my response, already excitedly discussing the fact that Weatherstone had three spellcaster students.

Exiting the room, it felt as if a ton of bricks had been lifted from my shoulders. I'd finished my assessment, and while I had no doubt I was far from the strongest student they'd seen, my energy was no longer completely locked away in my chest, and I knew I owed Logan a huge thanks.

A thanks I'd give first, and then I'd demand answers.

CHAPTER 38

"I'm so excited!" Belle shouted, shaking her ass around my dorm room. "We did it. We fucking passed freshman year, and now we're going home."

"I'll miss you guys," Sara said, pouting dramatically. "Can we try to organize a meetup somewhere during our break?"

"I'd love that," I said as I finished packing away the last of my crystals, slipping the necklaces on over my head. I hadn't worn them in weeks, and it felt right to have them on for graduation. "We'll be back in the land of technology and phone reception too, so text me every freaking day. I want to know what's happening in your lives."

"I'll be getting a job," Haley sighed with gusto. "I need to help with next year's tuition. I just wish it wouldn't interfere with reading time."

"Get a job at a bookstore," I suggested, closing my suitcase. I had my backpack for tomorrow's change of clothing and toiletries.

Haley threw her arms around me. "That's the best idea, Pais! There's this glorious romance bookstore in the downtown area near my house, and I've always wanted to work there. I all but live there when I'm not at school or studying. They know me well."

Haley wasn't the only one who had to find a job, and I wondered if the roller rink still had a spot available. As a former derby girl on the weekends, I never could resist a good skate season.

Glancing at my watch, I saw that it was almost time for the graduation ceremony. We were dressed in jeans, boots, tanks, and jackets once more, the icy weather setting in early this year. Tonight was Halloween, and while we didn't partake in human traditions of dressing in costumes and collecting candy, we'd still gone for a darker, more dramatic makeup effect.

We were witches after all. No brooms or pointed hats, but there was a sexy darkness to this night all the same.

"Let's head there now," I said, "I think I'm as packed as I need to be."

Students could stay and continue independent study for the winter, but most left for at least some of it. Jenna and Alice would be officially graduating their entire program tonight, heading home with Simon and Morris.

The last time I chatted with Dad on the phone, he'd been erecting their barn out back, keeping busy. My heart hurt to know he wouldn't be here tonight for my graduation. At least it was only freshman year for me; I knew it hurt a lot worse for the twins.

When we emerged into Florence Hall, it was packed with students. Some were dressed formally in suits and long dresses, while others like us, in jeans and boots. There was no dress code tonight, allowing us to be comfortable.

"I can't believe how quickly this year flew by," Sara said as we ducked into the crowd. "I swear it was only yesterday that I arrived through those gates, so nervous I thought I might vomit."

It felt like yesterday to me as well, while also being centuries ago. It was a year of growth and change and confusion.

My siblings waited at the doors to the assembly hall. "We'll save you a seat," Sara said as I hugged Alice.

"Thank you," I called. "I'll be in shortly."

We all sat with our years, and while I wished I could be with my siblings, at least I'd get to see the twins graduate and receive their coven assignments.

"Are you nervous?" I asked Jenna. She looked stunning in a simple blue knitted dress. She'd pulled her hair back into a chignon at the nape of her neck, and her makeup was as dark and smoky as mine.

"Yes and no," she said in a rush, gaze darting around. "I'm excited for the next stage of our lives, but what if Alice and I don't end up in the same coven?"

"We're twins," Alice said breathily. "They can't separate us. It's against the laws of nature."

She looked just as beautiful in a black dress that was buttoned right down the front and had a high neckline and long sleeves. She'd teamed it with knee-high black boots, leaving her hair lightly curled around her face.

"I'm so proud of you two," I said, trying and failing to keep my tears at bay.

"We're proud of you, Baby Sis," Jensen interjected, wiping away one of the escaped traitors. "We heard that the assessors were discussing the possibility of a third spellcaster. Anything you want to tell us? Has it been confirmed?"

Pressing my lips together, I looked between the four of them.

"It's not official," I told them quickly. "But . . . the assessment went well. My magic didn't fail me, and I'm really excited for what the next year at Weatherstone will bring in way of development and my affinity."

"You've always had the power." Jensen's expression was serious. "Maybe what you lacked was the belief in yourself. Your confidence has grown a lot this year, and I, for one, can't wait to see what year two brings."

"Aw, guys." I sniffed. "Don't make me cry more of my makeup off."

Trevor gently nudged me. "Go on. Go and sit with the freshmen. We'll find you at dinner."

"See you then," I said.

By now the hall was noisy and almost full. Hurrying down the center aisle, I caught sight of my friends about halfway along, and headed straight for them. As I crossed toward them, fate decided to throw me a bone, and Logan entered the same aisle as me.

Grinding to a halt, it was now or never. "Hey, spellcaster." I ignored the many faces turned my way as I focused on Logan. "Where the Hel have you been?"

He turned to face me, and the ass-chewing I'd been working on giving him died in my mouth as I stared. He was devastating. He'd chosen semiformal, and as I dragged my gaze over him, I noted the slacks pressed against muscled thighs, and the way the green of his shirt turned those icy eyes brighter than ever. He'd rolled his sleeves to midforearm too, leaving his ink on display, like an additional slash of color and art against his outfit.

"My eyes are up here, Precious," he drawled.

My cheeks were heating, even as I shot him a withering stare. "We need to talk." I ignored everything else. "This is our last opportunity. Will you meet me after dinner tonight?"

He sobered, and as always was completely unreadable. "I can meet you after dinner. Say . . . near the graveyard."

A tingle of awareness traced down my spine, but I was so desperate to get these answers that I didn't hesitate. "Yes. I'll be there by ten."

Headmaster Gregor walked onto the stage then, dressed in shiny black robes, so I spun and hurried over to the girls, slipping into my seat just as he started.

"Welcome to graduation!" the headmaster shouted, his voice booming. "We've had a year, I know, and many of you will be grateful to just have made it through unscathed. I feel the same. We will never forget Gerard Donovan. We lost a great student this year." He paused for a moment, and everyone remained silent with him. "Tonight, on All Hallows' Eve, when the veil between the living and dead is thinnest, remember to send a blessing to our lost witches and warlocks. We will lift the cloaking energy after the dinner tonight, so take advantage of the power while you can. And be safe."

The blanket of energy was at this moment keeping us from feeling the full effect of Halloween, but when they lifted it, we'd be inundated with power. This was my first All Hallows' since the bloom of my energy, and I wouldn't lie: I wanted to know what the energy felt like.

I hadn't had a necromancy section in my assessment because spellcasters couldn't touch that magic, even though I'd shown signs I could. I wondered if I'd feel the thinning of the veil tonight.

"With all of that," Headmaster Gregor continued, "it's time for our seniors to cross the stage and receive their coven placement."

Nerves kicked in for my sisters, and while I had no doubt they'd be offered excellent placements, there were two worries. One: they wouldn't stay together, and two: they'd be sent to a coven far from Spokane. "Jerry Adams," the headmaster called. "As a fire elemental, you're being welcomed into the Coven of Warriors in Dallas, Texas. Congratulations, Jerry."

Jerry, a burly guy, well over six feet tall, crossed the stage in long determined strides to accept the rolled parchment. "Thank you," he said.

The headmaster shook his hand, and murmured a blessing, before he moved on to the next student. "Flow Allorn."

The water elemental was welcomed into the Coven of Mystic Light, which had a Californian branch. Absolute joy lit up her face when she heard the news.

The graduation continued for some time, until eventually Jenna and Alice Hallistar were called to the stage. Together. A fraction of my nerves eased because they were going to the same coven. "Our lovely nature sprite twins are being offered a place in Blessed Souls of Spokane, in their hometown of Spokane, Washington."

"Wooooo!" Trevor's shout was loud across the room, and everyone laughed as they joined in the cheer.

My own joy couldn't be contained, even if there was a niggling worry that they would be accepted into the coven right as Mom and Dad got kicked out. But surely the coven could find Dad a different job. There were always options.

After Headmaster Gregor blessed them, the twins hurried off the stage, smiling broadly. The rest of the students continued, finishing with Yvonne Zuka, a necromancer who ended up in a European coven.

"Amazing," Professor Gregor said. "I feel this year of graduates are capable, powerful, and ready to lead the magical world for many generations to come. As will all of you. Our assessor scores were some of the best we've had in years, and I'm proud of every graduating year." He cleared his throat and looked around. "For the first time, we have the chance of three spellcasters in Weatherstone who will become part of our proud legacy. We are the most prestigious magic college in America not because of us but because of you. Thank you."

The room erupted in applause, and I clapped along, wishing that half the student body wasn't staring at me now. Apparently, it was no secret who the third possible spellcaster was.

When Headmaster Gregor left the stage, another professor stepped out and led the blessings for the year. I'd never been part of this, but I'd heard about it from my siblings. All of us joined hands, up and down the rows, and together, the energy of the room rose collectively.

"Blessed be to those who walk these sacred halls. Blessed are their lives outside these walls. Blessed are their magics."

We repeated after him in our ancient language, and by the time we were done, I felt as if I could run a marathon, or swim the lake ten times. My energy was refreshed and renewed and lighter. A sense of being closer to my magic, and to my fellow witches and warlocks, washed through me. I didn't know a fraction of the students here, but we were all part of Weatherstone.

A collective.

CHAPTER 39

The dinner portion of the graduation ceremony was very reminiscent of our welcome ceremony. The tables were all pushed together in long lines as family-style platters were whooshed in on the winds. My siblings sat with me and my friends tonight, along with some of their friends who I knew in passing, creating a celebratory atmosphere.

"Jensen and I will be coming home for at least a month," Trevor told me as he shoveled a huge spoon of Irish stew into his mouth. "We want to be there when Jenna and Alice are inducted into the coven."

The girls flashed huge grins. "I can't believe we're together and in our first choice," Alice said with a sigh. "Simon will be home with me, and I can finally settle into my new life."

"*Our* new life," Jenna cheered. "Morris is going to love the forests, and I've got his collar ready."

Our kind existed within the human world, and while they knew about witches, they believed them to be humans who studied our ancient magic. Which, as one would expect, led to situations where the crossover of our worlds got us into trouble. Worse, it was downright outlawed to induct humans into our way of life unless you married one and bound them with a secrecy spell.

That meant Jenna couldn't take Morris down to the local mall and check out the shops with him. At least not in his bear form. Just the way the witch wine was disguised to look like normal wine, a bear could be disguised to look like a shaggy dog.

She'd been working on his collar all year, and I couldn't wait to see how he looked in his cute puppy form.

"Cheers," Belle said, raising her tea. "I think this deserves a celebratory drink."

I picked up my lemon water, lifted it in the air, and we all cheered to the future. For this brief moment in time, there was no worry about monsters, wonky magic, enemies who were sometimes lovers but mostly assholes, or finding an affinity.

Tonight, it was perfect.

When dinner was over, I hugged my family good-night, and we made plans to meet at the gate tomorrow morning. "Don't be late," Trevor said to Jensen, our resident late riser.

He saluted with his middle finger. "I'll do my best."

Jenna shook her head. "One last winter at home. I love it. Okay, I'm off for a bear hug. See you in the morning."

I walked with the girls back to our floor. "What should we do tonight?" Sara asked, her stroll casual, even with the flush of excitement in her cheeks. We were all still riding those waves of the final blessing. "The blanket should come down any moment, so we could head out to try and commune with the energy."

"Yes!" Belle shouted. "I couldn't sleep if my life depended on it, and this is our first All Hallows' in Weatherstone."

Glancing at my watch, I saw that it was almost 10:00 p.m. "Guys, I arranged to meet up with Logan near the graveyard." I felt a fluttering of nerves in my stomach. All three of them swung around and gaped at me, and I sought to explain. "I need answers. I need to know if he was involved with my dad's suspension, and what his father has planned next, and really . . . what happened in the past to link us together. I can't miss this chance."

Haley grabbed my arm, slowing me. "Wait, is that safe? I know you somewhat trust Logan now, or at least trust he's not actively trying to kill you, and I know we haven't had any monster attacks lately, but with the veil lifting, the risk will return, right?"

I nodded. "Yes, there's a risk. But I think with so many students around, I should be relatively safe. It's my last chance. I don't even know if he'll be back next year."

He'd transferred in suddenly and could leave just as suddenly. His evil father already had a penchant for pulling him from the school whenever he felt like it.

"I understand," Belle said, her expression sobering. "It'll ruin your entire winter break if you have more questions than answers."

She knew me well.

"Alrighty, then—" Sara got on board quickly "—let's get you to the graveyard."

We linked arms, hurrying down the steps, and as soon as my boots hit the grass, I felt a shimmer of magic wash over and through us. We ground to a halt, along with every other witch and warlock in the vicinity. "Holy goddess," Sara breathed, tilting her head back, her breaths ragged. "Do you feel that power?"

I hadn't realized the full extent of the blanket until this second, when the power in my chest was released. Free and fluttering. Not like a swarm of butterflies but a murder of crows, wild and rapid, strong and drugging in its intensity.

"Fuuuuck."

"That just about covers it," Belle said with a snort.

There was no time for me to indulge in the power coating my skin, which was starting to glow in response. I was late.

The girls remained with me as we set off for the graveyard once more, dodging around the hundreds of students pouring from the college, ready to indulge in one last night of everything Weatherstone had to offer.

"Let's hope they never drop a blanket over us again," Sara trilled, waving her hands above her head, bringing the winds with her. "Now I understand that I've been doing magic with one hand behind my back."

"The assessors adjusted for that," Haley piped in. "Our test scores will be elevated to match national standard. I checked with them."

Of course she had. If she wasn't reading books, she studied magic, and already showed abilities far above freshman level for a nature sprite. "Are you excited to find your familiar next year?" I asked her, as we rounded another corner and the graveyard came into sight.

"I've dreamed about this my entire life," she said with a sigh. "In my dreams, though, it was unicorns and dragons." Her shrug was cute, and I expected nothing less from a hardcore fantasy reader. "But any animal companion who will elevate my magic and provide me with a friend for life is all I could ask for."

"Jealous," Belle said, her bottom lip popping out. "I think we should all get familiars. I'd choose a dolphin." A dolphin would work perfectly for the water elemental.

"An eagle for me," Sara said, still drifting breezes across us as she exercised her air energy.

All three looked at me, and I smiled. "Is it weird that I've always wanted a cat?"

Belle's lips twitched. "Girl, you can just get a cat. You know that, right? It's a normal pet."

A chuckle escaped. "Yes, I know. But it's such a witch cliché."

Haley's laugh was unexpectedly light and airy. "I think it's perfect. Your mission this winter is to get yourself a cat."

The idea settled in my chest, and I let it sit there for a few minutes. "Maybe I will."

My parents would no doubt have a lot to say about it, but I'd worry about that along with all the other "tomorrow problems."

"There he is," Sara said softly, and the three of them slowed their steps. "Call out if you need us, we'll be nearby."

Logan was propped against the fence of the graveyard, long legs out in front of him, his head tilted back to the energy. My breath caught in my chest, bringing forth another stupid cliché, because I knew there was no literal way for air to get caught in my body from the mere sight of a godlike warlock. And yet, what other explanation was there? Even my heart beat in a different pattern. I hated the sensation that Logan was remaking fundamental parts of me.

Remaking me into what was still to be discovered.

"See you soon," I whispered, sucking in a deep breath and hurrying over to the spellcaster.

He opened his eyes long before he heard me coming and met my gaze. In the moonlight, his features were shadowed, the handsome planes hidden in the darkness, giving him an ethereal look. "How does your power feel?" he asked, that rumble of his accent deeper than usual. I choked on a gasp as I felt the first crash of his power against mine. I'd forgotten the intensity.

I'd forgotten a lot, it would seem.

"It's like electricity," I said in awe. "Everything is buzzing."

He nodded. "When your spellcaster abilities are fully unlocked, that's how you'll feel all the time. Like you're plugged into the world's energy."

It was scary in a way because plugged-in meant no limits.

And no limits meant I had to always be careful with how I used my energy.

Logan pushed up from the wall, and before I could get started with my questions he strolled right into the graveyard. Hesitating, I hovered at the junction of the gates, aware that with the return of the energy there was a return of that feeling of unease.

But I needed answers.

Not more than I needed to be alive, obviously, but Logan had never hurt me. If anything, I wouldn't be standing here if he hadn't been with me multiple times, so there was no safer place in Weatherstone than by his side.

Sucking in a fortifying breath, I followed him into the darkness, the moon lighting a path between the stones. At first, I couldn't see Logan, but eventually I found him standing over a nondescript grave. It was just a flat stone, with flowers concealing the name until I stood right above it.

"Kingston," I whispered, desperate to reach down and shift the roses. "Your family?"

He didn't look my way, staring down at the stone. "My great-great-grandfather. We are Weatherstone legacy."

Legacy were those who contributed to making the college into what it is today. There were the two founding witches to start, but plenty came after them.

"Why did you not go to school here as a freshman?"

His chuckle was dark. "Amusing that you think anything in my life is my choice. I'm the dutiful son. Born to tragedy, and I'll no doubt die the same way."

That ominous feeling traced down my spine, less intense than usual, more like a drip, drip of fear. There was a metallic taste in my mouth, and I worried I'd royally fucked up in trusting Logan. "What does your father want you to do with me?"

That got his attention, as he lifted that enigmatic gaze from the headstone and met mine. "Why, destroy you, Precious. You should know that."

I took a step back, and Logan shook his head, chuckling with less force. "Not tonight. You're safe tonight. What do you want to ask me?"

Safe tonight wasn't exactly reassuring, but he wasn't attacking, so I decided to plow ahead.

"Did your dad get mine suspended?"

The tilt of his lips was all smirk, and I fucking hated when he was all sharp edges and broken pieces. "He did not. He's pretty upset that wasn't his doing. I think you'll find the culprit for that is a little closer to home."

Blinking at him, I tried to understand what he meant. "Who?"

"I can't give you all the answers, but it's worth checking in with the ones you trust. Someone told their daddy about the party, and he's decided that the Hallistars need to go."

Someone. The headmaster said it was a powerful and influential family, and there was only one option for that amongst those I considered friend. *Belle.* Belle who was bonding with her asshole of a father.

Breathing deeply, I pushed that anger aside and got to my next question.

"Okay, so what is it that ties you and me together? I mean, we're clearly enemies."

Despite wanting to remain calm, I found myself getting more and more fired up. Belle's betrayal, while unintentional—*I had absolutely no doubt of that*—set off the panic and worry over my father once more. Then this stupid reaction to Logan, all while the energy ramped up my magic until I wanted to burst.

The crystals burned against my chest, and I had the feeling

it had been a mistake to wear them outside on a night like this. A night when Weatherstone was bathed in the energy of All Hallows' Eve.

"Logan!" I snapped. "It can't be that fucking hard of a question. What happened when I was four and you were six?"

He stepped into me. "Your dreams haven't told you?"

All my dreams had told me was how many positions this warlock could twist my body into, each more pleasurable than the last. "I remember falling in the rain. I remember you standing over me." My words were short. Blunt.

"Do you remember the ceremo—?"

A scraping sound cut him off, and I spun to find a monster emerging from behind a huge tree.

For the first time, it wasn't panic that held me immobile, it was anger. I'd almost had a real answer from Logan, I'd seen that in his eyes, and here we were, interrupted again by someone else's magic.

"Who the fuck are you?" I shouted, staring into the darkened spaces around the graves. "Come out and show yourself. Don't hide behind your beasts."

The monster scraped closer, and I couldn't miss how spider-like this one was, but with far more legs than it should have, and a much larger body. For all its legs, though, it found it difficult to navigate the narrow paths, and I'd have laughed as it tripped if I weren't so angry.

Even with a monster closing in, I was once again looking at Logan, and he hadn't taken his eyes off me. "You're a coward," I continued, and I pointed my finger violently, even though there was no one in sight except Logan. "A fucking coward."

As I pointed, another monster popped into view, this one appearing twenty feet away, and completely out of nowhere. It was one of the single-eyed versions, with a huge bulbous body and tusks out of either side of its mouth.

"Another ridiculous creation," I shouted into the night. "You're a joke!"

My energy burned as I fought the urge to set it all on fire. I'd never been able to create my own fire, at least not in any classes, but the way I felt now, there was an inferno desperately seeking an exit from my power.

Another monster arrived, closer than the others, just behind Logan, who never even turned to stare at the alligator-headed beast. He just continued to watch me closely, expressionless and unblinking. "Do you see them?" I snarled. "Tell me you see or at least feel them with your spellcaster abilities? Who is doing this?"

Logan took a step closer to me, shaking his head, but not in a way that spoke of confusion. More as in he was confirming a thought he'd already had. "I think it's you, Precious."

My next shout died off as I gasped. "Impossible."

Logan had lost his mind and was trying to blame me. How the fuck would I be conjuring monsters? "I've not cast one spell since we entered the graveyard." And there I went, jabbing my finger in his face again.

With each jab, another beast appeared until we were surrounded. Completely surrounded by monsters, and I was forced to acknowledge that the only enemy I faced here tonight was . . . myself?

Letting my hand fall, my head spun as I tried to comprehend what I'd just learned.

All year I'd been the one calling the monsters. With my magic. With my energy.

And with no idea how to get rid of them, we were going to die. They did not hold any sentimental value toward the witch who created them. My ribs could attest to that.

With a curse, Logan stepped into me, his grip tight on my hips as he used air to shoot us above them. My brain was functioning at the pace of a snail as I pieced the information together with new knowledge, like my desperate pull for energy when I'd been in the lake, and how that monster hadn't quite been in this world until I caught a flash of it.

I could tie emotional upheaval to almost all the creatures' appearances.

Logan landed us outside the graveyard and stepped in front of me. "Connect your power to mine," he ground out.

My head still a mess, I moved on autopilot, pressing my hands to his spine. I'd never been the one to initiate our connection, but there was really nothing to it. Our power knew each other, intimately. More intimately than the witch and warlock containing it, and that said something considering my relationship with Logan.

Electricity sparked around Logan, zapping across my skin, and with the power of All Hallows' rolling across the lands, I couldn't imagine anything in this world as powerful as Logan Kingston felt beneath my touch.

If our energies weren't connected, I'd be dead, just from standing this close to him.

He didn't release his magic for many long moments, and if he didn't hurry, he would call everyone to us. This was a beacon of power in a school of magic. Everyone would want in on it.

Including the monsters, apparently, as they all came into view, scurrying, sliding, and raging toward us.

In a line, they almost looked like an army, charging into battle, most of them standing ten feet or taller, and filled with dark rage. "Use our energy, Paisley," Logan said. "Send them away."

A whimper escaped my lips, and true fear curdled in my stomach like old milk. "I—I don't know h-how."

Logan's rumble was darker than the beasts we faced as they came scurrying out of the graveyard perimeter. "Seems we'll have to do this the old-fashioned way, then."

I had no idea what he meant, until his power ramped up, and I realized that he'd been holding back. There was a tugging sensation in my gut, and it wasn't until my back arched and I cried out that I felt Logan draw from my energy as well as his own.

Which was impossible. We could connect and elevate power, but he couldn't steal mine unless I freely gave it to him—I didn't remember anyone asking permission.

"Use your fucking crystals," Logan grit out, sending forth a wave of power that knocked the monsters back. It didn't disappear this time, and it seemed that even Logan had a limit to what he could explode with magic alone. I managed to reach up with one hand, while keeping the other firmly on Logan, and grasp my necklaces. Closing my eyes, I prayed to Selene that we would make it out of here alive. Not just us, but every other student who walked the grounds.

The swirls in my gut grew, and if I wasn't locked in a power strong enough to shake the lands, I would have cried out. Just as Gran's photos had suggested, there was an immediate boost to my magical essence as soon as the crystals touched my skin. They'd been resting against my jacket, but on bare skin it was akin to plugging into that spellcaster energy.

Logan sent out another wave, and this one did what the others hadn't been able to, disintegrating the creatures into misty dust, and then we were alone once more.

Or so I thought.

A face appeared on the other side of the graveyard, one that was so familiar my heart clenched.

"Mom . . ." I sobbed my relief, releasing Logan's shirt. I'd been holding him so tightly my knuckles ached. "Mom!" I said again, stumbling toward her. "You were in there with them?"

Her arms wrapped around me, that familiar hug I'd felt a million times in my life, and would have called the most comforting embrace in the world. Only this time it felt different.

Pulling back, I looked her over. "What were you doing with the monsters, Mom?"

Her face was drawn as she sucked in a deep breath, and I noticed how disheveled she looked, as if she'd been pulled from bed into this spot. She even wore flannel pajamas and had bare feet.

"You called me, sweetheart," she whispered, her lips trembling. "And we have a lot to talk about."

I felt him at my back, his power along with the heat and chemistry that had drawn me to Logan all year. "Demon-witch," Logan murmured, and Mom's gaze snapped to him.

Stepping out from the two of them, I wondered why I was once again unable to catch my breath. "Demon-witch," I murmured. *Demon-witch*. I knew that term. I knew that fucking term. *Witch massacre*. From their own kind.

"You stay away from my daughter," Mom snarled.

Logan's smile wasn't nice. "Paisley belongs to me. You know that, and I'll kill anyone that takes her from me."

I waited for Mom to fight him, to hit back and refute his claim, but there was only a skitter of fear over her face. "Give me the rest of the year," she breathed. "Please. She needs to learn before they come for her."

Goddess of the damn moon. What was happening here?

A sniffle escaped me as I pressed my hand against my chest, the shock too much to process. Logan's gaze snapped to me, and he examined me in a burning sweep. "One month," he countered. "I'll give you one month and then I'm coming for you, Precious."

I burned and died under his gaze in that moment, before it was all over, and he disappeared into the air once more. "Mom," I breathed, shaking uncontrollably. Even as I continued to stare at the spot Logan had just vacated.

"I'll explain everything," she whispered, bundling me up into her arms. "I promise. But we need to get out of here now."

She used air to lift us above the land, just as Logan had done, and then we were outside the barriers. A portal was already set up there, and when she dragged me through, we were back home. On the porch. Like I'd done a million times. I was so shocked I didn't stop to think how she'd managed to get through the securities of Weatherstone in the first place, or use the air element when it wasn't her affinity.

There was no time to ask either, as Dad was already waiting for us, his expression wreathed in agony, which eased when Mom fell into his arms. "I got her, Tom," she sobbed. "I got her in time."

"What is happening?" I said in a huff, my body still vibrating from the power and . . . Logan.

Paisley belongs to me. The burning intensified, until I was in real danger of setting our house on fire. I couldn't think about that. I couldn't think about Logan. Not until I had other answers.

When my parents pulled apart, I got a front-row view to the panic, fear, and rage in their expressions, and I braced myself for what was to come. "Paisley, I need to tell you everything," Mom whispered, her face begging me for forgiveness. It terrified me that I didn't know what she'd done to warrant such forgiveness. "I need you to understand."

Dad stepped forward. "Not tonight, Beth. You're both exhausted and terrified. I'll let the others know Paisley is here. We can deal with the rest in the morning." He reached back to pick up a book from the ledge near the door, as if it had been sitting there waiting for my return.

He held it out to me, and I took it without thought, looking down to find the title: *The Reapers of Purgatory*. I jerked my head up. "How did you know I was searching for this book?"

"Read it," Dad said gruffly. "Read it first, and then in the morning we'll talk."

Mom hadn't moved her focus from my face. She looked absolutely devastated. As badly as I needed answers tonight, I would wait for morning. "Okay, we will discuss everything in the morning," I agreed. "But from here on out, no more secrets or lies. No more."

They both nodded, without hesitation, before shuffling me inside.

As I clutched the book to my chest, I had the real sense that I might have survived my first year at Weatherstone and made it through graduation, but it was clear that this year wasn't done with me yet. And neither was Logan Kingston.

I'll kill anyone that takes her from me.

He'd given us one month, and I was determined that by then I'd know everything I needed to know about demon-witches.

Demon-witches and the monsters they called.

★ ★ ★ ★ ★

ACKNOWLEDGMENTS

First and foremost, thank you to my husband, Travis. You're my book boyfriend inspiration, and I wouldn't be half the author I am without your support and love always propping me up in the background. I love you.

Thank you to my two beautiful daughters, who share their mother with fictional characters, and still find time to remind me what unconditional love is. You're the best thing I've ever done in my life. My greatest achievements. I love you more than words.

Thank you to my wonderful parents, who are always in my corner, no matter what life throws our way. I wouldn't be the person I am without your support and love, and I'm grateful every day for the life you built for me. Along with my brother, Cody, and sister-in-law, Laura, who are the most wonderful support system and family we could ask for. I love you all.

Thank you to my editor, Cat Clyne, (and the entire MIRA team) for believing in my story when it was only a rough three chapters and a basic outline. You saw the diamond in the rough and knew that we could polish this baby until it shone. Your faith in me is very appreciated, and I have immensely enjoyed our time working together. Let's do it again soon.

Thank you to my agent Flavia Viotti, Meire Dias, and the entire Bookcase Literary Agency for their incredible support and fight as they champion my books out in the world. I have so much respect and admiration for you and your team, and the amazing job you do. Thank you for believing in me.

Lastly, but never least, thank you to my readers. You've

been with me for over twelve years, through ups and downs, multiple series, and I truly would not be where I am today without your immense support. I will forever be grateful for the way you have changed my life. It's a kind of magic I could never put into words. Even when I try. So . . . With all my love, I thank you.